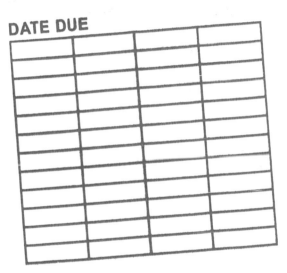

DATE DUE

The Sister Circle

Also by Nancy Moser
in Large Print:

Time Lottery

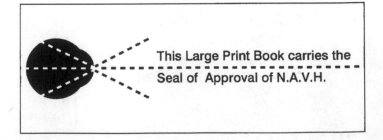

This Large Print Book carries the
Seal of Approval of N.A.V.H.

Vonette Bright
& Nancy Moser

Thorndike Press • Waterville, Maine

Published in 2005 by arrangement with Tyndale House Publishers, Inc.

Thorndike Press® Large Print Christian Fiction.

The tree indicium is a trademark of Thorndike Press.

The text of this Large Print edition is unabridged.
Other aspects of the book may vary from the original edition.

Set in 16 pt. Plantin by Myrna S. Raven.

Printed in the United States on permanent paper.

Library of Congress Cataloging-in-Publication Data

Bright, Vonette Z.
    The sister circle / by Vonette Bright & Nancy Moser.
        p. cm. — (Sister circle ; # 1) (Thorndike Press large
    print Christian fiction)
    ISBN 0-7862-7744-0 (lg. print : hc : alk. paper)
        1. Traffic accident victims — Family relationships — Fiction.
    2. Female friendship — Fiction.   3. Boardinghouses — Fiction.
    4. Widows — Fiction.   5. Large type books.   I. Moser, Nancy.
    II. Title.   III. Thorndike Press large print Christian fiction series.
    PS3602.R5317S57 2005
    813'.6—dc22   2005010548

The Sister Circle

As the Founder/CEO of NAVH, the only national health agency solely devoted to those who, although not totally blind, have an eye disease which could lead to serious visual impairment, I am pleased to recognize Thorndike Press* as one of the leading publishers in the large print field.

Founded in 1954 in San Francisco to prepare large print textbooks for partially seeing children, NAVH became the pioneer and standard setting agency in the preparation of large type.

Today, those publishers who meet our standards carry the prestigious "Seal of Approval" indicating high quality large print. We are delighted that Thorndike Press is one of the publishers whose titles meet these standards. We are also pleased to recognize the significant contribution Thorndike Press is making in this important and growing field.

Lorraine H. Marchi, L.H.D.
Founder/CEO
NAVH

* Thorndike Press encompasses the following imprints: Thorndike, Wheeler, Walker and Large Print Press.

Vonette Bright dedicates this book to the
sisters in the circle of my life:
My precious birth sister, Deanne Rice;
My sisters-in-love,
Martha and Arelie Zachary,
Florence Skinner, and Lucille Bright;
My daughters-in-love,
Terry and Katherine Bright.
I also wish to dedicate this volume (with
gratitude) to the more than one hundred
Campus Crusade Staff women who have
served with me as personal associates over
the past fifty-one years.
They have ministered to and with me,
making it possible for me to be available to
minister to others worldwide.
Without them my life would have been
very different, and I would not have
experienced the special joy of bringing
many new sisters into the faith.
I pray that all of these dear ones
will be blessed by God just
as they have blessed me.
They are living examples of biblical
sisterhood!

Nancy Moser dedicates this book to
the sisters brought to me through birth:
Lois and Crystie;
the sisters brought to me
through marriage:
Wendi, Deanna, Sheree, and Nikki;
the sisters brought to me through
this project:
Vonette, Brenda, Becky, Anne,
Kathy, and Danielle;
and the sisters brought to me over all the
days that are my life. . . .
Thank you and bless you, and may the
bonds of our sisterhood increase in love, in
faith, and in chocolate.

1

O my people, trust in him at all times.
Pour out your heart to him,
for God is our refuge.
PSALM 62:8

Evelyn wanted to throw the coffee in his face.

As if reading her mind, the man flinched. "I'm sorry, Mrs. Peerbaugh," he said. "I feel really bad."

Evelyn looked at the life insurance check in her hand. Ten thousand dollars. After paying the funeral expenses, there would be little left. "It's not your fault."

The man fidgeted in his chair, the china cup balanced precariously on his thigh. He looked down at Peppers the cat nervously, as she rubbed against the lower part of his leg.

Evelyn put a hand near the floor. "Come here, kitty." Peppers accepted the invitation and performed a graceful arc, finishing it against Evelyn's right ankle. She was rewarded with a scratch behind the ears.

"Perhaps your husband had other policies?" the man said. "People often have policies from more than one insurance company."

Evelyn shook her head. After the shock of Aaron's car accident a month ago, she'd gone through the drawer that held all their important papers and had found only the one effective policy — *effective* being the key word. There were other policies — one for two hundred and fifty thousand dollars and one for fifty thousand — but both had been cashed in, and Evelyn had no idea where the money had gone. Unbelievable. Now this insurance check, combined with their minuscule bank accounts, was it.

Why hadn't Aaron confided in her about their financial situation? Their lifestyle had been comfortable but not lavish. He had offered no clue that they were struggling.

And she hadn't asked.

Why *hadn't* she asked?

Of course, for Evelyn to have known the extent of their troubles meant that Aaron would have had to admit them, and that was a whole new cake to cut. Aaron had worn a cloak of confidence like a king wearing a royal robe. Whatever life had to offer, he could handle it.

Ha! Who was left to handle it now?

Aaron had been as impractical as Waterford crystal at a picnic. Evelyn doubted he had ever allowed himself to consider the possibility of death. He was always high on dreams and low on common sense. If it hadn't been for Evelyn's insistence that they hold on to the Peerbaugh family home that had been in his family since 1900, Aaron would have uprooted her and their son multiple times. They'd have left Carson Creek and ended up in Seattle or Tampa on some get-rich scheme that would have left them living in a rented trailer with a telephone line strung over the branches of the nearest tree. Holding fast to the house had been one of the few times Evelyn had taken a stand —

"Mrs. Peerbaugh?"

She blinked her memories away. "Mmm?"

"If there's anything I can do . . ."

She set her cup on the coffee table that separated them. A plate of cookies lay untouched, but she realized it was too late to offer them again. And the way the man shifted in his seat and avoided her eyes told her he wanted to leave ASAP. Even though she didn't mind his company, there was no reason to make him uncomfortable any longer. It wasn't his fault her inheritance was so pitiful, and she was sure he had better things to do than to sit around comforting a widow about her husband's lack of foresight.

She stood, signaling the end to their meeting. "Well, Mr. . . ." She felt herself blush. She'd forgotten his name.

"Walker. Jim Walker."

She moved toward the door. "Yes, Mr. Walker. Thanks for coming by. I really appreciate your visit — and the check."

He raised a surprised eyebrow as if he didn't believe her last statement, wisely held the platitudes to a minimum, and left.

Evelyn leaned against the closed door and listened as his footsteps traveled down the porch steps and onto the stepping-stone walk. A car door. An engine. Then silence. Utter, complete silence except for the ticking of the mantel clock counting down the seconds that were left in *her* life.

The silence became a vacuum that sucked away all her energy. She let the solidity of the door guide her as she slid to the floor. Her challis skirt got hung up on a knee, revealing her slip. She moved to pull it primly down, but when she realized there was no one around to see, let it be.

That would take getting used to, having no one around.

The tears began to flow uncontrollably — sobs she never expected. Thoughts of her life began to unfold like a book being opened. . . . She'd lived a pleasant, respectable life, enjoyed good friends, and reared an independent son. Now, in her golden years, was this all she had to show? This was it? Decades of humdrum, monotonous existence coupled with financial struggle?

She sniffed loudly and used her skirt to wipe her face. Then, without warning, she spoke aloud, "God, if You're out there . . . help! Tell me what I'm supposed to do next."

With effort, she took a deep breath, but the air entered in ragged pieces. Why did she feel so worn-out? She used to be full of energy, and yet now, as a widow, her strength vacillated between the frenzy of a worker ant and a bug squashed beneath someone's foot. As if sensing her mood, Peppers nudged her face into Evelyn's calf. Evelyn picked her up and let the calico find her favorite position on Evelyn's shoulder, like a baby going to be burped. Peppers' purring resonated against Evelyn's chest like the comforting sound of cicadas on a summer evening.

Balancing Peppers with one hand, Evelyn drew the check front and center and stared at it. Add another zero and it would have been doable. What had Aaron been thinking?

Yet she couldn't blame it all on him. Hadn't she *let* him be irresponsible? Maybe if she'd been another type of person she could have told him, "Enough, Aaron! Quit going after the quick money, the big break, and settle for a better, steady job that can provide for your family."

But she hadn't said that. She couldn't count the number of times she'd sat across from him as he'd explained his latest big idea. He had been just successful enough to keep up their hopes that the big break was soon to come, that his invention ideas would solve their problems. He'd taken such pleasure in his schemes, his projects. High hopes that were never realized. His failures stemmed from two problems. He had a penchant for being one step behind in his inventions (they'd first seen Velcro in a store the same week Aaron had shown her his prototype for a similar product). Plus, he had a habit of not finishing what he started before moving on to the next project. Add the two qualities together and you got nothing done. Nothing accomplished.

But Evelyn hadn't held her tongue because she was a lady, *or* superior. She'd held back and let Aaron do his thing because she was a coward. She hated confrontation and avoided it at all cost. Go along to get along. Aaron used to become angry at her for saying, "I don't care."

"Don't you care about anything, Evelyn?"

It's not that she didn't care, but she often found decisions daunting and figured it was much safer — and easier — if she let someone else make the choices. Besides, most of the time it made the other person happy, and that was always a good thing.

Peppers squirmed and Evelyn let her go. Then she carefully balanced the check on one knee and sent it flying with a powerful flick of her finger. It didn't fly very long but slid to the floor by the stairs, nudging a defenseless dust bunny. *Would a larger check have floated longer?* Garbage to garbage, dust to dust.

She wasn't without assets. The front hall of the Peerbaugh home loomed before her, the oak staircase a massive Victorian sculpture, its faded flowered runner held in place by brass rods that would cost a fortune to duplicate. Solid brass light fixtures and doorknobs, lovely antiques. The entry table was crowned by a carved mirror and held an azalea plant from the funeral, an anniversary clock they'd received on their thirtieth, and a pink Depression-glass dish forever empty of Aaron's keys and loose change.

Or *was* it empty?

Evelyn pushed herself to her feet, suddenly desperate to see if the dish held a souvenir of her husband's last days. For a whole month she'd walked past and never noticed. But there it was: a quarter, two dimes, and three pennies spotting the glass. She reached to grab them, then withdrew her hand. The array of coins was a still-life composition, each coin placed just so to give an air of haphazardness to its art. She would not move them. Those coins would remain in that dish, undisturbed, until further notice. They were her legacy.

Which left the grand total of her inheritance at ten thousand dollars and forty-eight cents.

Suddenly, a new thought: What about their son, Russell? Where was his inheritance?

An answer loomed. Emotionally spent and physically weary but with new purpose, Evelyn staggered up the stairs to her bedroom and opened the top drawer of Aaron's dresser. She pawed through a haphazard array of paper scraps, pens, and newspaper clippings.

There it is!

Her hand closed around the Peerbaugh family pocket watch, a valuable and coveted possession — even if it no longer worked. This would be Russell's.

It was better than nothing.

Closing the drawer, she noticed a thin five-by-seven box and read the printing on the top: *The New Testament.* Ah yes. It was the Bible Aaron had received from his mother one birthday when she'd been especially disgusted with his flitty ways. *"There's direction for your life in this book, Son. Read it,"* she'd said.

As far as Evelyn knew, Aaron had never even removed it from its box, much less read what was on the pages. The fact that it was still in its original package was testament to her husband's stubbornness at accepting his mother's — or anyone else's — advice.

Evelyn set her fingers upon it. Could there be advice for her within its pages?

She withdrew her hand and shut the drawer. Maybe. But not today. She had enough to think about today.

★ ★ ★

Evelyn spooned another helping of cashew chicken onto her plate, digging the final morsels from the white box.

Her son's fork stopped midway to his mouth. "Glad to see you've got some appetite back. What's the occasion?"

She retrieved a fallen cashew and licked her fingers. "Desperation."

Russell gave her a look that reminded her of his father. "Mom, it'll be all right. I'll help out. You know I will. What's mine is yours."

She shook her head vigorously. "That's not the way it's supposed to work, Russell. The child is not supposed to give money to the parent. The parents are supposed to leave money to the child."

"I wasn't expecting anything." His inability to look her in the eye told a different story.

She put one hand on his, and with the other pulled the gold watch from the pocket of her skirt. She held it out to him, its chain slithering off the side of her hand like a lifeline being extended. "I know it's not much, but I want you to have this."

Russell hesitated a moment, then retrieved the watch and turned it over. He flipped open the cover then held it to his

18

ear. "Does it work?"

"I . . . I don't think so." Her next words spilled out in a flood. "But it's been in the family for three generations, and you make four. I remember seeing your grandfather pull it out of his pocket and —"

"Dad never used this."

"But it was his."

"Did he want me to have it?"

All words died. *Oh dear.*

He looked up. Then down again. Then he set the watch aside, next to the salt and pepper shakers.

"I wish there was more to give you, Russell. And if there's anything in the house that would mean something special to you, just ask. I mean it." He shrugged, and her heart squeezed with the pain of inadequacy. "I'm just glad you're financially stable in your own right."

With a pause, then a shuffling of his shoulders and a blink, Russell seemed to erase the past minute and move on. "I *am* financially independent. Which means I can help you." His jaw tightened. "Like Dad should have done."

"Don't be bitter, Russell. I'm . . . I'm trying not to be."

"But ten thousand dollars . . . what was he thinking?"

"You know your father. He was thinking of a thousand ways to get rich. Always the entrepreneur, always expecting the big turnaround. He didn't mean to leave me in such a desperate situation. And he certainly wasn't contemplating a premature death."

Russell snickered and Evelyn let it go. It would do no good to rehash Aaron's failings. He was dead. She was alone. Those were facts that couldn't be disputed. "There has to be a way for me to earn some money."

"As in you getting a job?"

His incredulous tone pushed a button on her anger, and all intentions to be gracious were shoved aside. "Tell me what choice I have, Russell. After thirty-one years of marriage I'm left with nothing. Nothing! The way I figure it, I've either been a weak fool or a dupe. I sat back and let your father take care of me, never confronting his flighty ways, never making him look past the moment. So now I've gotten what I deserve — which is nothing. I feel like I'm the victim of a con, a thirty-year con in which I've handed over my life savings — both monetary and emotional — and come up with nothing. If your father were here, I would tell . . . I would . . ." She realized she'd been ranting.

"You'd want to yell at him, but you wouldn't. You'd escape to the porch, where you'd hope he would come find you to talk, only he never would. Then after a while, after you'd calmed down, you'd go back inside and pick up as if nothing had happened."

She retrieved her fork, focusing on the food. "Don't mock me, Russell. That's my life you're talking about. Our life. And your father . . . he's dead. I loved —"

He stopped her hand with his. "I don't mean to hurt you, but the issue is not whether you loved him or whether he loved you. Or even how you argued and made up. Right now the point is, he failed to provide for you. He was negligent. He was wrong."

"But it does no good for me to . . . it doesn't change anything."

"It doesn't change anything, but I disagree with you about it not doing any good to express your anger. Anger, in itself, is not wrong. You need to let it out. The trick is not to sit and soak in it."

She managed a smile. "Or your skin will prune?"

"Something like that." They each took a bite and chewed in silence. "You mentioned getting a job . . ." His head

21

shook back and forth.

"I promise not to become a brain surgeon — or a banker like you."

He looked at his plate. "I'm sure you can do anything you set out to do. But you have to be realistic. You've never had a job. Who's going to hire you with *no* experience? Plus, there's the issue of your age . . ." He glanced up, then down again.

He had a point. Getting a first job at age fifty-six was a stretch. "Isn't there a law against age discrimination?"

"Sure, but . . ." He shrugged.

"In an entry position between me and a pretty young thing, I'd lose?"

He shrugged again.

Evelyn took a big bite of rice, hoping the physical fuel would spark some brilliant idea that would solve everything. Her mind was blank.

Russell shoved his plate aside. "Moving on to another question . . . what are you going to do with this house? It was big when it was just you and Dad, but now that it's just you . . ."

"If only you'd do your part and give me some grandchildren."

"Gotta have a wife first." He grinned at her wickedly. "Actually, I don't *have* to have a wife . . ."

She pinched the tip of his nose. "You may be thirty but you're still my baby boy, and as such, you'd better watch your mouth — and your morals."

"I didn't *say* anything."

"But you were thinking naughty thoughts."

"Since when did you become the thought police?"

"Since I became your mother."

He didn't argue; he took his plate to the sink and rinsed it off before putting it in the dishwasher. He returned to his chair, and she was suddenly struck by how much he looked like Aaron, and Aaron's father, Oscar. The Peerbaugh nose made its recipients more interesting than handsome. And the receding hairline —

"Mom, you're looking at me funny."

Evelyn nodded. "You remind me of your father and his father." She looked around, realizing where she was. "In fact, the first time I met your Grandpa Peerbaugh was in this very kitchen. Your father had brought me to dinner to meet his family. It was a full house then, full of Aaron's younger brother and sister, and two renters who lived in two of the bedrooms upstairs. Your grandfather had even had an extra bathroom installed —"

Evelyn sucked in a breath. "That's it!"

"What's it?"

"Renters. I'll take in boarders!"

Russell shook his head. "Strangers in your house? I don't think that's a good idea."

"I would interview them, screen them. And once they moved in, they wouldn't *be* strangers."

Russell laughed. "You got that right. There are only two bathrooms upstairs. Two bathrooms and four bedrooms. Nobody's going to want to rent a room and have to share a bathroom."

"Who says?"

"People are used to having their own bathroom. Their privacy."

"People are spoiled."

"Maybe. Maybe not. And there's only one kitchen."

"We'd share that too. We'd even eat together when we could. Like a family."

"Where would people entertain guests?"

"The parlor, the porch, the sunroom . . . they'd have the run of the house. I think there are a lot of people who would enjoy living in surroundings like this — even if they only had one bedroom to call their own."

"But your antiques. This house is a showplace. Would you want people

24

touching Grandma Nelson's china or sitting in Aunt Mildred's walnut rocker?"

Evelyn stood and began to pace. Her hands danced as her thoughts pummeled her brain. "Those are just things, Russell. Things that have been used for generations. If something breaks, it breaks."

"You weren't that forgiving when I broke something."

"I've changed." She wasn't sure that was true. *If only Aaron were here. He'd take this idea and run with it.*

"How much rent could you charge?"

Evelyn stopped at the kitchen window, pinched a dead leaf off an African violet, and did the mental math. *There's no mortgage . . . just utilities and upkeep. And I'll be getting some Social Security . . .*

"Mom? How much would you charge?"

"I don't know yet. But I'll figure it out."

When she turned back to him, he was shaking his head. "Face it, Mom; you're the last person to tackle such a thing. You're the epitome of disorganization. The house is always clean, but if I asked you right now for a picture of Dad, you would draw photos from five different locations. Why, I've seen you hold a receipt in your hand for a full minute, trying to decide which drawer or purse to stuff it in."

Everything he said was true. "I'll be better. I'll work at it."

"And how are you going to manage rent and damage deposits, house repairs, and tenant disputes? If someone yells at you, you'll probably run out to the porch. Or if they came to you with a sob story about not being able to pay the rent, you'll make them a cup of tea and give them a hug before telling them not to worry about it. So then *I'd* end up worrying about it; I'd end up the bad guy. I'm not sure I'm up for that."

"I'll make it work. I will."

He scooted his chair back. "Would you forget the whole thing if I wrote you a check for a few thousand?"

She straightened her shoulders and shook her head vehemently. "A boarding-house is the answer; I know it is."

He stared at her, and there was a hint of disgust in his face. But also resignation. And even pride? "You've never come to a decision this fast in your life, Mom. *How* do you know? How?"

It was a good question that didn't have a clear answer. This feeling of certainty was foreign but undeniable. She put a fist to her heart, where her certainty was lodged. "How do I know? I just do."

★ ★ ★

Evelyn couldn't sleep. She used to fall asleep within thirty seconds of her head hitting the pillow, but since Aaron's accident the evenings and the nights were torture. Too quiet. Too much time to think, worry, and grieve. If only she didn't have to sleep.

The moonlight sprinkled through the lace of the curtains, falling across the floor and rising up the side of Aaron's dresser. She'd neglected to close the top drawer all the way, and it stood out an inch, calling attention to itself. Aaron's top drawer. The drawer that had held Russell's pitiful inheritance of a gold watch. The drawer that held . . .

She got out of bed and opened it. Her eyes fell on their quarry. She removed the box from the drawer and the New Testament from the box. She returned to bed. The maroon leather binding was a little stiff, but the pages whiffled against themselves as she fanned them. She opened to the first page, which began with the book called Matthew. As she read, she had to make herself concentrate, but what did she have to lose?

Soon, concentration wasn't a problem. She read the genealogy of Jesus, the visit of the magi, and the early life of Jesus. She was captivated with the man called John the Baptist, who risked everything to say what God wanted him to say. And then there were the amazing words of Jesus to those who chose to follow Him.

It was good stuff. As interesting as any novel and more heady than the best self-help book. Why had she been so absorbed with the routines of life that she had not given this book the attention it so obviously deserved? She was a spiritual illiterate. Not something to be proud of. But something that could be rectified.

She nodded at her conclusion and went back to reading the book: "So I tell you, don't worry about everyday life." The words hit home. Hard. She wasn't supposed to worry about anything, not even food or clothes. God would provide. Worry wouldn't add a moment to her life. "Your heavenly Father already knows all your needs, and he will give you all you need from day to day if you live for him and make the Kingdom of God your primary concern."

She pulled the Bible to her chest. It was as if Jesus were speaking to her. To *her!* He knew what she needed and would make sure she got it. She laughed with the pure joy of it.

She read more. And more.

Evelyn woke up to find the Bible opened on her chest and the light still on. She glanced at the clock: 2:13 A.M. She'd read until after midnight and smiled at the memory of her accomplishment. She set the Bible on the bedside table and reached for the light. But her hand stopped short.

Get up.

Compelled to follow the inner nudge, she put on her robe against the nip in the air and ventured into the second-floor hallway. She flipped on the light and found herself studying the layout of the rooms.

The house was a perfect square, with the staircase cutting a hole in the middle from the front entry. The upstairs hallway wound around the stairwell, providing access to the four bedrooms and passing by a window that overlooked the front porch. Each room had its own special perk. The two rooms in the front of the house each had a private balcony overlooking one side of the yard. The two bedrooms that looked out on the backyard had wonderful views of the garden, one even having a window seat. And sandwiched between the front and back bedrooms on each side of the upper level was a bathroom. If Evelyn kept

the front room that she and Aaron had occupied . . . she really liked the morning sun
that came onto their private porch.

But was she willing to share her bathroom with a stranger? Actually, there was a
third bath on the first floor. It was tiny and
only had a shower, but someone could use
it, if need be. And if she let in only woman
boarders . . . it could be like an extended
slumber party. That could be fun.
Couldn't it?

Her eyes were drawn to the cord hanging
from the hall ceiling that, if pulled,
brought down stairs that led to the attic
and its attached turret room. When was
the last time she'd been up there? A year
ago? Funny how you could forget a room
even existed.

Without thinking about it or even realizing she'd made a decision, Evelyn pulled
the cord on the stairs and climbed toward
the attic. Warm, musty air rushed down to
meet her. She flicked the light switch near
the top step. It was an attic right out of a
movie — with trunks, orphan lampshades,
crates, and assorted pieces of furniture.
When she and Aaron had first moved into
the house she'd fallen upon it like a treasure trove and had taken many days to sort
through, claim, and reorganize the heir-

looms of the Peerbaugh family. Over the years, when her own parents had died, she'd added a few of her own family treasures, things she didn't want to use but couldn't bring herself to give away.

Peppers did not hesitate a moment and began exploring the room — a bug smorgasbord. *Go to it, Peps. There's nothing I hate worse than spid—*

Evelyn spotted a dressing table with a trifold mirror and felt her heart flutter. She made a beeline for it, her eyes locked on the small drawer centered under the mirror. It had been so long since she'd looked inside.

She touched the drawer knob but then pulled her hand away. *No. This will do no good. You don't need to remember this right now. The past is past. Deal with the present and figure out your future.*

With difficulty, Evelyn stepped away from the temptation of the dresser. Then she closed her eyes and deliberately turned her back on it. After a cleansing breath, she opened her eyes. The first thing she saw across the room made her smile. Then laugh.

Russell had asked how she knew she was supposed to rent out her home. She strode to a wooden sign hanging from a rafter.

She unfastened the two eye hooks holding it in place. She balanced it against her abdomen and traced a finger along the painted letters. Here was her confirmation. Here was her answer.

Peerbaugh Place, Rooms 4 Rent.

2

*Cheerfully share your home with those
who need a meal or a place to stay.
God has given gifts to each of you from
his great variety of spiritual gifts.
Manage them well so that God's*
generosity can flow through you.
1 PETER 4:9–10

Because of her middle-of-the-night attic excursion, Evelyn slept until eight-thirty. Yet
before she had her first cup of coffee, before
she retrieved the morning paper, Evelyn
picked up the Peerbaugh Place sign, dusted
it off, and headed to the porch in her terry-
cloth robe. She knew she was doing things
out of order, but she felt the need to complete this first step before she moved on to
the myriad of tasks that needed to be done in
order to bring renters into her home.

She stopped at the top of the porch steps
and looked to the overhang. Sure enough.
There were two hooks, waiting decades for
the sign to return to its proper place. She
stood on her tiptoes and hooked it on. It
swung back and forth as if nodding its ap-

proval. She added a nod of her own. This felt right. Very right.

Thanks, God.

She blinked at the realization that she'd just prayed again. Before yesterday, the last time she'd talked to God had been at the hospital when Aaron was fighting for his life. And before that? Although she'd grown up going to Sunday school and knew the basic tenets of Christianity, she'd let her prayer life slide through the cracks of the busyness of her life. There'd been times over the years when she'd felt a need for God and had pulled out the Bible and prayed — and had received the comfort she'd been seeking. But then she'd let God slide back into the background until she needed Him again. It was a very one-sided relationship. God gave and she took.

But He took *Aaron . . .*

Although her logical mind knew that Aaron's penchant for speed and his tendency to be a distracted driver were responsible for his death, she'd needed to blame someone else and God made a good scapegoat. Taking Aaron before his time wasn't fair. Not to him, and especially not to her. She knew there were consequences to people's actions, and if the consequence of being a bad driver was death at the wheel, at least that made a certain kind of sense. But why should Evelyn have to suffer? *Bad plan, God. Definitely a bad —*

The sign proclaiming Peerbaugh Place stopped its swing, and the rays of the morning sun shone on it like a spotlight.

This is a good plan. Continue.

Evelyn sucked in a breath. The words had not been a prayer going *out;* they had formed a thought coming *in.* Clear and distinct. Not a voice, just an idea — and not her own. A strong idea, bonded with a sense of certainty; words welded with a feeling of peace.

"Okay," Evelyn said. She laughed when she realized she'd spoken aloud. On occasion she talked to herself or Peppers, but now she was talking to . . .

This was getting too weird. She shook her head and turned toward the front door.

Coffee. That was the ticket. She needed coffee.

Mae Fitzpatrick turned the volume of the Judy Collins CD to a level that handily drowned out her own singing. The volume adjustment was an act of self-preservation, the singing one of rebellion. Why she — a woman with a heart for music — had not

35

been given a decent voice was a twist of fate she defied with every off-key note she sang. She loved the song playing, "Marieke," and sang along, knowing that she was massacring not only the notes but also the Flemish or French or whatever language Judy was singing. Oh, well. It couldn't be helped.

She shifted her ancient VW bug into third, then reached across the passenger seat to open its window. Though the March morning was nippy, Mae preferred air on her face at all —

The mug of tea that had been wedged between her thighs splashed over at her effort, and she jerked the wheel, causing the driver behind her to honk.

"Whoa there, Mae!" she scolded herself. "You're over your limit of simultaneous acts." She pulled to the curb and yanked on the emergency brake. She dug a wad of Taco Bell napkins from the glove compartment and dabbed at the spilled tea, which had since run off her lap and into a puddle under her behind. Realizing that if she didn't act in the next few seconds her skirt would look as if she'd had another kind of accident, she threw open the car door and jumped from her seat as if she'd hit an ejection button.

She had not remembered that the mug of tea was in her hands. Her quick movement sent most of the amber liquid splashing onto the street, narrowly missing her fruit-adorned sandal. She set the mug on top of the car and backed away with raised arms, as if it were a ticking bomb and she chose surrender. *Step away from the car . . .*

Judy sang on, taking only a moment's break from singing Flemish to singing about a nightingale. The VW continued its putt-putt idle, acting annoyingly oblivious as if saying, *It's not my fault.*

Truth be told, the car was right. Ever since Mae had awakened this morning she'd been a bumper car run amuck. She'd had to speed through a shower when the hot water had decided to stop at lukewarm. She'd knocked the blackberry preserves to the floor, had been forced to use the microwave to heat her tea water when the stove decided not to work, and had found it nearly impossible to insert her pierced earring even though her ears had been that way since the summer of '68 when she and a friend had decided to make hippie beads to sell at rock concerts. In order to better show their wares, they'd pierced each other's ears with a needle and a cube of ice.

The friend was long gone, but Mae's interest in jewelry had remained and had turned from a hobby into her livelihood. No more hippie beads. Mae was the proud proprietor of Silver-Wear, where she turned silver into stunning pieces of wearable art. What the business didn't give her in financial rewards it gave her in satisfaction. It was a trade-off Mae was willing to accept. She'd never needed many material things and much preferred to spend what money she did have on eating out with friends, or taking a week to explore the Flint Hills of Kansas or the maple-syrup country of Vermont. She loved going on bus trips and meeting new people. Her address book was thick with the names of people she'd befriended.

She finished dabbing her skirt, moved to do the same to the driver's seat, and was about to get in when she heard the soft creak of metal against metal. She looked over her car toward a stately Victorian home and noticed a sign moving in the wind. *Peerbaugh Place, Rooms 4 Rent.* The first thought that came into her mind was *Why not?* And before she'd fully let the thought settle, she found herself turning off the car and marching up the front walk.

Who knew? Maybe her luck was about to change.

Evelyn was coming downstairs after getting dressed when the doorbell rang. She hurried down the last few steps and opened the door to a middle-aged woman with very long, very curly, graying hair. The woman thrust out a hip and dug her fist onto its ledge, making the tiny bells at the end of her tie belt twitter.

"I think I'm here for the room?"

Evelyn looked at her blankly, unsure if she'd just heard a statement or a question.

The woman pointed to the sign. "Rooms 4 Rent?"

"Wow." It was all Evelyn could say.

The woman laughed. "If that *wow* is a reaction to my charming personality and striking looks, I'll take it. But if there's another reason, you'll have to explain."

"I just put the sign up an hour ago."

"Oh. Well. First come, first served, I hope."

"I just got the idea last evening."

"I just decided I needed a room. . . ." She shook her head as if clearing it. "I didn't even know I'd decided I needed to move, but hey, here I am, and here you are. I call that good karma."

Evelyn took a moment to let the woman's mention of karma form a link with her long hair, Indian-dyed skirt, and sandals. She was an over-the-hill hippie, that's what she was.

"I'm Mae Fitzpatrick. And you are?"

Evelyn shook Mae's hand. "Evelyn Peerbaugh."

"Which explains the sign. You going to ask me in? Karma or no karma, I'd like to see the room before I say a definite yes." She looked at her feet. Peppers was doing a figure eight between them, across the threshold. "We're confusing your cat. . . ."

Evelyn stepped aside, letting both Mae and Peppers in. Once the woman was inside, Evelyn fought a swell of panic. It was too soon. She wasn't ready. She —

Mae strode from one side of the foyer to the other, peeking into the parlor and the dining room. "Nice place. It's a palace compared to the digs I'm used to."

"Where have you been living?"

Mae ran a hand over the carving on the banister. "Apartment over on Third. Moody plumbing and a kitchen that encourages eating out. It's also full of twenty-somethings with stereos. I like my music as much as the next person, but not at three in the morning. And my tastes lean to Judy

40

Collins, James Taylor, and Andrea Bocelli."

"Opera?"

"Sung by a handsome Italian? You'd better believe it."

"You're not married?"

Mae stopped her inspection. "I'm not sure what my appreciation of Bocelli has to do with me being single, but I'll let it slide. And why don't we hold the renter-landlord interview until after I've seen the room. That all right with you?"

Flustered, Evelyn put a hand to her collar. Why did this woman make her feel as if *she* wasn't in charge? It was *her* house. She put one foot on the stair, then turned to face Mae. "Like I told you, I just got the idea to rent out rooms yesterday, and I haven't even had time to fully think it through. I can show you the rooms I was thinking about renting and then —"

"Then I can help you get this rooming house going." Mae walked past her up the stairs. "I'm good at making things do what I want. Just wait. You'll see."

Evelyn didn't doubt it.

Evelyn and Mae sat at the kitchen table, Mae stirring a second spoonful of sugar into her coffee while Evelyn took notes.

"First off, I prefer herbal teas to coffee." She clinked her spoon on the rim of the cup. "Mae Fitzpatrick doesn't need any additional caffeine in her system. The world couldn't take it."

Evelyn believed it and wrote *herbal tea* on the list.

"Then there's the shared bathroom. I'm not too keen on that, but it's doable. Adds to the adventure. Besides, with my business, I can adjust my bathroom times."

"What's your business?"

"I make jewelry. I'm a silversmith. Maybe you've seen my shop? Silver-Wear?"

Evelyn brightened. "I've been in there. Got my son a money clip with an eagle on it."

"I remember that one. Does he like it?"

"Still uses it." She looked at Mae with new eyes. "You're a real artist. An *artiste*."

Mae laughed. "Ooh, I like foreign words. *Artiste*." She sighed as if soaking in the word. "Call me that and I'm apt to raise my prices." With a flip of her head, she returned to her coffee and looked around the kitchen. "You planning on cooking for us, or should we share the duties?"

"I like to cook, but I'd also like to share."

"Fine with me. Tell me what to do and I'll do it. But be warned: I'm into an

Italian cooking phase at the moment —
Mae's Marvelous Manicotti is my latest
creation. You'll find I live my life in many
such phases. . . ." Mae sighed.

Evelyn didn't ask and Mae didn't elabo-
rate.

"I've always loved Italian food but my
ex, Danny, he wouldn't have it in the
house. Had a thing against Italians. I think
it had something to do with his childhood
neighborhood. The Irish against the Italians." Mae shrugged. "I never was too keen
on Danny's prejudices. My ancestors are
gypsy — or at least that's what I'm
claiming. Sounds exotic, doesn't it?"

It suited her. "How long have you been
divorced?"

Mae waved a hand. "A smidgen past forever. Danny and I never should have married in the first place. Met in the free-love
sixties, had sex, got pregnant, got married,
popped out a couple kids, then he left."

Mae made motherhood sound as imper-
sonal as saying a couple pieces of bread
had popped out of a toaster.

Mae shrugged again, making her earrings
dance. "It's just as well. Sometimes living
alone is better than living a life of groan and
moan. It wasn't easy being a single mom
bringing up two kids, but we managed."

"Where are your kids now?"

"Unfortunately too far away to see often. Last I heard, Ringo lived in LA, and Starr in New York. I'd like to see more of them, but they have their own lives." She leaned close across the table. "I think I'm too much for them."

Imagine that.

She raised her coffee toward Evelyn. "And you? You got to jump in here with your own life story. You get me talking and I'll give you a three-hour movie, no intermission. What's up with you?"

Evelyn fingered the edge of the yellow pad. "I'm a widow. A new widow. Just lost my husband a month ago."

Mae sat back in her chair with a huff. "Zounds, sister. And here I am going on . . . how you doing? How'd he die?"

"I'm doing okay. He died in a car accident. Going too fast in the rain. Lost control. Ran into a tree out on Highway —"

Mae slammed a hand on the table. "On Highway 2? I heard about that one! That was your husband?"

Evelyn nodded. It was a little disconcerting to know that Aaron's death had been news.

Mae reached across the table and patted her hand. "You got kids?"

"A grown son, Russell. He's a vice president at the Carson Creek National Bank."

"Grandkids?"

"He's not married. Not yet."

Mae leaned back and smiled. Her finger did a curlicue in front of Evelyn's face. "I see Mama Matchmaker in your eyes. You got someone in mind for him?"

"I wish I did. He's thirty and seems in no hurry. He's a freewheeling bachelor."

"Ugh. No fair. A woman who's unmarried is a pitiful old maid. A man? He's a freewheeling bachelor. Not fair. Not fair at all."

Evelyn had never thought of such a thing, but she agreed. Being a woman was often hard. And being a widow was harder. "Aaron didn't leave me much. I decided to open the house to boarders to help make ends meet."

"Good for you. I like to see a woman with spunk — one who doesn't take adversity lying down. You and me will get along just fine. I know it."

"Me too." Evelyn was surprised that she meant it, but she did. She liked Mae, and the thought of her verve coming into the house was like opening a musty room that had been closed too long.

Mae stirred a third spoonful of sugar

into her coffee. "You'll have to get a permit from the city to do this, you know."

Evelyn let her chin drop. "No, I didn't know. How do I do that?"

"Oh, I'll do it for you," Mae said. "Being a business owner, I know all the people at city hall by their first name, last name, and the names I call them when they cause me trouble."

"Do you think it'll be hard to get one?"

"Not with Mae on your team." She pushed herself away from the table. "I gotta get to the shop now. I'll stop at city hall over lunch."

Evelyn stood to see her out. "What should I do next?"

Mae thought a moment. "I'd start by clearing the knickknacks out of the rooms you want to rent. People will have their own doodads. And clean out the dresser drawers and the closets." She opened the front door, then turned back. "Oh. And get me some tea. Almond Sunset or Bengal Spice would be good."

It would be Evelyn's pleasure. Peerbaugh Place was now open for business. This would be a piece of cake — or rather a cup of tea. Herbal.

Tessa Klein hunkered over the steering

wheel, her eyes locked on the street in front of her. It was hard seeing over the huge hood, and once again she thought about trading in her boat of a car for a smaller model. Although this vehicle had been her late Alfred's pride and joy, and though at one time in her life she *had* taken her own joy in owning it, now that she was the one driving it around Carson Creek, she felt it both a burden and a challenge. The only way Tessa could even reach the pedals was to put the driver's seat as far forward as it would go. And that meant that the person in the passenger seat had to be as tiny as she was. But most of the time, that seat was empty anyway, so leg room or no leg room didn't matter.

Room. Or a lack of it. That was the issue that seemed to consume Tessa lately. And it wasn't that the bedroom she was staying in at her daughter's house didn't carry enough square feet. It was the mental room Tessa was lacking. She felt as welcome there as a red bean in a bag of dried peas, like something to be plucked out and tossed away so it didn't defile the rest. She'd tried to be tolerant and had used every ounce of her willpower to keep her mouth shut — even though her daughter's hubby and Tessa's grandson fairly begged for some outside intercession. Those two could argue over the existence of air. The constant tension squeezed Tessa dry, making her feel like a sponge being wrung out and set precariously on the edge of a sink.

Yesterday had pressed her nearly to the point of walking out. She'd just gotten a new book on Elizabethan history and had settled into her room with a notepad at her side, all ready to study, when her grandson had brought a friend home from school and had proceeded to park in front of the computer, filling the house with the insipid *boink-boink* and *crash* sounds of some game. Why couldn't they defeat the aliens with the mute button pushed? Plus their constant shouting as they competed against each other. And then Naomi had come home from work and started dinner, flipping the stereo on, filling what was left of the noise capacity of the house with a moronic bass beat.

Tessa had felt as if her nerves were on the verge of sprouting through her skin. She'd found herself clutching her new book to her chest so tightly that she'd actually folded a page back. To desecrate a book . . . unthinkable.

She'd marched into the family room and flipped off the stereo.

Naomi came out of the kitchen at the same time Leonard and his friend looked up from their game. "What's wrong, Mother?" Naomi asked.

"Noise is what's wrong. God did not intend for ears, minds, or souls to be constantly filled with junk noise."

Naomi rolled her eyes and finished wiping out the salad bowl. "It's not junk, Mother. The boys are playing a game. And the music I was listening to was Sibelius. Hardly junk." She turned her back and returned to the kitchen. Leonard seemed quick to note that his mother was not paying any attention to Grandma, so he didn't see a reason to either. He and his friend turned back to their game, and the noise resumed.

Tessa had returned to her room, and only through an enormous amount of restraint, did *not* slam the door. But she hadn't studied either. She'd set the Elizabethan history book aside for a more appropriate time, sat in the chair, and fumed. She knew it was childish but —

Her eyes were temporarily pulled off the street to a beautiful Victorian house, complete with gingerbread, a turret, and a big porch. A sign swung back and forth as if saying, *Look at me! Look at me!* It said *Peerbaugh Place, Rooms 4 Rent.*

She slammed on the brakes. Her eyes shot to the rearview mirror; she was grateful no one had been behind her.

And Tessa smiled.

Evelyn put the swan figurine in the box with the rest of the pretties. The front bedroom Mae had chosen was now full of boxes containing a lifetime of bric-a-brac as well as the contents from the closet and the dresser. She scanned the room. She'd leave the pictures on the wall. If the tenants wanted to remove them, they would be free to do so. Now all she had to do was dust and vacuum. Evelyn picked up one of the boxes to move to the attic. *If only Aaron was around to help with the heavy —*

She heard a car door slam and pulled the lace curtain aside to look out the window. An elderly black woman walked around the front of a huge car and paused at the end of the front walk. She looked at something on the house and nodded as if she'd asked a question and received an answer.

What's she looking at? It was too early for flowers in the porch planters, and the daffodils were just starting to burst through the ground.

The sign!

Evelyn dumped the box on the bed, glanced in the dresser mirror, decided her marginal hairdo would have to do, and ran down the stairs. She paused at the front door and took a deep breath. *Okay, God. Here we go again.*

Another prayer. Quite phenomenal.

She opened the door and casually walked onto the porch. Peppers slipped out with her, giving Evelyn something to do. She picked her up, cuddling her close. "There, there, Peps, want to take a turn around the porch with me?" Only then did she allow herself to look at the woman coming up the walk. She proceeded with a lame expression of surprise. "Oh. Hello. May I help you?"

"Your sign . . . you have rooms to rent?"

Evelyn smiled. This was amazing. "I sure do. Are you looking for a room?"

"It appears so." She pointed to her car. "I was just driving by on the way to my Bible study when I happened to look over and see the sign. Never saw it before —"

"That's because it wasn't up before. I just hung it this morning."

The woman put both hands in the air. "Well, praise be! That's that, then." She strode onto the porch as if rushing to accept a prize.

Evelyn found herself taking a step back. The woman stopped within a foot of her, the top of her head barely reaching Evelyn's chin. They shook hands, and Evelyn found a surprising power in the woman's grip.

"Tessa Klein," she said. "God's mighty servant — in spite of my size. And you are?"

Evelyn was at a loss. Although she and God were back on speaking terms, "mighty servant" was definitely not a title she could claim. "Evelyn Peerbaugh. . . . uh . . . landlord." *Kinda. Sorta. Hopefully.*

"Glad to meet you, Mrs. Peerbaugh."

Evelyn held Peppers up for inspection. "And this is Peppers. She's a dear. I don't know what I would do without —"

Tessa ignored the cat completely, not even patting her head. She looked to the wicker furniture in the corner of the porch. "Can we sit? I've never been one to stand and talk. That's what chairs are for."

Evelyn set Peppers free and led Tessa to the settee. "Would you like some coffee? I've got some made." She thought of Mae. "Or maybe tea?"

"Coffee would be grand. Strong and

black. Never did abide with tea. It's like drinking tan water." She shuddered with disgust.

One vote for coffee. "I'll be right back."

Evelyn returned with a tray holding coffee and butter cookies. She'd even used Grandma Nelson's rose china. Somehow Tessa Klein seemed the type who would appreciate such a thing.

"Here we are." She handed Tessa a cup and offered a cookie.

Tessa took one. "I love sweets."

Evelyn patted the extra ten pounds that congregated around her midsection. "Me too. Unfortunately."

Tessa raised a bony finger. "As I was saying, I love sweets but only allow myself one a day. Self-control is essential to godly living."

"You said you were looking for a room?"

"Only thought of the idea last evening, and then, when I saw your sign . . ." She shook her head. "Mmm, mmm . . . God is never late and never early; that's what I always say. It's pretty clear He put the idea in my head, you put the sign up, I drove by, and —" she spread her hands — "the rest is His will being laid out like slices of birthday cake. All we have to do is reach out and take a piece. Totally logical."

Evelyn felt an eyebrow rise and, with determination, lowered it. She wasn't used to hearing people talk like this. It wasn't offensive, just different.

Tessa pinched a piece of lint from her skirt and dropped it in her napkin. "Since I was widowed eleven months ago, I've been living with my daughter's family. And that's been fine and dandy, but it's a bit tight for my taste. Though the thought of living by myself. . . . In all my seventy-five years I've never been on my own — went from my parents' home to my husband's." She took a deep breath. "And yet 'It is better to live alone in the corner of an attic than with a contentious wife in a lovely home.' "

"You lost me. You're a contentious wife?"

A hand flew to her chest. "No, no, not me. My daughter and her family. They'd get a blue ribbon for bickering. I don't know where they get such an attitude. I've never been one to argue — at least not for argument's sake. Though when a person is right . . ." She shrugged.

There was a warning of a sort there, but Evelyn didn't have time to dissect it.

"So." Tessa put her coffee down and slapped her thighs. "May I see my room?"

It sounded like a done deal. Things were going so fast. . . . Evelyn led Tessa upstairs, noting that although the woman took the stairs well, she took them slowly and held on to the railing with extra care. Surely she could find a one-level retirement home to rent rather than a two-story house with steep stairs.

Evelyn turned into the smaller of the two back bedrooms. "I have two rooms left. This one has the best view of the garden, but the other one is slightly bigger and has a window seat." She pulled the dotted-Swiss curtains aside and looked down on her garden. The plants were just starting to come up. She thought of past years and the gardening chores she would have already accomplished by now. "I'm behind in my yard work. I'm a little late because of my husband's death."

"You're a recent widow?"

"A month now." She told Tessa about the car accident, the lack of insurance, and the need to open her house to boarders.

"Shame on him!" Tessa said, wagging a finger. " 'Those who won't care for their own relatives, especially those living in the same household, have denied what we believe. Such people are worse than unbelievers.' " She cocked her head. "Unless . . .

55

was he a believer?"

"I . . . I really don't know."

Both of Tessa's eyebrows rose, causing a washboard on her forehead. "You don't *know?*"

Evelyn felt a sudden need to be busy. She smoothed the yellow-and-white quilt on the bed. "We didn't talk about such things."

"Such *things?* God is not a *thing,* Evelyn. He is the Almighty, ruler of heaven and earth. He is —"

"I know that."

Another look. "Do you?"

Evelyn straightened and smoothed her shirt over her hips. "Actually, Mrs. Klein, I don't think the level of my faith is any of your business. That's a personal matter between me and God."

"Humph. Well, that's something at least."

"What's something?"

"At least you acknowledge His existence. That's a start. Now, let's see that other room."

She followed Tessa into the hallway. Acknowledged or unacknowledged, Evelyn hoped God knew what He was doing.

Evelyn pulled the covers over her shoulder and shut off the bedside lamp.

Peppers had already found her place in the crook of Evelyn's legs. The darkness tucked around them, providing the perfect backdrop for some heavy-duty thinking.

It had been a well-spent day — a miraculous day, when she really thought about it. She'd found the sign, put it up, and had gotten two paying renters without advertising. Tessa had ended up taking the smaller of the two back rooms, opting for its better view. Yet truth be told, Evelyn was a little disappointed that the third — and final — room hadn't rented. Now *that* would have been a real miracle.

Should I put an ad in the paper tomorrow?

The thought came — and went as quickly as it had come. She wasn't ready to resort to normal means to rent out the last room. Wouldn't that be an affront to God or fate or whatever was at work here? No, she'd hold off taking matters into her own hands.

For a little while.

3

Be humble and gentle.
Be patient with each other,
making allowance for each other's faults
because of your love.
EPHESIANS 4:2

Evelyn had taken only one sip of her morning coffee when the doorbell rang. She drew her robe tight around her and peeked through the leaded glass of the door. A mass of orange undulated in the bevels of the glass.

"It's me, Evie. It's Mae. Let me in."

Before Evelyn could pull the door fully open, Mae Fitzpatrick had opened the screen door wide and was inside, heading toward the kitchen with two sacks of groceries. The sleeves of her orange peasant blouse billowed in her own wind. Her orange-and-fuchsia flip-flops marked a syncopated rhythm below denim capri pants edged with an embroidered ribbon. Evelyn dutifully followed rather than be left in Mae's dust.

Mae set the sacks on the counter and

began unpacking — and talking. "Top o' the morning to you, Evie. I come bearing gifts. Of course I also come bearing the bulk of my worldly possessions out in the car, but first things first." She displayed a can of artichoke hearts. "I have a recipe for a super artichoke dip. I'll make us some to-night — as an appetizer." She gave Evelyn a sideways glance. "You do like artichokes, don't you?" Mae made it sound like a character requirement.

"I've rarely had the pleasure," Evelyn said. "Aaron didn't like vegetables."

"Well, *I* love 'em, so I will take it upon myself to educate you to the delights of the veggie kingdom: asparagus, squash, and peppers of every color and intensity. That sound okay with you?"

Mae didn't wait for an answer. She opened cupboards, found the pantry before Evelyn could point it out, and emptied part of her wares inside, distributing the rest into the refrigerator. She folded the sacks in half and found the place under the sink where Evelyn stored them. Suddenly, Evelyn had the feeling her kitchen was not her kitchen anymore. She'd been invaded by a tall gypsy with painted toenails and a butterfly comb in her frizzy hair.

Mae stopped her movement and put her

hands on her hips. "Uh-oh. I'm getting bad vibes. Have I overwhelmed you?"

Evelyn felt herself redden. "A bit."

Instead of apologizing, Mae left the kitchen. "You'll get over it. At least I'm a friendly invader." Evelyn heard the front door open, and Mae's words took on the echo of the foyer. "You did get my room cleaned out, didn't you?"

Evelyn moved after her, feeling like a puppy looking to its master for direction. "It's all ready for —"

"Mighty fine," Mae said. "Now if you'll hold the screen door open, I'll do the hauling. No need for both of us to get sweaty. I took the entire day off, but it won't take that long. I've promised myself never to accumulate more things than I can move in two hours."

Evelyn thought of the three decades of stuff that filled Peerbaugh Place.

Mae handed the screen door off to Evelyn, then stopped at the top of the porch steps and adjusted the butterfly comb. "Uh-oh. There I go again, giving offense when I don't mean to. There's nothing wrong with having stuff, Evelyn — if that's your thing. Not to have many things is a decision I made. Simplify and unify. We are all one in the universe, even without our toaster ovens and matching handbags. Doesn't that sound grand?"

Evelyn opened her mouth to answer — by saying what, she wasn't sure — but once again, Mae moved on before she had a chance to reply.

Just as well. She'd have to get used to the fact that Mae Fitzpatrick left her speechless.

Evelyn had just packed the last box of knickknacks from the other two rental rooms when Mae appeared, a glow to her forehead, a flush to her cheeks.

"Ready or not, I'm in."

"Is the room satisfactory?" Evelyn asked. "Can I get you any — ?"

"Yes to the first question, no to the second. It's great. Though I *did* take down the landscape above the bed to make room for a Picasso print I got in San Francisco. I assume that's okay."

Only if you like Picasso.

Evelyn lifted a box and headed to the attic stairs. "Would you pull down on that rope, please?"

Mae got the stairs down, retrieved a box, and followed Evelyn up. "Wow. Quite a treasure trove up here."

"Kind of the opposite of your 'simplify'

lifestyle, isn't it? I really should have a garage sale or something."

Mae tried on a straw hat, leaning over to see her reflection in the dressing table. "Don't do such a thing on my account. You is what you is, and I is what I is. It's not my job to try to change you or make you see things my way. We can be unified in our differences by believing in one mind, one spirit. A world based on peace and brotherly — or should I say sisterly — love."

It sounded easy enough, and it handily removed Evelyn's guilt. For the moment at least.

They took another load to the attic, then both rested by sitting on some trunks. "Tell me about the other tenants," Mae said.

"Tenant. I still have one room to rent."

"Tell me about her then."

When you say po-ta-to, she'll say po-tah-to.
. . . "She's seventy-five, a widow who's been living with her daughter. This is the first time she'll be on her own. Ever."

Mae rubbed her hands together. "Oh, goody. We'll have a chance to break her in good."

"I'm not sure Tessa Klein will take kindly to any 'breaking in'."

Mae's legs stopped swinging. "Which means?"

Evelyn's mind scrambled to find a diplomatic way to say what needed to be said. "She seems a bit set in her ways."

"Meaning she always has to brush her teeth *before* she combs her hair?"

"I don't know about that . . . I was referring to how she seems set in her opinions of things." Evelyn was quick to add, "It sounds like she's a deeply religious woman."

Mae threw her hands in the air in a mock revival stance. "Praise the Lord! Hallelujah! Come to me, sweet Jesus!"

Although Evelyn shared some of Mae's distaste for in-your-face religion, she didn't like the mocking tone. If they were going to get along, live together . . . "There's nothing wrong with believing strongly in God."

"Just so her God doesn't interfere with my God."

Oh dear. "I'm sure she'll be tolerant if you'll be tolerant." Evelyn wasn't sure at all.

Mae slid off the trunk. " 'Whatever works for you' is my motto." She brushed the dust off the back of her capris. "How did you choose her anyway?"

"I didn't choose her; she chose me."

"But you're the landlord. You don't have to take the first person who comes to your door."

Evelyn smiled. "But I did. That would be you."

Mae shrugged. "Point taken. But that doesn't mean you have to take the second one. Or the third. Any applicants for the last room?"

"None."

"Hmm. Well, we'll see what happens. I'm tolerant, but I *do* have my preferences. And certainly not a man. Though that would make things interesting." Mae headed down the attic steps. "You ready for lunch? I make a mean tuna salad with bean sprouts and celery chunks."

Yummy.

The doorbell rang, and Mae was up to get it before Evelyn twitched a muscle. *You'll have to be faster than that to keep up with me.*

Mae thought the woman at the door looked like she could have snapped in two with a good sneeze. But it was more than her physical frame that looked brittle; there was an edge to her eyes and a tilt to her jaw that proclaimed, *Don't tread on me.*

"May I help you?" Mae asked.

"Who are you?"

"I'm Mae Fitzpatrick. I live here."

The woman pulled open the screen door, forcing Mae to step aside and let her in. *Glad to meet you too.* Mae shut the door behind her and thrust her hand out. "And you are?"

"Tessa Klein."

The woman did not meet Mae's eyes. She was too busy giving Mae a once-over. Mae wished she were wearing her leopard leggings, black off-the-shoulder shirt, and metallic gold mules. That outfit would have deserved such scrutiny.

Mae decided to fight fire with fire and did her own sweep of Tessa's outfit. The woman could have been the poster child for frumpy. Pull-on pants, a floral overblouse that screamed, *I'm elderly,* and an enormous purse that most likely contained at least two embroidered hankies hanging from her crooked forearm. Pitiful.

"You always dress like that?" Tessa asked Mae. She flicked a finger to encompass the extent of Mae's fashion.

"Only on Saturdays. The rest of the week I get really funky."

When Tessa's left eyebrow lifted, Mae slipped her hand around her arm and led her toward the kitchen. "Tell you what. Maybe next week, you and I can go shopping. The Fashion Bug on the square has the cutest halter top in the window, which I'm dying to strap on. Who knows? They might have a matching one for you. What do you think, Tessie?"

Tessa pulled her arm out of captivity, none too gently. "It's Tessa, and I'll thank you not to impose your fashion machinations on me."

Mae raised her arms in surrender. "Hey, *no problemo.* I don't *machinate* anybody until I've known them at least an hour, so don't pull your polyester out of shape for me."

Suddenly Evelyn came rushing out of the kitchen like a referee ready to pull two boxers apart. Her eyes darted nervously between them. *What does she think I'm going to do?* Mae wondered. *Arm wrestle the old lady to the ground?*

"Mrs. Klein. How nice you're here."

"Thank you, Mrs. Peerbaugh."

Mae made a time-out *T* with her hands. "Okay. Don't you think we should drop this Mrs. stuff? We're going to be housemates. Share each other's blow-dryers, Cracker Jack prizes, and the intimate details of our lives." They both looked at her as if she were an alien being. These ladies needed more shaking up than a bottle of Yoo-Hoo. "Okay. So forget the Cracker Jacks."

Evelyn pinched her lower lip, then let it go. "I do think first names might be more appropriate. Is that all right with you . . . ?" She hesitated and Mae could tell she was weighing whether to use "Mrs. Klein" or "Tessa."

"Tessa will be fine."

Evelyn looked way too relieved. If everything was going to be this draining, they'd need to schedule afternoon naps to recharge.

Tessa looked at her watch. "I said I'd be here at one — and I was. Now it's after. My things are in the car."

Her voice implied that she expected someone else to retrieve them. And the way her ugly — but comfortable — shoes seemed glued to the foyer floor, Mae was sure of it. It took all her self-control not to say, "So?"

Evelyn jumped in, her voice too loud. "I'll get them!" She started to push past the two women, but Mae pulled her back.

"Gracious goose, Evie. I'll help too, if you give me a minute." *Give me a minute to turn my patience button on full blast.*

"I'd like something to drink, if you don't mind," Tessa said, looking toward the kitchen.

The idea that Tessa expected to sip tea while she and Evelyn worked was totally unacceptable — an expectation that had to be nipped in the bud. Now. "That sounds grand," Mae said. "I could use some refreshment myself."

Evelyn looked between them, her face a mask of turmoil. Mae tried to give her a look of encouragement, and after a moment of hesitation, Evelyn swept her hand toward the kitchen like a courtier making way for the queen. "Right this way."

Tessa walked past. "I'd like coffee, please. Black."

Coffee? It was not a good sign.

Mae headed upstairs with the eleventh box of Tessa's twelve. Her pace had slowed, as had Evelyn's, who carried the final box.

Tessa was getting moved in — no thanks to Tessa. Not that she could have helped much if she'd been so inclined — which she obviously wasn't. The very idea of Tessa carrying a box up the steep stairs made Evelyn shudder. So without verbally sharing their decision, the two younger

68

women had emptied Tessa's car of Tessa's worldly goods. All twelve boxes and two suitcases full.

Mae stopped halfway up to re-situate a box with her knee. "Are you sure there aren't rocks in these boxes, Tessie?"

Tessa answered from her station in the bedroom doorway. "No. Just books."

"All of them?"

"Of course."

To Evelyn, there was no 'of course' to it. She and Aaron had plenty of books, but there were more unread than read ones on the shelves. And Tessa's books were much more scholarly than Evelyn's romances and mysteries. Tessa's books covered a wide range from biographies to world politics to thrillers. And Bibles . . . Evelyn had never seen so many Bibles and books about Bibles.

Evelyn reached the hallway and leaned the edge of her box on the railing. "Do you read all these?"

"Of course."

"I sure hope there's room on the bookshelf," Tessa said, glancing in her room.

Evelyn hoped so too. At Tessa's instruction, they had transferred a bookshelf from the unclaimed bedroom into Tessa's, she, willingly sacrificing a second dresser to obtain a home for her beloved books.

Mae dropped her box on Tessa's bed. "Maybe you can build a Leaning Tower of Pisa with them?"

"I will not have my books stacked haphazardly." Tessa eyed the last two boxes, chewing on a fingernail. "Do you have extra shelf space downstairs for these, Evelyn?"

Evelyn did a quick mental scan of the first-floor shelves. "I'm afraid not."

"Then where am I going to put them?"

"There's an attic."

"That will have to do." Tessa's eyes lit up. "Perhaps I can use it as a study?"

"It's unfinished," Evelyn said. "But there is room for your boxes."

Tessa sighed deeply. "Let me go through these more thoroughly, separating the ones I want to keep out. Then you can take the boxes to the attic — if that's our only solution."

Evelyn felt rebellion brewing. It wasn't the work Tessa made for the rest of them that riled her, it was the I-deserve-it attitude. But surprisingly, if Evelyn thought she was going to get an ally in Mae, she was wrong.

Although Mae's earlier if-Tessa-has-a-break-let's-all-have-a-break mutiny had been an interesting prologue to the atmosphere of the household, Mae had behaved herself the rest of the afternoon, as if making her point up front was satisfaction enough. It was the tension of waiting to see which way the mood would swing that rattled Evelyn's nerves the most. Would Tessa say something to upset Mae? Or vice versa?

Actually, in spite of her tolerant ways, Evelyn *was* pleased that Mae had taken a stand against Tessa's attitude. It was the principle of the thing. Like the law of the land, the law of Peerbaugh Place was going to have to be created according to precedent. Evelyn realized that allowing the strong will of Tessa to overpower them once would be akin to letting a child eat chocolate only once and then trying to get him to stop.

There would be a lot of adjusting to do, and in her exhaustion Evelyn decided she wasn't going to be the only one doing the adjusting.

At least she hoped not.

Evelyn picked the box of pink stomach tablets off the grocery shelf and opened it. She wasn't in the habit of using a product before paying for it, but this was an emer-

71

gency. Her first landlord moment. She popped two into her mouth and chewed, hoping they would counteract the surges of acid that were wreaking havoc on her tummy.

She'd escaped the house, needing time alone. Evelyn had been used to having Aaron around during the day, and they'd found a kind of rhythm in his work and her household activities. But somehow having two other women underfoot. . . . The past three days had been something altogether different. So this afternoon when Tessa had gone to the library (for *more* books?), Evelyn had taken advantage of the moment to run errands. Luckily, Mae had not offered to come along.

It was odd leaving a stranger in control of her house. Would Evelyn return home and find her possessions cleared out, stolen by Mae and her gang of thugs? Ridiculous or not, her renters *were* virtual strangers. Strangers trying to mold a life together.

And yet . . . there was an air of excitement about that. Perhaps the stress invading her stomach wasn't all negative. Perhaps Evelyn was feeling wound up because she found herself on an adventure — something bigger than herself, something

God had drop-kicked into her corner. Evelyn the Adventurer. She liked the sound of that.

She tried to concentrate on the task at hand. Adventurers needed to eat. She turned down the pasta aisle. As landlord, Evelyn had volunteered to make the meals until they brought in the last renter and had a chance to make a proper schedule. Except for the coffee-tea thing, no one seemed overly picky. That was a blessing.

Evelyn stopped in front of the lasagna noodles. Mae had mentioned she liked Italian. Evelyn remembered her mother's recipe. She'd made it once for Aaron when they were first married, but he had pooh-poohed it as too fancy. But now, fancy could be good. In fact, fancy could be downright fun.

She put a box in her cart.

Back at home Evelyn had to park on the street because there was a strange car in the driveway. She walked past it with an armload of groceries and noticed a doll and an empty juice box on the backseat. Who was visiting?

She went in the kitchen door and found Mae sitting at the table with a young woman who had spiky dark hair and wore horn-rimmed glasses that reminded Evelyn of the sixties. A little girl colored in a coloring book nearby.

Mae stood immediately to help. "Evelyn! Just in time. Let me take those. Are there more in the car?"

Evelyn smiled tentatively at the young woman and nodded.

"Then I'll get them. Come in and meet our newest tenant, Audra Taylor."

In her shock, all Evelyn could do was nod. She was out of the house an hour, and in her absence Mae had rented the last room? To a mother and child? Who did Mae think she — ?

Audra stood and extended her hand. "Nice to meet you, Mrs. Peerbaugh. Mrs. Fitzpatrick showed me around the place. It's beautiful." She turned to her daughter. "Summer, say hello to Mrs. Peerbaugh."

The little girl looked up from her coloring, assessed Evelyn with one glance, held up her picture, and said, "Hello. I like dogs to be purple, don't you?"

Evelyn was taken aback. She'd expected a shy hello. "Purple's a pretty color."

Summer looked at the picture and nodded. "That's what I think too." She went back to her play as if it were work. "This picture's for you."

"Why, thank you." Evelyn turned to Audra. "She's a bright one."

Before Audra could answer, Summer chimed in, "Mama says I'm percocious."

"It's *pre*cocious, baby," Audra said.

"Yesterday was my birthday," the child continued. "I'm five now."

Evelyn found herself softening to the two of them. And yet . . . two in one room? And a child? Talk about adjustments.

Mae came in with the rest of the groceries, closing the door with her foot. "You three get acquainted yet?"

"We're getting there." *As if I had a choice?* Evelyn moved to help with the groceries, but was passed by Summer, who'd gotten out of her chair and had skipped to Mae's side.

The little girl picked up a can of tomato sauce. "Where does this go?"

"My, my, you are the little helper, aren't you?"

Her mother spoke up. "It's best to let her help. If you say you can do it yourself, she'll stew."

"I'll stew," Summer said, pulling the kitchen stool over to the counter as if it had her name on it. She climbed the steps in front of the open cupboard of canned goods and held out her hand to Mae.

75

"Well, then," Mae said, "I guess I'd better let you help."

Her own help not needed, Evelyn was forced to return to the table and sit across from Audra. It was an awkward moment. Audra looked to Evelyn as if waiting for final approval.

Evelyn figured she had two choices. She could either be gracious and accept what was done as done, or she could take a stand and claim Peerbaugh Place as her own and insist that proper renter-landlord etiquette be met; tell Mae to cool it. She could give in or fight.

But what was she fighting for? Was it the addition of a young mother and child she objected to, or Mae's stepping over the line?

She'd never been a fighter, and most of the time in their marriage it had been a blessing. Aaron didn't like *any* emotional outbursts, and Evelyn had discovered it was easier to remain quiet and in control rather than deal with his reactions to her highs and lows. It wasn't that *he* was so controlled or calm . . . he'd had more highs and lows than a roller coaster. Yet maybe one excitable person was enough for one home. While Aaron commandeered the role of emotional thrill ride, she'd accepted the role of passenger, along for the ride. While he'd thrown his hands in the air with reckless abandon during the thrilling moments of their lives, she'd closed her eyes and held on tight.

She had to open her eyes now. She had to let go of the handrail. She was in the roller-coaster car alone. *If that's the case, then I want out! Out, right now. I don't want any more roller coasters in my life. I don't —* She stopped her mental ranting. She wasn't alone in this. God was around. He'd help.

"I really appreciate this, Mrs. Peerbaugh," Audra said.

Audra's politeness broke through her thoughts. It was done. The house was rented. So be it. Who was she to argue? As for Mae? She was just being Mae — definitely someone who thrived on roller coasters.

Evelyn cleared her mind of any inkling to wobble what was already in place and managed a smile. "You're welcome, Audra. But what brings you out looking for a room? Where's your . . . I mean . . ."

"Where's my husband?"

Evelyn felt herself redden. "Well, yes, that *is* one of the obvious questions."

"There is no husband, never was a husband. Summer is the product of a teenage spree into sexuality. Her father wanted to marry me, but I knew that wasn't the answer to our situation. Luke's a nice guy but not husband material."

"But he *was* nice enough to sleep with." As soon as the words were out, Evelyn slapped a hand to her mouth. "I'm sorry. I hadn't meant to say that aloud."

"Might as well say it. Everybody thinks it anyway. And you're right. We had fun, but that was the extent of it." Audra sighed deeply. "And so, here we are."

An unwed mother. Evelyn couldn't get that label out of her mind. "Why didn't you give her up for adoption?"

Mae swung around. "Evie! You don't say such a thing in front of the . . ." She nodded at Summer.

Evelyn felt herself redden again. "Sorry. That was inappropriate. I didn't mean to imply that you made the wrong decision; I just —"

"It's okay," Audra said. "That's the right choice for a lot of women, but I . . ." She looked at her daughter and seemed to weigh her words. "Though the whole situation came as a shock, my parents were very supportive. Perhaps if they hadn't been . . ."

Evelyn couldn't help but be impressed

by the love she saw in the look Audra gave her daughter. Its intensity made her own heart ache with envy.

Audra continued. "She's the sun in my sky, aren't you, baby?"

Summer didn't look up from her grocery unpacking. "I'm your sweetie baby. Sweet as sugar sprinkles with a cherry on top." The little girl looked down at Peppers, who had her front legs on the bottom step of the stool. Summer momentarily forgot helping and sat down on the top step, dragging a resigned Peppers into her arms. "Ooh, kitty, kitty. What's your name?"

Audra broke in, "No, Summer. You leave the kitty alone, she might not like —"

"She loves attention, and her name is Peppers," Evelyn said. "She likes you."

Audra fingered one of Summer's crayons and seemed to willingly let the Peppers issue slide, as if she'd only spoken up out of a sense of duty to be polite. "Anyway, Summer and I have been staying at my parents' while I went to college. But now I've graduated and it's time we made our own way. I just got a job at the Carson Creek National Bank. I start in two weeks. A good friend of mine helped me get the job." She sighed. "I'm lucky to have Gillie — and Piper. She's another of my friends who's hung with me. I feel very blessed."

"The bank?" Evelyn said. "My son works there. Russell Peerbaugh? He's a vice president."

"Oh? I didn't meet him during the interviews."

"What an interesting coincidence," Evelyn said.

"Karma," said Mae.

And Tessa would call it an act of God. But still, an unwed mother and a child. "The room's pretty small for two of you."

Audra waved the comment away. "It's great. We're used to sharing a room. Been together since she was born. My parents' house isn't very big. This is perfect. If you don't mind, we'll move in this weekend. Then I'll have plenty of time to get settled and spend some time with Summer before my job starts."

Mae raised a loaf of French bread like a sword. "I hereby declare Peerbaugh Place full up. There is no more room at the inn." She tilted a head to Evelyn. "And she likes tea instead of coffee, which makes it two against two."

Well then. That settled it.

Evelyn was helping Tessa hang a picture on the wall of her bedroom when she heard the front door open.

"Mom? You home?"

Evelyn wished she had a camera to catch the look on her son's face when she, Tessa, *and* Mae appeared at the top of the stairs.

"I'm . . . I'm sorry. I didn't know you had company."

Mae leaned on the railing. "We're not company, brother; we live here." She turned to Evelyn. "This your son who works at the bank?"

Evelyn was suddenly flustered, as if she were a teenager who'd been caught with a boy in her room. She handed the hammer to Tessa and went down the stairs. "Russell, this is Mae Fitzpatrick, and this is Tessa Klein. They are my new tenants."

Mae gave Russell a salute. "Nice to meet you, Russ. I don't have an account in your bank, but maybe I'll change over to try to keep it in the family, eh?"

"Don't stand there like a codfish, boy," Tessa said. "It's not polite."

Russell looked toward his mother, his eyes asking questions. Evelyn took his arm. "Why don't we go into the kitchen?"

Mae's voice called after them, "Nice to meet you, Russ."

As soon as the kitchen door swung shut, he pounced. "You've rented out the rooms

81

already? I saw the sign . . . where did you get that so quickly? It hasn't even been a week since we talked about this. I was against it and yet you went ahead anyway? This is not like you."

Knowing it was preferable to have an argument eye-to-eye, instead of looking up at her six-foot son, Evelyn sat down, hoping Russell would follow suit. He did.

"You weren't against it, Russell. Not exactly. And it's worked out. All of it. I found the sign in the attic, left over from when your grandparents rented rooms. I took that as a sign that this was something I was supposed —"

"The sign was a sign?" He shook his head in disgust. "Don't get strange on me, Mom. Since when do you live your life according to signs?"

She shuffled her shoulders. She thought he'd be happy for her. Because of the tenants, she would be financially secure. "There were other things that happened —"

"More *signs?*" He snickered.

Why couldn't he be open to things beyond black-and-white? Evelyn fingered the edge of a place mat. "How else do you explain the fact that I rented out all three rooms without even advertising?"

"Luck."

"I'm not sure I believe in luck." She was uncertain how to say this. "I . . . I prayed about this. It all fell into place." She decided to pass the buck. "Tessa says it's God's doing."

Russell laughed and made the salt, pepper, and sugar containers form a line just like he used to do with his toy soldiers. "I think you're reading too much into this, Mom. I've never heard you talk about God much. We rarely went to church. . . ."

"Perhaps that was a mistake."

His eyebrows rose. "*Now* you're getting religious? Suddenly? After all these years?"

She wished she could still send him to his room — never mind it was currently inhabited by a middle-aged hippie with a Picasso above her bed. "Is there a time limit on knowing God?"

"Of course not —"

She stood and looked down at him, enjoying the feeling of power her stance created. "Then if I choose to start praying — at my advanced age — I will. And if I choose to believe that God had something to do with these wonderful ladies moving in here and solving my money problems, I will. And nothing you can say — and no money you can give me — will stop me. Is that okay with you?"

He raised his hands in surrender. "I guess it has to be."

Exactly.

"But, Mom?" His voice and his eyes hinted he was her little boy again.

"What, Russell?"

"I thought that maybe, since Dad's gone, I'd be the man of the family now."

Oh dear. "You can be. You *are* the man of the family." She leaned over and kissed the top of his head. "You're my *only* man. I need you very much."

"But I didn't help. We talked, but you did this on your own."

She lifted his chin. "Is that a bad thing?"

"No, but —"

"Because to tell you the truth, it felt pretty good."

He nodded, and she hoped it was a nod of understanding. "Dad never let you do much, did he?" His hand jerked upward, as if he wanted to stop the words. "I didn't mean that the way it sounded — like you haven't *done* anything. I just meant that he didn't let you blossom. He never wanted you to have a job. He kept a tight lid on you." He took her hand and ran a thumb over her wedding band, making it turn. "I always had the feeling you had a lot more potential than anyone ever saw. Like you were a caged bird, just waiting to sing."

Evelyn felt tears in her eyes. That's exactly how she'd felt. It was a feeling she'd stifled for the sake of the marriage. She'd tried to break free a few times, but Aaron had always caught her and put her back in her cage. Eventually she'd stopped trying because the reconfinement after her short flights of freedom hurt too much. The feeling of lost possibilities was like being told about a sunset, yet never being allowed to look out the window to fully enjoy it. And certainly never being allowed to go outside to experience it firsthand.

Russell stood and pulled her into his arms. Her head rested on his shoulder and she felt small. How had this man come from her body? It didn't seem possible.

"If renting out this house makes you fly, I'm all for it, Mom. I won't cage you up. I promise."

His declaration was a total surprise. Her throat tightened. "Thank you, Russell."

It was a moment she would always remember. The moment when the cage door flew open and she was free to soar.

"May I join you?"

Evelyn looked up from the morris chair in the sunroom to find Mae standing in the doorway. "Have a seat." She flipped on a lamp. The room was nearly dark and she hadn't even noticed.

Mae settled into a rocker. "Did you have a nice visit with your son? I hope we didn't shock him too much."

"It was very nice," Evelyn said. "In fact, quite enlightening."

"Ooh, sounds interesting. Tell me more."

Evelyn tucked her feet beneath her. "He *was* shocked to find the rooms rented out. We'd talked about it, but he didn't know that I'd gone ahead with the idea."

"Was he upset?"

"Not really." She leaned forward, resting her arms on her knees. "And this is the strange part. He told me that he'd noticed how his father used to hem me in. He said I was a caged bird wanting to be let out to sing."

"That's pretty poetic stuff for a banker."

Evelyn smiled. "Yes, I suppose it is. And I guess that's part of what touched me so deeply. Neither Russell nor Aaron was very demonstrative in their words or actions. They both like — liked — control."

Mae put her feet on the footstool, crossing them at the ankles. "Ah, I get the picture. You were a good wife; you did what your husband wanted you to do. You even thought what he wanted you to think, right? You encouraged him, but in the process discouraged yourself."

Evelyn hadn't taken the idea that far, but yes, what Mae said was true. "I had dreams once. . . ."

Mae raised a finger and recited, " 'If there were dreams to sell, what would you buy?' " She smiled. "Thomas Lovell Beddoes."

Evelyn nodded. "I like that. But I don't know the answer to that question: what would I buy? I haven't thought about my dreams in a long, long time."

"What were they?"

Evelyn thought a moment and found her mind a blank. "It's obviously been *too* long. I don't even remember."

"Well, I bet they've changed anyway. The dreams we have as young marrieds have a tendency to evolve over the years. But isn't it exciting that you've felt the spark to start thinking of them again? And isn't it wonderful that your son was the one who ignited that spark?"

Evelyn's heart swelled with possibilities.

4

*Dear friends, since God loved us
that much, we surely ought
to love each other.*
1 JOHN 4:11

Audra took hold of the box of Summer's toys and closed the hatchback of her ancient Pinto with an elbow. She had just stepped onto the curb when Gillie Danson drove by, tooting her horn. While Gillie did a turnaround in the neighbor's drive so she could pull up behind Audra, Audra set the box on the roof of the car and waited to greet her friend.

She couldn't help but notice the contrast between her own rust-and-dust vehicle and Gillie's shiny BMW; her own torn jeans and sweatshirt, and Gillie's tailored pants and top. Though Audra wasn't into designer clothes, she was pretty sure Gillie's were an expensive brand from an expensive store — the kind Audra only walked *through*, never shopped *in*. Audra couldn't imagine spending big money on clothes. It was pure extravagance. But that was Gillie.

The fact that they were friends was a fluke. When they'd met a year previous, they'd both been taking classes at the university — Audra toward her degree in business and Gillie to pass the time. Wealthy, divorced socialites didn't need to take classes or work at the bank, but Gillie did both, as if staying busy and being out in public were essential to her well-being.

Gillie got out of her car, and took one large package and one small one out of the backseat. Both were wrapped in pink-and-silver foil paper with huge bows. "I come bearing housewarming gifts. Is the little princess around?"

Audra lifted the box of toys and headed up the walk. "She's inside. You didn't have to do that, Gillie. You already gave her such an expensive birthday gift."

"So?" She glanced at Audra's car for the first time. "Is that the last box? Did I miss helping you move in?"

As always. Gillie had a habit of showing up at just the right moment to miss the bulk of the work. "This is the last of it. Can you get the door for me?"

Gillie hurried up the porch steps and opened the screen door wide. Audra slipped in and headed to the stairs. "Come on up and we'll give you the grand tour."

Gillie lagged behind, scanning the entry, and Audra knew she was mentally going through a checklist. From her nod and smile, it appeared Peerbaugh Place passed. Audra wished she didn't need her friend's approval, but she did.

Summer called from the landing. "Gillie!" Her eyes immediately moved to the presents. "What's in the boxes?"

"Summer!" Audra didn't like how Gillie was spoiling her daughter or how much Summer enjoyed it.

Gillie continued up the stairs. "Goodness, Audra. Don't get after the girl. She can't help but notice that this biggest, best, prettiest gift —" Gillie presented it like a courtly lady-in-waiting — "is for her."

Summer squealed. *"Me?"*

"You, princess. Let's go in your apartment and open it."

Audra inwardly groaned. "It's not an apartment, Gillie. I told you. It's a room. One room." She went through the door and set the toys on the bed. "This is it."

Gillie did her scan thing again, but this time there was less approval in her eyes. "This is it?"

"This is it."

"Where does Summer sleep?"

Summer patted the far side of the bed. "This is my side. Mommy gets the other."

"You had more room at your parents' house."

"More room but less independence." Audra avoided Gillie's eyes by transferring Summer's Lego sets to a shelf.

"I suppose you have that right," Gillie said, fingering a doily on the dresser. "Since the divorce I certainly am enjoying my independence — as long as Jerry pays the alimony on time."

"As long as he keeps you living in the lifestyle to which you were accustomed?" Audra immediately realized how mercenary it sounded. "Sorry, that was rude."

"Rude or not, it's the truth. I don't hide the fact I like nice things." She smiled and curled her short blonde hair behind her ear in a youthful gesture that erased five years from her thirty-five. "I also like to give nice things." She handed Audra the smaller package. "So . . . open your presents."

Summer looked to Audra for permission. "Go ahead, baby."

Summer carefully removed the bow, setting it on the bed as if it were a delicate butterfly. The ribbon was taken off next and wrapped around her hand. Next the tape was removed from one end —

"Sake-a-day, Summer! Just rip into it. The suspense is killing me and I know what it is."

But Summer shook her head. "We should keep the paper. It's too pretty to mess up."

Gillie threw her hands in the air. "Who am I to argue with self-control?" She shook her head. "Who'd have thought I'd be taught patience by a five-year-old."

Summer handed the wrapping paper to Audra, who folded it carefully. Then she took the lid off the box and gasped. Audra added a gasp of her own. It was a gorgeous doll at least two feet tall. It had waist-length blonde ringlets and was dressed in an intricate gown of pale teal tapestry, ivory satin, and gold braid.

"Oooh, Mommy, look."

"I see. It's beautiful."

Gillie reached across the bed and lifted up the dress. "Look underneath: pantaloons, a ruffled petticoat, and lace-up boots." She fingered a tag attached to the doll's wrist. "Her name is Margaret."

Summer lifted her out of the box. "It's a princess doll."

"For my princess."

Summer set the doll down and hurled

herself toward Gillie, giving her a hug. "Thank you, thank you. I'll take very good care of her."

"I know you will." She turned to Audra. "Now it's Mommy's turn."

Not to be outdone by her daughter, Audra opened the package with the same care. Inside was a brightly colored silk scarf with a horse on it.

"It's a Hermés scarf," Gillie said. "Real silk, made in France."

Audra held it up, hoping it looked better unfolded. "It's lovely," she said. But in truth, she found it too much for her simple tastes. Yet she was sure Gillie had spent a fortune on it. Gillie gave only the best.

"Here," Gillie said, expertly folding it and wrapping it around Audra's neck. She pulled her to the dresser mirror. "The royal blue complements your dark hair and eyes."

Audra had to admit she was right but couldn't imagine ever wearing it. She turned and hugged her friend. "Thank you, Gillie. You're far too generous."

"Not at all. If I can't give pretty things to my friends . . ." She adjusted the folds of the scarf at Audra's neck. "To tell you the truth, I'm getting a bit weary of spending money on myself."

Audra gasped dramatically and put a hand to her chest.

Gillie tugged at the scarf. "Be nice."

Audra adjusted the scarf back to the way Gillie had originally placed it. "I'm not making fun — not too much anyway. It's just that I've never been around anyone who had money to spend in any way they wanted — whenever they wanted."

"Yeah, well, let me tell you, it's not all it's cracked up to be. A person gets used to it way too fast."

"I can imagine."

Gillie eyed her suspiciously. "Is that said sarcastically or for real?"

Audra considered this a moment. "Both. I can imagine, and yet I can't. But somehow I know imagining is as far as I'll get. I don't think material riches are going to be a part of my life."

"You need to find yourself a rich executive."

"Oh sure. They'll be real attracted to a bank teller who has a child. I don't think I'm on the wish list of most corporate dynamos."

"As much as I am as a divorcée. Don't put yourself down. You're quite a catch."

Audra watched as Summer fingered the doll's finery. "My desirability factor doesn't matter. I've made my choices and I don't regret them." She nodded toward Summer. "At least not one of them."

When Gillie spoke her voice was soft. "Sometimes I envy you."

Audra laughed. "You, envy *me?*"

"You're richer than I am in so many ways."

Together they watched Summer play. Two incredibly rich women.

It seems all I do is pack up my personal things.

Evelyn placed a porcelain cardinal in a box. Now that the walnut whatnot shelf was empty, she could move it —

"What are you doing?" Tessa stood in the doorway, her toes in the parlor, her body in the foyer.

"Just putting some things away."

"Childproofing, that's what you're doing." She nodded to the room at the top of the stairs where they could hear the *bump-de-bump* sounds of Audra and Summer moving in.

"Actually, I'm not —"

"That's the trouble with having kids around," Tessa said. "The tendency is to give in to them. When my daughter was little, I refused to move any of my nice things. She soon learned what *no* meant."

I bet she did. Evelyn carried the shelf away from its place between the piano and the grandfather clock, leaving an empty space. "But as I was saying, I'm not moving these things because I'm afraid Summer will break them. I'm moving them to make room for her toy box."

Tessa made a face. "It's not one of those horrid plastic footballs, is it?"

Evelyn stifled a smile. "Of course not. Summer's a girl."

Tessa cocked her head. "You know what I mean."

"Yes, I do. And no, it's not a plastic toy box, but an old-fashioned wooden box with her name on it. I saw it myself."

"But they have a room. Why can't it go up there?"

For the same reason two boxes of your books had to be put in the attic. "It can. In fact, they've already taken it upstairs, but I don't see any reason why they have to cram it into that room when there's plenty of space down here. I was just trying to be nice."

Mae sashayed in. "What's cooking, sisters? Isn't it grand Peerbaugh Place is full?"

Tessa pointed to the empty space along

the wall. "There's going to be a toy box there."

Mae gave a quick glance before turning away. "Sounds appropriate. Boy, that Summer is a smart one for five. I told her how to spell my name one time, and now she can do it all by —"

Tessa stood in the space that would soon hold the toy box. "You don't understand. It's going to sit right *here*. Right in the middle of our parlor."

My parlor.

Mae looked at Tessa as if she were wearing something distasteful. "Who pinched your pantaloons, Tessie? The kid's a kid. Do you expect her to play quietly in a corner, not making a sou—" She clapped her hands. "That's it, isn't it? You're of the 'children should be seen and not heard' philosophy. I thought that went out with windup cars and the Charleston."

Tessa straightened to her full five-foot status. "Children can be heard, but there are limits. Respectable limits." She turned to Evelyn. "We're going to need a lot of rules now."

Mae rolled her eyes. "Here we go . . ."

"Like what?" Evelyn said.

Tessa counted on her fingers. "A rule that says no cartoons early in the morning on the television, and no leaving toys on the couch so a person can't sit down without moving them."

"Heaven forbid," Mae said.

"And no jumping up and down so a person's nerves jangle, and no laughing loudly, and no running, and no —"

"No being a kid?"

"You know what I mean." She looked to Evelyn. "*You* know what I mean, don't you, Evelyn?"

Two sets of eyes blazed into Evelyn. Maybe if she snuck into the kitchen, they could duke it out. She hadn't meant to cause a stir over a toy box.

"Evelyn? You're the landlord."

Rookie landlord. "I think we *will* need a few rules."

"Ha!" Tessa said, nodding in victory.

"For all of us."

"Ha!" Mae said, nodding in victory.

"Maybe you two would like to get together and make a list?" *There. That was good. Pass the buck.*

"You chickening out on us, Evie?"

Evelyn took in a breath, then let it out, along with her answer. "Yes."

Mae laughed. "Smart woman." She turned to Tessa. "So what do you say, Tessie? Shall we withdraw to the dining room and see what rules, regulations, by-laws, and executive orders we can dream up?"

Without saying a word, Tessa walked past Mae, across the foyer, and into the dining room.

Mae turned to Evelyn. "I guess that's a yes. Evie, if you don't hear from us in two days, send a search party."

As she heard dining-room chairs being moved, Evelyn moved out of their sight line and sank into a chair. *Oh dear.*

Gillie arranged the top of Audra's dresser with a jewelry box and assorted perfume bottles. She glanced back toward the bed, directly opposite. "You really need a TV here. It would be nice for Summer to be able to lie in bed and watch Saturday morning cartoons."

Audra popped her head out of the closet. "We don't have money for a TV."

"I'm not talking a big screen. You can get a small one for under one hundred dollars."

"Which is one hundred dollars we don't have. Besides, we don't need it."

"You don't *need* a lot of things, but that doesn't negate the fact that it would be a nice thing to have."

"Drop it, Gillie." Audra retreated into the closet.

Gillie sidestepped to her purse and retrieved her wallet. She pulled out five twenty-dollar bills. She looked around the room for a place to slip them unobtrusively. Her eyes fell on the jewelry box. She opened it, lifted the fabric-lined tray, slipped the bills beneath it, and shut the lid. *There. Now Audra has no excuse.*

She gave the jewelry box a final pat. It felt good to be generous.

Audra heard voices below. Animated voices. She went down a few stairs and listened. The light was on in the dining room and she could see the back of Tessa, seated in a chair. "But I need quiet for my studies," Tessa said.

"So the rest of us are supposed to tiptoe around?" It was Mae. "Dream on, Sister Tessie. I will not agree to a house rule about no noise after seven. That's ridiculous. The world's just coming to life at seven."

House rules? They were making rules without her?

Audra backtracked into her room, grabbed Gillie's arm, and pulled her into the hall.

"What — ?"

Audra put a finger to her lips. "Shh. Listen."

Tessa's voice continued. ". . . a child around makes an enormous difference in the decibel level of the house. I'm not used to such disturbances. House rules are a logical consequence of —"

"Summer's a consequence?" Audra whispered to Gillie.

Gillie pointed at the stairs. "You'd better get down there."

Audra stuck her head in the room where they had left Summer arranging her clothes in the bottom drawer of the dresser. Somehow she'd cajoled Peppers to jump in. Audra could hear the cat purring from the doorway. "Gillie and I are going downstairs for a few minutes, baby. You okay up here alone?"

Summer barely looked up. "We're fine, Mommy."

They left the door open and took the stairs quietly, not wanting to interrupt. Was Evelyn in there too? If all three of them were meeting without her . . .

Audra walked through the doorway of the dining room with Gillie close behind. She was relieved to see that Evelyn was not a participant. At least she wasn't being shunned. Audra caught Mae in the middle

101

of listing her favorite television programs.

"And on Fridays I like to watch —" Mae spotted the two of them. "Hey, girlie girl. Hey, Gillie. You all moved in?"

"Pretty much." Tessa and Mae sat across from each other at the table. Audra moved between them, to the head. Gillie took a place at her shoulder. "What were you two talking about?"

"Rules," Tessa said. She pointed to a piece of paper in front of her. The list was written in an elegant cursive that Audra found impossible to read from the side.

Audra weighed her words carefully. No need to be overly sensitive, yet it was important she take a stand right away. She was not going to be a bystander in this house; she was going to be an equal partner. She put a hand on the back of an empty chair. "I'd like to join in," she said.

Mae reached under the table and shoved the chair outward. "You bet. We weren't trying to exclude you. Tessie and I started talking and took off with it. Actually, it was Evelyn's idea."

"Then shouldn't she be here too? If we're making house rules?"

Tessa pointed her pen at the list. "She told us to do it."

"But she *is* the landlord. She needs to be involved."

"Even if she doesn't want to be?" Tessa asked.

This woman can argue about anything. "I'm not going to force her, but I think it would be logical. And respectful." She looked to Gillie. "Don't you agree?"

Gillie put a hand to her chest. "I'm just a bystander here, but yes, I think it would be the right thing to do. I live in Highacre Park, and our neighborhood has periodic meetings to address covenants and —"

Mae wiggled a hand at her ear. "Woo. Highacre Park. La-di-da."

Audra noticed the slightest of blushes fall on Gillie's cheeks. "It's nice."

"Like Buckingham Palace is nice." Mae removed her hoop earrings and tossed them on the table. "Calling in Evelyn is fine with me. I heard her in the kitchen. Go get her. Let's do this right."

Audra found Evelyn peeling potatoes. The woman turned around when Audra entered, a potato peel hanging precariously from the sleeve of her shirt. "Everything okay, Audra?"

"It's fine." She peeked in the oven and saw a meat loaf. Down-home cooking.

"I'm making scalloped potatoes too. And corn."

"You're making quite a feast."

Evelyn shrugged. "It's an easy meal."

"Are you planning to cook *every* meal?"

"No, but we haven't thought that far."

Audra glanced toward the dining room. Maybe there *was* a need for some house rules. The key was to make everyone feel at ease and not put out. "We are in the dining room, going over a few things, and —"

Evelyn nodded. "Ah. So Tessa and Mae conned you into joining them."

It seemed an odd choice of words. Could it be that Evelyn didn't want to be involved? That seemed impossible. "I think — we all think — it's important you're in on it too. Can I help you finish in here so you can join us?"

Evelyn's cheeks flushed like a girl being asked to a dance. "Well, I suppose. If you're there too . . ." She rinsed a potato. "Actually, I'm nearly done. These have to be sliced and the milk and cheese added. You can help if you want."

Audra finished the potatoes and put them in the oven while Evelyn rinsed out the sink and put some lotion on her hands — the scent of freesia filled the room.

Within minutes, they were ready to join the others. They entered the dining room to Mae's applause.

"Hear, hear! The Fearsome Foursome is complete. Now we can get down to some real business."

They settled in around the six-seat table. Although Audra was tempted to take the head chair, she left it empty for Evelyn and took a seat next to Mae. Gillie stood by awkwardly.

"Can Gillie sit in?" Audra asked.

"Fine by me," Mae said. "We need an impartial moderator."

"She's not impartial," Tessa said. "She's Audra's friend."

Gillie raised a finger. "I prefer to think of myself as a friend-in-waiting to all you ladies."

Mae slapped a hand on the table. "Hear, hear, again! I'm all for adding to our sisterhood. Take a seat, Sister Gillie."

Gillie sat next to Tessa. Then Mae got up and pulled out the head chair for Evelyn. "And for you, Madame President, the seat of honor."

Evelyn eyed the chair as if it could cause her harm. "No, I don't need to sit . . ."

"Of course you do. You're the head of the household."

Evelyn sat down, but reddened. Audra was shocked to realize the woman had probably never ever sat in that spot of honor. Had it been an old-fashioned household with the head spot reserved for the husband? Mae had told Audra about Mr. Peerbaugh's recent death. The fact that Evelyn could even function at all was an amazing thing. Not that Audra had any experience in long-term relationships, but she couldn't imagine her mother surviving very well without her father. Or vice versa.

Tessa pushed her list in front of Evelyn. "As you see, we haven't gotten very far." She cast an accusing glance at Mae. "We seem to have different ideas about the proper atmosphere of Peerbaugh Place."

Evelyn looked at each of their faces, as though searching for clues that would determine her next words. She looked totally uncomfortable, and it took all of Audra's willpower not to jump in. "I think we all want the same thing —," Evelyn said.

Tessa shook her head. "I fear you're wrong there, Evelyn. I took a room at Peerbaugh Place to get away from noise and busyness. I want a quiet sanctuary where I can study and read and —"

Mae shook her head. "Sanctuary, schmanctuary. You want that, go to a church. You aren't the only one living here, Tessie."

Tessa's jaw tightened. Audra wasn't sure if it was because of Mae's comment or the fact she'd called her Tessie. Tessa did *not* look like a Tessie. Nor act like one.

Tessa folded her hands on top of the table. "I'm willing to compromise, but the fact that there is now a . . . a child —" She glanced at Audra and raised a hand. "I love children; please don't misunderstand. But I have a right to be concerned about the noise level that a five-year-old creates."

Audra felt her heart flutter. "She's a good girl. If this is going to be our home — the home of all of us — then we'll all have to adapt. To a lot of things."

"And I'm willing to do so," Tessa said. "Rules will simply clarify those things."

Evelyn laid her hands flat on the table. "I'm sure something can be arranged if we all make an effort to get along."

This was getting nowhere. Round and round, saying the same thing, talking about how they should have rules but not making any decisions. Audra raised her hand. "I have an idea."

The others turned silent. "Sounds promising," Mae said. "Shoot."

Audra eagerly accepted control. "Give

me that pad of paper, and we'll need four pens." She nodded to Gillie. "Sorry, Gil, but you don't get a vote on this."

"No problem."

Evelyn slid the pad across the slick walnut tabletop while Mae headed for the kitchen. Audra quickly scanned the list Tessa had made before ripping it off the pad. It was pretty useless. One-word phrases: *noise, bathrooms, meals.* But if nothing else, it was an outline for their future discussion. Audra tore off four pieces of paper and passed them around.

Mae returned with three additional pens. "I just want to make it known that if this is a test, I'm going to flunk. I forgot to study, and a dog ate my homework."

Tessa rolled her eyes. Audra noticed she had positioned her paper and pen like a teacher's pet eager to get another A.

Yet Tessa's willingness *did* soften Audra's opinion of her. A little. She'd take any eager participant over the wariness Evelyn exhibited by biting the end of her pen.

"Okay," Audra said. "Number your paper from one to three. Then write down the three most important aspects of a household — this household. Things that are essential for you to be happy here."

"Like what?" Evelyn asked.

Audra nodded toward Tessa. "Like quiet time or meals together — or not together. Do you want to entertain friends? Do you want a special night for us tenants to socialize together? Is this merely a place for you to sleep — are you gone most of the time? That kind of thing."

The women nodded and hunched over their papers. Tessa had her three things listed immediately. Mae wrote one item down with flourish, turned her head in the opposite direction a moment in thought, then added another, then repeated the process.

It was worrisome that Evelyn was still biting her pen. It seemed logical she would have the most finely tuned expectations. After all, the rooming house was her business venture. Certainly she had visions of how it should play out.

But maybe not. Audra watched her a moment longer, and when the woman still didn't write anything down, Audra decided to concentrate on her own list. It didn't take long. She knew what she wanted out of Peerbaugh Place. Three *S*s: security, sisterhood, and solace.

Mae's eyes made the rounds, trying to read what was on everyone's papers. Tessa pulled hers to her chest as if hoarding the correct answers. Mae tapped an orange fingernail on Evelyn's blank sheet. "Zounds, sister. You've got to want something from all of us." She tapped her fingernail two more times. "You better say your piece or else we'll take advantage of you."

"We certainly will not," Tessa said.

Mae slapped her hand on the table. "Glad to hear it, Tessie!"

Evelyn pushed her paper toward the center of the table. "I'll wait until I hear what the rest of you have to say."

A landlord who's a follower. Interesting. "If that's what you want," Audra said. "Who volunteers to go first?"

Tessa and Mae both raised their hands. Audra suffered a silent sigh. She made a choice. "Tessa? Why don't you share your list."

Mae crossed her arms with a *harrumph,* but Audra could tell it was all for show. "Yes, Tessie. You go first. I'll defer to age before beauty anytime."

Audra exchanged a glance with Gillie. *Hoo-boy.*

Tessa wisely ignored the comment and angled her paper toward the light. "I've already said the first one. Silence, or quiet time as Mae calls it. Number two is stability. I don't like surprises. And three is order. I like things neat and tidy." She gave Mae a scathing look.

Mae gestured to herself. "Why are you looking at me?"

"I've seen your room."

"I just moved in."

"You moved in first. You've had plenty of time to get organized. Even Audra's settled. I think if you had your way you'd live out of boxes."

"Would it help if I drew pretty pictures on them?"

Audra interceded. "Mac, what's on your list?"

Mae cleared her throat. "Unlike Tessie, who sounds like she'd do best in a cloister somewhere, I —"

"That wasn't necessary," Tessa said.

"Maybe not, but you've made it pretty clear that our presence is a burden to tolerate."

"I just want things orderly and under control."

"You want to strangle the life out of this house."

"I do not!"

Mae made a twisting motion with her hands. "You want to wring us dry until the only sound you hear is our last dying breath."

Evelyn put a hand to her mouth to stifle a gasp, and Audra reined in a laugh. Obviously tolerance did not come naturally with age. She put a hand on Mae's arm, and the woman sat back in her chair. "As you see," Audra said, "we have vastly different views of what's ideal. But that's okay. That's what this meeting is about."

Evelyn looked relieved and hopeful — and far too dependent on Audra to fix everything. It's not that Audra minded assuming control, but it would have been nice to have the strength of the landlord behind her, instead of her desperate pleading eyes.

Audra turned to Mae. "Your list please?" *And only your list and nothing but your list.*

"Friendship." She set the list down and explained. "I really like your idea of a tenant night where we have a special dinner and talk, and maybe have special themes. One night we could have a luau; another a video night; another, play board games. . . ."

"That sounds like fun," Evelyn said.

Tessa remained silent.

"What's number two?" Audra asked.

Mae consulted her list for only a moment. Obviously her answers couldn't be condensed into one word. "I want happiness. I want joy. I want this to be a place I run home to every evening after work, knowing it's a refuge, a —"

Tessa sat forward. "A sanctuary?"

Mae grinned. "A sanctuary full of life and laughter, of peace and —"

Evelyn raised a finger. "I vote for peace." When all eyes turned to her, she reddened and lowered her finger. "Well, I do."

Audra stepped in. "I think we all vote for peace — in all its forms."

"And number three is tolerance." Mae met Tessa's eyes for just a moment. "I want this to be a place of sharing, of bonding, of accepting each other for who we are. Even in our diversity. Diversity can be a good thing, you know."

Audra nodded. "Indeed it can."

"That's it for me," Mae said. "Now, it's your turn, Audra."

Audra straightened her shoulders, taking strength from Gillie's supportive nod. "I want security, sisterhood, and solace."

The other women sat on these terms a moment as if defining them. It was Tessa who spoke first. "I think that pretty well sums it up."

Audra was pleased. She'd always had that ability — to sum up, to capture the essence of a situation. The fact that she had done so *before* anyone else had shared their list was inner proof that her view of life was right on target. Not bad for a twenty-three-year-old.

But her satisfaction was short-lived when Mae asked, "So now what?"

"Yes, now what?" Tessa asked. "What rules can we make out of all this?"

Good question.

Audra was stunned when Evelyn was the one to answer. "I don't think we need set rules. Since we all know what's important to the other people in the house, we can be mindful of these things. And with a little common sense and kindness . . ." She looked around the table.

Mae clapped. "Bravo, Evie. I think you're right. As long as we make a point of being polite —"

"But wouldn't it be safer to have some written guidelines?" Tessa said.

Mae scribbled on the back of her paper, then held it up for all to see. "Here. It's written down. *Thou shalt be nice.*"

"You're mocking God," Tessa objected.

"Huh?"

"You're making it sound like an eleventh commandment. *Thou shalt . . .*"

"Well, isn't it?" Mae said.

"Of course not," Tessa said, sounding appalled. "There are the Ten Commandments. Certainly you know that."

"I've heard of them once or twice," Mae said. "Didn't Charlton Heston have something to do with writing them up?"

"Oh, pooh," Tessa said.

Gillie and Audra laughed.

Mac continued. "I think my 'thou shalt' is a good one. I'm sure God and Charlton wouldn't mind an addendum."

Tessa's head shook no, no, no. "You cannot amend the Word of God. You cannot —"

Audra's mind had been reeling, but now it landed on something she hoped would appease them both. "Didn't Jesus say to love your neighbor as yourself?"

"Luke 10:27," Tessa said. "Among other verses. But —"

Audra wasn't going to let her get off track. "But isn't that virtually the same as Mae's commandment? Doesn't loving your neighbor as you love yourself involve being nice to them?"

"I suppose. But it doesn't say —"

Evelyn spoke up. "I vote for Mae's commandment."

"That's three ayes, Tessie." Mae's look had a hint of confrontation in it.

There was a moment of silence. *Come on, Tessa. You can do it. For the good of the house.*

"I suppose," Tessa said.

"Yay!"

"But I will not call it Mae's Commandment."

"How about the Nice Nugget, the Nice Notice, the Nice Nudge, the Nice —"

Tessa made a face. "I'd take Mae's Commandment over any of those."

"Then Mae's Commandment it is."

All but Tessa giggled. "You tricked me," she said.

Mae tried to look innocent but failed. "Now how could little ol' me possibly do something like that to little ol' you?"

"I . . . you . . ."

"Be *nice*, Tessie," Mae said.

Tessa crossed her arms and turned to Audra. "Let's move on to other things."

"Like what?" Audra asked. Her stomach began to knot.

Tessa retrieved her original list. "Use of the bathroom. And meals. Who makes what, when?"

Audra's stomach relaxed. *Those* issues were easy.

Evelyn held her dirt-caked hands like a surgeon and walked through the foyer toward the kitchen to wash them. After last Saturday's Tenant Forum — as Tessa had dubbed their first meeting — she'd gotten a good start on planting the porch flower boxes, and today she'd finally been able to finish the job. About time, since it was already a week into April. Tomorrow she might tackle the backyard.

Evelyn stopped at the entry table and stared at the pink dish that held Aaron's last change.

It was gone.

She whipped around, dirt flying from her hands. "Hey!" she yelled for anyone to hear. "Who took it?"

Audra and Summer appeared on the upstairs landing. "Evelyn? What's wrong?"

Evelyn pointed at the empty dish. "Who took the money that was in this dish?"

Summer slunk onto the top step as if trying to hide. She peered through the railing.

"Did you take it, Summer?" Evelyn asked.

No reply.

Audra moved toward her daughter. "Summer? Answer Mrs. Peerbaugh. Did you take the money in the dish?"

The little girl looked up at her mother, then down to Evelyn. She was surrounded.

Finally, she stood and dug her hand into the pocket of her jeans. She pulled out some coins.

Audra grabbed her other hand and led her downstairs. "You don't take other people's things, especially not money."

"It was just sitting there."

"That doesn't matter. If a bike was sitting in the front yard, would you claim it as your own?"

Summer's face fought for the right answer.

"Well?"

"No?"

"Exactly. The same applies with money in a dish." They reached the table. "Put it back."

With a tentative look to Evelyn, Summer held her hand over the dish and dropped the coins. A penny was reluctant to leave her soft palm, so she nudged it loose.

"Now say you're sorry."

Summer's eyes were huge and repentant. "I'm sorry." She looked to her mother. "Will God forgive me, Mommy?"

Audra's face lost its stern edge. She nodded. "Of course He will, baby."

Her repentance was a moving sight, but Evelyn didn't feel like being merciful; she didn't feel like being forgiving. It wasn't the taking of the money — it was only forty-eight cents. It was taking *that* particular money. Aaron's money. She knew it was petty, yet it was hard to let it go. Feeling embarrassed at her own struggle, Evelyn had to force herself to say, "It's okay."

Audra led her daughter upstairs, giving her an extended lecture. Evelyn pounced upon the task at hand: she moved the coins around in the dish, trying to re-create their previous positions. *If only I can get them back to the way they were . . .*

She sensed she was not alone. She looked up and found Audra and Summer on the stairs, watching her.

"What are you doing?" Audra asked.

Evelyn stared at the dish and at her fingers poised above the coins, desperately trying to re-create a moment in time. Aaron's moment in time. *He'll never have any more moments.*

Without warning, a wave of sorrow engulfed Evelyn. She covered her face with her hands, appalled that it was happening with an audience yet helpless to do anything to stop it. At first, the surge of tears offered release, like a refreshing rain on a dusty day, but they soon turned into a torrent of floodwaters threatening to pull her under. Logic had no authority. She sank to the floor, seeking smallness, tightness, comfort. *If only I could disappear.*

Evelyn felt a hand on her shoulder and found Audra stooped beside her. "They were *his* coins, weren't they?"

Evelyn looked at the young woman through her fingers. "How did you — ?"

Audra shrugged. "My dad always empties his pockets when he comes into the house."

At this simple statement of fact, the storm clouds parted ever so slightly, and Evelyn let her hands fall away. She swiped the tears aside, their dampness revitalizing the dried dirt on her hands.

"Run and get Mrs. Peerbaugh a tissue, Summer."

The little girl ran to the bathroom and back, waving two tissues like white flags. Evelyn dabbed at her face and blew her nose. "I know it's absurd. They couldn't stay in place forever."

"But you wanted them that way a little while longer, right?"

Evelyn nodded, relieved — and surprised — so young a woman would understand.

Summer stood before them. She dug her hand in her other pocket and pulled out a penny. "I found this on the sidewalk. I don't know who it belongs to so I can't give it back. But you can have it if you want."

"No, honey, Mrs. Peerbaugh doesn't want more money; she wants to keep her husband's —"

Evelyn looked at the dear little girl who was offering everything she had to make *her* feel better. She pushed herself to standing. "Actually, I think your penny will make a wonderful addition to the dish. Do you want to put it in?"

With a look of relief, Summer carefully placed the penny in the pink dish. Somehow the addition of the new penny in a *new* moment in time made the necessity of hanging on to the *old* moment moot.

Summer looked up at Evelyn and smiled. "I like it there."

Mindful of her dirty hands, Evelyn used her forearm to draw the tiny head toward her side. "I do too. It looks as if it belongs."

Belonging. That was the key to so much.

Evelyn set the fork just so. To celebrate their first week together, they would eat in the dining room tonight using china, crystal, and sterling. Company setting for a family fare of pot roast, potatoes and gravy, carrots, hot rolls, and peach whip salad. The aroma of the roast cooking in the Crock-Pot had grown in intensity all day, teasing their taste buds.

Mae appeared at Evelyn's side. "Wow. Now *that's* a table."

"You approve?"

Mae ran a hand along the gold rim of the china. "What's not to approve? I never had any china or other fancies. Danny and me were Melmac people."

Evelyn turned a plate a quarter inch so the floral pattern was seated correctly. "We were too when Russell was growing up. Only brought these out for special occasions." She straightened a spoon. "I often wonder if that was the right thing to do."

"Every day's a special occasion? That sort of thing?"

"Actually, every day is *not* a special occasion, but maybe it wouldn't hurt if we aimed a little higher in our expectations."

"Expect the expected and get exactly what you deserve."

Evelyn smiled. "Who said that?"

Mae thought a moment. "Me."

"I'm impressed. It's a talent to be profound *before* dinner."

"Ha! You aimed too low by expecting the expected."

"Guilty as charged." Evelyn stood back and studied the total effect of the table. "I think we're ready. Will you call everyone?"

Mae moved a half-dozen steps into the foyer and yelled up the stairs. "Dinner! Come and get it!"

That was one way to do it.

The women sat back in their chairs, full and content. Summer was off playing in the parlor — using the toys in her toy box.

"Wonderful," Mae said, squelching a belch, "absolutely wonderful."

"Home cooking at its best," Tessa said.

"I especially like this lemon cake," Audra said. "You had a busy afternoon."

Evelyn felt herself blush. "Actually, the cake's still left over from the funeral. All I did was thaw it."

Tessa flipped a hand. "I ate funeral leftovers for months after, too. No use letting good food go to waste."

Mae pushed herself back from the table. "Well . . . with our innards full, I think this is the perfect time to spill our guts."

Tessa's eyebrow raised. "Excuse me?"

Mae leaned forward to make her point.

"Tell our stories, share our little secrets. Spill it."

Tessa raised her eyebrows. "I barely know you ladies."

"When has that ever stopped a good woman-to-woman chat? Women can get to the heart of things faster than a man can eat a second helping of pie. Speaking of men . . ."

"Who said we were talking about men?" Audra asked.

"Just a suggestion. The point I was trying to make is that women don't need to know each other well to share their innermost secrets. I'll give you an example. On the last day of our son's first semester of college he told me that he and his roommate talked all night — the *first* time they'd really talked after living in a twelve-by-twelve room together for four months. Can you believe such a thing?" Mae flipped the absurdity away. "Two women would have had their life histories, their dreams, and their favorite shopping spots covered in one evening — the *first* evening. And since Peerbaugh Place has been full for a whole week now, we're way behind." She looked around the table. "Am I right, or am I right?"

She was right. Sharing was like air to women. Evelyn had often bemoaned the fact that Aaron had never been interested in hearing her thoughts — deep or superficial. She'd fought it at first, cried about it, argued too. Finally, she'd surrendered, realizing that the image of her and Aaron sitting up into the wee hours of the morning discussing how they *felt* about things wasn't going to happen. If it hadn't been for the willing ears of a few friends, Evelyn would have clammed up permanently. Yet even those visits into the sharing sisterhood had become more rare over the years. Had she forgotten how to partake in some old-fashioned woman talk? Was she out of practice? Maybe these ladies could help each other discover the truths about the important issues of life: love, careers, family, hopes and dreams . . . maybe even God.

There was a moment of silence. Mae shook her head. "Green grasshoppers, sisters. I'm just asking for a few facts. Barbara Walters stuff. This is your life."

"Where were we born?" Audra asked. "That kind of thing?"

Mae smashed a cake crumb with a finger and licked it away. "I'm betting we can do better than that." She thought a moment. "How's this for an icebreaker? What's the worst thing your husband —" she nodded to Audra — "or boyfriend, ever did?"

Evelyn raised a finger. "Aaron used to pick his teeth with one of his business cards."

Mae rolled her eyes. "That is the most pitiful thing I've ever heard — and I'm not talking about his bad etiquette. I'm not interested in whether or not they leave the toilet seat up, sisters. I'm talking about big things. Like this . . ." She adjusted herself in the chair as if setting a good foundation for her story. "One time Danny and I had a fight while we were driving — we were master arguers, us two. Anyway, he got so mad that he stopped the car, pushed me out, and drove away. It was night — and raining."

Audra's eyes widened. "What did you do?"

"Hitched a ride. Then he got mad at that — said it was unsafe and I wasn't being smart." She shook her head. "I couldn't win with Danny."

Evelyn was getting ready to tell about the time Aaron took all their money out of the savings account and sent it to some shyster who promised millions in minutes, when she noticed Tessa's head shaking in a steady rhythm.

Mae noticed it too. "What's got your

noggin waggin', Tessie?"

"I will not partake in man bashing. It's wrong."

"Actually, it proves the men were wrong," Mae said.

Tessa gave her head one final shake. " 'Let those who have never sinned throw the first stones.' "

"Yeah, yeah," Mae said. "Even I've heard that one. But I'm not saying I'm without sin. I'm not perfect — only near perfect."

The laughter helped break the tension. A little.

" 'Do not testify falsely against your neighbor,' " Tessa said.

"False nothing," Mae said. "I'm not telling lies. I'm telling the truth. He left me on the side of the road."

"I think she's talking about gossip. We're not supposed to gossip," Audra said. She looked away and fingered the edge of her napkin, and Evelyn could tell she was about to share something delicate. "I used to think it didn't matter, talking about other people behind their backs." She looked up. "But it does matter. It hurts."

Evelyn understood completely. There'd been one horrid time in her life when she'd been sure the unkind words of others possessed the power to kill her. Evelyn closed her eyes on those memories, then opened them, determined to concentrate on the moment at hand. "Are you talking about your pregnancy, Audra?"

Audra nodded. "People were nasty about it."

"Now that surprises me," Mae said. "In this day and age? It's not like we shun unwed mothers and send them to a secret baby factory anymore."

"No," Tessa said. "Now we close our eyes and pretend it's okay." She nodded toward Audra. "You know what you did is wrong, don't you? You *do* admit that."

Mae tossed her napkin on the table. "Now *that* was subtle, Tessa. Who's throwing the first stone now?"

"*I* didn't have an illegitimate baby."

"How do we know?"

Tessa put a hand to her chest. "Well, I wouldn't, I couldn't . . ."

"Stop!" Evelyn found herself standing but couldn't remember how she had gotten from point A to point B. All eyes were on her — a situation she deplored. But this talk of gossip and doing wrong and condemning others . . . it hit too close to home. "I don't want to discuss anything if we're going to turn it into an I'm-right-and-you're-wrong fight. Although we may not approve of the situation Audra found herself in, we —"

Audra shoved her chair back, also standing. "I don't need any of you to approve or disapprove."

"Then maybe we should stop talking about —"

Audra shook her head. "No, Evelyn, it's good to bring it out in the open. That's the bad thing about gossip; it's done on the sly. I'd much rather have you ladies attack me to my face than —"

"We're not attacking you, Audra," Mae said.

Audra nodded to Tessa. "She is."

Tessa unfastened and refastened the top button of her blouse.

Mae put a hand on Audra's arm, urging her to sit. "But if she apologizes . . ." She flashed a passionate look in Tessa's direction.

Evelyn was relieved when Tessa accepted the challenge. "Well, for the good of the house, I do apologize for casting any disparaging remarks that might have offended, Audra. But the truth is, fornication outside of marriage is —"

"Is a choice everyone has to make for themselves," Mae said.

Tessa jumped in. "That's a lie, Mae

Fitzpatrick, and you know it. The Bible says —"

" 'Love your neighbor as yourself,' " Evelyn said.

Mae slapped a hand on the table. "There it is. Twice in a week. Even we can't argue with that, can we, sisters?" Mae took Audra's hand and pulled gently. "Sit down, Audra. Nobody ever claimed girl talk was easy. That's what's so great about it. Women can have disagreements and then move on to talking about the cute pair of shoes they got on sale, in a situation where men would come to blows."

"Exactly," Tessa said. "We may be the weaker sex in terms of muscles, but I've always believed women were stronger than men in handling diverse — and adverse — situations. We adapt well." She looked around the table. "I can give you examples from dozens of biographies."

The phone rang and Evelyn left to answer it. It was a friend from her Women's League. A condolence check. She said what the friend wanted to hear and was back at the table in less than a minute.

"That was quick," Mae said.

Evelyn resumed her seat. "A friend checking up on me. I think she was disappointed I wasn't weak and weepy." She sighed. "People seem to want me to be in tears all the time. They think because I don't break down when they call, I don't feel anything." She looked around the table. "I feel. I ache. I hurt. But that doesn't mean I have to let the world see." She remembered the incident with Aaron's coins. She glanced at Audra, who remained blessedly silent. And yet . . . it *was* strange she could be collected and in control one minute, and sobbing on the floor the next. But she'd always been that way.

"I'd cry at the sight of a can of cream of mushroom soup," Tessa said. "My Alfred loved the casseroles I made with it. I could sit in a room full of friends and talk about him for hours and never shed a tear, but let me spot a can of soup . . ." She shook her head. "I finally took all the cans out of my daughter's pantry, set them on the kitchen table, and had it out with them. Cried till I could cry no more. I was fine after that."

Mae laughed. "Now *that* makes for an interesting image. As for me, I never cried when I lost Danny. Of course Danny is still alive — at least as far as I know. *Lost* can be a relative term."

Audra ate a bite of Summer's leftover cake. "I didn't cry when Luke left. And it *was* a mutual decision. Marrying him would have been a disaster."

Mae nodded. "That's where I think you made the better choice than I did. I got pregnant and married my guy, knowing full well he wasn't the right man. And so I ended up getting divorced. You'll never have to go through that."

"God hates divorce," Tessa said.

Mae rolled her eyes. "Oh, please . . ." She fueled herself with a deep breath. "Tessa, I think if we're going to get along in this house you are going to have to rein in your judgmental God. Personally, I've had just about enough of Him for one day."

"He's a loving God," Tessa said.

"Not according to you."

Although Evelyn was no expert on God, she had the feeling He *was* more loving than Tessa had expressed this evening. At least she hoped He was. "You know what?" she said. "My father always used to say it wasn't polite to discuss religion and politics at the dinner table."

"Sounds good to me," Mae said.

"Don't censor the conversation on my account," Audra said. "I'm no weakling. I can take whatever you can dish out."

"I'm sure you can," Evelyn said. "But maybe —"

Tessa shook her head. "I disagree. If we're going to live in the same house, if we're going to get to know each other and be a part of each other's lives like most of you want, then I think we need to feel free to speak our mind." She nodded toward Mae. "Even if we don't agree."

"Well, well. Amen to that, Tessa," Mae said. "I'm proud of you."

Evelyn felt foolish for quashing their discussion. Although she would have liked to steer clear of conflict, the other women were obviously not as timid.

"I agree too," Audra said. "Anything goes."

Mae turned to Evelyn. "It's three votes for truth. What say you, Mrs. Peerbaugh?"

Well, when Mae put it that way . . . Evelyn cast her vote. "Truth it is."

This could get interesting.

5

The young women will dance for joy. . . .
I will turn their mourning into joy.
I will comfort them and exchange
their sorrow for rejoicing.
JEREMIAH 31:13

Evelyn woke to a light tapping on her bedroom door.

"Evelyn?"

It was Tessa's voice. Evelyn slipped out of bed and opened it, trying to focus in her half sleep. "What's wrong?"

"I was just wondering if you'd like to go to church with me this morning."

At that point, Evelyn realized Tessa was fully dressed, hose and everything. She was even wearing a little hat with a feather in it.

"What time is it?"

"Seven. I like to go to the early service at 7:30. Then Sunday school. I generally go out to lunch with friends after. Care to join us?"

The bed called to her. *Come back to me . . . this is a day of rest.*

"I don't think so, Tessa. I have things to do this morning."

"Oh. Really." It was not a question and was thick with contempt.

"But thanks for thinking of me."

There was a quick flash in Tessa's eyes as she pivoted toward the stairs.

Evelyn returned to bed and hugged her pillow. Peppers jumped up, but instead of finding her normal place in the crook of Evelyn's knees, she stood in front of her accusingly. *I thought you were up.*

Evelyn tried closing her eyes, but when Peppers nudged a nose into her arm, she surrendered and got up.

Penance.

Evelyn poured herself a cup of coffee and chose the front section of the Sunday paper. This was the extent of her plans for the morning. *So much for having a lot to do.*

She held the cup under her chin and let the steam caress her face. *Why didn't I go with Tessa? What would it have hurt?* The look on Tessa's face had been one of condemnation — and resignation. A so-this-is-how-it's-going-to-be look.

Could Evelyn help it if she was a creature of habit? She and Aaron used to sleep until nine on Sundays, and then she'd make her Aunt Betty's coffee cake, and they'd share a pot of coffee over the morning paper. When it was nice out, they would sit on the sunporch, and when it was cold, in the kitchen. Evelyn had chosen the kitchen this morning because . . . because she could.

Their breakfasts together were times Evelyn cherished — though she didn't realize the extent of her fondness for them until Aaron was gone. But now that she was facing a lifetime of Sundays without him . . . she'd be hanged if she was going to give up this tradition of over three decades and suffer a guilt trip because of some woman she'd known only a few weeks.

She heard footsteps on the stairs and guessed, because of the lack of children's footsteps, it was Mae. She was right.

Mae's mint green chenille bathrobe made Evelyn think of her childhood. If she'd been wearing fuzzy slippers, the memory would have been complete. But Mae was barefoot.

"Morning," she said. "Water on?"

Evelyn nodded, glad she'd thought to put a pot on for Mae's tea. "Coffee cake is in the oven."

"So that's what I smelled." Mae pulled out a chair and schlumped into it. Her eyes were barely open, and she yawned widely, exposing a myriad of silver fillings. "Why are you up so early on a Sunday morning?"

"I always get up this early," Evelyn said. As soon as the words were out of her mouth, she wanted to take them back. Not only were they a lie — and they had vowed just the night before to tell the truth — but her words were setting a precedent she didn't want to keep.

"You're blushing," Mae said.

Evelyn put her hands on her cheeks and felt their heat. "I hate my face."

"Why?"

"Because it betrays me. I can't lie without it giving me away."

Mae raised an eyebrow. "You were lying?"

Evelyn nodded. "I generally sleep until at least nine every chance I get. I am not a morning person. The only reason I'm up this morning is because Tessa knocked on my door at seven and invited me to go to church with her."

"I take it you said no."

"I said no." Evelyn sighed. "But I should have said yes. That would have been the polite thing to do, right?"

Mae got up to make her tea. "Polite, sure. But I'm not sure that's the proper attitude to take to church. I'm no Holy Roller myself, but I always figured if I were to go, it had better be because I wanted to be there, needed to be there. Not because it was the polite thing to do."

"You have a point. You always have a point."

Mae waved a hand in a courtly gesture. "Why, thank you. I do my best to have an opinion about most everything." She dipped a tea bag in a mug of hot water. "Now you, Evie, you don't seem to be the type to spread your views much. Is it because you don't have any opinions, or you're just too shy to share them?"

It was way too deep a question first thing in the morning. "I honestly don't know."

Mae hesitated a moment, then burst out laughing. "Gracious gyroscope, Evie. You don't even have an opinion about having an opinion?"

She had to laugh too. "I guess I don't."

Mae returned to her seat. "Well, then I'll make it a point to drum up a few extra opinions for you, just to take up the slack. We can't have a household of five females without five different opinions."

The smell of the coffee cake was stronger. Evelyn glanced at the oven. They still had a few more minutes. "Speaking of the household . . . how do you think it's going, the five of us? Do you think the talk last night was a good thing?"

"Of course it was a good thing. Talking is always a good thing." Mae leaned close. "Of course, talking is my thing, so I'm biased." She leaned back. "But I think it's essential we keep things on the table, whether we like what's spread out there or not."

Evelyn's thoughts immediately flew to Tessa. She seemed to be the burr under their —

"Tessa's a pistol, that's for sure," Mae said. "And I can foresee some mighty arguments looming."

"Oh dear."

"No, no, that's perfectly fine. Mae Fitzpatrick has never been one to shy away from a little lively discussion, though I can't stand to have people mad at me, that's a fact. They can disagree with me all they want — as long as I know about it — but people holding a grudge or getting all silent and pouting about something they think I've done wrong . . ." She shook her head hard enough to make her sleep-frizzed hair sway. "Tell me to my face so we can clear it up. Or not. It's the creepy crawly silent conflicts I can't tolerate, the ones that slither under the baseboards when the lights come on. Get 'em out in the open where we can squash 'em good."

Evelyn smiled and pretended to write something down. "I'll remember that. No creepy crawly conflicts with Mae."

Mae tapped a nail on Evelyn's imaginary list. "And no blame games either. Truth or nothing. That's what we decided, right?"

For better or worse.

Evelyn was putting Grandma Nelson's china back in the hutch when the doorbell rang. She answered it. A pretty, thirtyish woman stood before her. She had chin-length brown hair with a hint of wave to it but not much style, as if whatever style her hair possessed was an afterthought. A wisp blew upward in the breeze. Her hair wasn't her strong point. That distinction went to her smile.

"Hi. I'm Piper Wellington. I'm here to see —"

"Hey, Pipe!" Audra raced down the stairs with Summer close behind. "It's about time you visited. Come on in and see our new digs."

Evelyn let Piper in and was about to introduce herself when Summer nearly knocked the young woman down with a hug.

"Hey, pip-squeak. I missed you at church and at lunch after, but don't worry, I sang extra loud during the hymns and ate an extra order of french fries in your honor."

Summer looked up at her mom, her face stricken. "Mommy! Why didn't we go?"

Piper looked to Audra. "Yes, Mommy, why didn't you go?"

The look on Audra's face was that of a small animal surrounded on all sides. There was no way out. At least Evelyn wasn't the only one feeling guilty today.

Audra suddenly slipped her hand through Evelyn's arm. "Piper, this is our landlord, Evelyn Peerbaugh. Evelyn, this is Piper Wellington, my ex-best friend."

Piper shook Evelyn's hand. "Best friend, guilt monger. I'm a woman of many talents."

Evelyn liked her immediately. She couldn't help but notice the difference between Piper's attitude toward Audra's choice not to attend church and her own experience with Tessa.

Summer pulled Piper's hand. "Come see my room."

"Our room," Audra said. She led the way upstairs.

"Nice to meet you, Mrs. Peerbaugh," Piper said.

"Evelyn. Call me Evelyn."

"Glad to, Evelyn."

Nice girl. Nice.

Ten minutes later Audra, Summer, and Piper came downstairs, Audra carrying a small box. "Evelyn? I noticed you have a CD player in the parlor. It's dumb I keep all my CDs upstairs. I'd be happy to share them, if you have extra room."

"And extra tolerance," Piper said.

"Hey, go easy on me," Audra said. "The Nylons happen to be a very cool group."

"Whatever you say."

Evelyn put the last of the crystal water goblets away and shut the door to the hutch. "I'm sure we can find some room." She led the way into the parlor where the music system was located. Aaron had been a big music lover and had insisted on keeping abreast of the latest equipment. She opened the storage cabinet. "Just as I thought; there's plenty of space."

Piper sat on the couch and had Summer in her lap before she had time to even cross her legs. She adjusted Summer into the crook of her arm and pumped her hand into her tummy as if fluffing a pillow. Summer giggled. "Put something on, Evelyn. Something from *your* collection."

Evelyn couldn't remember the last time she'd played music. She wasn't even sure what they had. Audra started to move away from the CD storage, but Evelyn stopped her. "No, you're fine. Most of my music is in here." She opened a separate cabinet revealing nearly a hundred records.

"Wow," Audra said, "you have real records?"

Summer looked up at Piper. "What's a record?"

Evelyn sighed. "My age is showing."

Audra pulled one out. "No, this is fabulous." She held a Beach Boys album for her daughter to see. "A record is music, baby. Like a big CD." She turned to Evelyn. "Play this one."

Surfin' Safari. "You like the Beach Boys?"

"Doesn't everybody?" Piper said.

"Exactly," Audra said. "Is this an original?"

"I don't know. I suppose it is."

Audra looked on the back. "Evelyn, it is. It's from 1963. Do you know how much this is worth?"

"I haven't a clue."

"It's worth nothing unless I get to hear it," Piper said. "Quit yer yappin' and put it on."

Evelyn put the record on the ancient turntable and started it. The title song filled the room. Within seconds Piper was on her feet, holding Summer's hands, dancing wildly. Audra joined in, doing the swim.

Before she knew it, Evelyn was dancing with them. She suddenly remembered how much she loved to dance. It made her feel as if a power switch had been turned on.

Audra turned it up so it sounded as if the Beach Boys were jamming in the corner.

Mae appeared at the bottom of the stairs and entered the parlor doing the frug — if Evelyn remembered her dances correctly. All of them danced with total abandon, laughing, singing horribly, and having the most fun Evelyn could remember having in a long, long —

The front door opened and Tessa walked in. The look on her face could have been an illustration for shocked horror.

"Hey, Tessie, come on in; the water's fine."

Though the other three kept dancing, heedless of the intruder in their midst,

Evelyn couldn't do it. She went to the record player and lifted the play arm. "Sorry it's so loud, Tessa. We got a little carried —"

"Indeed you did."

"Hey, Tessie, you can't argue with the classics. Come join us."

"I wouldn't think of it."

Evelyn's stomach tightened, readying for another fight. "I guess that's enough for one afternoon, ladies."

Tessa raised a hand. "I said I wouldn't think of joining you in dancing to that . . . that ridiculous go-go music." She wagged a finger. "However, if you have some Glenn Miller, I'm in."

They all stood in stunned silence.

"Well? Do you have it? 'Little Brown Jug' is my favorite."

Evelyn snapped out of it. "Actually, I believe I do."

And she did. She put on the record and found "Little Brown Jug." By the second measure, Tessa Klein had dropped her purse, shucked off her shoes, and was jiving with the best of them.

That Tessa knew a thing or two about dancing.

Tessa eased herself onto her bed. It took

some effort to lift her legs off the floor. She hadn't danced like that since Glenn Miller wasn't a golden oldie.

She closed her eyes and rested the back of her hand on her forehead. She tried to breathe deep, but her heart stitched at the effort. But the pain felt different this time. As if its claws had put on mittens. Muted. Bearable. Almost worth it.

Dancing with her roommates, her friends . . .

Were they her friends? Her friends were the characters in the books she read and the historical figures who led such fascinating lives — lives that were worthy of writing about. What was worthy about her life? What had she ever done that could be put in a book and read about by anyone? That she would *want* people to read about, anyway.

Nothing. Not a thing.

And that fact grieved her greatly and made her heart pull with a different kind of hurt.

Evelyn paused at the mirror above the entry table and put on her earrings. She could hear Audra, Piper, Gillie, and Summer in the kitchen, making dinner for the three of them. Their laughter nourished the house, seeping into the dry hungry cracks like lemon oil on wood. It had been less than two weeks since Audra and Summer had moved in, but they — and Piper and Gillie — already seemed like an essential part of the household. If she hadn't already had this dinner planned at Russell's, she would have been content to join them until their oil of happiness ran over her in excess.

Mae came down the stairs in her unique *one-two-three, one-two-three* rhythm. She was also dressed up, wearing a chartreuse broomstick skirt, matching off-the-shoulder blouse, and yet another pair of sandals — these sporting a yellow daisy.

"You look snazzy, Evie. You got a date too?"

"Oh no . . . I —"

Mae joined her at the mirror, fluffing her already fluffy hair. "Don't make it sound like a sin, sister. You're single now. It would be allowed if you'd be so inclined and found some gentleman to incline with you." She laughed. "Or recline, as the case may be."

"It's only been seven weeks today."

Mae stopped fluffing and stared at Evelyn's reflection. "Six weeks, six days, four hours, ten minutes, and twenty-three seconds?"

Evelyn fished her car keys from her

purse. "I don't keep track. Not like that."

"Glad to hear it. I, myself, keep tabs on how long Danny's been gone by celebrating. Like tonight. I'm going out with the most dashing man. Harry, of Harry's Plumbing fame? You ever use him?"

"No —"

"Well, I have — for plumbing *and* other things." She laughed at her joke and turned toward the laughter in the kitchen. "Who's eating in?"

"The two girls, Gillie, and Piper. Tessa had a potluck at church."

"Figures. That woman spends more time at church than God."

"She's a good dancer though, isn't she?" Evelyn said, remembering last Sunday.

"Totally shocked the VapoRub offa my chest."

"We saw a side to Tessa that wasn't so —"

"Drawn up tight like a raisin? Yup. It was nice. Hope it continues — for all our sakes." She ran a finger along the edge of her lipstick, fending off a wayward pink smudge. "You never said where you're going. If it's not a date, then who you so gussied up for?"

"Russell."

"Oh. That's nice." She looked disappointed. "He taking you out or cooking in?"

"He's cooking. He's a good cook."

Mae cocked her head. "And you say he's single — and a banker?"

"Mae! He's only thirty and you're . . . you're . . ."

"Much too much for him no matter how old he is." She turned on her heel, making her skirt wave good-bye. "Ta-ta. I'm off to stun the world. Don't wait up."

Evelyn wouldn't think of it.

Russell greeted Evelyn at the door. "You look pretty, Mom."

"Thanks, honey." Evelyn appreciated how Russell had gotten more generous with the compliments since Aaron's death.

He took her sweater and purse, setting them on the entry chair. "Is that a new skirt?"

"I've had it for years."

"New hair?"

"Russell . . ."

"Well, there's something different about you. You're . . . glowing."

She laughed. "It must be my new housemates. You wouldn't believe the things they've got me doing. Last Sunday afternoon, we even had a little dancefest. The Beach Boys and Glenn Miller."

"And where was this?"

"In the parlor."

"Of our house?"

"*My* house. Yes. It was quite . . ." She searched for the word.

"Undignified?"

"You sound like your father. Actually, it was quite joyful. I love to dance."

"Since when?"

"Since always. When I was little I used to dance around the house to my own music. Your grandma used to accuse me of having a radio on in my head. 'Evelyn, turn that thing off and sit still. You're acting like a crazy person.'" Without intending to, Evelyn found herself swaying. When she saw Russell notice, she stopped.

"Did Dad ever take you dancing?"

"Once. When we were first dating. He wasn't very good at it."

"Did that matter?"

"Not to me. I suggested lessons, but you know your dad. Self-made men don't need lessons on anything." She heard the bitterness in her voice and shucked the attitude away. Bitterness was not good for the appetite.

Russell brought out a plate of ribs and placed it in front of his mother. She leaned

150

her face toward it and took a deep breath. "This smells delicious."

"They're called Waimanalo ribs. I have raspberry mandarin salad, snow peas with papaya relish, homemade buttermilk biscuits, and cheesecake with cherries and chocolate topping for dessert."

She patted his hand. "You'll make someone a wonderful husband."

"Mom . . ."

She served herself three ribs. "I was bragging about you to Mae, and she offered to go out with you."

"Which one is she?"

"The hippie with the long gray hair. Actually, she reminds me of Aunt Meg in that tornado movie *Twister*. The metal artist who feeds them half a cow."

"She wants to go out with me?"

Evelyn delayed her answer to take her first bite. Tangy yet sweet. "Yum. Actually, I think Mae's criteria for a date is anything male and breathing."

"Are you sure you want that type of woman in your home?"

"Oh dear . . . I exaggerate. I'm sure Mae's quite the proper lady. I like her a lot. It's as though she's the main character in a marvelous movie that never ends, and she's giving an Oscar-winning performance."

"Sounds like a histrionic eccentric."

She shrugged. "Maybe a bit."

"Tell me about your other tenants."

"You met Tessa Klein. She's —"

"The lady who made the codfish comment?"

Evelyn blinked, finding the memory. "Well, yes, she did say that. Tessa *is* a bit opinionated about things, but I think her heart's good. She's just used to having her own way — and letting everybody know what that way is."

"That doesn't sound good."

She took a sip of her water. "Nice goblets, honey. These new?"

"They're Waterford. I found a place online. . . ." He cleared his throat. "You were telling me about Tessie?"

"Tessa. Though Mae insists on calling her Tessie. I think Mae does it on purpose — a continuous power game. She calls me Evie, but I kind of like it."

"What does Tessa call Mae?"

Her spoon stopped halfway to her mouth. "Mae. Tessa's formal. I'd bet she was a very strict mother. And she seems to only tolerate Summer."

"Who's Summer?"

"Audra's little girl."

"You only have three rooms, Mom. I'm

152

hearing four names."

"That's because Audra and Summer share a room. I told you about them."

"You have two women sharing the same — ?"

"Don't be ridiculous. Audra is Summer's mother. Summer is five."

"Oh yeah. You did tell me. So how is it? Having a child in the house?"

"She's a good girl. Very polite. Always wants to help. I moved her toy box down to the parlor so she has more space to play."

Russell lifted a rib to eat it, then set it down. "Where's the father?"

"Never was one. Never a husband, that is."

"This Audra's an unwed mother?"

She set her fork down and stared at him. "I've never heard you sound so vindictive, Russell. Audra made a wonderful, unselfish choice to have the child. From what I can see, she's a good mother. Things like this happen, and a girl's got to handle it the best she —"

"So, living in your house you have an overaged floozy, an unwed mother, an illegitimate child, and a judgmental grandma. Sounds lovely."

"I don't like your tone."

153

"And I don't like the sounds of your household. You are completely new at this, Mom, and it seems you've taken the first people who walked in off the street. You can't tell me that of all the people you interviewed these were the best?"

She took another sip of water.

"You did interview other tenants, didn't you?"

She set the glass down. "I didn't need to. These ladies showed up and they seemed right, and I . . . I trusted my instincts."

He snickered, then cut it off. "Sorry. I didn't mean to do that."

She adjusted the napkin in her lap. "You sounded like your father just then."

He held his hand across the table and waited until she gave him hers. "I think it goes back to experience, Mom. Dad didn't give you a chance to gain much experience in a lot of things."

"So now I have the chance. Now I've *got* to do it on my own. And I think I'm doing all right. Maybe it won't all work out perfectly. So what? I'll deal with that when I have to."

"The Scarlett O'Hara syndrome: 'I'll think about it tomorrow,' right?"

"Scarlett had her good points too. She was very tenacious. And so am I."

"Tenacious and stubborn."

"And so am I?"

"You have your moments, Mom."

She gave a quick nod. "You bet I do. So get used to it."

Evelyn unwrapped the two Waterford goblets Russell had given her as a present and put them in the hutch. She'd told him it wasn't necessary, that she'd merely mentioned liking them in passing because they were beautiful, not because she'd wanted them for herself. But Russell had insisted. If it made him feel he was helping . . .

She'd had such a nice dinner with her son in spite of his doubts about her tenants. Eating at Russell's had been a rare occurrence when Aaron had been alive — for no reason other than they just hadn't done it. But now, eating together twice in one month . . . Evelyn supposed Russell felt responsible for her. Did she come across as needy?

As she reached the top of the stairs, Tessa's door opened and she crooked a finger. "Psst."

"What — ?" Before Evelyn could finish her sentence, she heard a man's laugh. It came from Mae's room.

Tessa crossed her arms and nodded.

"I've been waiting for you to get home. She has a man in there." She checked her watch. "And she *has* had a man in there for fifty-two minutes. What are you going to do about it?"

Evelyn was totally confused — confused about what she should do *and* what she thought about the situation in the first place.

"Well?"

Evelyn opened her mouth to answer, but then shut it. "I'm tired. I'm going to bed. Good night." Then she hurried to her bedroom and shut the door.

Chicken.

6

The Lord remembers us, and he will surely bless us. He will bless the people of Israel and the family of Aaron. . . . He will bless those who fear the Lord, both great and small.
PSALM 115:12–13

Audra waltzed into the kitchen and did a three-sixty. "How do I look?"

"Very pretty," Evelyn said.

Summer spoke through a mouthful of cereal. "Pretty, Mommy."

"Don't talk with your mouth full, baby."

Mae handed her a cup of tea. "You'll knock 'em dead, girlie girl."

"I'll settle for not dumping the cash drawer on the floor."

Tessa stood at the counter and poured a cup of coffee. "I'm missing something. Why are you so dressed up?"

Mae answered for Audra. "She starts her job at the bank today, Tessie. Get with the program."

"I beg your par—"

Evelyn jumped in. "She's working with

my son, or at least at the same bank." She nodded to Audra. "You make sure to look him up, all right? Introduce yourself. Tell him hi."

Audra couldn't imagine the tellers having much contact with the vice presidents. "I'll see what I can do." She sat at the table at the same moment Summer slipped off her knees, nearly spilling her cereal. She reached over and caught her. "Baby! Careful!"

Evelyn popped out of her seat. "It's not your fault, sweetie. You shouldn't have to sit on your knees for every meal. So I've been thinking about a solution." She brought the step stool over to the table. "How's this? A special chair, just for you."

Summer slid off the big chair, stepped onto the stool, turned herself around, and sat on the top step, her tiny hips fitting like a puzzle piece finding its place. She wriggled proudly. "I have my *own* special chair."

The women laughed, and Audra flashed Evelyn a look of thanks. She was a dear woman who seemed to sense what people were feeling, anticipating their needs. Yet she did it in a way that made no one uncomfortable.

Mae poured sugar on her cornflakes. "I

158

sure am liking this. All five of us gathered for breakfast."

"Just like a family," Evelyn said.

"A family of women," Audra said.

Mae raised her mug. *"Vive les femmes! Vive la famille!"*

"Yes, yes, that's all well and good," Tessa said. "But there were more than just females here the other night." She cast an eye at Mae, and Audra wondered what was going on. "You've been avoiding me, Mae Fitzpatrick."

Mae glared at Tessa over her mug. "Now why ever would I do that?"

"You know very well why. Guilt."

"For what?"

"For having a . . . you know . . . in your room."

Mae rolled her eyes. "Oh that. Did we disturb you, Tessie?"

Evelyn's head was doing a Ping-Pong between them. "Ladies . . ."

"What's going on?" Audra asked.

Tessa glanced at Summer, and Audra took the hint. "Baby, would you run upstairs and get my pearl earrings? They're in the jewelry box on top of the dresser. Can you reach it?" Always eager to help, Summer nodded and left the room. "What's all this about?" Audra asked.

Mae dunked her cereal with the back of her spoon. "Tessie's got her bloomers in a bunch because I had a man in my room the other night."

"You did?" Audra hadn't meant to sound so incredulous.

"There is life after forty, girlie girl."

Evelyn smiled. "Forty?"

Mae shrugged. "All right. Fifty then. The point is, what I do or do not do in the seclusion of my private space should be my business and no one else's."

Tessa tapped a spoon on the edge of the jam jar. "I do not agree. There have to be limits, for the sake of the safety and —"

"Safety?" Mae said. "Harry Mathison is hardly a threat to the safety of this or any other —"

"Harry the plumber?" Audra asked. "I know who he is. He worked on Piper's shower."

"Quite a looker, isn't he?"

Audra shrugged, remembering a balding man whose work shirt with *Harry* embroidered on the pocket had been pulled to bursting by a more than ample belly. "Sure. I mean, I suppose —"

Tessa returned her uneaten toast to her plate. "Whether Harry the plumber looks like Robert Goulet or Bob Hope is inconsequential. He should not —"

"I've heard of Bob Hope, but Robert who?" Audra asked.

Tessa gave an exaggerated sigh. "Robert Goulet happens to have a voice that can melt metal. Compared to him, today's singers sound as if they're clearing their throats."

Evelyn sighed. "Robert Goulet as Lancelot." She began to sing, " 'If ever I would leave you —' "

Mae joined in. " 'It wouldn't be in springtime . . .' "

Audra was stunned as all three ladies finished the verse with gusto, apparently forgetting they were in the middle of a heated argument.

When they finished, Mae shuddered with pleasure. "He was dreamy. Still is dreamy."

"I'll give him that," Evelyn said. "But if we're talking dreamy . . . there's no one like Frank."

"Sinatra?" Tessa asked.

Evelyn looked hurt. "Of course Sinatra. Is there any other Frank?"

Tessa shook her head. "He was too short. I like my men tall."

Mae laughed. "As if Frank was going to ask you out. Besides, you're bitsy. Height

161

shouldn't matter to you. If you'd ever had the pleasure of even standing next to Frank, you would have come up to his armpit."

Tessa straightened her spine. "I was taller once."

"When? When you stood on a chair?"

Audra couldn't believe the direction this conversation had taken. She looked to the door leading to the foyer and the stairs. Summer would be back any minute. "Ladies? Don't we have an issue to resolve?"

The three older ladies blinked themselves back to the present. Mae spoke first. "The point is, my private life is my business, and I will not have —"

"So you admit you were being intimate?" Tessa asked.

"I will admit no such thing," Mae said. She spread peanut butter on a piece of bread in a thick swath. "Actually, we were just talking and I wouldn't even consider 'being intimate' with Harry." She snickered. "I mean, he's a nice guy and all, but please . . ."

Audra raised a hand to comment, then realized it wasn't necessary, and lowered it. "Perhaps we should limit our male contact to the public areas. It's not that I object to a little romance, but there is Summer to consider. And though neither of us was aware of Harry's presence the other night, I don't want Summer seeing things she shouldn't." She hoped she wasn't being too strong. She was an equal partner here, but a junior partner in seniority.

"I think that's doable," Evelyn said. She looked to the others. "For Summer's sake, right?"

Mae nodded. "I still don't think I was doing anything wrong."

"But you —"

Audra jumped in before Tessa could fan the flame again. "I appreciate it, ladies." She looked at her watch. She'd wanted to get to work a little early for her first day. Impress them. She pushed herself away from the table just as Summer came back with her earrings — and something else.

"What do you have there, baby?"

Summer displayed five twenty-dollar bills.

"Where did you get this?"

"It was in the jewelry box. Right under the little tray thingy."

"I've never had that much money lying about, and I would never put money in —" Then she knew.

"You know where it came from?" Mae asked.

Audra nodded and folded the bills in half. "I can guess. It's from Gillie. She's always giving me things. Worried about my finances. This would be just like her."

"Boy," Mae said, "I'll have to be extra nice to her."

Audra put the earrings on. "We've got to go."

"Where are you taking the girl?" Tessa asked.

Audra hated the way Tessa always called her that. "I'm taking Summer to a babysitter who lives over on Cosgrove." She drew Summer's head close. "So this is her first day too."

"Have a good day, both of you," Evelyn said. "You'll be here for dinner? I was thinking of making chicken and rice."

Audra felt bad. They'd each contributed fifty dollars a week for food and had discussed taking turns cooking. Audra had volunteered to draw up a weekly chart, but she hadn't done it. In fact, she'd forgotten all about it. "Evelyn. I'm so sorry. Here you are cooking again. I was supposed to make the schedule and didn't."

Evelyn flipped her concern away. "No problem."

Audra moved to her side and put a hand on her shoulder. "But it is a problem. I said I would do it and I let you down."

"Goodness, Audra," Mae said. "It's not that big a deal."

"It is to me." Audra prided herself on her organizational abilities. She was a natural at lists and schedules and found joy in turning chaos into order.

Tessa didn't say anything but nodded her agreement. At least there was one other tenant who would hold her accountable.

The question remained whether that would be a blessing or a curse.

Although Audra had visited the day-care home right after she and Summer had moved into Peerbaugh Place, today the house looked shabbier; the day-care provider, Rollanda Sims, more disheveled. And had the house smelled like cigarette smoke when she was here before? She'd obviously been in such a hurry to start her new life that she hadn't fully considered the quality of that life.

"We'll have a great time today, won't we, Sunny?" Rollanda said. A three-year-old boy peeked shyly from around her ample backside. He clearly needed to have his nose wiped.

"Her name's —"

"My name's Summer."

Way to stick up for yourself, baby.

"Oh. Summer. That's a pretty name for a pretty girl."

Somehow the compliment — that Audra had heard dozens of times before with no adverse reaction — struck her as false and oozy. A baby cried from another room, the tenor of the cry revealing its newborn status.

Rollanda did not so much as glance in its direction.

"Shouldn't you go check on the baby?" Audra asked.

"Oh, she's fine. Probably just needs changing."

There was a crash from the kitchen, and at least two children started arguing.

"Shut up in there!" Rollanda turned back to Audra. Her teeth were decidedly yellow. "Those kids. If I'm not at their backs every minute, they'd destroy the place."

If that was supposed to reassure Audra, it didn't. And as far as the house being destroyed . . . Audra noticed a large stain in the carpet heading toward the bedrooms, and the arms of the couch were threadbare, the decorative welting frayed and ripped.

Audra felt Summer press against her side, one hand hooking itself into the back of Audra's belt. She clearly didn't want to stay, but the clock was ticking and Audra had to get to work for her first day.

Rollanda held her hand toward Summer. "Come on, girl. Let's go get some Sugar Puffs. Would you like that?"

Audra felt Summer's negative shake.

Rollanda's eyebrows furrowed. "Come on. You're not the only kid in the castle."

That was it. Audra grabbed Summer's hand and escaped outside, running to the car.

"Hey!" Rollanda called from the porch. "What're you doing?"

"We've changed our minds."

"But I reserved a place for you. You're still going to have to pay me for at least a week. I —"

Audra shut Summer's car door and turned on Rollanda. "I don't owe you anything, lady. I don't know what I was thinking. And if I were you, I'd quit yapping at me and get in that house and show those poor kids a little love and care."

"Don't go judging —"

Audra stormed to the driver's door. "Clean up your act or I'll sic the authorities on you."

The tires squealed.

"Now what, Mommy?" Summer asked.

Audra's heart beat in her throat. She glanced at the speedometer and eased down to the speed limit. "I have no idea." The clock on the dash said 7:45; work started at eight. So much for being early.

"I want to go home, Mommy."

"But I have to go to work."

"Aunt Evelyn can take care of me."

Audra looked in the backseat. "Aunt? Where did you get that?"

Summer shrugged and looked out the window. "That's what Opie calls his grandma lady. Aunt Bea."

Audra had to smile. Good old Andy Griffith. "But we don't know if Aunt Evelyn will agree to take care of you."

"We can ask, can't we?"

That they could do.

Evelyn stood in the parlor with her hands behind her back like a sergeant in an empty barracks. The clock on the mantel seemed a half step behind her heartbeat. There were no other sounds. One minute the kitchen had been alive with women's conversation and the clattering of break- fast, the next quiet and still. Everyone gone, with her left behind. Once again, alone.

She knew she should enjoy it. She realized in a house full of women these solitary moments were a thing to be cherished. During the first week, hadn't she escaped to the grocery store for this very reason? Had she already become used to — and dependent upon — having people around? Is that why she felt like an empty box waiting to be filled?

The truth was, she'd never spent much time alone. Although Aaron had held a few out-of-house jobs, most of the time he'd found employment he could do at home, with the excuse that it gave him more time to work on his own projects. And so, more often than not, he'd been here with her. But that didn't mean she couldn't be alone, did it?

Did it?

"You're pitiful, Evelyn. Snap out of it."

This empty house was reality. As of today, both Audra and Mae worked and Summer was off at day care. Tessa took adult ed classes and was involved in numerous church organizations. If Evelyn wanted company, she could rejoin the committees she'd been involved in before Aaron's death.

The trouble was, she didn't feel like it. They all seemed frivolous. What difference did it make if the park planted twelve more trees, or whether the caterer at the library dinner served pâté or nachos? Was the world changed by any of those things?

Stop right there, Evelyn. Don't take on the world. You've got enough to handle.

Unexpected tears brewed and she flicked them away. This was ridiculous. One minute she was overwhelmed by being alone and the next, overwhelmed by thinking beyond —

The front door opened and Summer burst in, with Audra right behind her. Evelyn swiped a finger under her lashes and cleared the tears out of her throat. "What are you doing home? I thought —"

"Yeah, I thought too," Audra said. Summer was already at her toy box. "Don't get things out, baby. Not until we know if you're . . . if you're . . ."

Summer froze, then looked at Evelyn expectantly.

"If she's what?"

"If I'm staying. If you'll take care of me," Summer said. She stood and took hold of Evelyn's hand. "My other baby-sitter was icky. Can I stay here with you?"

Evelyn looked from Summer's upturned face to Audra.

"She's telling the truth, Evelyn. Her baby-sitter was beyond icky. I just couldn't leave her there. And I really, really have to get to work. We were wondering — actually it was Summer's idea — if Aunt Evelyn could take care of her."

Evelyn felt her heart tug. "Aunt Evelyn?"

Summer nodded solemnly.

Audra took a step toward the door. "This wouldn't be a permanent thing. Just until I find a day care that doesn't remind me of a place we see on the evening news being raided by Social Services."

"That bad?"

"Pretty close." Audra dropped her chin and peered through her lashes. "Have we made the situation sound desperate enough?"

Evelyn laughed and made a decision on the spot. Actually, there was no decision in it. They needed her. How could she say no to that? It had been fun having Summer around for the past three weeks. How different could it be to care for her while her mother worked? "I'd be happy to take care of Summer."

Audra's sigh spoke a thousand words. She was at the door within seconds.

"Thank you, Evelyn. I owe you big time." She blew a kiss to Summer. "See you later, baby. Have fun with Aunt Evelyn, don't make a mess, and mind what she says."

The door closed and there was a moment of silence as Evelyn and Summer assessed each other. It had been twenty-five years since Evelyn had been alone with a five-year-old. Then she had an idea . . .

"How would you like to do some dancing?"

"Yeah!"

In minutes they were boogying to "Barbara Ann."

It was nice to be needed.

Gillie gave Audra the once-over. She looked nice for her first day of work. A navy suit was a good choice, though in a way, it looked odd on Audra, whom Gillie was used to seeing in the clothes of a college student. Yet beyond the suit, Gillie was disappointed that Audra wasn't wearing the scarf she'd given her. It would have matched perfectly.

And why hadn't Audra mentioned the money she'd left in her jewelry box? Not a word. Certainly she'd found it after all this time.

Gillie looked closer. Maybe not . . .

Audra wasn't wearing any jewelry beyond a watch and pearl earrings. Maybe the money was still sitting there, untouched.

Oh well, Gillie could only give the gifts; it wasn't up to her how people used them.

Unfortunately.

Audra wasn't sure how to broach the problem of the hundred dollars. She didn't want to hurt Gillie's feelings, but she also didn't want Gillie to get into the habit of being her sugar daddy, or to be more apt, her sugar sister.

Finally, there was a lull in the customers and the first day's instruction. Audra got the folded bills out of her purse and called across the teller partition to her friend. "Gil?"

Gillie looked up. "Hmm?"

Audra held the bills across the divider between them. "Here."

Gillie had them in her hand before she realized what they were. She tried to give them back. "This is yours. Now you can get that TV we talked about."

Audra shook her head. "I'm not taking your money."

"But I want to give it to you. Don't look a gift giver in the mouth . . . face . . . whatever that saying is."

Audra adjusted her stance, trying to look stronger than she felt. "You already gave us a doll and a scarf." She put a hand to her throat, suddenly realizing what she *wasn't* wearing. Maybe Gillie hadn't noticed . . . "Part of my being on my own is providing for myself — or not providing, as *I* can afford. Not you. Not my parents. Not anyone. Do you understand?"

"I was just trying to help." Gillie looked so hurt, so broken.

"I know, and I don't mean to sound ungrateful."

"So I can't give you presents even if it brings *me* much joy?"

Hoo-boy. Audra felt her resolve weaken. Since Gillie's divorce, her friend had no focus for her familial feelings. She and Jerry had never had children. Who was Audra to prevent her from giving if her heart told her to give? Wasn't that a type of selfishness?

Audra sighed deeply. "Okay . . . tell you what. You can give us *reasonable* presents if the spirit moves you, but no more cash. Understand?"

Gillie palmed the twenties. "No more cash. Gotcha."

A friend who was *too* generous. What a problem to have.

★ ★ ★

Audra was startled when Gillie suddenly called out, "Mr. Peerbaugh!"

A man with an aquiline nose and a strong jaw detoured toward Gillie. He glanced at Audra and nodded. He had soft eyes that lit up when he smiled.

Gillie took over. "Mr. Peerbaugh, I want you to meet our newest employee, Ms. Taylor. And Audra, this is Mr. Peerbaugh, one of the vice presidents."

"You're Evelyn's son, aren't you?"

"And you're the Audra who's one of my mother's —"

"Tenants. Yes, that's me."

Gillie beamed. "Well, isn't this nice. You two know each other."

"Not really," Russell said. He seemed to realize his comment sounded rude because he quickly added, "But we know *of* each other."

"Well, that's a start, isn't it?" Gillie said.

Audra held out her hand. "Nice to meet you, Mr. Peerbaugh. I'll try to do a good job and make you proud."

He held her hand a moment too long, then noticed and let it go. Was he blushing? "Yes . . . well . . . it's nice meeting you too, Ms. Taylor."

He fled.

Gillie leaned close and whispered, "He's interested."

"I'm sure he's interested in all the new employees."

"Uh-uh. More than that. Didn't you notice how you scared him to death?"

"I did not."

Gillie wiped off her counter. "Think what you want, but I know what I saw."

Audra saw Russell Peerbaugh slip into one of the front offices. He glanced over his shoulder at her, then quickly looked away.

"By the way, he's rich."

She flashed Gillie a glance. "That doesn't matter to me."

Gillie rolled her eyes. "Give me a break. It might not matter, but presented two equally wonderful men — one with money, one without — you'd pick the rich one, wouldn't you?"

"You put me in that exact position and I'll decide then." Audra lowered her voice. "Shouldn't we get back to work?"

"Party pooper."

"I'll get the jelly." Evelyn watched as Summer spread peanut butter to the edges of the bread as if painting a white wall with caramel-colored paint.

Summer concentrated, biting her tongue. She was something else, always wanting to help. After their dance session, Evelyn had suggested they take some toys outside so Summer could play while Evelyn planted impatiens and marigolds in the back flower bed. But Summer had refused, asking instead to help. And then when it was lunchtime, Summer had pulled her stool to the counter and stood on the bottom step before Evelyn had even taken the bread out of the pantry. It was as though helping was Summer's play. Evelyn had noticed Audra's discipline and knew the mother expected a lot of the daughter, so part of Summer's eagerness was probably her desire to be the good girl Audra demanded. Yet it seemed more than that. There was a level of joy in the serving.

"Do you like strawberry jam?" Evelyn asked, setting the jar nearby.

"I like any jam. Honey too."

"Honey on peanut butter?"

Summer delayed answering while she painstakingly dipped the knife in the jam jar and plopped a huge glob in the middle of one of the sandwiches. That accomplished, she answered, "Yup. My grandma taught me that. Warm honey."

That *did* sound good.

Evelyn perked up at the mention of Summer's grandma. Maybe this was a chance to find out a little more about Audra. "Your grandma with the honey, is that the grandma you lived with until you moved here?"

Summer licked jam off her thumb and started making Evelyn's sandwich. "Grandma Nellie."

"Did you like living with her?"

"We made cookies."

"Was there a grandpa around?"

Summer nodded. "Grandpa Howard. He looked at books about Mooie a lot."

"Mooie?"

"It's a place in Hawaii."

Evelyn smiled. "Maui."

"Yeah, that's it."

"Were your grandparents taking a trip to Maui?"

"Grandma didn't want to go 'cause she wanted to take care of me while Mommy was at class, but Grandpa said that was no excuse — Mommy was a grown woman and it was about time she got out her own."

"Got out *on* her own?" Evelyn asked.

Summer handed Evelyn the knife. "You cut them, okay? I'm not allowed to use a knife that way. I scratched Grandma's counters once."

Evelyn cut the sandwiches into triangles, her mind mulling the issues of a multigenerational household. Would her parents have been so accommodating? When would they have reached their limit?

She'd never know.

"I like it cut 'agonal best," Summer said, getting off the stool and moving it over to the cupboard with the plates. "I like to bite off the corners."

She was a joy. But Evelyn reminded herself it had only been four hours. Could she do this day after day? Would Summer's need to help become a burden, forcing Evelyn to have to think up jobs for her to do? It was obvious she was not the type to mindlessly sit in front of a Disney video.

The doorbell rang and Summer was off to answer it. Evelyn had to run to catch up. "No, sweetie. You can't answer the door without me." Evelyn opened the door to Piper, who immediately zeroed in on Summer. "Hey, pip-squeak. What are you doing here?"

"Aunt Evelyn's taking care of me. I made sandwiches. Come see." She was off to the kitchen, leaving the ladies behind.

Piper brought forward a framed picture with a bow on it. "I just stopped over to bring Audra this picture for her room. It used to hang in my living room and she's always admired it, so I thought it would make a nice housewarming gift." It was a picture of a flower stall on a European street. Very refreshing and happy.

Summer swung open the door leading to the kitchen. "Piper! Come see my sandwiches."

"Yes, ma'am!"

"Join us," Evelyn said. "That is, if you like peanut butter and strawberry jam."

"Couldn't live without it."

The two women poured drinks and washed some oranges while Summer made Piper a sandwich. Slowly but surely . . .

Finally, they were all seated at the table. Evelyn was reaching for her sandwich when Piper held out her hand, palm up, also extending one to Summer. "Would you like me to say grace?"

"Sure," Evelyn said. She'd never heard of grace being said at lunchtime, but if Piper wanted to do it, why not?

Piper took their hands, and Evelyn reached across the table to join with Summer. When the circle was complete, Piper bowed her head. "Lord Jesus, we thank you for this yummy food and for the friends sharing it. Be with us today and help us to do Your will. Amen."

"Amen!" Summer said.

Evelyn had the feeling God would have preferred the word *delicious* rather than the casual *yummy* but wasn't about to bring it up. "So," she said, picking up her sandwich, "I forget . . . where do you work that gives you the freedom of slipping over our way?"

"I'm a counselor at the high school. It's my lunch break, so time is a bit tight, but I really wanted the picture to be here when Audra got home from her first day at work."

"I've been wanting to ask . . . how did you meet her?"

"Audra was one of my students."

Evelyn struggled to swallow so she could talk. "You were her counselor?"

Piper glanced at Summer and gave a small nod. *Ah, so that's it.*

Summer was making half of her sandwich walk across her plate, bowing to the other, smaller half.

"You don't look that much older than Audra," Evelyn said. "And she's only . . ."

"She's twenty-three. But I'm plenty old. I'm thirty-three."

Evelyn dropped her chin. "No way."

"Yes, way." She sighed deeply. "Somehow I've slogged past the big three-O."

"Then you're married?"

Piper laughed, and Evelyn realized the judgment she'd just made. "I didn't mean to imply if you're over thirty you *have* to be married, but —"

"But that *is* the norm. I know."

"Do you want to be married?"

Piper took a bite of sandwich and didn't answer until she was through chewing and had taken a drink of tea. "I used to. I was brought up old-fashioned. A girl got married, had babies, and they lived happily ever after. I gave it a good try."

"We all do." Evelyn realized her statement sounded odd. She quickly added, "Were you engaged?"

"Once. He backed out."

"I'm so sorry."

"Don't be. It was the best thing all in all. It stung like a salted wound for a long time, but I think that was more due to the humiliation of it than the loss of his love. I think I was going after the dream instead of living the plan God wanted me to live."

"What plan? If there's some great plan I need to know about, tell me the details. I'm floundering a bit myself."

"It's not *a* plan, not one plan for all of us," Piper said. "We each have an individual plan. God made us unique and has special jobs for each of us to do."

Evelyn laughed. "So far, I think I've missed the *special* part."

Piper studied her a moment, and it took effort for Evelyn not to look away. "I didn't mean special in the sense of something earth-shattering or huge in scope. But God does have a unique plan for each of us. What He wants *you* to do with your life is different than what He wants me to do, and sometimes even different from what *we* want to do."

"That doesn't seem right."

Piper shrugged. "Sometimes we get off track and only *think* we're doing what we're supposed to be doing. We may even think we like it. Like me and marriage. But the thing is, since I've stopped pursuing marriage like a running back racing toward the goal line, I've felt more peaceful. Which means I'm on the right track."

"Feeling peaceful means that?"

"Sure." Piper wiped her mouth with a napkin. "I've chosen a Bible verse to live by. It helps me remember what to strive for. Do you want to hear it?"

"I can use all the help I can get."

Piper cleared her throat. "It's John 14:27. It's Jesus talking. He says, 'I am leaving you with a gift — peace of mind and heart. And the peace I give isn't like the peace the world gives. So don't be troubled or afraid.' "

Troubled and afraid. Evelyn could relate to that. Piper was looking at her, waiting for a reaction. "That's nice."

Piper's sigh forced her shoulders to rise, then drop. "When I get agitated about something it's generally because I've gone off on a detour, or I'm stalled on the shoulder of the road I'm supposed to be on."

"What do you do then?" Evelyn had to admit this topic of discussion was a new one for her, but she found it quite intriguing — as intriguing as the young woman sharing so openly with her.

"Pray," Piper answered simply.

"Then you feel peace?" Could it be that easy?

"Not always right away. But I try to listen to God as much as I talk *to* Him. And He always answers."

"Always?"

Piper laughed. "Not always right away and not always how I want, but He does answer. Yes, no, not yet . . ."

Evelyn wanted to share something, but she wasn't used to talking about her faith to other people. And yet Piper spoke so easily about hers, even about the times when she'd failed at it. Maybe it was safe to —

"You look as though you want to say something but are scared to."

"Not scared, but . . ."

"Hey, I'm no guru with all the right answers. And I realize we don't know each other all that well yet. But I'd be happy to listen to whatever it is that's dug a rut between your eyebrows."

Evelyn put a finger between her eyes and felt the deep wrinkle that had etched its way into her face.

Piper pointed to her own face. "I'm getting one of those too. Deep thoughts equal deep lines. A marking on the road map of life."

Evelyn smiled and touched her sandwich, but did not pick it up. "It seems my road map has been folded so many times it can't be folded any other way."

"You're caught in a rut — or a crease?"

Evelyn smiled at the creative metaphor. "I was. Until my husband died. Now it's as if the map has been laid open. To tell you the truth, it scares me."

Piper nodded. "Were you and your husband happy?"

"Of course."

Piper didn't respond but kept looking at her.

"As happy as most."

"You don't sound very enthusiastic."

Evelyn watched as Summer got down from her chair and put her plate and glass in the dishwasher. She went off to play in the parlor. Whether the little girl left because the conversation bored her, or whether she sensed it was more comfortable for the women to talk alone, Evelyn didn't know. But she appreciated her absence.

Had she and Aaron been happy? "I loved him."

"That's good."

"He loved me."

"That's double good. And yet I hear a *but* hovering."

Evelyn sighed as she prepared to voice what was sure to sound disloyal. "I loved him, but a lot of the time I didn't like him."

"Why not?"

Good question. Evelyn scooted her chair back. "Do you want some more tea?"

"No, and you're stalling."

Evelyn filled her half-full glass to the top, then returned to her seat. She couldn't believe she was having this conversation.

186

And yet somehow she felt more comfortable with Piper than she'd felt with anyone in a long time. It might feel good talking about things — not that it would do any good. Aaron was gone. She didn't have to deal with his failings as a husband anymore — or with her failings as a wife.

Or did she?

She took the plunge. "Aaron didn't make me feel very good about myself. I was talking to my son the other day, and he mentioned that he'd seen how his father often stifled me. He suggested that now I should allow myself to fly." She smiled, feeling sheepish. "Me? Fly? At fifty-six?" The smile faded. "It's a little late for that."

Piper put a hand on Evelyn's forearm and gave it a shake. "There will be none of that too-late business. That's a bunch of hooey. Moses didn't get started until he was eighty, and Abraham was nearly one hundred and —"

Evelyn wasn't sure about the details of these men's achievements, but she remembered enough from her childhood to recognize their names. She raised a hand. "I'm no Moses or Abraham."

"How do you know?"

The dialogue died.

Piper smiled and patted Evelyn's

forearm again, more gently this time. "I didn't mean to overwhelm you, Evelyn. But my point is there's no unemployment in the workplace of God. And no discrimination of any kind. You say yes to Him, He'll use you. You say no, and He'll find somebody else to do it — after giving you a jillion chances to say yes. He's persistent. And patient."

"You act like He actually asks people questions."

"He asked you if you wanted to start this boardinghouse, didn't He?"

"What?"

Piper made a sweeping gesture. "You started this place and have provided a home for three women in need — and a little girl. It's a good thing, don't you think?"

"Yes — yes, I do, but —"

"*But* nothing. God asked you a question, and you said yes." Piper shook her head. "That's all it takes, Evelyn. He provides the incentive and the opportunities, and steps back while we make a choice for Him or against Him."

"I wasn't making a choice for God when I decided —"

"You may not understand exactly how He plans to use this place, but be assured,

He *does* plan to use it." She put a fist to her heart. "I know it. I feel it."

"You do?"

"And I bet if you let yourself, you feel it too. Am I right?"

Evelyn's heart began to beat a little faster. Her throat tightened and before she realized what was happening, she started to cry.

Piper was at her side in an instant, an arm around her shoulders, her cheek against her hair. "Oh, dear lady. You *do* know it, don't you?"

Evelyn could only manage a nod.

Piper kissed the top of her head. "Welcome to the road, Evelyn. He's got you exactly where He wants you."

It was a truth Evelyn didn't understand but could not deny. And the feeling was awesome.

Tessa got the idea right in the middle of her Thursday morning Elizabethan history class, right in the middle of the teacher's lecture about Walsingham's part in the purging of Queen Elizabeth's foes. Tessa wasn't sure why sixteenth-century court intrigue had made her think of asking her classmates over to Peerbaugh Place, but it did. At least three of them were coming over at seven for dessert and discussion.

It was nice to have a place to invite scholarly associates.

Mae put the "Out to lunch, back in a bunch" sign on the door of Silver-Wear and headed to Ruby's diner. She'd eaten at Ruby's every weekday for six years, meeting up with three other gals who worked downtown. They'd eaten their way through the menu multiple times, having made a daily vow never to eat the same thing as another person at the table. Nibblers all.

The other ladies were already seated, three iced teas and a diet Coke in place.

"Hey, Mae, how are the new digs? Or should I say old digs. You've been in nearly a month, right?"

That's when she got an idea. "How 'bout seeing for yourself? Come over tonight at seven. We'll play cards."

"I'll bring the chips and salsa."

"I'll bring molasses cookies."

"I'll bring raspberry iced tea."

It was nice to have a place to bring old friends.

Audra liked her job. There was something very satisfying about dealing with numbers. One plus one always equaled two. She could hardly believe that tomorrow she'd complete her first full week.

To celebrate, she asked Gillie to come over for the evening. Maybe they'd rent a movie. She'd call Piper too.

It was nice to have a place to bring old friends.

Summer stood at the counter mixing bread crumbs and spices into a bowl of ground beef — with her hands. Peppers sat on the floor at her feet, waiting for spills.

"This feels icky."

"But it will taste good," Evelyn said. She readied a baking dish for the Swedish meatballs. They'd be delicious with mushroom gravy.

"Now what?" Summer asked, giving the meat a final squeeze.

"Now we form the meat into balls." Evelyn did the first one and placed it in the dish. "That big, okay?"

Summer nodded and dove into the work.

Tessa came through the kitchen door carrying a sack from Dalton's Grocery. She set it down and moved between them, peering over their shoulders. "Meatballs. Good choice."

"We're having a grand old time making

them, aren't we, sweetie?"

Summer held up a meatball for inspection. "Is this right?"

"Super."

Tessa pointed at Summer. "I see the girl's still here."

Evelyn noticed how Tessa never addressed Summer directly. Only as "the girl." Odd.

"Aunt Evelyn is my baby-sitter now."

Tessa raised an eyebrow. "So is this a permanent situation?"

"I don't know yet," Evelyn said.

Tessa went back to her sack and pulled out a pint of strawberries, then returned them to their place. She shook her head. "If I were you, I'd watch it, Evelyn. You get yourself hemmed in with baby-sitting and you'll lose the chance to better yourself."

"What?"

"Better yourself. Like taking classes as I do. Expanding your mind." Tessa glanced at Summer as if she were a speck on a clean floor. "You can't do that if your time is consumed with patty-cake and *Sesame Street.*"

Summer turned toward Tessa. "I'm too old for *Sesame Street.* I know my ABCs. I'm going to kindergarten next year. I can spell lots of things." She looked across the

192

counter. "Like *sink*. S-I-N—"

Again, Tessa didn't address Summer but responded directly to Evelyn. "You *do* understand my concern for you, Evelyn. I detest wasted time."

Evelyn watched Summer's face. The child's eyes searched Tessa's profile like a desperate miner searching for gold. Finding no hint of treasure, she went back to making the meatballs. Poor little thing. All she wanted was to be acknowledged. Why couldn't Tessa do that? It's not as if she hadn't been around kids. Evelyn had heard her speak of a grandson.

But what had Tessa said about him? Complaints, mostly — about the computer games, the noise, the arguing. No words of endearment, no anecdotes about time spent together. In fact, it sounded as if Tessa had spent most of her time trying to avoid him.

Evelyn felt sudden pity for the woman. She would have given anything if Russell were married with children. She'd spoil her grandchildren with love. Chocolate-chip cookies fresh from the oven, Popsicles from the ice-cream man, and outings to the zoo. But there were no grandchildren and didn't promise to be for a long time.

But there *was* Summer.

Evelyn flashed the little girl a smile that surpassed reassuring and suggested pure joy. Summer seemed a little shocked by it, but returned it just the same. There was a what's-going-on? look on her face.

What *was* going on?

It didn't take more than a few seconds for Evelyn to realize what had made her smile, what had made her heart swell with anticipation. "There's no need to be concerned about me, Tessa. I'm not about to waste my time. I think the way I can better myself — and others — right now is to take care of Summer. Permanently."

Summer beamed.

"Would you like that, sweetie?"

Summer extended her arms toward Evelyn in an awkward hug from the stool.

"Watch the messy hands," Tessa said, taking a step back.

Evelyn ignored her completely and accepted the hug, messy hands and all.

Tessa moved her grocery items to the other side of the kitchen. Evelyn was a fool. Taking care of a child was going to condemn her to mediocrity. If a person didn't continually work at bettering her mind, then what was the use of living? Use it or lose it.

Tessa removed strawberries, kiwi, and Cool Whip from the sack.

Evelyn saw. "Ooh, that looks good. I love strawberries, don't you, Summer?"

"Uh-huh. They're best dipped in sug—"

"They're not for you. Either of you." Tessa caught the stunned look on their faces and realized she might have been too harsh. "I've invited three classmates over for dessert tonight and thought I'd whip up some meringues and serve them with fruit and topping." Now Evelyn looked absolutely crushed. "I suppose there might be enough to share . . . later . . . after they've been here."

Evelyn turned her back on Tessa and buddied up shoulder to shoulder with Summer. "That's okay. We'll find our own dessert, won't we?"

Tessa looked down at the strawberries. Perhaps she'd made a faux pas. Perhaps it was rude of her to not *plan* on sharing. There would probably be enough, but the fact that she hadn't even considered it, hadn't bought extra so there would be enough . . .

Oh, Lord, this isn't good. I see what You're trying to tell me. Selfish, that's what I am. Help me make amends.

She turned toward the others, but they

had created a wall with their backs and were giggling over something. Tessa's anger loomed. So be it. She didn't need them.

Evelyn looked up from cutting lettuce with Summer to see Mae use her shoulder to swing open the kitchen door. Mae stopped behind Tessa, eyeing the meringue circles she was placing on a cookie sheet topped with brown paper.

"Zounds, sisters. It's another feast in the making. If I don't watch it, there's going to be too much Mae." She raised her grocery sack. "And I've got some nibblies to add to the mix. Little carrots, celery, green peppers, and spinach dip." She tossed the sack on the kitchen table. "Actually, I have ulterior motives. If you don't mind, Evelyn, I've asked three of my friends over later to play cards and these goodies are for them, but you guys are welcome to share. There's plenty."

Tessa did an about-face, one hand holding a spatula, the other forming a cup beneath it to catch any drips. "You can't have people over. *I'm* having people over."

"When did this happen?" Mae asked.

"This afternoon while I was at class. We were discussing Elizabethan history and how Walsingham —"

"Walsing-who?"

Tessa's back straightened. "Sir Francis Walsingham. He was the secretary of state to Queen Elizabeth I and developed a secret service of sorts that purged the queen of her enemies. Quite ruthless but very loyal."

"Sounds like a fun guy."

Tessa pursed her lips. "He's an interesting man. Which is why I have three friends coming over at seven to continue our discussion." She nodded toward the batter. "I'm making fruit meringues."

Summer spoke over her shoulder. "We don't get any."

Tessa flashed the child a look that surprised Evelyn. But Summer took it well by turning back to her work.

"Well," Mae said, "everyone can have as much of my food offering as they want." She moved to the sink to wash the celery.

Tessa had not moved and the spatula threatened to drip into her hand. "But you don't understand. This is not acceptable. We can't both have people over at the same time."

"Afraid we'll corrupt your discussion, Tessie? Bring in some of the rebellious Irish influence from my Fitzpatrick name?"

Evelyn tensed as Tessa did a quarter turn in her direction. "What are *you* going to do about this situation?"

Mae did her own quarter turn, but added a smile. "Yes, Evelyn, what *are* you going to do about this *situation?*"

"I . . . I don't really know what —"

Audra came through the door just then, her eyes seeking her daughter. "Hey, baby. Did you have a good day?"

"It was great, Mommy. We cooked and cleaned and —"

Evelyn was glad to change the subject. "How was work?"

Audra hugged Summer from behind. "Oh, it was —"

"Excuse me?" Tessa said. "We have a crisis here."

Audra scanned their faces. "What's going on?"

Mae did the honors. "It seems Tessie and I are engaged in a battle for the parlor. She's invited three of her snooty scholar types over to discuss dead people, and I've invited three of my fabulously amiable friends over to play cards, and —"

Audra put a hand to her mouth. "And I've invited Gillie and Piper over to watch a movie."

"This —" Tessa punctuated the air with

the spatula once, spraying a blob of meringue onto the floor. Her hand returned to its place beneath it. "This will not do."

Evelyn wanted to flee. "Oh dear."

Mae stepped into the middle of the kitchen, her hands raised. "Take your corners, sisters. We *will* work this out."

"I don't see how."

Mae pointed a finger at Tessa. "Would you and your group be comfortable in the sunroom?"

Tessa glanced toward the room at the back of the house off the kitchen. It was clearly not her first choice. "I was hoping for the parlor. After all, that *is* the most elegant —"

"I won't argue with you there. But my friends and I need a table. If we use the dining room and Audra and her bunch watch a movie in the parlor where the VCR is located . . ." Mae dropped her chin and challenged Tessa. "Unless you and your friends wouldn't mind the sounds of a hearty card game rising from the next room?"

Tessa opened her mouth, then shut it, then opened it again. "You're not giving me much choice."

Mae shrugged. "Yeah, well . . ."

Tessa shuffled her shoulders. "I want a choice."

Mae dropped her jaw. "You . . . ? You have a choice. You can either join our card game in the dining room or watch a movie in the parlor. Or you can have your meeting in the relative quiet of the sun-room. Take your pick."

Tessa's eyes flashed. "What happened to the democracy of Peerbaugh Place? Since when does one tenant get to dictate —"

"But you want to dictate —"

Tessa looked surprised. "Me?"

Mae took a step toward Tessa, bran-dishing a celery stalk. "Who has pro-claimed herself the dictator of this house from the first moment she — ?"

"I did no such —"

Audra moved between them. "Ladies!"

Mae lowered the celery. "She always has to have her way."

"Only because my way is the best way."

Mae's snicker was thick with contempt. "Our own little Napoléon. How did we get so lucky?"

"Technically, Napoléon was not a dic-tator. He was an emperor and —"

Mae raised her arms in a mock bow. "Oh, Empress Tessie, how may we serve you?"

Audra pulled one of Mae's hands down. "Come on, you two. We can work this out."

"Not me," Mae said. She suddenly took a musketeer stance with the celery as her sword. "I say *en garde!*"

When Tessa picked up a spoon, Evelyn fled the room. This was ridiculous. She headed to the solace of the front porch. When no one followed to offer their apologies, her anger grew. They were completely missing the point. It didn't matter who used what room — the point was that not one of them had even asked permission to use *any* room. After all, it was her house.

She looked toward the kitchen where loud voices could still be heard.

At least it used to be her house.

Evelyn had planned to sustain her pout all evening, but it was hard to do when her tenants seemed oblivious. So, short of standing in the foyer and making a very vocal announcement, her anger would have to wait for another day, another battle. And there *was* the possibility she was overreacting. It *was* kind of nice seeing her home full of life.

By seven-thirty, Peerbaugh Place was bulging. Mae and her friends were settled around the dining-room table with a deck of cards, snack foods, and iced drinks all around. Mae introduced her friends to

Evelyn, but Evelyn forgot to make a point of remembering their names, so she left the room as ignorant as she was when she'd entered it. She also left marveling at the ability of all four women to talk at once and yet carry on conversations.

Tessa and her three classmates — two men and another woman — were ensconced in the sunroom with the French doors closed. Tessa had asked if she could use Grandma Nelson's china, and Evelyn had given her permission. And so the fruit meringues were served with hot tea in rosebudded teacups. *I'm glad I had Summer dust in there.*

Audra, Gillie, and Piper were in the parlor watching one of Evelyn's favorite movies, *Dave*, with Summer digging through the toy box nearby.

And then there was Evelyn. Alone again. After making the rounds, her anger made room for sadness. Everybody had someone — except her.

Feeling a new pout coming on, Evelyn — with Peppers close behind — trudged up the stairs and closed the door of her room, leaving the noise of the house behind her. The sudden muffle of the sounds against the envelope of her silent room was eerie.

She leaned against the door and looked

at the bedroom — the room that, up until several weeks ago, had housed her and Aaron for over thirty years. And yet it was not a room she had spent much time in. What was the point? After all, it was a *bed*room. Once she was up for the day, she rarely returned until night.

She shook the odd thoughts away. It was too carly to go to bed. Maybe she could read. There was a chair in the corner she could sit in. An unused chair. Neither she nor Aaron had sat in it much. It had mostly been a place for Peppers to sleep in — as she did now — or for Aaron to toss his clothes across at the end of the day. A place where, the next morning, Evelyn would pick up the discarded clothes and put them in their proper place. The chair was still in great shape, covered with a green ivy chintz she'd found on sale for a dollar and forty-nine cents a yard in Kresge's basement back in . . . back in . . .

She looked to the ceiling, trying to remember the year she'd decorated this room. It had been the year Aaron's parents had died. 1976? She did the math. That would make the blue-and-green chintz over twenty-seven years old.

No, it couldn't be. This room has looked the same that long?

But as she scanned the space, Evelyn realized it was true. Grandma Peerbaugh's Seven Sisters quilt still covered the bed as it had when the old woman had lived here with Grandpa Peerbaugh. White lace curtains framed the windows — the same ones that had been in the room when she and Aaron had moved in. The walnut, four-drawer dresser with a matching bedside table, and a mirrored, oak dresser sat in the exact spots they'd sat in for decades. In fact, the only reason Evelyn had recovered the chair was because the original upholstery had been worn and frayed — back in 1976.

The truth was it had never really been her room at all.

Why hadn't she changed the room's décor as she had changed? Despite the fact that she wasn't talented in this regard, certainly she wasn't the same woman who'd moved in here with a young child? Certainly, after so many years, she'd earned the right to make the Peerbaugh master bedroom match her personality and tastes.

Why had she been so hesitant to change things? Why had it taken years for her to feel that the Peerbaugh family home was *her* family home? How ironic that now that it was *just* her home, it was no longer her home alone but the home of people who weren't even family.

She listened to the muted noises below. Mae's laughter stood out among the other voices. She heard Summer's giggle. Her previous anger was absurd. She was being petty, caring if they asked permission. She wanted them to feel at home, didn't she? And it had all worked out — no thanks to her.

Evelyn grabbed a book from the bedside table, nudged Peppers to the side, and sat in the chair. Peppers rearranged herself and went back to sleep, purring with contentment.

Contentment. Evelyn could use a little of that. *If everything's worked out with the evening's arrangements, then why are you up here alone while they're downstairs having fun?*

"No one asked me," *she said aloud. The hurt swelled.*

Evelyn opened her book, determined to think other thoughts. But she didn't even glance at the open pages. From this new perspective, seated in the chair, she saw the room like a stranger — and she didn't like it. It oozed age and mustiness and faded colors that slept a deathly sleep.

Then change it.

Evelyn suddenly found herself at the tall

dresser, looking over the items that had sat there for years: a small lamp with a porcelain base shaped like a woman in a wide pink skirt, a small crystal dish that held rubber bands, two full bottles of men's cologne, and an oak jewelry box that Aaron had received for Christmas from his mother. Aaron and jewelry were a laughable notion, like putting a bow on a Doberman pinscher.

Then what had he used it for?

Evelyn was shocked to realize she'd never opened it — or if she had, she'd long ago forgotten what was inside. She'd dusted it often enough, but why had curiosity never caused her to open —

She opened it now, expecting to find a stray pair of cuff links, a few coins, or even a stack of old-fashioned handkerchiefs. Maybe a set of keys or —

The inside was crammed with greeting cards.

Evelyn slid onto the bed, setting the box on her lap. She recognized the top card. It was the Valentine's Day card she'd given Aaron just two months earlier. In fact, all the cards were Valentine's Day cards from her to him. She flipped to the one at the bottom, thankful for her habit of putting the year on the back of each card.

This one was dated 1972. Their first Valentine's Day as husband and wife. She looked at her flowing cursive. So young. So full of hope. And the sentiment: *I'll love you forever and ever. Evelyn.*

He'd kept them. Gruff, unsentimental Aaron Peerbaugh had kept them all.

This one act did not fit with the man she thought she knew, the man who had rarely remembered their anniversary, or who had often commemorated her birthday with a quick, "Here's twenty bucks; go buy yourself something."

And as far as her getting a Valentine's Day card from him? It had never happened. She'd cried many tears over that — though the tears had waned a bit in recent years. What was the use? He was what he was, and she obviously wasn't going to change him.

Evelyn flipped through the cards, fascinated at how dated some of them were. A person never thought about greeting cards going out of style. Some were romantic, some sentimental, and some almost cold — as Valentine's Day cards went. She picked up one that displayed a simple red heart in a field of blue. *I love you* it said inside. That's all. No flowery words or verse about forever. She remembered picking it out. It had been a bad year for them, a year of many arguments. No specific conflict stuck in her mind, just a dissatisfaction and frustration that the marriage they were living was not the marriage she'd wanted.

She'd spent more time choosing that card than she'd taken during good years when she'd felt their marriage was thriving. All the rosy sentiments and gushy verses had seemed totally wrong, hypocritical. At that time, she hadn't wanted to love him forever, and she certainly hadn't thought he was the best thing that had ever happened to her. And as far as not being able to live without him? On that particular Valentine's Day, if someone had given her a hard nudge out the front door, she would have gone for good. Standing in the store that year, card after card had spoken of a love she did not feel. So she had chosen a card that merely said *I love you.* But even that had been a stretch.

Good, bad. Hopeful, hopeless. Love and even hate.

Evelyn pulled the stack of cards to her chest, and with a sudden *knowing,* understood that finding these cards could be a good thing at this moment in her life — or a bad thing. For Aaron was not with her. "Forever and ever" was just the romantic passion of a newlywed wife who couldn't even fathom that on some days they might not like each other, much less that someday she might be left alone. And at this moment, those words and that memory of high expectations that were never realized could bring Evelyn down and make her despair. Or . . .

Evelyn stood and began placing the cards on the bed in order, years one through thirty-one. And with each addition, she felt herself grow stronger. Year added to year. Two lives joined through love — flawed but constant. Thousands of days. Tens of thousands of hours. Had their time together been perfect? Far from it. Had it been happy? Yes. But there were levels of happiness.

Who could judge such things? And who said life was supposed to be happy all the time? Like the conversation and laughter she could hear ebbing to highs and lows in the rooms beneath her, life was ever changing, filling itself up with every sort of emotion and experience. Life was not a boring straight line — whether that line be the measure of happiness or sorrow. Life was a wave, rising high and crashing low.

It was an achievement. And that, in itself, was good.

When Evelyn was finished laying out the cards, she stood back and admired her handiwork. Splashes of red and pink hearts covered the bed, and though there was room for a few more, it was not to be.

Evelyn knew that she wasn't supposed to look upon the years that *weren't* there but the many years that were. She and Aaron had been blessed with an extended time together — more than many couples ever received.

Now another time had begun — the time to move on. She, alone, but not —

A tap on her door. "Evie?"

Evelyn opened the door to Mae.

"I've come to collect you."

"Collect me?"

Mae took her hand. "Audra, Summer, Gillie, and Piper have decided to join us for a rousing game of Uno. And so your presence is requested in the dining room. The more the merrier."

"But I don't know how to play —"

"Gracious game-o-rama, Evie. It's Uno we're talking about, not bridge. Come join us."

Evelyn glanced back to the greeting cards. She felt Mae's eyes slide over her shoulder.

"That's quite a collection of love notes

210

you have there," Mae said.

"Aaron kept them. Thirty-one years' worth. I didn't know he'd done it. I didn't know they mattered to him. I didn't know —" She was shocked to realize how she was about to complete that last sentence. *Where is this coming from?*

"You didn't know your love meant that much to him?"

Mae had pegged it.

"It makes me . . . mad."

"That he kept them and didn't tell you?"

Evelyn shook her head. It went deeper. "That he didn't love me enough to . . . to . . ." *To what?* She let her eyes scour the cards, trying to pinpoint the core of her thought.

Mae put a hand on her shoulder. "If he didn't love you, he wouldn't have kept them. It's evidence of his love."

That was it. Evelyn had suppressed the desire so long she hadn't been able to bring it front and center. What she really wished Aaron had done, what she really wanted beyond a few cards tucked away in a box was — "I wanted the words, Mae. Three little words." On the edge of tears, she looked to her friend. "I was aching to *know*. Why could he never let me *know?* Why do I feel so sad about what I could have had rather than what I lost?"

Evelyn walked back toward the bed. Mae followed and put an arm around her, and together they looked at the cards. Finally, Mae gave her a squeeze. "I have no excuse for your husband. He should have let you know how much he loved you. But now, with the cards, you know a little more than you did before. And that's good. It's a bit of comfort, isn't it? Belated though it might be?"

She was right. Just when Evelyn had felt lonely, the cards had given her a modicum of comfort — along with some pain. Yet beyond that, they had spurred her to ease up on the tie that bound her to the past. The taut cord that had wrapped around her since Aaron's death had loosened, letting her breathe a little easier. It was one more step toward an independent future.

"So, Evie? You coming?"

"Mmm? In a minute."

"You want something to drink? Doris brought some great raspberry tea."

"That would be nice."

Mae left her alone. Evelyn looked at the cards strung across the bed — unmistakable evidence of two lives joined by God.

She smiled. For reasons she could not understand, *Mrs. Aaron Peerbaugh* did not exist anymore. But *Evelyn Peerbaugh* did.

And as she returned the cards to their box and closed it with a satisfying click, she knew that whatever she had or had not accomplished in her life so far had only been the beginning of something more. Something better?

Piper's words came back to her: *"Welcome to the road, Evelyn. He's got you exactly where He wants you."*

She turned to the door to go downstairs and join the others. *Ready or not, here I come.*

7

Be humble and gentle. Be patient with each other, making allowance for each other's faults because of your love.
EPHESIANS 4:2

Tessa entered the kitchen last. Everyone else was already eating breakfast and chattering away about the fun time they'd had the night before, but the pulled look on Tessa's face told Evelyn that their laughter was not pleasing to her.

As the others noticed her entrance — and her stiff jaw — they quieted. Evelyn was quick to fill in the awkward silence. "Morning, Tessa. Coffee's ready."

Tessa poured herself a cup and wiped up the counter where someone else had spilled.

"Aren't you pleased with last night, Tessie?" Mae asked. "I knew it would work out if we all —"

"I am *not* pleased." She put an English muffin in the toaster, avoiding their eyes. "It was far too noisy. My friends and I could barely hear each other, what with the ruckus caused by the card game."

"We asked you to join us," Mae said. "In fact, it would have been fitting. I've heard Henry VIII enjoyed his own rousing game of cards — in between cutting off his wives' heads."

Tessa readied her knife with margarine. "Whether I like to play cards or not is hardly the issuc. The issue is that last night, Peerbaugh Place was more like a bawdy house than a rooming house."

Evelyn raised a hand, ready to say that personally, she'd enjoyed every shriek, hoot, and giggle, but Audra beat her to it.

"I think you're overreacting. It was one of the most delightful evenings I've had in months. We were just having a little fun."

"And certainly even you can't disapprove of fun, can you, Tessic?" Mae said.

"I like fun as much as the next pers—"

"Then it's settled. The fun will continue unabated." Mae plunked a tea bag in her mug. She looked at Tessa, a challenge in her eyes. "Drink your coffee, Tessie; it's getting cold."

Oh dear. As was Tessa.

Evelyn stood at the doorway to her bedroom, giving the room a good once-over in daylight.

Summer came to her side and peered in. "What you looking at?"

Before she could answer, Audra appeared, poking through her purse. She stopped beside the two of them. "What's going on?"

"We're looking at Aunt Evelyn's room."

It sounded strange. As if her room were a tourist attraction. "Last night I got the idea to redecorate it. It's been the same for decades."

Audra took a look. Evelyn couldn't tell whether she approved or disapproved of the present décor. Mae came into the hall and joined them.

"What's so interesting?"

"Aunt Evelyn's going to decorate."

Evelyn suddenly had the awful thought that if she redecorated her room the others would expect to have their rooms changed too. She didn't have enough money for that.

"What do you want to do with it?"

"That's the rub," Evelyn said. "I don't know. I'm not very good at decorating — being original."

Mae headed downstairs. "I *wear* my originality. As far as decorating goes, I don't know the difference between chintz and prints." She called up from the front door.

216

"Ta-ta, sisters. Have a nice day."

Audra dug her keys out of her purse. "If you want help, Piper's great at this kind of thing."

"You think she would?"

"To have a chance to spend someone else's money? She'd love it."

"But that's just it. I don't have a lot —"

Audra kissed Summer and headed downstairs. "Don't worry about it. I've never seen Piper buy anything at less than 40 percent off. Have a good day, you two."

Evelyn was left with Summer, who dutifully stayed by her side, looking at the room. "What do you think, sweetie?"

"I like yellow best."

Evelyn cocked her head, trying to envision yellow walls. It was a thought.

Tessa sat on her bed, listening to the footsteps of Evelyn and Summer go downstairs. The tenants' discussion at breakfast had riled her so much that it felt as if all the atoms in her body were bumping against each other. Was it too much for her to expect a few guidelines to be enforced? She'd presented her point only to have Audra and Mae — especially Mae — tear it apart. And Evelyn . . . her effectiveness as a landlord could be compared to the effect of one drop of rain in an ocean.

And then just now, the entire household had been in on Evelyn's discussion to redecorate her room. Everyone except Tessa. Had they sought her out? Had they made an attempt to include her?

Did you make an effort to be included? Why did you stay safely in your room after you heard them talking? It's not their fault; it's yours.

Tessa closed her eyes against the traitorous thoughts and took a cleansing breath, but it didn't do its job. Her chest was still tight. It *wasn't* her fault. It wasn't. There were certain foundations that were necessary to live a life in a civilized way, and if some people — like Mae — insisted on making those foundations wobble, it was her responsibility to tell them the truth. Set them straight.

Tessa pressed a hand against her chest, trying to calm the racing of her heart. It was such a burden being right.

She thought of Evelyn and Summer downstairs, probably chatting and giggling, or worse — dancing. And though Tessa didn't have to be at her Bible study class until noon, she felt the need to get away from this place ASAP. She checked her hair in the mirror, took up her purse, and headed downstairs to escape to the world of her classes and church, where people understood and appreciated her.

Evelyn looked up from the dining-room table where she and Summer were getting ready to do a puzzle. Tessa stood in the doorway. "I'm going."

"Where to?"

Tessa moved to the front door and put one hand on the knob. Her mouth was tight, like she'd eaten a pickle. "I have errands and then I have to teach a Bible study class. I've been the leader for seven years now."

Evelyn dumped the puzzle on the table. Summer had picked it out: a kitty tangled in yarn. It was a black cat, not a calico like Peppers. "Will you be here for lunch?"

"We've gone over this before. Bible study is held over lunch so working people can come." Tessa held up a sack. "We each bring our own." She paused a second. "Anything else?"

"No . . . except have a good day."

Tessa gave one curt nod and left.

The house felt better with her gone.

Summer got on her knees and helped turn the pieces right side up. "She's not very happy, is she?"

Evelyn stopped turning. "Why do you say that?"

"She doesn't like us. None of us, but especially me."

"Oh, sweetie, it's not that she doesn't like us; it's just that she . . . she's . . ." Evelyn shrugged and sighed. "I'm glad you're a happy girl."

Summer found the two pieces that made the kitty's nose and snapped them together. "Being happy's best."

"I think so too."

Summer stopped and Evelyn felt her eyes. She looked up. "What?"

"Are you happy?"

"Well, I don't —"

" 'Cause Tessa's not, but Aunt Mae is. And I was just wondering if you are too."

"Why don't you call Tessa, Aunt Tessa?"

Summer bit her lip. "I don't know."

Evelyn could only nod. There were so many things people did without knowing why — herself included.

"So . . . are you happy or aren't you?"

Evelyn looked over Summer's right shoulder, the image of Aaron springing to mind. Why did the notion of happiness bring about memories of him? And how could such a simple question be so difficult to answer? After a few moments she blinked and managed a smile. "Actually, I think I am happy, or at least I'm starting to be." She reached a hand across the table and touched Summer's cheek. "You're a big part of my happiness, little girl. I'm so glad your baby-sitter was icky."

"Me too."

Yes, indeed, sometimes icky was good.

The doorbell rang. A few moments later there was a knock on the door. Someone was impatient.

Summer ran to open it, and Evelyn had to rush to get there first. "Uh-uh, little girl. Remember? Only I answer the door."

Summer pulled up short and let Evelyn open it. It was their neighbor from across the street, Collier Ames. His graying eyebrows nearly touched.

Uh-oh.

Evelyn opened the screen door, hooking a foot in front of Peppers to prevent her from escaping outside. Summer came to the rescue, scooping her up. "Hi, Collier. I haven't seen you since . . ." She was going to say, "since the funeral" but didn't want him feeling bad about not checking on her. "I haven't seen you for a while."

"And I haven't seen you either. Haven't seen *you* but have seen a virtual caravan of cars and women."

He made it sound like she was running a brothel. "They're my tenants, Collier."

He turned around and flicked a hand at the sign. "Yes, I saw that. Do you really think Aaron would approve of you turning his family home into . . . a . . . a . . ."

The brothel image returned. "A boardinghouse?"

Collier shook his head and scuffed a shoe on the porch, showing Evelyn his bald spot. "Aaron would never approve."

Evelyn's heart revved up as if someone had ordered, "Drivers, start your engines!" Collier had no right to criticize her. And what did he know about what Aaron would approve or disapprove of? Although Aaron had talked to Collier occasionally, Evelyn had rarely shared more than a polite wave across the street.

She felt Summer at her side, Peppers still in her arms. She pulled her close. "I'm sorry you feel that way, Collier, but opening the house to boarders was a necessity."

His eyes had traveled south. "Is she the only child?"

"So far."

"Aunt Evelyn's my baby-sitter 'cause my other one was icky."

Collier raised an eyebrow. "I hope you're not thinking about starting a day care here too."

It was an interesting idea. "Maybe."

His head started shaking again. "I'm not sure I can go along with that, Evelyn."

"Not sure *you* can . . . ?"

He made a sweeping gesture toward the neighborhood. "This is a nice street, full of single-family homes. We don't want it turning into renters' row and certainly don't want it swarming with kids playing everywhere."

"Heaven forbid."

He reddened. "You know what I mean."

"Not really." *Where am I getting this chutzpah?*

He sighed deeply, like an impatient parent telling a child for the twentieth time what was expected of her. "Truth be told, Evelyn, I'm not sure what you're doing is legal. There have to be rules. Building codes. Licenses."

Evelyn's stomach flipped. *Mae was going to check into that. . . . What if all this was for naught? What if Peerbaugh Place has to close down because of some legality?*

Evelyn closed the door halfway, feeling a desperate need to be rid of her neighbor. "I can assure you, Collier, everything is on the up-and-up."

"So you have a license? You've checked with the city and —"

"Afternoon, Collier. Nice talking with you." She shut the door. She did not hear his footsteps recede for a good thirty seconds. She let out the breath she had been holding. Summer looked up at her. She had moved Peppers close to her ear, as if the cat's purring was a comfort. "Are we in trouble?"

"I hope not, sweetie. I hope not."

Tessa sat at the head of the table in the Sunday school classroom and readied her Bible and notes. A tuna sandwich and a sliced apple sat neatly on a napkin nearby. The group ranged from five to eight people — usually women. All the regulars were present except Marla. But Marla always *did* nudge the tardy button.

Tessa heard the door open. *Like today.* She looked up, expecting to see Marla, but instead saw Marla and a newcomer — who looked familiar. It was Audra's friend. *What was her name?*

Marla stood at the edge of the table. "I've brought a guest today. I've been trying to get her to come with me for ages. She's a counselor at the high school. This is Piper Wellington. Piper, this is the gang."

Greetings were exchanged as they sat down and took out their lunches. Piper gave Tessa a special nod. "How are you this morning, Tessa?"

"Fine." She clipped her answer and looked down. Piper's presence was disconcerting, though Tessa couldn't pin down why. She fueled herself with a bite of sandwich, then clasped her hands on top of her Bible. "Shall we begin?"

Tessa was in her element. Nothing made her feel more alive than being in the midst of a learning environment, or better yet, being the one in charge. "Let's open our Bibles to John 4. Today we're going to study the famous story of Jesus and the Samaritan woman at the well."

"The naughty, naughty woman," Helen said with a wink.

Although Tessa hadn't planned on starting with the woman's reputation, she went with Helen's opening. How normal for people to jump on the scandal. "Helen, since you started it, how was she, as you say, naughty?"

"She'd had five husbands and was living with another man — out of wedlock." Helen looked around the table as if gauging the other women's reactions. "That's why she was at the well at noon. All the other women came in the morning and evening, but she didn't dare go then."

Helen was enjoying the woman's sin far too much. "But that was only part of her problem, correct?" Tessa asked. "The reason it was unusual for Jesus — or any man — to talk to her was that —"

Marla interrupted. "She was a half-breed, a Samaritan — only half Jew. And she was alone at the well. No respected Jewish man would speak to a woman who was alone like that."

"But Jesus *did* speak to her," Piper said, "which proves —" She stopped talking as all eyes turned to her. "I'm sorry. Aren't I allowed to contribute?"

Marla put a hand on Piper's. "Of course you are. That's why I asked you along." Marla turned to the rest of the group. "Piper's the smartest Bible person I've ever met. She has a way of knowing things, of understanding things, that's way beyond me."

Yes, yes, enough of the Piper fan club. Tessa cleared her throat. "Getting back to the subject . . ."

"Sorry," Piper said. "I didn't mean to cause a stir."

"Moving on —"

Josie pointed the corner of her sandwich at Piper. "Actually, I'd like to hear the rest of what you have to say. You said, 'which proves' . . . which proves what?"

Tessa had had enough of this. She was losing control of the class. "Which proves we have to get back on track. I think it's interesting that Jesus doesn't let this woman get away with anything. He's the one who brings up her past and when she tries to change the subject, Jesus goes back to it, pouncing on the fact that she's a sinner."

Piper raised a tentative hand. "I don't think Jesus 'pounced' on anything. The woman doesn't deny she's done bad things. She just doesn't want to talk about it. She's embarrassed. Isn't that human nature?"

Helen laughed. "You start talking about my flaws, and I'll start talking about the weather faster than a spring shower popping up on a cloudy day."

"The point is," Tessa said, raising her voice to a level of authority, "Jesus knew all about this woman's sins and wasn't about to let her get away with them. He condemned her as anyone would."

There was a moment of silence. Piper and Helen looked back to their Bibles. The rest of the women gave Tessa odd looks.

What is their problem? Can't they see — ?

Piper spoke first. "Pardon me, but I believe you're mistaken, Tessa."

There was a hushed intake of breath as the group registered their shock. *Rightly so. How dare she come in here and question my ability, my knowledge, my —*

Piper raised her opened Bible, a hand supporting its spine. "I don't see any condemnation in these verses. She asks Jesus how He can draw water from the well because He doesn't have a bucket, and then He tells her *He* is the living water. He tells her He is the Messiah she's heard about. He shares that wonderful message with her — a Samaritan and a woman shunned for her sins. There's a reason for that and it has nothing to do with condemnation."

Josie's finger was following the verses. She looked up. "I think Piper's right, Tessa. I don't see Jesus yelling at her in any way, literally or figuratively. He's giving her great news —"

Helen interrupted. "Which, considering who she is, means that the good news of Jesus is for everyone, not just special people."

Piper laughed and clapped. "This is wonderful, ladies. Absolutely wonderful."

Tessa shook her head. "I don't see what's

so wonderful about it. We've gotten way off track. I wanted to point out that when the woman mentions bucket, the Greek word for bucket is *antlema*. This is the only time this word appears in the New Testament. But in that time in history, their buckets were very different from our concept of bucket, for they were probably made of —"

"That's all very interesting, Tessa," Josie said, "but what we're talking about seems more . . ." She looked to the ceiling, searching for the word. ". . . more vital. It's applying the Bible to our lives. And isn't that one reason we study it in the first place?"

Tessa shook her head. "I don't approve of the 'What's in it for us?' mentality. There is knowledge here, important knowledge."

Piper again. "But what good is knowledge if it's limited to facts we can spout off like the names of the fifty states?"

Marla snickered. "And who cares about water buckets when Jesus is talking about drawing an entirely different kind of water — living water?"

Piper stroked the opened page. "There's more than knowledge here — there's wisdom." She scanned the eyes of everyone at the table. "Did you know wisdom is the only thing God always gives to those who ask?"

Ha! Gotcha. Tessa shook her head. "I don't think that's correct, Piper. I don't remember seeing any such thing —"

Piper turned the pages of her Bible. "Here it is, James 1:5–6: 'If you need wisdom — if you want to know what God wants you to do — ask him, and he will gladly tell you. He will not resent your asking. But when you ask him, be sure that you really expect him to answer, for a doubtful mind is as unsettled as a wave of the sea that is driven and tossed by the wind.' "

"Ooh, cool," Helen said. "So asking for wisdom and having faith you'll get it . . . super cool."

Tessa was shocked. She could not remember anyone ever saying *cool* in a Bible study. It was a totally inappropriate —

"Absolutely cool," Piper said. "That's what God was giving the woman at the well. Wisdom about how He could change her life, wisdom about who He is."

Josie fidgeted in her chair as if the words were going to burst out if they didn't find release immediately. "And then the woman got so excited that she went to the town and told everyone to come listen to Him."

"Which shows how the Good News is for everyone who will come listen, not just a chosen few."

Tessa didn't like this. Not one bit. "I disagree — again. A person has to work at being saved." She decided it was best to sound self-deprecating. "I know *I* have to work hard at it."

Piper opened her mouth to speak, closed it, then drew in a breath. "Oh, Tessa . . . I'm sorry, but you're wrong. Very, very wrong."

Tessa drew her arms across her chest. "I am not." How dare Piper accuse her of being wrong! If there was one thing Tessa refused to do — ever — it was to be wrong. "God's not going to give something as wonderful as heaven to people who haven't earned —"

Piper leaned forward on the table. Her voice was soft but full of emotion. "You can't earn your way to heaven. It's a gift. The apostle Paul said, 'God saved you by his special favor when you believed. And you can't take credit for this; it is a gift from God. Salvation is not a reward for the good things we have done, so none of us can boast about it.' We do good works *because* He has saved us, not to earn anything. Besides, we don't deserve it. If we got what we deserve, if we got the due punishment for all the things we do wrong daily, we'd —"

"Have to hang on a cross, just like Jesus did." Helen gave a nod that sealed her words.

"Jesus took the punishment for all of us. He got what *we* deserved. Deserve. All God asks as a qualification to go to heaven is that we accept this act and let Him forgive us. What we do isn't as important as pinning our faith on what God has done — and is willing to do — for us."

Tessa's heart pounded, and for a moment she reminded herself to calm down or the pain might take over. But how could she calm down? This . . . this intruder had barged into her Bible study that she'd run for seven years and usurped her power and authority. It wasn't right and she wasn't going to . . . going to . . .

Without realizing she'd made a decision, Tessa pushed her chair back, stood, and closed her Bible with a loud *whap*. She gathered it, along with her notes, and strode from the room.

If they didn't appreciate her, they could do without her.

★ ★ ★

Tessa was at her car when —

"Tessa!"

She turned around to see Marla hurrying toward her. Tessa put her back to the car door, applied an appropriate look of indignation, and waited for the upcoming apology.

Marla was out of breath. "Why did you walk out?"

"I wasn't needed."

"That's ridiculous. Of course you're needed. Why would you say such a thing?"

"You all rallied around Piper. You agreed with her. Even when she disagreed with what I said."

Marla bit her lower lip. "Tessa . . . you're a smart lady. I've never known anyone who knows more facts and definitions and dates and —"

Tessa flipped a hand toward the church. "What does any of that matter? According to Piper, knowledge isn't important." *Therefore, I'm not important.*

"You're blowing this out of proportion."

Tessa raised her chin. "You women let this stranger come into our well-established class and take over, and you follow her like mindless rats following —"

Marla's eyes blazed. "Excuse me?"

"You want me back, you need to apologize."

"*We* need to apologize?"

"An apology from each of you would be preferred, but I'll settle for one from you, as their spokesperson."

Marla took a step back and laughed, her head shaking in disbelief. "You are one piece of work, Tessa Klein. You are so caught up in thinking you own the rights to being right. Well, let me tell you, you are not right all the time. This isn't the first time you've nearly led us astray in Bible study. Other times, we've talked about things after class and fixed the damage you've caused by your arrogant insistence that only you can be —"

"Damage? *I* caused?"

Marla walked toward the building. "Bye, Tessa. Hope to see you next Friday at *our* Bible study."

Tessa knew she shouldn't be driving in her emotional state, but she didn't care. She had never felt such anger. At Marla. At Piper.

At God.

I'm trying to do Your work here, Lord. You've given me a gift for teaching, and I'm trying to use it.

She braked at a corner in front of the

Methodist church. The sign out front told the service times and had an inspirational message: *Love your neighbor as yourself.*

As she pulled away, Tessa pointed an angry finger at the words. "That's what I'm trying to do. I love to teach them and share with them."

But you love yourself more.

She shook the thought away. She'd tried to love the women she'd just left, and look at the thanks she got. Overthrown as the head of her very own Bible study. It wasn't fair, not fair at all.

She hit her palm on the steering wheel. "I'm not going to take this. I'm going to walk right into Pastor Bill's office and make him force those ungrateful women to give me my class back."

She turned at the next corner, heading back toward her church. A billboard loomed to her right. It was one of those witty God-boards. A black background with a simple message, signed simply *God.* She usually enjoyed these boards and found them clever. But today the message boomed in her ears as if the words on the board had become audible.

Don't make Me come down there. . . .

At the same moment, the Christian radio station she'd been listening to ended a song. The DJ came on: "Our verse for today comes from Proverbs 16:18. 'Pride goes before destruction, and haughtiness before a fall.' "

Tessa slammed on the brakes, causing the car behind her to honk and swerve to miss her bumper.

"Hey, lady! What do you think you're doing?"

It was a good question.

She pulled to the curb and shut off her car. She closed her eyes but found that the torrent of words that had consumed her just moments before had retreated like bedbugs in the light. Love and pride. Water and oil. Living water. Jesus.

Her mind was suddenly weary and contrite.

It was a good beginning.

Gillie poked Audra in the side, leaning close. "He's back."

Audra looked up and saw Russell Peerbaugh pass through the lobby, a single piece of paper in his hands. He glanced her way. Gillie offered a flippy wave.

Audra hit her arm. "Don't!"

"Just being friendly." She put a rubber band around a stack of twenties. "If looks were Morse code, that man's been

SOSing you all week."

"What?"

"SOS: Sending Out Signals. The question is, are you catching what he's sending?"

Audra straightened a pile of tens. "Maybe."

Gillie rolled her eyes. "As a fellow single woman who wouldn't mind the attention of a man who had looks, brains, *and* more than fifty bucks to his name, I'd start sending something back, lady. In a fast staccato rhythm." She tatted her fingernail on the counter.

They saw Russell return from his errand. But instead of taking his normal parallel pathway, he turned toward them. Before walking away, Gillie gave Audra a nudge and whispered, "SOS, lady. SOS."

Audra's heart took up the staccato rhythm. She met his eyes. He looked down. She looked down, only to look up and find him looking at her. *This is ridiculous. I'm acting like a schoolgirl. He's my boss — not my immediate boss, but still a higher-up. He probably just wants to see how things are going.*

"Ms. Taylor."

"Mr. —" She found the need to clear her throat. "Mr. Peerbaugh."

"Things going well?"

"Yes."

"Would you like to go out to dinner with me?"

If there'd been a transition from boss to date, she'd missed it. "I don't know."

He looked around the lobby. Audra did too. There were far too many eyes. Some looked away. Some blatantly watched.

It was his turn to clear his throat. He changed his weight to his other foot. "I know this is unusual, but —" he leaned toward her an inch — "I really would like to get to know you better."

"Thank you."

He smiled as if he'd gained a victory. "So? Dinner? At seven?"

"Tonight?"

"You aren't eating tonight?" He waved his flip comment away. "I know the etiquette police would issue me multiple tickets for this short notice, but if you're not busy . . ."

"I'm not. That would be great."

He beamed and bounced twice on his toes. "Wonderful. Would you like me to pick you —" He stopped, got a wrinkle between his brows, then lost it. "If it's all right with you, I'd rather we didn't let my mother know we're seeing each

238

other. Not just yet."

She wasn't sure if this was good or bad, but before her insecurities took over, he added, "More than anything she wants me married off, and if she found out about our date, I'm afraid she'd pounce on you like an overzealous yenta."

"Matchmaker, matchmaker, make me a match?"

"Exactly."

"No problem," Audra said. "I'll meet you at the restaurant. Which is . . . ?"

"Chez Garsaud."

She must have made a face because he laughed. "You act like I mentioned the moon or something."

"Might as well be. The chances of me ever eating at Chez Garsaud are about the same as me going to the moon."

He looked pleased. "All the better. I love giving people something they've never had before."

"Then I'm your girl." She realized the double entendre in that phrase. "I'm in."

"Excellent. See you at seven."

As Russell walked away, Gillie came toward her. "Way to go, Audra. Chez Garsaud."

Audra shrugged, but she felt like pumping a fist. "It was nothing."

It was something.

Gillie was glad the rest room was empty. She stepped before a mirror and took a look. *I'm a pretty woman. Why can't I find a nice man like Russell Peerbaugh?*

She flicked a fingernail against the mirror. "Because he wasn't attracted to you, the quick-to-flaunt-my-alimony Gillie. He was attracted to unpretentious, unaffected, unwed mother, Audra."

She sighed, watching the lift and drop of her shoulders. *So be it.*

She noticed a stray wisp of hair and wet her fingers under the faucet to tame it. She let her fingers flow past her hair, along her jawline. It was nicely sculptured, even at age thirty-five.

Jerry used to trace my jawline, used to gaze into my eyes. Used to tell me he loved me. She shook such memories away. Jerry was gone. Remarried to a younger version of herself.

Unfortunately, even though she wanted to give Jerry one hundred percent of the blame, she couldn't. Their life together had been a partnership in self-absorption. They hadn't had children because they didn't want to be bothered. Their offspring consisted of a house, three cars, clothes with designer labels, and vacations in

240

places that were hot, luxurious, and just a bit decadent.

They'd bought the finest *things* and indulged in the best life money could buy. So with all the focus on obtaining the best, it was nearly inevitable that Jerry's eyes and desires would fall on a better, younger woman. To Jerry, trading in Gillie for a new improved model was akin to trading in their Jeep for a Lexus. A logical progression of their lifestyle.

"Good riddance," Gillie told the mirror.

She had to look away, her eyes unable to face the lie. Good riddance? Baloney. She missed Jerry, even if he was a flawed two-timing specimen. They'd had something special for a while. Before they'd let themselves become consumed with lifestyle over life, they'd felt devotion for each other more than for things.

Where had that love gone?

It had dissolved like fog burning off in the sun, and no matter how hard Gillie had tried, she had not been able to grab onto the dissipating mist.

She straightened her shoulders, lifting her jaw defiantly. *What's done is done. Who needs a husband when I have the husband's money?*

She felt a shopping spree coming on.

"I'm home —"

Before Mae could close the door, Evelyn was at her side, grabbing her arm. "Mae, I'm so worried."

"Whoa there, Evie. Let me get both feet in the door before you swoop down on me."

Evelyn let go and took a step back. "Sorry."

Mae removed her shoulder bag over her head. "No problem. Or by your actions, I guess there is a problem. What's going on?"

Evelyn moved to the parlor. "Let's sit down."

"That bad?"

"Maybe. Possibly."

Mae tried to think of something that could get Evelyn so riled, but her mind was blank. In their short acquaintance, she'd never seen Evelyn get riled about anything.

They both sat on the couch. Evelyn angled her body toward Mae. "We had a visitor today — Collier Ames from across the street."

"I take it this isn't a good thing?"

Evelyn shrugged. "Truthfully, I've never paid much mind to him one way or the other."

"Until now."

"Until now. He's complaining about me opening up Peerbaugh Place. Having tenants. Extra people on the block. He asked if I had a license or a permit or something and —"

Mae had the picture. "A nosy troublemaker, eh?"

Evelyn wrung her hands. "Did you get the permit at city hall like you said you would?"

A memory surfaced. She *had* promised to do that, the first day. "Oh no, I'm afraid I didn't. I forgot."

Evelyn stood and paced. "But what if Collier gets to them first and complains, and they decide that I can't have a permit, and they send someone out and inspect the house and decide the halls aren't wide enough, or there are too few toilets, or I need a different roof." She stopped in front of Mae. "What if they close me down?"

Mae reached out and touched her arm. "They're not going to —"

"But what if they do?" Her eyes were wild. "I *have* to have this income to survive. This felt so right. And all of you are such a joy to me, and now, taking care of Summer . . ." She looked toward the back of the house, and Mae wondered if that's where Summer was playing.

She stood and took Evelyn's hands in hers, waiting until she had her eyes. "I'll take care of it on Monday, Evie. I promise."

Evelyn nodded.

"Now take a deep breath with me." Evelyn followed directions, then glanced toward the front door as if reliving something.

"But what if Collier comes back?"

"Invite him in for Uno and a cup of tea."

"I can't imagine him liking tea."

Goodness . . . "Evelyn, I was kidding. Don't worry about him. Worse comes to worst, I'll take care of Collier Ames."

Evelyn smiled. "He won't know what hit him."

"Exactly." Mae headed for the stairs. "You remembered that I was going out tonight, right? Dinner and a movie? So I won't be here to eat?"

"I remembered," Evelyn said. "Actually, Audra called. She's got a date."

"Really? How nice."

"And Piper's picking up Summer. They're going to McDonald's. So tonight it's just going to be Tessa and I."

Lucky you.

Piper stood in the doorway of Evelyn's room.

"What do you think?" Evelyn asked. "Audra said you were good at this decorating stuff."

"I am."

Evelyn laughed. "I like a confident woman."

Piper strolled around the furniture, her eyes busy. "It comes and goes. You caught me on a good day, confidence-wise." She stroked the top of the high dresser. "Nice antiques."

Evelyn laughed. "Funny how I never thought of them as that. When Aaron and I moved in here, we just thought of them as used — and even more importantly, free."

Piper traced a carved finial of the four-poster. "These are more than used; this piece and the high dresser are lovely."

They both looked at the low dresser with the mirror. "But that?" Evelyn asked.

"Less lovely."

"I know it doesn't match."

"It doesn't have to match, but it's too . . ." Piper waved her hands, trying to come up with the right word.

"Too ugly?" Evelyn offered.

"I was going to say too heavy-looking."

"But *ugly* will do?"

"I was trying to be nice."

Evelyn sat on the bed as Piper looked around. "I don't want you to be nice, Piper. I want you to do what needs to be done to make this room wonderful."

"That's a little vague."

Evelyn shrugged. "I trust you."

Piper turned on a funny little lamp made of a lady in a big skirt. She turned it off. "That's nice of you, but the only way I'm going to agree to do this is if you and I go shopping together. That way I'll be able to figure out what style you like."

Evelyn hung her head. "Oh, no, no . . . shopping . . . that's too much of a burden. I don't think —"

"What?"

Evelyn smiled. "You don't have to ask twice."

Piper was relieved. She ran a hand over the quilt, touching a finger to each of the seven stars in one of the quilt blocks. "Actually, I like this quilt a lot. Does it have a story? Quilts often have stories."

"It was Grandma Peerbaugh's. I know the pattern is called Seven Sisters. If I remember correctly, her sisters made it for her as a wedding present. There were seven sisters in the Peerbaugh family."

The number seven stuck in Piper's head, and she did a quick accounting. "And now there are seven women making up the life of this house. Interesting."

"Seven — ?"

Piper counted off on her fingers. "There's you, Mae, Tessa, Summer, and Audra. And Gillie and I are always hanging around Peerbaugh Place. Seven females."

Evelyn nodded, obviously pleased. "Seven sisters. I like that."

Piper looked over the room again. "Maybe we should keep the quilt since it has added meaning."

Evelyn ran a hand across the fabric as if seeing it fresh. "You don't think it would be bad keeping it? After all, I was trying to start over. Get something new in here."

Piper scanned the room. "We can make the room look new in other ways. It will be a challenge and I love a —"

Summer appeared in the doorway with a jump. "I'm ready!"

Piper held out her hand and Summer grabbed on. "Chicken nuggets or a hamburger?"

"A cheeseburger and lots and lots of french fries."

"You're my kind of girl, pip-squeak."

Audra joined them, wearing a pink dress that set off her dark hair and eyes.

"Wow," said Piper.

"Thanks," Audra said, swishing to the stairs. "That was just the reaction I was hoping for."

They headed down after her. "Who's the lucky man?" Evelyn asked.

"Oh, just someone I met recently."

At the bottom of the stairs Piper looked between Audra and Evelyn. Audra had confided that Russell was her date and that she'd agreed to keep it quiet. The question was, *could* she?

"What's his name?" Evelyn asked.

Piper saw Audra's face draw up in a moment of panic. The girl did not like to lie — it was one of the things Piper loved about her. But how would she not tell Evelyn —

Audra checked her hair in the foyer mirror. "I do not reveal the names of my dates until we've been out at least three times. Which means, if past experience can be trusted, you will never hear me utter the name of *any* date."

"Your relationships don't last long?"

"Uh . . . no."

"That's too bad. You're a pretty girl.

And young, and —"

"And picky," Piper said, opening the front door.

"Rightfully so," Audra said.

"But, hey, what do I know? I can't remember the last man I went out with who lured me beyond a first date."

"Exactly." Audra kissed Summer and they all left together.

Evelyn stood at the door. "Isn't he picking you up here? A gentleman always picks a lady —"

Audra kept walking. "It's fine, Evelyn. See you later."

As Evelyn withdrew inside, Piper paused at Audra's car. "That was close."

Audra got in the driver's seat. "As I said, if experience serves, I won't have to do it again."

Somehow, eating a salad at McDonald's didn't seem quite right — or possible. The smell of french fries was like the call of the Sirens luring Odysseus to his death — or Piper to an extra pound around her middle. Super-size it, please.

Piper sat in the play area of the restaurant with Summer. The little girl dragged a french fry through a puddle of catsup, bit off a fourth of an inch, and dipped it again.

"Those fries are a good way to eat catsup, aren't they? Better than using a spoon."

Summer nodded and shoved the rest in her mouth and champed dramatically.

"Chew with your mouth closed, please."

Summer's lips glued themselves together, making Piper smile. Summer always made her smile.

It was one of Piper's biggest regrets, not having children. Of course you needed a husband to do that. Actually, you didn't — as Audra had proven — but Piper wouldn't even consider doing it any other way. Marriage first, kids second. That was God's order of things, even if it wasn't the way of the world.

If she followed the way of the world, she'd have slept with a dozen men or gone to be artificially inseminated, with the full intent of raising a child on her own. None were options she would consider.

Piper was still a virgin, a fact the students she counseled found either hilarious or appalling. Oh, she'd come close a few times. With her fiancé, Jason. And with Barry Minion. He'd been a contender back in college, but his view of living a moral life had little to do with what God had deemed right and a lot to do with what

Barry Minion had wanted to do. Piper had tried to tell him about God and Jesus, to share her heart and explain to him how *everything* changed when a person made that one, eternally important commitment. But Barry had only laughed at her and called her Pious Piper. At first it had been in jest, but then he'd started to use that nickname in an inflammatory way every time she disagreed with something he did. Bye-bye, Barry.

Being a part of Audra's and Summer's lives was a salve to what could have been. It's not that she didn't pray that God would send her a soul mate, but so far He'd said no. At age thirty-three, Piper was beginning to wonder if it would be a permanent answer. If so, she knew that no amount of "Please, Daddy, please" would change the Almighty's mind. She wasn't entirely reconciled to the idea yet, but she did trust her loving heavenly Father to do what was best for her.

"Why are you looking at me funny?" Summer asked.

Piper hadn't realized she'd been staring. She smiled. "You have your mother's eyes. Lovely brown eyes."

"Thank you." Summer ate another fry

and studied Piper's face. "Whose eyes do you have?"

The question took her by surprise. "Why . . . I don't know."

"Who has green eyes, your mom or your dad?"

Actually, neither. Piper thought of the blue eyes of both her parents. And their blond hair. And the petite frames. She remembered times in her life when people would comment on the tall, brunette, hazel-eyed girl with the short, light-haired, blue-eyed parents.

Summer was waiting for an answer.

"Actually, I'm adopted. I don't know what color my birth parents' eyes were. Are." *Are they alive? I don't even know that.*

Summer nodded and chewed. "Mandy Rice is 'dopted. She lived next to Grandma and Grandpa. She said she was special 'cause her parents chose her."

"All children are special."

"But Mommy didn't choose me. She had to have me."

Piper wasn't sure exactly what Summer meant by this, but was sure it had nothing to do with the abortion Audra *had* considered having when she'd first found out she was pregnant.

Piper dipped a fry in Summer's catsup.

"Your mommy had to have you because she knew what a fabulous little girl you'd be."

"How did she know?"

Piper hesitated only a moment. "Because God made you." She thought of a psalm. "God made you 'wonderfully complex.' He knit you together in your mother's womb!"

Summer considered this a moment. "Wow. Cool."

"You betcha."

Evelyn looked at her watch. Six-thirty. The rule was that dinner was at six, unless other arrangements were made. Tessa had not made other arrangements. Tessa was a stickler for rules.

Evelyn was worried. She called the church but there was no answer.

She went into the foyer and looked out the front window until two cars went by that weren't Tessa's. She stepped onto the porch and sat on the wicker settee. And waited.

God, keep her safe.

Russell was waiting for her.

Audra parked in the lot of Chez Garsaud. But before she could even open her door, Russell had done it for her.

"Hi," he said, offering her his hand.

She got out. "Such service. I'm impressed."

"The least I can do for a lovely lady." He offered his arm and they headed to the entrance.

Audra was taken aback by the manners and flattery. She'd never been around men who gave compliments right out of a Cary Grant movie. The most Luke would have ever offered was "Nice dress" before possessively putting his hand on her back and leading her into Coney's or Ruby's, where he might or might not have remembered to open the door for her.

Coney's or Chez Garsaud. Both good food. Both good places in their own ways. *Don't go getting uppity.*

But as they moved through the double doors, Audra's senses were thrust into a wonderland of brass, leather, and walnut.

"Good evening," the maître d' said. He looked like a model in a magazine, and Audra was glad she'd worn her pink dress instead of the challis skirt.

"We have reservations," Russell said. "Peerbaugh?"

With a quick glance to the podium, the man picked up two menus and flashed a smile. "Yes, Mr. Peerbaugh. Miss. Right

254

this way, please."

Her chair was held for her; a napkin was placed in her lap with a flourish; leather-covered menus written in French were set before them. There was lemon in the iced water served in crystal goblets, fresh flowers, the music of a string quartet, and a rich aroma that made her want to skip the menu and just say, "Bring me a bit of each, please."

Russell looked up from his menu. "Don't be intimidated by the French. The only French I know is menu-French from coming here."

"You come here that often?"

Russell shrugged. "The bank does. To entertain big customers."

"By 'big' I assume you mean they have to have more than eighty-nine fifty-two in their checking account?"

"I think one hundred dollars is the minimum."

"Ten dollars and forty-eight cents short. I'll work on it."

"Math in your head. Now *I'm* impressed."

"I work at a bank, you know."

"Good place for you."

"Yes, it is."

He closed his menu and set it aside. He

reached over the top of hers and pointed. "The veal's excellent. Otherwise I'd recommend the salmon." He sat back. "So something besides the need for a job — just any job — brought you to the bank?"

Audra decided on the salmon and closed her menu. "I've always liked numbers. I'm good at them. Did you know two plus two is four?"

"You don't say."

She nodded. The waiter brought them a basket of bread covered with a burgundy napkin. He took their order and left.

"What's your background?" Russell asked. "Do you have a degree?"

"I thought I already had the job."

His cheeks reddened. He unwrapped the bread and offered her a hard roll before taking one himself and tucking the bread back in. "I don't mean to be nosy. I'm just interested."

"In your employees in general, or . . ." She'd started the sentence, but suddenly chickened out at finishing it. *What are you doing? You're forcing him into making a statement saying far more than —*

"Or specifically you?"

She tore her roll apart and applied butter from an iced bowl, glad for something to do. "Something like that."

He reached across the table and gave her hand the lightest touch before withdrawing it. "Let me assure you, Audra, I am not in the habit of dating any of the bank's employees. In fact, I've never done it before."

"Dated? Or dated an employee?"

The fact that he smiled was very important to her. She'd dated enough guys who took offense easily or who couldn't handle the sarcastic banter she preferred.

"I can't rest a moment with you, can I?" he said.

She took a bite of roll. It was warm and melted in her mouth. "Is that what you want? To have easy conversation? To rest?"

He raised an eyebrow and set his roll and butter knife down. "Actually, no. To be truthful, I'm rather bored with easy conversation that circles around and ends up where it started."

"You want to be challenged."

"Now that you mention it . . ."

She sighed. "So shall we discuss world peace, hunger, stocks, or the finer points of making a peanut butter and jelly sandwich? My daughter's an expert."

"At world peace?"

She couldn't rest a moment with *him*. This was good. Very, very good.

"You have a daughter?"

"I assumed you knew."

"Oh, I did. Mom mentioned it. Perhaps I should have phrased the question differently: Tell me about your daughter."

Audra was surprised by his interest. Having a five-year-old child was usually a date-killer. And maybe Russell was just being polite. He obviously was a whiz at doing that.

"She's a mistake that became the joy of my life."

"Oh?"

Audra felt a large plank of pride set itself on her shoulder. "Want to hear all the gory details? Premarital sex, unwed mother, absent father. I've been living with my parents for the past —"

"What's her name?"

Audra was shocked — and chastened — to silence. Summer was not a cause to hold up like a trophy nor a burden brought forward to gain sympathy. Audra was over-reacting big time.

She adjusted the napkin in her lap. "Her name's Summer after my favorite season of the year." She glanced up. "Actually, *she's* my favorite season. I love being a mother."

Russell nodded. "What's her favorite thing to do?"

Make me happy. Audra put it in less personal terms. "Help."

"As in . . . ?"

"As in she has a need to serve. She seeks out what needs to be done and takes care of it. Whether it is getting me a napkin, straightening my perfume bottles, or climbing onto my lap at just the right moment."

"How old is she?"

"She just turned five."

"Has she always been like that?"

"Always. It's like it was born into her."

"Maybe it was."

"How so?"

Russell spread the butter on his roll from edge to edge. "I think people are born with certain abilities or traits or gifts. I'm not sure what to call them, but we seem to be innately different and it's not a choice we've made. It just is."

"My friend Piper would say God did it."

"God gave us the abilities?"

Audra nodded. Actually she liked the notion and hoped it was true. "She'd be able to give you a Bible verse to prove her case, but I've heard her say many times that we each have a unique purpose and unique gifts, and it's up to us to figure out what they are and say yes."

259

"Yes to what?"

"Not to what. To whom."

"Okay, to whom?"

"God."

As he nodded, his face tightened ever so slightly. Audra's first inclination was to pull back and not mention God again. After all, she was pretty new to this faith business and wouldn't know a thing about it if it weren't for Piper. But something inside yanked at her reticence, and she felt a sudden surge of boldness.

Their salads came and it was the perfect time to let the subject drop. But she couldn't. She didn't. "Do you believe in God?"

Russell muffed the bite going into his mouth, and most of it landed back in the bowl. He dabbed at his chin. "Banish the small talk, eh?"

"You wanted to be challenged."

He nodded. "The answer to your pointed question is yes, I believe in God."

"Really believe or just say-so believe?"

"If you're asking if I stand on the street corners shouting 'Praise the Lord' —"

"No, no, nothing like that." Audra said a quick prayer that she'd get the words right. This was all so new to her. . . . "Until I got pregnant, I was a say-so believer. I prayed. Sometimes. But most times no. It was Piper who got me to realize there was more to it than that."

"Who exactly is this Piper? Is that a male or female?"

"A female. Actually, she was my counselor in school when I got pregnant. But we've gone way beyond that. Now we're best friends."

"And she got you tuned in to God."

Audra nodded. She couldn't answer because her mouth was full. Finally, "There's such a difference between going through the motions and knowing He's real. That He's right here all the time." She put a hand on her heart. "It's such a comfort."

"I suppose. If you need comfort."

This one comment set him back three paces in her eyes. "That's a cocky thing to say."

He blinked twice in quick succession. "I didn't mean it to be. But it's a known fact that people turn to God when they're having a bad time. You can't deny that."

"And once the trial is past, a lot of people forget about Him. I'd done that many times in my life. But with Piper's help, I realized if I expect Him to help me in the bad times, then I owe Him my attention during the good times. We can't be foul-weather believers."

Russell cocked his head and nodded. "That does sound logical."

She felt herself relax. Perhaps this was a victory of sorts. Perhaps this was all that was to be accomplished this first time talking about God — this first time talking about anything. This first date.

Audra was suddenly struck by how much they'd covered beyond normal conversation. And the entrée hadn't even come yet, much less dessert.

First date? She was already looking forward to the second.

When Tessa pulled into the driveway, she immediately saw Evelyn sitting on the porch, and watched her rise and walk to the railing.

"Tessa! Where have you been? I've been so worried."

Tessa looked at her watch: 7:05. She was over an hour late for dinner. Where had the time gone? She'd sat at the curb for ages and then had driven over to the park, where she'd continued her introspection on a bench.

She tried to straighten her spine, to take the offensive, but found it difficult. "Sorry," she said, taking the steps to the porch. She leaned extra hard on the railing. "Time got away from me."

She went inside and headed to the kitchen with Evelyn close on her heels. "Didn't your Bible study end hours ago?"

Don't mention the Bible study. Please don't mention it. "I hope dinner isn't ruined."

"It's fine. It's just goulash. You can't hurt goulash. But —"

Tessa whipped around, causing Evelyn to pull up short to stop from running into her. "Evelyn, I've had a hard day. I don't feel like talking about it. I would appreciate it if you would respect my privacy and leave it be."

"Well, sure . . . I didn't mean to pry. I was just worried that something had happened to you."

Oh, something happened, all right.

Tessa washed her hands. "I should have called. For that I apologize. I won't do it again. Okay?"

Evelyn looked anything but sure. "Whatever you say."

Tessa wasn't sure she'd ever say much of anything again.

Evelyn felt more alone with Tessa *in* the house than she had with Tessa out of it. Tessa did not say a word all through dinner, and afterwards, withdrew to her room, asking not to be disturbed.

What had happened to her?

While Evelyn cleaned up the kitchen she found herself praying. It was all she could think to do.

Evelyn was out of her chair the moment Mae came in the door. "Mae!"

Mae put a hand to her chest and took a breath. "That's the second time you've done that today, Evie. We need to get you a warning bell or something to let me know you're lurking." She took another breath. "The nosy neighbor hasn't been bothering you again, has he?"

"No, no." With a glance upstairs, Evelyn drew her into the parlor. "It's Tessa."

"What's wrong?"

"She came home an hour late for dinner, all upset. She didn't say a word while we ate. She went up to her room saying she didn't want to be disturbed."

"Tessa not say a word? That is bad."

Evelyn nodded. "I'm really worried."

"Did she give you any clues?"

"Just that she'd had a bad day. I know she had her Bible study this afternoon, but that shouldn't upset her."

They turned toward the porch, where

the sounds of Summer and Piper could be heard. Evelyn rushed to the door to quiet them.

"Shh!"

Piper shut the door gently. "What's — ?"

Mae crooked a finger, drawing the two new additions into the parlor. "Tessa's upset. Shut up in her room."

Piper's face changed from interest to concern to understanding. "I wonder . . ."

"You know something?"

"I was at Tessa's Bible study today."

"*You* were there? Why?"

"I went with a friend. Plus I thought it would be nice since Tessa lives here and —"

"Did anything happen?"

"She walked out. She quit the group."

Mae raised a finger. "I thought she was head of it."

"She was." Piper looked past them, deep in thought. "Uh-oh . . . it's my fault."

"What did you do?"

"I contradicted her. Someone asked a question and Tessa gave the wrong answer. So I corrected —"

Mae waved her hands in the air as if fending off evil. "Whoa, there. The all-wise Tessa wouldn't take that lying down."

"That explains it," Evelyn said. "Knowing things is life to Tessa. Being proved wrong is death." She looked up-stairs. It made sense.

Piper took a step toward the stairs. "Should I go apologize or something?"

Mae pulled her back. "Not tonight. Maybe we need to think of the larger issue here."

"Which is?"

They all looked at each other as if none of them dared talk. Mae fueled herself with a breath. "I'll be the one to say what we all know as true. Tessa is an arrogant know-it-all. She needed to be knocked from her pedestal. She can always climb back up."

"You think so?" Evelyn asked. "She acts strong, but tonight . . . I've never seen her so broken."

"I know so." Mae leaned toward Summer, who'd been taking the whole thing in. "How was McDonald's, doll face?"

Evelyn let their chatter fill the room. But no matter how hard she tried, she couldn't stop looking upstairs.

Before she went to bed, Evelyn knocked on Tessa's door. There was a weak "Yes?"

"You okay, Tessa?"

"I'm fine."

"You need anything?"

"No."

Evelyn had rarely felt so helpless. "Good night, then."

There was no good night from Tessa.

No good night *for* Tessa?

8

Love wisdom like a sister; make insight a
beloved member of your family.
PROVERBS 7:4

Mae entered the kitchen for breakfast
Monday morning and was immediately
struck by the silence. Audra, Summer, and
Evelyn sat around the table eating, but they
weren't talking. Even Peppers was quiet at
Evelyn's feet. And Tessa was absent. Come
to think of it, she didn't recall seeing Tessa
all weekend.

Mae was appalled by the relief she felt at
this fact. She made an exaggerated show of
tiptoeing to get a mug for tea.

"What are you doing?" Audra asked.

"Trying not to disturb the hush." She
put a finger to her lips. *"Shhhh."*

Summer giggled.

"Were we that bad?" Evelyn asked.

"Positively muzzled." Mae poured her
hot water, purposely making as much noise
as possible. "We shouldn't give in to her
moods, sisters. It's not healthy for the
house or Tessie."

"But she's upset," Audra said.

"I understand that. But having the rest of us walk around on eggshells while she pouts doesn't do anybody any good."

"She won't talk," Evelyn said. "I tried all weekend. She hardly comes out of her room."

Mae dunked a tea bag. "That's her choice. We need to make it known we're here for her, but then we move on with our lives."

Audra was nodding. "By doing otherwise, we're being enablers. I've heard of that for alcoholics and addicts. We're enabling Tessa to remain mired in her troubles instead —"

"Instead of yanking her out of them." Mae stood by the table. "So what will it be, sisters? Enabling or yanking?"

"She's not a wishbone, Mae," Evelyn said.

"We're not going to snap her in two, Evie; we're just going to give her a little tug." She looked around the table. "Well?"

"Now?" Audra said.

"If we don't do it now, it will have to be after work, and I, for one, don't want Tessa to waste another day of her life moping." She put a hand on Evelyn's shoulder. "There's another reason for doing it now. Evie and

Summer. They're the ones who'll have to be with her all day, stormy or sunny."

Audra laughed. "I'm not sure you could ever call Tessa's mood sunny."

Evelyn pushed her chair back. "I'm in."

"That's the spirit. Audra?"

Audra shoved the last corner of toast in her mouth and stood. "Why not? I'm always ripe for quelling insurrection first thing in the morning."

"Can I come?" Summer said.

Mae ruffled her hair. "Hold down the fort, doll face. If you hear screams, call the Coast Guard."

Summer's forehead wrinkled. "What?"

Audra pointed to her cereal. "Eat your breakfast, baby. We'll be right back."

Evelyn wrung her hands. "I think you're being optimistic."

As they headed to the stairs single file, Mae was rather surprised they'd agreed to do . . . whatever it was they were going to do. She realized too late that it was her fault. Once again her freedom with words had started something far beyond her original intention. *Why do I do this? Speak before I think?*

It was too late now. She led the women upstairs, and they gathered outside Tessa's door.

270

"Now what?" Evelyn whispered.

Retreat sounded good; her tea was getting cold.

"Shouldn't we knock or something?" Audra said.

They looked to Mae. She took a deep breath and fired on Fort Sumter. "Tessa?"

No sound.

She knocked again.

Nothing.

Mae turned to Evelyn. "*You* call her. She likes you best."

Evelyn cleared her throat as if she had been asked to give a speech. She stepped forward and tapped her knuckles on the door. Her tap was far softer than Mae's aggressive knock. Could a knock be deemed friendly? Friend or foe?

"Tessa? It's us. Breakfast is ready. Did you oversleep?"

Mae gave Evelyn a thumbs-up. She was good. It was wise not to mention Tessa's troubles or that they were worried about her. That would only play into her mood. It was best to act as if everything was normal.

"I poured you a cup of coffee, Tessa. It's getting cold. I was going to make eggs. Do you want one or two?"

Mae put a hand up as they heard sounds

from inside. Footsteps. They all took a step back, giving Tessa space. The door opened.

Tessa looked awful, her hair mussed from sleep, her skin mottled, and the collar of her robe half turned under. She eyed the crowd. "It takes all of you to tell me it's breakfast?"

Audra stepped away as if she'd been passing by on her way to her room. "I was just getting a belt. . . ."

Mae pretended to adjust the clasp on her watch. "And I just can't stand to have anyone sleep later than I do, so I came to get you up. You lazy bum, you."

Evelyn shook her head. "They're lying."

Mae was shocked to silence. Audra froze on the way to her room.

Evelyn continued. "We didn't just *happen* to be passing by your door; we came here specifically to see how you're doing. You've been in your room far too long."

"You've passed the legal limit," Mae said, tapping her watch. "It's time you joined us."

Tessa looked at each one of them, her mouth a droopy frown. *Come on, Tessie, lift up those corners and smile. You look like a hound dog, scowling at us like that.*

Audra rejoined the circle. "If you're upset about something, you need to tell us about it. That's what we're here for. We miss you."

Mae wasn't sure about that . . .

"We need to be like family and be able to share the good times and the bad," Evelyn said.

"Piper told us what happened and —"

Tessa's eyes flashed. "She told you? How dare she tell you!"

Audra hurried to correct the mistake. "It wasn't anything bad. And we don't know the details. She just told us that you got upset at Bible study and walked out."

"Whether I walked out or not is no concern of yours. And for Piper to tell you about it . . ." She put a wrinkled hand to her chest as it heaved. "That's gossip, pure and simple."

"Piper is not a gossip," Audra said. "She didn't mean anything derogatory. She's just concerned, like the rest of us. We want to understand. We want to —"

Tessa took a step back into her room and grabbed hold of the doorknob. "I don't need you to understand or to help. And I certainly don't need you to be my family. I need to be left alone!"

She slammed the door with such force

that the air current moved their hair. The three women stared at each other. Mae had never considered this would be the result of their friendly intervention. She felt anger rise like the temperature in a cartoon thermometer. *Watch out! It's goin' to blow!*

Evelyn took her arm. "Come on, Mae. Let's leave her alone."

Mae shook her hand away. "This is what we get for being nice?"

"She's just upset," Audra said, heading for the stairs.

"Well, so am I." Mae placed herself squarely in front of Tessa's door. Her mind flooded with angry words. She considered — briefly — that she shouldn't actually say them, but her will overturned common sense. "Hey, Tessie! Speaking of family . . . are you sure you're not here because your family kicked you out?"

Evelyn gasped. "Mae!"

Audra spoke from the stairs. "Mae, leave it alone. You're making it worse."

She knew they were right, but her anger was slow to dissipate. She turned on her heel and headed downstairs, passing Audra on the way. With each step, regret was thrown over her anger like a blanket on a flame. Unfortunately, there was no telling which would consume the other.

And frankly, Mae didn't care.

Tessa stared at the closed door as if her friends were still in front of her. But they weren't. They were gone. She'd heard their footsteps fall away and their voices fade into the kitchen. At the rate she was going, they weren't going to be her friends much longer.

"Are you sure you're not here because your family kicked you out?"

Mae's words stung. They were a lie. And yet they skimmed the truth enough to burn. Her family hadn't kicked her out, but she certainly had given them ample reason to do so. She had moved into her daughter's home like a dictator conquering a country. She'd insisted on her way, her schedule, her likes and dislikes to be honored. She'd expected them to do the adapting, while she sat in her room and ordered them about like slaves. But it was worse than that. For even in the most horrible slave-master relationships, the master provided something for the slaves. Food. Housing. Minimal for certain, but something. Yet Tessa had provided nothing to her daughter's household. No financial compensation, no offerings to help with dinner or chores or even to get groceries.

And especially, no kind words. Or interest. Never a "How was your day?" to daughter, son-in-law, or grandson. She'd accepted their kisses and hugs as her due but had never so much as touched one of them on the shoulder in an act of attachment and affection.

Tessa backed toward her bed and dropped onto it, her legs unable to sustain the burden of her faults any longer. She raised her face toward heaven and let the tears slide past her ears.

"What's wrong with me, Lord? I've turned into a tough, unlikable shrew. I put on airs like I'm special; like I'm the epitome of a good Christian woman, but I'm far from it."

Far from it.

An hour later, Tessa stood at her dresser, brushing her hair. Each stroke was deliberate and took effort. It was as if all her actions were in slow motion, compensating for the flurry of thoughts that assailed her mind like machine-gun fire. She could think fast or move fast, but not both.

There was a quiet knock on the door. Evelyn again?

"Yes?"

"Tessa?"

It was the girl. Tessa opened the door.

Summer raised a plate holding a sandwich. "I made this for you. You missed breakfast."

The thoughts stopped firing and Tessa pressed a hand to her heart, this time for a good reason. There was no pain — not in the usual sense — but her chest *did* tighten.

"Come in, girl."

Summer came in the door with wary eyes, as if entering enemy territory. Tessa took the sandwich, parting the slices to see what was inside. Peanut butter and jelly. She detested peanut butter.

An inner voice chastised. *Tessa* . . .

She assured the voice with a nod and asked, "Did you make this all by yourself?"

The girl nodded. "I told Aunt Evelyn it was for me, that I was extra hungry this morning."

"Where is *Aunt* Evelyn?"

"She's watering the flowers out back." She pointed to the sandwich. "Take a bite. It's good. I promise."

Tessa braced herself for the horrid taste. She took a small bite and chewed. It wasn't *that* bad.

"Do you like it?"

"It's very tasty."

The girl beamed. "I was going to bring milk too, but I was afraid I'd spill it on the stairs, and coffee's too hot. I'd get in trouble."

The innocent wisdom of the girl assailed her. An extraordinary child come to comfort a bitter old woman. Tessa let herself be softened. "That was a wise choice," she said. "How about I come downstairs and finish this in the kitchen? Then we can both have a glass of milk."

"I'd like that," the girl said. Then she took Tessa's hand, shocking Tessa with its smallness yet its soft strength. Little beige fingers curled around wrinkled walnut ones. The girl looked up at her and smiled. "I'm glad you're happier now, Aunt Tessa."

Aunt Tessa. The words were a soothing elixir. "Me too . . . Summer."

Piper was just getting out of her car in the school parking lot when her cell phone rang. It was Audra's ring. "Morning, Aud. What's up?"

"Tessa's still upset."

Piper closed the car door and leaned on the hood. "It's all my fault."

There was a condemning moment of silence before Audra said what friends were

278

expected to say. "I'm sure you didn't do anything wrong. Tessa overreacts to every-thing."

"That might be true, but I . . . I said too much."

"Don't beat yourself up over it, Piper. You're a smart lady. You know a lot about God and the Bible. I'd know nothing if it weren't for you. What you said was the truth, wasn't it?"

"Well, yes . . ."

"Then don't worry about it. I think Tessa has issues to contend with beyond what happened at the Bible study."

"Like what?"

"I'm not sure. But a woman doesn't get judgmental and bitter for no reason."

"Which means she needs our help more than ever."

"I'll have to start calling you Saint Piper. You are *way* too good."

I wish.

"Didn't mean to squelch your day, but I thought you should know. And I figured you, above all people, might know what to do."

"I'll go talk to her."

"I was hoping you'd say that. When?"

Piper checked her watch. School would be starting soon. She needed to see Tessa, but it would have to be later. "I'll try at lunch."

"I hope she's out of her room by then."

Me too.

Piper closed the door to her office, sat at her desk, and bowed her head. *Lord, I'm sorry if I've offended Tessa, or more especially, You. For a long time I've realized that You've given me the gift of insight, but have I gone too far? Do I need to learn the gift of tact?*

There was a knock on her door. Another day of education began.

For all of them.

Evelyn went in the house, wondering what was taking Summer so long. The little girl had wanted to eat a sandwich, but the time had long passed for her to be —

Evelyn stopped in the doorway, shocked to see Tessa and Summer at the kitchen table. Peppers lapped milk from a bowl.

Tessa lifted a glass of milk. "Care to join us?"

"Well . . . sure." Evelyn got a glass and sat at the table. She watched, fascinated, as Summer grinned at Tessa and Tessa grinned at Summer, like they shared a secret. "Did I miss something?"

Tessa filled the glass. "Quite a lot actually," she said. "I've experienced a catharsis."

Evelyn felt a little dumb for not having that word in her vocabulary. Tessa must have sensed her hesitance. "A cleansing. Purging." She shrugged. "I'm sorry for being such a bother."

"You're not —"

"I am. In more ways than one. And I know it." She clinked her glass against Summer's. "And I'm determined to change, with God's help."

Evelyn was totally confused. The last she'd seen of Tessa was her angry face as the door slammed. She looked to Summer, trying to silently ask, *What happened?* But Summer just smiled and wiped a milk mustache from her upper lip.

Whatever caused the cath . . . the carth . . . the *change* in Tessa, Evelyn was all for it.

Evelyn took her purse and headed for the door. "Are you sure it's all right?"

Tessa carried a book into the parlor and settled on the couch. Summer played at her toy box nearby, pulling out farm animal figurines. "We're fine. You need to see your old friends. I'm a widow too. I know."

Evelyn nodded. When Yvonne Freidricks had called asking her to go to

281

lunch, Evelyn had told her no. She had Summer to take care of. Yvonne had graciously said, "Bring her along," but Evelyn knew it was said out of politeness more than sincerity. From what Evelyn had seen, Yvonne liked children about as much as Tessa did.

Did might be the key word. Evelyn watched as Summer climbed next to Tessa on the couch, opening a picture book between them. *Miracles do happen.*

And so, because of this particular miracle, Evelyn had called Yvonne back. They were meeting for lunch. The fact that Yvonne was a fairly new widow herself was the clincher. It had been eight months since Yvonne's Harry had died of a heart attack. Evelyn could use some encouragement, and maybe even a few pointers about how to move from months into years.

Drake's was a middle-priced restaurant a block off Carson Creek's square, serving everything from burritos to ribs to chicken salad. Aaron had loved the chicken-fried steak, extra gravy please. As soon as Evelyn walked in the door, she spotted Yvonne, who waved at her from a booth by the window. Water had already been served and a menu sat at her place. Yvonne scooted out and hugged Evelyn tightly.

"Oooh, my poor friend." She let go and stared into Evelyn's eyes. "How *are* you doing?"

Yvonne wasn't a close enough friend for Evelyn to tell her the complete truth, so she fudged and said the word that would propel them into lunch. "Fine."

They sat across from each other. Yvonne tugged at her blazer, smoothing it. "I know you're lying about the 'fine' business, but that's okay. I've found that one of the perks of widowhood is that we're allowed to lie." She leaned over the table and put a hand on Evelyn's. "In fact, it's almost encouraged." She winked.

Evelyn was so disconcerted by Yvonne's suggestion, she had to look away. She looked down. And saw Yvonne's hand. And Yvonne's ring. A huge sapphire surrounded by diamonds. She pulled it close to get a better look. "Gracious, Yvonne, when did you get this?"

Yvonne made her hand teeter, catching the light. "Just a little something I bought last week."

"Why?" The question had slipped out. "I mean . . ."

"I know what you mean, and the answer is, because I could. Because I always wanted pretty jewelry, but when Harry was alive, it wasn't possible — or allowed."

Evelyn understood the *possible* part. "Allowed?"

Yvonne shrugged, the exaggerated shoulder pads in her out-of-date blazer nipping the bottom of her silver pageboy. "You know how it goes. After being married nearly forty years, there was always something breaking down. The dryer, then the refrigerator. I found it quite annoying that the mechanical items in our house seemed to follow our own aging process." Her face clouded. "But at least they could be replaced." She snapped herself out of it by adjusting the ring on her finger. "Anyway, there was little extra money for jewelry, no matter how many catalogs I left open or hints I gave. And I don't blame Harry. He was a wonderful man and a good provider. But romantic he wasn't." She sighed. "Every time I nudged him toward getting me jewelry, I knew it was out of the question, but . . ." She sighed again and gave her ring hand another teeter. ". . . a girl can dream, can't she?"

"So, if you don't mind my asking, where did you get the money to buy it now?"

"Insurance. We might not have been able

to live extravagant lives when Harry was alive, but he certainly made sure I'd have no money troubles after he was gone. No sir, not a one."

Evelyn wanted to ask the next question, she *needed* to ask it, even if it promised to make her feel worse than she already did. "How much did he leave you?"

"A quarter million."

Evelyn fell back against the booth.

"Goodness, Evelyn. Close your mouth. I didn't think it would shock you that much. Especially not after you've been through it too."

Evelyn tried to speak. Tried to think of something appropriate to say. Tried not to be mad at Yvonne, at Harry, at Aaron . . .

"How much did Aaron leave you?"

Evelyn shook her head. No way was she going to tell.

"Ah, come on, Evelyn. It doesn't matter if it's a little less. There's no set number."

Evelyn took a sip of her water and cleared her throat. "Let's just say that the biggest ring I'll be able to afford is the one that comes in a box of Cracker Jack."

It was Yvonne's turn to sit back in shock. "No. He didn't leave you anything?"

Evelyn's resolve not to tell dissipated.

"Ten thousand. And after the funeral expenses . . ."

Yvonne's ring glimmered as she raised her hands in horror. "That's terrible! What was he thinking?"

Although Evelyn had lost her appetite, she picked up the menu. It was a good place to hide.

Tessa set down her book on Elizabeth I, removed her reading glasses, and rubbed her eyes. She couldn't read for extended periods like she used to.

At the other end of the couch, Summer stopped feeding her doll and looked at the cover of the book. "That's fancy."

Tessa put her glasses back on to see the object of Summer's attention. The little girl was pointing at the portrait of the queen on the cover; she was dressed in her royal regalia, including a bejeweled crown and exaggerated ruff. "She was the queen of England a long time ago."

Summer traced a finger across the picture as if trying to touch the finery. "She sure wore a lot of jewelry. Mommy has some jewelry."

"But not like this. This is real."

"Real?"

Tessa realized Summer had no understanding of diamonds, rubies, and emeralds. She remembered the book on the crown jewels she had upstairs. She stood and held out her hand. "Come with me. I have something to show you."

Up in Tessa's room they spread the oversized book on the bed and pored over the pages. Tessa was able to tell the story behind each tiara, scepter, and ring. Summer responded with the appropriate *ooh*s and *aah*s, and even asked a few good questions.

It felt good to be a teacher again — and to have such a willing pupil.

"And I'd really like to have some of those doodads around the side," Gillie said.

At the mention of the odd term Mae blinked. "What?" The younger woman had dropped by Silver-Wear and asked Mae to create a silver bracelet for her sister. They sat together next to one of Mae's display cases. Mae was trying to pay attention, but thoughts of Tessie kept intruding.

Gillie made an exasperated face. "If you're not going to listen to me, Mae, I might as well go to the mall and buy my sister a birthday present from a chain store. But after meeting you, I wanted to give you the business."

Mae shifted in her seat, vowing to concentrate on the designs Gillie wanted on the bracelet. She looked down at the sketch she'd made during their conversation. "Doodads, you say?"

"Yeah, those curly things, like the ones you have etched in your earrings." She waved a finger toward her ears.

Mae put a hand up to remind herself which earrings she was wearing. Once she remembered, she understood. "I can do that for you. No problem."

Gillie sat back, appeased. "Good. And you'll have it done by a week from Monday?"

"Absolutely." Mae wrote up an order form for Gillie to sign, then noticed there was still a line etched between the woman's eyes. "You look bothered."

Gillie looked up and blinked. "I do?"

Mae pointed to the wrinkle. "I'd say that's the Grand Canyon in the making."

Gillie pressed a finger against the wrinkle, as if trying to iron it out. "I've been thinking about my husband lately. My ex-husband."

"Oooh, I've learned it's best not to do that."

Gillie shrugged. "It doesn't hit me often, but when I see another couple really hit it off like Russell and Audra . . ." She shrugged again. "It makes me want what they have. Want that spark. That hopeful intensity."

"I understand completely," Mae said. "I've been divorced for eons, yet witnessing a moment of romance still does me in. How long has it been for you?"

"A year."

"Why, you're still a rookie."

"I feel much, much older than a rookie."

"I think it goes with the territory."

Gillie gathered her parcel. "I'd better go."

"What'd you find shopping?"

Gillie brightened, put the shopping bag down, and pulled out a beautifully wrapped baby blue box with a royal blue bow. "This is for Audra and Summer. It's a little TV to go on their dresser. A house-warming."

"But didn't you give them that fancy doll and a Herman scarf?"

"Hermés." Gillie returned the gift to the bag. "I'm a present junkie. I admit it." She let the sack alone and looked at Mae intently. "I used to love buying myself things. I was an Olympic-caliber shopper. But now it's losing its luster, and to be honest, I find that fact a little disconcerting."

"You like being self-indulgent?"

Gillie smiled at Mae's bluntness. "I had it down to an art. It's all I've ever known. Rich parents. Rich husband."

"But now?"

"I'm finding I like to buy for others more than for myself."

"Sounds like a good progression. If you don't mind my asking, what brought on this burst of philanthropy?"

Gillie looked past her, deep in thought. "Actually . . . the divorce."

Mae laughed. "Usually women get greedy during a divorce, but you've gotten generous?"

Gillie shrugged. "The desire for more broke my marriage. And now, though I still have money for plenty, I need less. Does that make any sense?"

"Absolutely. Now you want to give more to others."

"But giving to others is new to me. Actually, I'm beginning to think successful giving is an art."

"And becoming an artist takes practice."

Gillie nodded and looked down at the display case full of Mae's wares. "You should know. Your work is beautiful, the quality exquisite." She grinned. "Believe me, I only buy the best."

"Thank you, sister. I appreciate the com-

pliment, especially from such a connois-
seur as yourself." Mae pointed to the
sketch. "Your sister will love this bracelet. I
promise."

Gillie took Mae's hand and squeezed.
"I'm so glad I've met you and the others at
Peerbaugh Place. It's like gaining a whole
new set of sisters." She gathered her bag
and left Silver-Wear, the bell on the door
announcing her exit.

Mae stared at the sketch a good minute
before she realized she wasn't *in* the moment, her mind still rehashing this morning's foray with Tessa. Her stomach and
heart fought, as if they'd physically moved
toward each other within her torso, grabbing onto the other in a wrestling match
where there would be no winner.

Sisters.

It was such a wonderful title that Mae
passed around without a second thought.
And yet it was such a strong designation,
conjuring up feelings of a bond, a link, a con-
nection. Even a pact. A cozy closeness where
a woman could feel at ease and wanted.

Wanted, not unwanted. Mae's words to
Tessa flashed front and center: *"Are you
sure you're not here because your family
kicked you out?"*

Mae dropped the sketch on her desk and

placed her elbows on top of it, her head in her hands. "Why did I say such an awful thing?"

True or not true, Mae didn't have a right to say it out loud, no matter how exasperating, annoying, frustrating —

Mae curbed her list of Tessa's faults, realizing they were often her own. Hadn't Tessa mentioned some Bible verse about letting those who had never sinned throw the first stones?

Mae sat up. "I've thrown more than a stone. How about a boulder?" Some sister she was. She'd moved into this special circle of women at Peerbaugh Place only to hurt one of them. She'd created a chink in her circle of sisters, the circle that should remain unbroken.

Circle. Sisters.

An idea popped into her mind. She grabbed a pencil and a fresh piece of sketching paper. . . .

Mae was feeling positively giddy when she went to the city offices to do her favor for Evelyn. Although her newest project for Tessa would take some time, she would rectify the immediate bad feelings by apologizing this evening. And then she would try harder to be a better friend. She was always calling the ladies "sisters." She needed to start treating them as such.

And now it was time to help another sister. A few minutes in the city offices and Evelyn would be in business for real.

No one was at the counter. A hand-written note stating *Ring for service* was propped against a domed bell. Mae popped it twice. A tiny woman who looked as if she might have been around for the groundbreaking of the aging city hall eased her way from a gray metal desk to Mae's presence. Where the counter hit Mae at rib level, it cut the lady at her armpits. She wore a name badge that said *Lyndie*. The name did not suit her.

"Yes?" It was said as a challenge.

"I need some questions answered about a boardinghouse."

Lyndie shook her head. "No such thing."

"Excuse me?"

"No such thing in Carson Creek. And hasn't been since that Peerbaugh Place shut down, back in —" she looked to the water-spotted ceiling — "1962 or three. I could look it up if you want —"

"No, that won't be necessary," Mae said. "And actually, it's Peerbaugh Place I'm talking about. It's reopened."

Lyndie's neck bobbed back like a strutting rooster's. "Can't be."

"Why not?"

"Because we don't have the paperwork."

"So an establishment doesn't exist if you don't have the paperwork?"

"Exactly."

"Uh-huh." What should have been a simple jumping-through-the-red-tape hoop had now become a leap off a high cliff that you couldn't even get to without hiking up steep rocks with a fifty-pound pack on your back, barefoot, in a blizzard.

"I hate to disagree with you, Lyndie. But it *can* be. I live there. Now."

Behind her thick glasses Lyndie's eyes squinted. "Then you'll have to move."

"What?"

"You can't live there if we don't have the paperwork."

"But that's why I'm here. I want to get the paperwork and turn it in. Then Peerbaugh Place will exist — officially and otherwise."

"But if it's already open . . ." Lyndie's head shook again. "This is all backward. Highly irregular and I don't see how I can —"

A man in a polo shirt walking by Lyndie's desk overheard the conversation and detoured to the counter. "Is there a problem?"

Lyndie turned sideways and extended a disdainful hand in Mae's direction as if she were a smear on an otherwise shiny clean window. "This woman says she's living at a boardinghouse, and according to our records it doesn't even exist."

Mae spread her hands like a holy man offering a benediction. "Therefore, I do not exist."

The man smiled ever-so-slightly, giving the impression he was used to Lyndie's ways. He put a hand on the old woman's back. "Actually, Lyndie, if you don't mind, I think I'll handle this special case and let you get back to your work."

Lyndie looked between the two of them, as though assessing if her *not* having to help Mae was a positive or negative bend to her day. She finally nodded and returned to her desk without another word.

The man — wearing a name badge, *Matthew* — opened the swinging partition to the counter and held it for Mae. "Why don't you come back to my desk, and we can get this cleared up. How would that be?"

"That would be grand." Mae strode behind the counter like a queen, giving Lyndie a haughty nod as she passed. *How's this for existing, Lyndie dear?*

Matthew's desk was across the office, with its own window. He offered her the only chair. He was a nice-looking man with wonderful wavy hair, but when Mae made note of his wedding ring, she let all further thoughts in that direction scatter.

Matthew settled behind his desk. "Now, what can I do for you?"

"I am a resident of Peerbaugh Place, a boardinghouse which *does* exist."

"Actually, I've heard of it." He shuffled some papers. "We've had some complaints about it."

Mae resisted the urge to gape at him. "Collier Ames?"

Matthew checked the paper — papers. "Yes. Do you know him?"

"He's the nosy neighbor from across the street." Although Evelyn had told her Collier's complaints, she decided to act innocent. "What's his beef?"

"He doesn't like the extra cars and says the house has become . . . here's his quote, 'noisy, with elevated levels of laughter and loud conversation,' unquote."

Mae raised her eyebrows. "We're too happy?"

"Apparently."

"Would he prefer that we all sat around in the evening and wailed and keened? I'm sure we could rile ourselves up about some sadness: hunger, child abuse, the extinction of some snail darter in the waterways of America."

Matthew laughed. "I'm sure that won't be necessary. We're not dumb, Ms. . . . Ms. . . ."

She reached across his desk and shook his hand. "Mae Fitzpatrick."

He continued, "Ms. Fitzpatrick. We get complaints all the time that are without real merit. The bottom line is, people don't like change, especially in the neighborhoods where they've lived for years."

"But Mrs. Peerbaugh needed to open her house to boarders. Her husband just died, and he left her practically penniless. So this is not some whim. This is her livelihood."

Matthew opened his drawer and dug through files. He pulled out a form. "Then let's fill this out and get it all legal."

Mae felt a wave of relief. "So it's okay for her to keep the house open to tenants?"

"How many rooms are rented out?"

Mae did a mental count. "Three."

"As long as she's got five or under, there are no special rules. Is there a garage?"

"Two-stall."

"I'd suggest you use it. And the

driveway. Avoid parking in the street in front of Mr. Ames's home as much as possible. And keep your levity to a respectable level. Do that, and you'll be fine."

"Whew."

He laughed. "Mrs. Peerbaugh's full name?"

Everything was going to be all right. Peerbaugh Place was officially open for business.

As for Collier Ames? Mae wasn't done with him yet.

Piper wasn't looking forward to seeing Tessa, but she knew it had to be done. The need to apologize for the Bible study fiasco had eaten at her all morning. So much so that she took an early lunch and headed to Peerbaugh Place. It would be awkward dealing with her flaws in front of Evelyn too, but so be it.

When she drove up, Tessa and Summer were on the front porch. *Since when does Tessa like being around kids?*

Piper got out of her car. "Hey, pip-squeak."

Summer came running, meeting Piper on the walk. "Come see. I'm making a crown."

"So you can be Princess Pip-squeak?" Piper let herself be pulled up the porch steps and into Tessa's presence. Yellow construction paper and crayons littered the table in front of the wicker settee. "Hi, Tessa."

A curt nod. "Piper."

Summer picked up a paper crown, colored with pretend jewels. "When I'm done, we're going to tape it in a circle and I can wear it, just like Queen Elizabeth."

"The first," Tessa said.

"She was the queen of England for forty-five years. She had red hair and led a war with Spain."

"Wow. Where did you learn that?"

"Aunt Tessa."

Aunt Tessa? Piper looked to Tessa and saw her shrug. "She's a good little pupil."

Summer went back to coloring. "I get an A plus."

"Yes, you do."

Piper was confused. This was the troubled Tessa that Audra had spoken about? The one who wouldn't come out of her room? The one who'd had it out with Mae?

"What can we do for you, Piper?"

Ah. There it was. A slight edge in her voice that was vintage Tessa. "I just stopped by to apologize for the other day. I shouldn't have challenged

299

you at *your* Bible study."

Tessa hesitated a moment as if she wanted to say one thing but was choosing to say another. "Apology accepted."

And that was that. Piper nodded and headed for her car.

"Piper!" Summer said. "Don't go. We were going to have lunch." She turned to Tessa. "Can Piper have lunch with us?"

Piper intervened before Tessa had to answer. She didn't *want* to have lunch with them. Not today. "No thank you, pip-squeak. I have to get back to school. I just wanted to stop by and tell Tessa I was sorry." She headed down the steps.

Out of the corner of her eye, she saw Tessa stand and move to the railing. "Piper?"

Piper stopped on the stone walk. "Yes?"

"I'm sorry too. You were right to share the truth, no matter who's talking or who's in charge. The truth. That's what's important."

Piper realized what a concession this was. She smiled. "Thanks, Tessa. I'll see you later."

On the way back to school, Piper splurged on a Big Mac and fries. She had something to celebrate.

Audra heard a loud sigh from Gillie as the last of a long line of customers left. "Whew. What brought on that rush? You'd think it was Friday or something."

Audra agreed. For the past hour they'd barely had a moment to look up.

Gillie came into Audra's teller station. "I haven't even had a chance to ask you how your date with boss-man went Friday night." She wiggled her eyebrows suggestively.

Audra straightened the deposit slips. "It was very nice."

Gillie looked stricken. "Nice? Going to Chez Garsaud deserves at least a 'great' just walking in the door. I know. Jerry and I used to go quite often. Plus the fact you shared the experience with a man who's obviously smitten."

"He's not smitten."

Gillie grinned. "Your blush says otherwise."

Audra decided telling Gillie *something* was the best way to shut the conversation down. "We had a nice — a great — evening getting to know each other. He's a fascinating man."

"Oooh, *fascinating*. That is much better than *nice*."

"Glad you think —" She looked up to see Russell coming toward her. His smile was genuine and she returned it. Before leaving, Gillie whispered, "No more slinking through the lobby to catch your eye, huh?"

Nope. No more slinking through the lobby.

"Morning," Russell said.

"Afternoon."

He looked at his watch. "That's the trouble with meetings; they make me lose track of time."

Audra was going to say, *That's my department* but didn't, realizing it might sound too flirty. It was a good line though. If only she were a different kind of woman.

Audra saw people coming in the bank's foyer. "I'd better get back to work. Wouldn't want the boss to think I'm slacking off."

Russell nodded, then added quickly, "Do you like jazz?"

"I love jazz."

"Friday night?"

"That would be grand."

He walked away, and Gillie mouthed over their shared divider, "Grand?"

Definitely grand. Not *nice*, not *great*. *Grand.*

★ ★ ★

Mae was confused. This morning at breakfast, they had all been nervous Nellies because of Tessa, and yet this evening, when they sat around the dinner table, Tessa was positively chirpy, going on and on about her day, and more surprisingly, helping Summer cut her almond chicken.

The vibes were all wrong. The world was out of whack and Mae didn't like it. When Tessa asked Summer to join her in singing a song they'd heard on the radio for the others, Mae couldn't stand the suspense any longer. She made a *T* with her hands. "Okay, that's it. Time out."

"Excuse me?" Tessa asked.

"I feel like I've walked into the middle of a Stanley Kubrick movie." She waved a hand toward Tessa and Summer. "This does not compute. It's as if Cuba and Kansas have made an alliance."

"Is it a crime to be happy?" Tessa applied her huffy face, and its appearance made Mae relax a little. Huffy she could handle.

"Let's just say my curiosity chimes are clanging loudly."

Tessa put a hand on Summer's arm. "Summer and I had a chance to spend some time together today while Evelyn had

303

lunch with a friend. It turns out this little girl is quite smart and inquisitive. She let me teach her all about Queen Elizabeth I and Elizabethan —"

"So you found a sap for your schooling. Really, Tessie, you shouldn't prey on the young. They are far too innocent."

Tessa pulled her hand away from Summer's arm and clenched it under her chin as if Mae had struck her. "That was uncalled for."

Mae replayed her last line to try to figure out what the hubbub was about. "She's just a kid, Tessie."

"A smart kid who showed genuine interest in —"

Was the woman that gullible? "She's a loving kid who would do anything to make any one of us feel good. She wants our approval." She looked at Summer, "No offense, doll face," then back to Tessa. "But to take her kind indulgence of your scholarly tribble as genuine interest . . ." She shook her head. "You're deluding yourself."

Tessa's fingers grappled with her collar.

Evelyn jumped in. "I don't think you're being fair, Mae. Tessa wasn't forcing Summer to be interested. She really was interested, weren't you, sweetie?"

Summer put a green bean in her mouth and touched the yellow construction paper on her head. "We made me a crown."

"You helped her make that?" Mae asked.

Tessa's spine straightened. "I most certainly did."

"Wow. How . . . normal of you." As soon as she said it, Mae realized she'd gone too far. Everyone's face registered varied levels of shock. *What are you trying to do here, Mae? Rile up what has been calmed down? What happened to the lofty bonds of sisterhood? What happened to the Mae Commandment: Thou shalt be nice?*

With great deliberation, Tessa pushed her chair back and stood. "I've lost my appetite. If you'll excuse me."

Audra pushed her plate away. "Me too. If you'll excuse me."

Evelyn watched them go, then got up, her forehead furrowed. "I'd better . . ." She left.

Mae was left at the table with Summer. Summer looked at Mae and then toward the kitchen door. She got off the stool and followed the others.

"Where you going, doll face?"

"They need a hug."

Mae was left alone. A hug sounded good — but unavailable at the moment.

Mae finished cleaning the kitchen, carefully putting away the food so the ladies could heat it up later. She'd expected one of them to return to the kitchen, but none had. Her comment had been just a little thing. A joke. *"How normal of you."*

How normal of you, Mae. To say too much. To be so sarcastic your words chide. Why can't you keep your mouth shut?

Mae left the kitchen to find the others. She heard voices and glanced upstairs, but Audra's and Tessa's doors were open, the rooms quiet. She listened again. The conversation was coming from the front porch. She stood at the door, listening.

Evelyn was talking, "It just galled me that she would be so flip."

Mae's stomach clenched.

Audra spoke. "She was just showing off. It's her way, isn't it?"

"I suppose so. And she didn't mean to be offensive."

"But she was," Tessa said. "She was being impudent and hurtful, whether she meant to or not."

Mae felt her blood boil. *You should talk, Tessie. You own the hurtful concession. I was just renting it.*

"Just stay away from her for a while,"

Audra said. "That's probably best. At least until you feel stronger."

"And she feels nicer."

Okay. That was it. There was no way Mae was going to stay quiet. How would Peerbaugh Place survive such a situation? It had to be cleared up now. Even if it meant she had to . . .

She burst through the front door and into their presence. "Okay, sisters. That's it. I hereby present myself before you, ready to eat crow any way you want it served: boiled, fried, fricasseed, or raw." She stood before them, her face raised to the sky, her eyes closed, her arms outstretched. A willing sacrifice.

When they didn't say anything, she opened one eye and peered at them.

"What are you doing, Mae?" Audra asked.

"You look like a zealous scarecrow," Tessa said.

Mae dropped her arms. "I'm willing to sacrifice myself for the good of the house, and this is the thanks I get?"

Evelyn looked at the others. "We have no idea what you're talking about."

Mae leaned against the railing for support. "I heard Evelyn complaining about me. And then Audra said I was showing off, and Tessie said that I was being impudent and hurtful."

"But —"

Mae put up a hand. "And though I may be all of those things, I have to tell you that I don't want any of you to avoid me. Just tell me to my face so I can put a lid on myself. I can do that, you know."

With a sudden burst, they all laughed. The sound was unnerving. Mae stood erect and drilled her fists into her hips. "What's so funny?"

Audra used a finger to wipe a tear from under her eye. "Oh, Mae, this is too funny. For you to think . . ."

"We weren't talking about you," Tessa said.

"We were talking about Yvonne Freidricks," Evelyn said. "She's a friend of mine who was widowed eight months ago. I went to lunch with her, and she showed me a huge ring she'd bought with her husband's insurance money."

"She's the one who's impudent and hurtful," Tessa said. "Though I must admit, you do have your moments."

"So this isn't about me?"

"Not this time," Audra said.

Mae sank onto the rocker. "So I wasted all this good repentance for nothing?"

"Oh, no, no," Evelyn said. "We'll take it. We're not ones to turn down a good confession."

"Especially if it's warranted." Audra grinned.

"And it was good, wasn't it?" Mae asked.

"A-number one."

Tessa's head was nodding in a constant motion. "God likes confessions." She glanced at the others, then down. "And I guess it's time I offered my own. I'm sorry for being so difficult. Besides upsetting the household, I know God doesn't approve of difficult people, so I wasn't pleasing Him much either. Will you ladies forgive me?"

"Certainly."

"Of course."

Tessa turned to Mae. "And you? Do you forgive me?"

Mae was confused. Although Tessa had been a pain, Mae couldn't see that she'd done anything that warranted her being forgiven.

"Mae?" Audra asked. "What's wrong?"

"I was just thinking that all this forgiveness talk is a little harsh. Saying *I'm sorry* is one thing, but asking for forgiveness?" She shook her head. "Isn't that going overboard?"

"Not at all," Audra said. She looked to

Tessa as if asking permission to answer for them both.

Tessa extended an opened hand, urging her to speak. Mae was glad. Whatever was going to be said, she'd rather hear it from Audra.

"Since Jesus died to forgive all our sins — past, present, and future — it's up to us to forgive each other."

Tessa spoke up. "And to try to be the best people we can be — to make Him proud."

They were getting too heavy for her tastes. Mae shook her head. "But sin . . . Tessa and I just had a little disagreement, exchanged a few harsh words; that's hardly a sin."

"I disagree," Audra said. " 'A truly wise person uses few words; a person with understanding is even-tempered. Even fools are thought to be wise when they keep silent; when they keep their mouths shut, they seem intelligent.' "

Mae had heard that somewhere before. Then she remembered. "Didn't Mark Twain say that last part?"

Audra smiled. "The Bible said it first."

Mae raised an eyebrow. *What do you know?* She'd never considered the Bible to hold anything especially wise — and certainly not witty.

"So you see, most words said in anger are in the wrong. And being in the wrong is not being in the right. And being right is good and what God wants for us. Therefore, being wrong is a sin." Audra laughed at herself. "I think that makes sense. Doesn't it?"

"It makes sense to me," Evelyn said.

Tessa slapped her hands on her knees. " 'Be kind to each other, tenderhearted, forgiving one another, just as God through Christ has forgiven you.' That says it all."

It certainly said a lot. The words hung in the air and Mae tried to digest them. All this God-talk was new to her. How ironic that she, a woman who'd left God behind decades ago, would end up in a house with not one but two Bible-quoting women. And Piper too. Zounds, she was surrounded.

She cleared her throat. She may not have completely understood this forgiveness process, but no one would say that Mae Fitzpatrick couldn't apologize and feel contrite with the best of them. "I'm sorry too, Tessie." She nodded to the others, including them. "Sorry to all of you. I know my mouth often breaks away from my brain and I say too much." She suddenly remembered Audra's recent words. "And so I apologize and ask your forgiveness for my words, past, present, and unfortunately — but inevitably — future."

The women laughed. "You're forgiven, Mae," Audra said.

"You didn't need to do that, but I forgive you too," Evelyn said.

Tessa nodded once. "Well done."

Mae experienced a surge of pride and grabbed onto the feeling. Perhaps this forgiveness stuff was also a part of sisterhood. Interesting.

The others went inside, leaving Mae on the porch. It had already been an eventful day. An emotional day. Relationships were so complicated. If only people would just get along.

She spotted Collier Ames with a broom out on his porch. But he was doing more than sweeping. His gaze repeatedly strayed across the street toward her. Most likely he'd witnessed the entire incident with her dramatic act of repentance. Would the city receive another complaint?

Mae made an instant decision. She strode down the porch steps and across the street toward Collier's home. He stopped sweeping and stared at her approach as if determining whether to retreat or prepare his broom for battle.

"Mr. Ames!"

He took a tentative step to the edge of his porch, the broom held diagonally across his chest. "Yes?"

Mae thought about positioning herself at the bottom of the steps, but then realized she would be forced to converse looking up at him. Hardly a power position. So she continued her stride up the steps to his side. He took a step back, his eyes registering his shock. She tried to appease him with a smile and an extended hand. "Mae Fitzpatrick. Your neighbor."

He had to let the broom resume its rightful position touching the floor. He wiped his palm on his pants. "Collier Ames."

The greeting obstacle hurdled, Mae took a moment to recognize that Collier Ames was a nice-looking man. Six-foot, sixtyish, with a face that reminded her of Anthony Hopkins in his non–Hannibal Lecter roles. And he had very nice eyes that she imagined could twinkle if he let them.

"What can I do for you, Ms. Fitzpatrick?"

"Call me Mae." She cocked a head toward Peerbaugh Place. "You saw? And heard?"

He nodded. "I didn't mean to."

Yeah, right. I wouldn't be surprised if you had a set of binoculars at the window.

He continued. "This is a quiet neighborhood, and I really don't approve of domestic squabbles held on the front porch for all to witness."

"So you'd prefer they were held inside, behind closed doors?"

His eyebrows furrowed as though he was afraid this was a trick question.

Mae was not about to discuss the problems of Peerbaugh Place with this man, no matter how handsome he was. She decided to take the offense. "I heard you've been to the city complaining about us."

His nod came after a moment's hesitation. "I'm glad they contacted you —"

"They didn't contact us. They realize your grievances are frivolous, the interference of a bored man who has too much time on his hands."

His eyebrows raised. "But —"

She stopped his words with a hand. "Let me assure you that Peerbaugh Place will be an asset to this neighborhood. Evelyn is a dear woman who has opened her home to us, and slowly but surely, we are creating a family. And isn't that what neighborhoods are about? Family? And though I apologize for any extravagant laughing or frivolity that may occur within those walls, I — we — refuse to let you rain on our parade."

"But —"

"But if you have any valid beefs, then I'd ask that you come talk to us directly. We are not unreasonable women, Mr. Ames. But we are women full of zest for life, and we will not let any cantankerous neighbor —"

She noticed he was smiling. "Are you married?"

For once in her life, Mae was speechless.

Tessa left the house, on her way to choir practice, when she heard Mae's laughter coming from across the street. She squinted her eyes to see in the light of dusk. Mae was leaning against the porch column while the neighbor man leaned against a broom. Their talk was animated, and the way they bent toward each other and away made Tessa think of a courting dance.

Mae looked her way and lifted a hand in a wave. Tessa flipped a quick motion but hurried to her car. She didn't want to en-courage Mae's love life.

The woman had no morals. None at all.

* * *

Mae walked back to Peerbaugh Place in a daze.

Evelyn met her on the porch, worry in her eyes. "I saw you go across the street, saw you talking with Collier . . . what happened?"

Mae used the railing to climb the steps. She looked back to Collier's. He stood on the porch and waved. She didn't have the strength to wave back.

Evelyn took her arm and helped her up the last step. "Goodness, Mae. Did he yell at you? Did he hurt — ?"

Mae motioned that she wanted to go inside. Evelyn held the door. Mae moved to the couch in the parlor and sank onto the cushions. She needed to preface the answers to Evelyn's questions, but by doing so, she found the entire thing even more confusing.

Evelyn sat beside her. "Mae. You're scaring me."

She shook her head, clearing her thoughts. "I went to the city today and got the license taken care of."

It took Evelyn a moment to change the direction of her thoughts. "That's great. But what — ?"

"Collier hasn't just been complaining to

you; he's been complaining about us to the city."

"Oh no . . ."

"But it's all right. I talked to a nice man at the city offices who says it's just frivolous stuff about loud laughter and parking on the street. But he did suggest we use the driveway for parking as much as possible."

"That's not a problem, but the laughing . . . ?"

"I know. It's ridiculous. That's why I went across the street to talk to Collier. Especially after my confession to the world. I'm afraid he saw and heard everything. Fuel for the gossip grist."

"Oh dear. Is he going to complain again?"

Now came the confusing part. "Actually, no. At least I don't think so."

"You talked him out of it?"

"Maybe."

"Mae, you're not making any sense."

Exactly. The last ten minutes hadn't made *any* sense.

Evelyn leaned closer to Mae, whispering as if Collier was within earshot. "I think the best course of action is to stay away from him as much as possible."

"That's going to be difficult."

"Why? We've never been close, just a

wave here and there."

"For you, it's possible. For me . . ."

"Mae . . ."

"I have a date with him Friday night."

Evelyn's jaw dropped. "You what?"

Mae stood and began to pace. "I was ranting at him, giving him my best shot, when all of a sudden he grins at me and asks if I'm married. Then the next thing I know, he's asking me for a date."

"But you don't like the man. You don't even know him."

Mae tossed her hands in the air. "He caught me off guard. For some bizarre reason he was charmed by my ranting and became charming himself." She looked toward Collier's house, trying to replay the turn of events. "Before I knew it, he was asking me out, and I was saying yes. He blew me away."

Evelyn laughed. "Glad to know someone can."

9

Return, O Lord, and rescue me.
Save me because of your
unfailing love.
PSALM 6:4

Piper was met at the office door by Heather, one of her fellow high school counselors. "Where have you been, Piper? We left a message."

Piper thought of her cell phone turned off in her purse. And had she checked her messages last night at home? Probably not. She'd had a committee meeting at church and had stayed late to help organize the library. Then it had been a hot bath and bed.

Piper noticed the entire office was agitated, people moving about with a determined step instead of the usual casual gait. "What's going on?"

"Justin Warden's house caught on fire last night, and his six-year-old sister was killed. Justin's in the hospital. He's doing okay, but he's suffered severe burns."

Since Justin was a sophomore and Piper

handled the seniors, she only knew *of* him. As the sophomore counselor, Heather would be taking the brunt of the counseling. "What's the plan? What can I do?"

"Besides dealing with the grief and Justin's injuries, the family doesn't have any insurance — medical or otherwise. The house is horribly damaged. We want you to be in charge of setting up a fundraiser for the community. Maybe distribute some collection boxes to local businesses."

Piper's mind was already buzzing with a to-do list. "I'll call Carson Creek National and have them set up a fund where people can send larger amounts."

The principal came out of her office and crooked a finger at Heather. She turned to leave. "Go to it, Piper. I trust you completely."

Audra was surprised to see Piper in her line. They exchanged a smile. Audra handed a receipt to a customer. "Thank you, Mr. Beasley. Have a nice day."

Piper moved front and center.

"I didn't know you had an account here."

"I don't," Piper said. She pulled out a small cardboard box with a slot in it. A sticker proclaimed *Warden Family Fund.*

Gillie looked over from the next station. "Who are the Wardens?"

Piper told her the story of the Wardens' tragedy. "Can I put this on the counter?"

"You'll have to ask Russell."

Piper grinned. "Oh, I'd love to meet your elusive Mr. Peerbaugh."

"Piper . . . he's not my —"

Gillie interrupted. "He most certainly is. Chez Garsaud is not a place you take a coworker — unless you want it to be more."

Piper drilled Audra with a look. "Speaking of . . . you never did tell me the details of your dinner."

Audra shrugged. "I didn't want to make a big thing —"

Piper glanced around the lobby, then reached out and touched Audra's hand. "Make a big thing. *Please* make a big thing. Don't you know I'm living vicariously through you?"

Audra couldn't remember the last time Piper had had a decent date. And it wasn't because she wasn't attractive, smart, witty. . . . Sometimes romance — or the lack of it — didn't make sense. "You want romance, you'd be best to rent a Cary Grant–Deborah Kerr movie."

Gillie sighed. "She always got to wear

the most luscious clothes. Tiny waist, flowing skirts."

Piper made a flipping motion off the right side of her head. "And funny little hats with feathers in them."

Gillie laughed. "I know the one you're talking about. She wore it with a ball gown in *Indiscreet*. Silly looking thing. But other than that —"

Audra realized they'd been chatting far too long. "Can the fashion patrol wait until later? We have work to do."

Piper straightened her shoulders. "So right. Actually, I need to talk to Russell about establishing a fund where people can send larger contributions for the Wardens."

Audra saw Russell walking by and caught his eye, motioning him over. "Here he is now."

Piper stood aside, waiting for him. Her face was blatantly transparent, showing she approved of what she saw. How could she not? Russell was a striking man.

"Do you need something, Audra?"

Audra introduced Russell and Piper, then let Piper take over the explanation.

"Certainly, you can set a box here. One at each teller station if you'd like. And if you'll come into my office, I'll get that fund account set up."

Piper beamed at Audra. Russell's cache of brownie points was near to overflowing.

Suddenly out of nowhere, Gillie retrieved her purse from beneath the counter and pulled out a bill. "I'll be the first to contribute," she said. Audra thought that was nice — and so like Gillie — and reached for her own purse to give a few dollars. She could even top Gillie's one bill — until Gillie displayed the bill and Audra saw its denomination. Ben Franklin's face smirked at his audience.

Piper grabbed the bill on its way to the collection box. "Gillie! This is a hundred dollars."

Gillie shrugged, but Audra noticed a fresh glow to her cheeks. "It's nothing." She looked around the bank at the other employees who were within earshot, as well as two customers who were coming through the door. "We all should give as much as we can. This poor family needs us."

Then, to Audra's horror, Gillie grabbed the contribution box, came around to the front of the teller area, and began going desk to desk collecting — shaming people into giving. Audra looked at Russell to check his reaction. He kept fingering the sleeve edge of his suit coat. His eyes repeatedly glanced at Gillie, then looked away as if he couldn't bear to watch but was drawn to do exactly that.

Even Piper seemed a bit uneasy. She was smiling, but her face was flushed. Audra was sure she hadn't meant to draw so much attention, nor disrupt the bank's business. When Gillie finished her rounds and headed straight for Russell, Audra's stomach clenched. Russell's fingers stopped their tracings and flinched in the direction of his wallet. Nothing like pushing their boss into a corner.

Gillie stopped front and center. "Your turn, Mr. Peerbaugh. What do you say?"

What does he say? How about "You're fired, Ms. Danson."

Russell opened his wallet and pulled out a bunch of bills — Audra caught sight of at least three twenties — folded them in two, and shoved them in the slot. There was no flashy one-hundred-dollar bill.

Gillie shoved a corner of a bill all the way in. "There. How's that?"

If she expected wild displays of gratitude, she was no doubt disappointed. Piper mumbled, "Thanks," Audra turned her attention to a customer, and Russell looked to Piper and extended an arm in the direction of his office.

"Shall we go set up that fund account, Ms. Wellington?"

They left, leaving Gillie standing alone in the lobby with the contribution box. Other eyes looked away. Gillie's face fell, and the word *what?* formed on her lips.

More than anything, Audra wanted to get her out of the middle of the lobby. The odd thing was, Gillie hadn't done anything wrong. Not really. Gillie looked to the floor awkwardly, then returned to her station. She set the box on the ledge spanning the front of the counter. With the soft brush of the paper box against laminate, Gillie seemed to snap out of her daze. "So. What's the problem here, Audra? I don't get it."

It was a loaded question that would be better addressed later. In private.

Evelyn watched as Summer disappeared into the tent made with blankets. In a moment, her face filled the opening. "This is so neat, Aunt Evelyn. It's my very own house."

Evelyn adjusted the clothespins holding two of the blanket-tents together. "I used to help Russell make these. One time he had the entire dining room covered with tents." She knelt to see inside.

Summer scooted between two dining chairs and gave Evelyn a tour. "This can be my kitchen, and under this chair can be where my baby sleeps." She suddenly lunged for the exit, forcing Evelyn to move back. "I have to get my dishes. And my doll stuff."

Little girls were so different. If only . . .

While Summer ran to gather her toys, Evelyn went in the parlor and retrieved some pillows, an afghan, and some picture books. The two met in the foyer. "Here's stuff to make a bed for you and some books to read."

"Reading in bed. Just like Mommy does." Summer's voice revealed that this was the greatest luxury. She crawled into the tent, pushing her doll stuff ahead of her. "Can I have a lamp like Mommy?"

"That can be arranged." Evelyn did a survey of the parlor, but all the lamps were too large. Then she remembered seeing one in the attic. "You get settled. I'll go find you a lamp."

Summer popped her head out, repeating her mantra. "This is so neat, Aunt Evelyn. Thank you."

"You're welcome, sweetie. I'll be right back."

Evelyn went upstairs and pulled the attic steps down into the hallway. It's a good thing she'd been up there recently, or she never would have remembered a lamp Summer could use.

Evelyn climbed the stairs, flipped on the attic light, and spotted the lamp right away. But as she passed the trunks she thought of another addition to Summer's play-house. Clothes. She flipped open a lid and was assailed with the smell of mothballs. She lifted a red crepe dress from its folds. It had beading on the shoulders — very thirties. She remembered Aaron's mother wearing it in a picture.

Evelyn dug through the other garments, feeling like a little girl herself. That was her one regret about having only a son. She'd never gotten to share the joy of playing dress-up with a daughter.

Her daughter.

Evelyn's eyes were drawn to the dressing table across the room. To the drawer. To the picture.

She set aside the clothes and moved toward it, needing to bond with what could have been. For she'd had a baby. A little girl wrapped in a pink blanket, her Gerber-baby mouth pulled tight as if she were waiting for a kiss.

I gave her kisses, over and over, until they took her away.

Evelyn pulled open the drawer and retrieved the one picture she had of her daughter: a color photo taken at the hospital by a kind nurse. Evelyn, holding her baby in her arms, gazing at her eyes, trying to lock in the sight of her so she'd never forget.

And she hadn't forgotten. Not for a moment. But the memories had been forced underground. For not even Aaron had known about the baby that had come before him. She'd often wanted to tell him, but as the years flew by, it had seemed safer — and easier — to let the past be the past.

Keeping it to herself had also made the secret special. Having this one picture in this one drawer that was hers alone. Evelyn and her baby girl. Mother and child.

Evelyn kissed the picture. Where was her daughter now? Was she thriving? She looked down at the picture. She was probably married by now, with many children. Evelyn's grandchildren she would never know.

If only Russell would get married and give her grandchildren. Maybe their presence would ease the pain of the could-have-beens.

"Aunt Evelyn? Are you up there?"

Summer. Evelyn put the picture back in its drawer. She needed to count her blessings. She *did* have a little girl to love. Not her blood, but a little girl, just the same. And she planned to do a good job of it too.

"Coming, sweetie."

Evelyn made grilled cheese sandwiches and brought a tray into the dining room, to Summer's tent city. She bent down at the opening. "Lunch is served. I thought we'd eat in your —"

She saw Summer lying on the pillows, but the little girl wasn't reading or even taking a nap. She was wrapped in the afghan, drawn up like a cocoon. Wisps of hair were matted against her face by sweat.

"Sweetie!" Evelyn dove into the tent, her hand on Summer's forehead before her feet made it through the opening. "You're burning up."

Summer opened one eye. "I don't feel too good."

Evelyn's first instinct was to pick her up and hold her close, but in the cramped quarters, that was impossible. Instead she peeled off the afghan and backed out of the tent, urging Summer to follow her. "Come out now. We need to get you to bed."

"But my tent city . . ."

"You can play in your tent when you're better."

Summer reluctantly followed, her movements like those of an old person, as if each one took effort. Once they were free of the tent, Evelyn took the girl in her arms and carried her upstairs.

In Summer's and Audra's room, Evelyn pulled back the covers and set her on top. "Get in, sweetie, and I'll get —"

Summer did not snuggle into the softness as Evelyn expected. Instead she scooted off the bed and began pulling the covers back up. "Mommy doesn't like the bed mussed up during the day." She carefully pulled the heading of the sheet over the edge of the blanket and smoothed it. She replaced the bedspread, a maid doing her duty.

What the — ?

Evelyn took a quick inventory of their room. She hadn't been inside since that first day. It was in perfect order. Almost too much order. A hanging jewelry rack on the wall had longer necklaces to the left, progressing to the shortest ones on the right. Stuffed animals were lined up on the window seat, each placed at attention, like toy soldiers guarding their post, not a single floppy ear out of place. A stack of magazines sat in the corner, their spines even and in the same direction. It was a good bet they were stacked in chronological order.

Summer's head met her rib cage. "Can I lie down in your room?"

"Sure, sweetie."

When they moved to Evelyn's room, she was struck by the difference in tone between the two spaces. Though Evelyn's may not have been decorated in the most stylish manner, it was cozy. It was inviting. It was lived in.

Summer took to the soft mattress and quilt immediately, snuggling in, accepting the comfort. Evelyn tucked the quilt around her, like she used to do with Russell. "There. Is that better?"

"Mm-hmm." Summer's eyes closed, then opened. "I like the stars on the blanket. Pretty."

"It's called the Seven Sisters quilt. Seven stars in a circle, just like the seven of us."

Summer nodded and snuggled deeper.

"I'm going to get a thermometer and take your temperature."

Summer tried to nod, but before she could finish the motion, she was asleep.

Peppers jumped on the bed and snuggled into the crook of Summer's legs. Evelyn tiptoed out of the room. Summer was in good hands. Sleep was the best thing. It would take Evelyn awhile to find the thermometer anyway. As she headed to the bathroom she shared with Tessa, Evelyn detoured, ending up back in Audra's room. No, she wasn't mistaken. It was sterile, cold. Too . . . planned. There was no living here, just order.

On impulse, Evelyn opened the walk-in closet. Her expectations were realized. The clothes were smooth and color coordinated, blues leading to greens, to yellows, and finally to oranges and reds. Everything was hung on identical white tube hangers. Three little-girl dresses hung at one end. Color-coordinated boxes filled the shelves, all neatly labeled: Sweaters, Purses, Winter Pants. Shoes hung on a rack on the back of the door, every pair situated properly, left to the left, right to the right. Evelyn took a black pump from the rack and studied its leather. Polished. No scuffs. She chose one of Summer's shoes and found it in similar condition. *I wonder if she has to polish them herself.*

She was surprised by the question, and yet, in light of Summer's actions, it didn't seem out of line. Although Evelyn had never seen any evidence that Summer was mistreated in any way — though Audra *was* strict — the basis for her always needing to help became clearer. It was expected of her.

And yet . . . Summer seemed to really enjoy helping. There was probably no way to pinpoint which came first, the helping or the desire to help. Some of that helping instinct had to be natural or Summer would be a different kind of child. Rebellious. And she was anything but that.

Evelyn suddenly remembered the sick child in the bed. Enough of this snooping and psychoanalyzing. She had a thermometer to find. Yet as she headed back to her bathroom, she had the thought that Audra wouldn't have to search for such a thing. She'd know exactly where it was.

"I'll come home right away."

Evelyn calmed her. "Audra, there's no need. She'll be fine. It's just the flu. Temperature of one hundred point four."

Audra looked to the bank's exit, wishing to flee. "But I don't want her to be any trouble."

"Nonsense. You've only been at the job two weeks.. You have no sick time built up. It's under control. I promise. Right now she's cuddled into my bed, taking a —"

"Your bed?"

"Uh . . . yes. I tried putting her in your room, but she didn't want to muss the covers. I didn't think you'd mind, but she was adamant."

Audra took a deep breath, finding calm. Why couldn't she ease up on her need for order? How many times had her own mother chastised her, saying, "Audra, she's just a little girl." Audra knew what she *should* do, but found it incredibly hard to do it.

"Audra, if you want, call me later."

Audra's guilt rode her shoulders like a burdened pack. "I'm sorry you have to handle all this, Evelyn. And I'm sorry . . . she could've slept in our room." It sounded as lame as it was.

"I know that. But be assured, she's doing fine here with Aunt Evelyn. Truly."

Audra said her good-byes and went back to work, fighting a twinge of an emotion she had a hard time defining. And then it hit her like a two-by-four across the back of the legs, and she felt herself buckle at the knowledge.

Summer *was* doing fine at home, snug in Aunt Evelyn's bed.

Better off there than with her mother?

★ ★ ★

Gillie searched out Audra during her break and found her seated at the breakroom table, looking at a magazine. Gillie cut herself a brownie from the pan someone had brought in. "Want one?" she asked.

Audra looked up, shook her head, then looked down.

Gillie took a seat across from her. "That's real nice of Piper to start the donation drive for that poor family."

Audra turned the page. "Yes, it is."

"I heard Russell say the donation account is set up too."

Another page. "Good."

She squashed a brownie crumb with a finger and ate it. "Are you mad at me?"

Audra glanced at her. "Summer's sick. I'm mad at myself for not being there."

"What kind of sick?"

"Evelyn says it's the flu. She'll be all right." Audra said the words as if trying to convince herself. "But truth be, I'm a little peeved at you too."

"Why's that?"

Audra ran a hand across her face. "Oh, never mind. I'm in a bad mood. I shouldn't say anything."

"No, go ahead. I want you to." Gillie

wasn't sure if that was the truth or not. She braced herself.

Audra took a deep breath. "I'm disappointed in you. Because of your donation."

I gave a hundred dollars. What does she want? She cleared her throat. "What's the problem? I gave more than anyone."

Audra shook her head and adjusted her glasses. "It's not the amount. The amount was generous."

"Then why are you looking at me as if I just robbed the bank?"

Audra closed the magazine and clasped her hands on top of it. "It's the way you did it, Gillie. We've been friends for a long time, and I know you're the one who got me this job." Audra took a breath. "Please know that I'm far from perfect in this respect either, but —"

"Audra, if you preface another sentence with a disclaimer, I'm going to toss all these brownies in the trash and hold you responsible."

"You gave so everyone saw."

Gillie replayed the moment in her mind. She'd taken the hundred-dollar bill from her purse. . . . "I don't get it."

"Giving so publicly . . . it makes everyone else feel guilty if they *didn't* give or couldn't give as much."

"I'm not responsible for what other people give or don't give. Besides, the bank encourages charity giving. It's good for business."

"And good for your career?"

Gillie drew back. "Now that's a slap in the face."

Audra looked down. "Forget I said anything. I never meant to hurt —"

"No, no. I can take whatever you've got to dish —"

"Gillie . . ."

Gillie pushed her brownie aside. "If I could take the money back, believe me, I would. Far be it for me to offer tainted money." She thought about the TV she had wrapped in her car. She'd meant to drop it off all week, but things had come up. She'd planned on dropping by and giving it to Audra this evening. But now . . .

Audra pushed her chair back, standing. "I shouldn't have said anything. I'd better get back. You coming?"

"In a minute. Eventually." The door to the break room closed and Gillie sat in the silence, taking little comfort in the company of her motives.

Russell caught up with Audra as she settled in after her break. "We still on for tonight? There's live jazz at the Grace Note and —"

"Oh dear . . . I'm sorry. I can't. Summer's sick."

She was pleased to see concern on his face.

"What's wrong with her?" he asked.

"It's just the flu, but your mom's had to take care of her all day, so I need to be there tonight."

"I understand. Though that doesn't mean I'm not disappointed . . . maybe tomorrow night?"

"We'll see."

Piper's day had been spent running around town, distributing donation boxes. It wasn't difficult work, but for someone used to being in a school office all day it was draining. By the time school was out, she was ready for a little fun. And that meant shopping. It didn't matter that she didn't need anything; it was the process that was relaxing. Besides, even if *she* didn't need anything, she knew someone who did.

Evelyn answered the door holding a bed tray. She put a finger to her lips. "Shh. Summer's sick."

Piper's eyes were drawn upstairs immediately. "What's wrong?"

"I think it's the flu. Fever, body aches." Evelyn lifted the tray. "I was bringing her some chicken soup. She wasn't hungry at lunchtime, but just now she said she felt like eating something, so that's good."

"Can I see her?"

"Come on up. Tessa's up there too."

Piper was confused when, at the top of the stairs, Evelyn bypassed Summer's room.

"She's in my room." As soon as Evelyn made this statement, she paused in the hall. "Maybe you can explain something for me. Summer didn't want to be in their bed because she said her mom didn't like it mussed up during the day. It seemed a little —" she made a face — "a little compulsive."

"That's Audra. Everything in its place."

"A virtue, I'm sure," Evelyn said. "But when it goes so far that a child doesn't feel comfortable getting in her own bed . . ."

Piper tried to think of some defense for Audra, but there wasn't any. Only facts. "I think besides being her nature, Audra has found comfort in being organized. She's had to be in order to survive her situation."

Evelyn nodded.

Piper pointed to the soup, which was

getting cold. "She's hungry?"

They went in Evelyn's room, where Summer was holding court in Evelyn's four-poster. Tessa sat in the chair, reading aloud, " 'One fish, two fish, red fish, blue fish . . .' "

"Lunch is served," Evelyn announced. "Sit up, sweetie."

Summer scooted back against the head-board, and Piper adjusted the pillows. "When did you get here, Piper?"

"Just a minute ago." She remembered her mission, and though she wasn't sure it was possible anymore, decided to mention it. "I came to take your Aunt Evelyn shopping for her bedroom reconstruction. But now —"

"Go on," Tessa said, flipping a hand at them. "I can take care of Summer." She patted a stack of books she'd brought in. "We have plenty to do."

"She needs to rest too," Evelyn said, tucking a napkin under Summer's chin.

"Gracious green eggs and ham, Evelyn. I'm not going to bore the girl or keep her up when she wants to sleep. I'm not insensitive, you know."

Evelyn smiled. "Gracious green eggs and ham? You sound like Mae."

Tessa shook her head. "Heaven forbid."

"So . . . ," Piper said. "Shall we go?"

"Is it okay with you, sweetie?"

Summer nodded as she slurped a spoonful of soup.

Tessa woke up and found herself slumped in a chair. It took her a moment to remember where she was. Evelyn's room. With Summer.

But Summer wasn't there.

Tessa stood quickly, making her muscles scream. The covers of the bed were turned back. "Summer? Where are you, girl?"

"I'm down here." The voice came from the foyer.

Tessa went into the hall and looked over the railing. Summer was negotiating the last step, carrying the bed tray full of dishes.

"What *are* you doing, child?"

Summer got to the foyer floor and looked up. "I'm taking the dishes to the kitchen."

"I can see that. But why? You're sick. You're not supposed —"

"Mommy says I should always put my dishes away."

"That's true — under normal conditions. But when you're sick, we're supposed to wait on you."

Summer looked down at the dishes. "I don't have to . . . ?"

"You don't have to. Wait right there." Tessa held the railing and went downstairs. She took the bed tray and headed into the kitchen.

At the kitchen door she glanced back and saw Summer following her. "Get back to bed, Summer."

"I can help put them away. I feel better."

This was ridiculous. Tessa set the tray on the counter and pointed upstairs. "You turn around right this very minute, and get back —"

Summer's shoulders sagged as if Tessa had pulled the plug on her air supply and she was deflating. Her lip quivered.

"What's wrong?"

Summer's eyes flitted back and forth as if she had no idea how to answer the question, or that she knew an answer but couldn't find the words.

Tessa knelt beside her. "Summer. Tell me."

Tears filled Summer's eyes and overflowed in one huge tear per eye that dive-bombed to the floor. "I don't want Mommy to get mad at me."

What? "Your mommy won't get mad at

you for being sick, Summer. She loves you very much."

Summer shook her head. "She might. If I don't help. She always likes it when I help."

Tessa's heart grabbed at the implication of the little girl's thought. The poor child felt she needed to earn her mother's love.

Though Tessa couldn't remember the last time she'd hugged anyone, she grabbed the girl and pulled her into her arms, feeling it necessary to hug such absurd ideas away. "Oh, child; dear, dear, child . . . you can be sure your mother loves you just because you're you. She's not going to love you more because you put the dishes away or make your bed or —"

Summer pulled back enough to see Tessa's face. "— make my animals stand in a straight row?"

"Or make your animals stand in a straight row." Tessa let go and used her thumb to wipe Summer's cheeks. "Mommies love their children just because. Do you believe me?"

Summer nodded; then she cocked her head as if she remembered something. "Jesus loves me too."

Tessa was impressed. For a five-year-old to know that . . . Audra must be doing something right.

"Mrs. Berry at Sunday school says God loves us all the time, even when we're bad."

"That's true. And so do mommies."

"And if I'm really, really good, then I get to go to heaven." Her forehead created a wrinkle. "Right?"

Tessa's mind soared back to the Bible study. Hadn't she virtually said the same thing? And hadn't Piper and the others pounced on her, saying she was wrong?

"Isn't that right, Aunt Tessa?"

Tessa moved from kneeling to sitting, right there on the kitchen floor. She felt as if someone had knocked the wind out of her. Maybe Someone had.

For hadn't she just witnessed the lie in such a belief? Summer had mistakenly thought she needed to do things to earn her mother's love. It was absurd. But no more absurd than Tessa's belief that she needed to do things to earn God's love, to earn the ultimate reward of God's love: heaven. Piper and the others were right.

And I was wrong. Oh, so wrong.

"Are you okay, Aunt Tessa?"

She wasn't sure. She reached for Summer, drawing her in. "You don't have to do anything to make your mommy love you, and you don't have to do anything to make God love you. You just have to believe in your mom and believe in Jesus. The love is a gift. And we don't get to heaven by doing good things, either. That's a gift, too."

"Like a present?"

Tessa smiled. "Like a present."

"I like presents."

"Me too." And Tessa felt as if she'd just received a big one. The present of another chance. "Help me to my feet, child. And let's get you back to bed so you can get well."

"But I feel well now."

"You may feel well now, but you still need to take time to completely heal."

As they climbed the stairs hand in hand, Tessa realized her words to Summer were applicable to herself as well.

Evelyn took the receipt from the clerk and juggled the huge sack with the smaller ones.

"Here. Let me take some of those," Piper said. She took the sack containing the throw pillows and the new eyelet shams. They left the store for the main concourse of the mall.

"I can't believe we've found all this stuff in so short a time," Evelyn said. "And on sale. You have sale radar."

"Glad to be of service."

Evelyn felt giddy. It had been so long since she'd been shopping with a friend. There was no real reason, but now that she'd experienced it again, she remembered the wonderful camaraderie of it. Buying something wasn't as important as the process of sharing time, trying things on, and *ooh*ing and *ahh*ing over pretty things.

She checked her watch. It was after five. "I need to get home and get dinner."

"We're going. But didn't I smell chili brewing?"

Evelyn nodded. "It's in the Crock-Pot."

"Then everything's under control. Ease up a bit, Evelyn. Let loose."

The mall's music system played "In the Mood." *She wants me to let loose?* Evelyn found herself moving to the beat, even doing a little two-step in front of the health-food store. Piper laughed. "Take it away, Evelyn!"

Other shoppers looked her way, but Evelyn didn't mind. Their smiles revealed that they wanted to dance too, but didn't have the courage.

But I do have the courage? Since when?

"You like to dance, don't you?"

"I do. I'd forgotten . . . but I really, really do."

"You should take dance lessons. Learn the fox-trot, the merengue."

"The meringue?"

Piper laughed. "I'm not talking egg whites, Evelyn. I'm talking Latin sizzle."

Evelyn shoved the thought of dance lessons away but found another thought in its place. "Actually, I have always wanted to take cooking classes."

"Really? It just so happens my parents take a cooking class every Wednesday afternoon. You could join —"

"I can't just barge in on their —"

"They don't own the class, Evelyn. They pay for it. At the community college. Twenty-five bucks for ten weeks. Something like that. They keep the price low because most of the participants are retirees. My parents have been doing it for six months. They love it." She shook her head and smiled. "Speaking of meringues, you should taste my dad's banana cream pie. His meringues are positively fluffy."

"I love banana cream pie."

"So what do you say? I could call my parents and have them pick you up for the next class."

"I don't know . . ."

"Sure you do." Piper dropped the sacks to the ground and dug her cell phone out of her purse. She dialed a number. "Mom? Hey, I've got a proposition for you. . . ."

Fluffy meringues, here I come.

Audra hurried home after work, needing to see her poor sick baby. She raced inside, letting the door slam.

"Shh!" Tessa was coming down the stairs. "Summer's sleeping."

Audra caught a breath and tried to calm herself. "How's she doing?"

Tessa reached the foyer. "Better. It appears to be one of those twenty-four-hour things."

Audra wrapped the long handle of her purse around its body and placed it on the stairs. "Where's Evelyn?"

"She and Piper went shopping."

Shopping? Wasn't she supposed to be taking care of my — ?

Tessa seemed to read her mind. "Don't get after her for it. It was plenty fine with me. Summer and I read some books and . . ." She hesitated. "Can we sit down a moment? I need to talk to you."

It seemed out of character for Tessa to ask anyone to sit down to talk. Tessa just talked; she didn't prepare her victims.

Audra turned toward the dining room, but found it covered with blankets. "What's this mess?"

"Evelyn and Summer made it before she got sick. A tent city, they call it."

I call it a disaster. "I'll clean it up as soon as we're done talking."

"There's no reason to take it down."

"But we can't get to the table."

"We can eat in the kitchen."

"But it's a mess."

"A mess is in the eye of the beholder, Audra." Tessa took her arm and steered her toward the parlor. "Which leads mc to what I wanted to talk to you about."

Audra let herself be led to the couch. Her mind raced with things that could have upset Tessa. "What did Summer do wrong now?"

Tessa blinked slowly, clearly incredulous. "What makes you think that? About Summer?"

Audra squeezed the bridge of her nose. *What* did *make me think that?*

"Summer's a good girl. I've yet to see her do anything wrong."

But just a few days ago her very existence was wrong. Audra snickered, but then stopped herself. "Why don't you tell me what's going on."

Tessa ran a finger along the crease of her pants. "It *is* Summer I want to talk with you about. But it's not her behavior that's in question." She glanced up, then down again. "I'm not sure how to best put this . . ."

"Just say it, Tessa."

Tessa nodded, apparently making a decision. She stilled her hand and looked Audra in the eye. "Summer thinks your love is conditional on what she does to earn it. The reason she's so helpful is linked to her thinking that you'll love her more, the more she does."

Audra's right eye twitched. "That's ridiculous."

"Yes it is, but it's the way she feels."

"She told you this?"

"I caught her taking her dishes downstairs — while she was sick — because she knew you'd want her to. The need to help overpowered even her sickness. She wanted you to be proud of her."

Audra could see it in her mind's eye. A little five-year-old scraping her plate, putting her dishes in the dishwasher . . .

"That's why she isn't in your bed. She didn't want to mess things up."

It sounded just as bad the second time she heard it.

"You really need to ease up on her,

Audra. Order is one thing, but this patho-
logical need for it . . ." Tessa shook her
head as if Audra were a mental case that
was hopeless. "I know you *want* to be a
good parent but . . ."

Audra let Tessa's words fade away. She
did want to be a good parent. Wasn't she
doing her very best in the tough situation
she was in? Didn't she deserve a little sympathy rather than condemnation? Didn't
she deserve —

She heard multiple voices and steps on
the porch. Piper and Evelyn came inside,
their arms full of sacks. Mae was right behind them. Then Gillie was the last inside,
carrying a shopping bag. "Come one,
come all," Mae said. "We all drove up at
the same —"

Tessa was at their side in seconds,
shushing them.

They all understood immediately,
glanced upstairs, then came into the
parlor. Evelyn set her sacks down. "How's
she doing?"

Audra was on her feet. "Physically, fine.
But mentally and emotionally?" She shot
Tessa a look. "According to Tessa, I'm too
hard on my own daughter. I make her think
she has to earn my love by doing chores."

Evelyn adjusted a sack that had fallen

over. "I know. I've seen it too and —"

"You think Tessa's right?"

Evelyn froze, then slowly straightened. "Well . . . actually . . . maybe I'm mistaken."

Mae nudged Evelyn from behind. "What's with you, Evie? You're like a Ping-Pong ball, first on this side of the table, then the other. Say what you think."

Evelyn crossed her arms one way, then another. "I think . . ."

"Come on," Mae said, "you can do it."

Evelyn nodded. "I think you're too hard on her. Sometimes."

Mae laughed. "You just had to slip that qualifier in there, didn't you?"

"I . . ."

Mae crossed the room and put an arm around Audra's shoulders. "We're not against you, Audra. We're trying to —"

Audra shucked her arm away. "You *are* against me. You're attacking me by saying I'm not a good mother." She began to pace. "I don't need this. Summer only has one parent and I do the best I can."

"Which brings up the point . . . is the father around? Do you ever let him see her?" Tessa asked.

"It's best he doesn't."

Tessa persisted. "But a child needs a father."

Mae sat in the rocker and began rocking furiously. "I don't agree with that one. My kids were better off without Danny. We *all* were better off."

"See?" Audra said. "Sometimes, it's best they have no contact."

"I may not know Summer's father directly," Gillie said, "but I know *of* him. From what you've said he's a little selfish and immature, but maybe if you let him see Summer and spend some time with her, he'd change."

Audra popped out of her seat. "I'm not using my daughter as a guinea pig to help her father become a better man."

"Maybe I said that wrong . . ."

Audra felt as if a heavy blanket had been thrown over her head, making it hard to breathe. All this advice, when they were clueless. "You have no idea what kind of man Luke is. None of you have any right —"

"But I *do* know him," Piper said. "I got to know him when you first found out you were pregnant. I'm not saying you should have married the guy then, nor do I think you should marry him now. But maybe he should be allowed to see —"

"No!"

The women's faces registered their shock. "We were just trying to help," Evelyn said.

"You can't help. Don't you get it? I've done the best I can, on my own, and I think I've done pretty good. But in order to survive, I need to be in control of the few things I've got left to control. I need —" She looked across the foyer and saw the tent city in the dining room. She strode toward it and yanked a blanket off the table, causing clothespins to fly and another tent to fall in on itself like a deflated soufflé.

"Audra, no!"

Don't tell me no . . . Audra began folding the blankets. "I need order. I need cleanliness. I need method. I need organization." She spotted Summer's play dishes stacked neatly beneath a chair. And under another chair, a doll was put to bed with the blanket pulled up just so, the doll clothes neatly folded in color-coordinated piles. . . .

This was no *play* tent city. Her daughter didn't frolic with reckless abandon, letting her imagination run wild. She stacked. She smoothed. She organized. She was controlled and eager to please. She was the daughter Audra wanted. Needed.

Insisted on?

Her voice lowered to a whisper. "I hate messes . . . my life is a . . . a mess . . ." Audra dropped the blanket, covered her face with her hands, and began to sob. Within seconds, she had five sets of arms touching her, holding her, comforting her. They led her to a chair and she sat, feeling as if air was too heavy a burden to bear.

A tissue appeared and she used it. "You want to know why I don't ever want Luke in my life?"

Mae stroked her hair. "Why?"

"Because he's done this before." Audra blew her nose. "He's fathered two other children outside of marriage. There was one before Summer, and there's been one since. I heard about both of them at the beauty parlor. I didn't know." Her head shook with a steady rhythm. "I didn't know." She looked up at them and sniffed. "That's why I don't want him around Summer. He's not a good man. He lives for fun and instant gratification of his own needs. He leaves a wake of pain wherever he goes."

"Oh dear," Evelyn said.

Tessa wagged a finger. "I told you, you shouldn't have slept with him. It was a sin, plain and simple."

The condemnation of the wagging finger pushed her over the edge. Audra felt the last vestige of energy burst forth. "Stop it, Tessa! Stop having to be right all the time. It's sickening. And it's just as much of a sin as me sleeping with Luke."

Tessa took a step back. "There's nothing wrong with being right."

"Yes, there is! The way you do it, anyway. Daily, you stand before the rest of us as if you're better than us. You act like you have all the answers and the rest of us are idiots for not seeing things the way you do. For not living the perfect life. Frankly, your *rightness* is a pain and a bore."

Everyone looked to Tessa, and Audra knew they were waiting for the volcano to erupt. But instead of fighting back — which Audra knew she deserved — Tessa sank onto her chair. When she spoke, her voice was small.

"But I'm not always right. I'm not. No matter how hard I try. I'll never be able to make up for the time I was truly wrong."

Silence. It seemed to Audra that all the women were holding their breath, waiting to see whether Tessa would continue. When she did, her voice was so soft Audra had trouble hearing her.

"It wasn't indigestion. It *was* his heart."

Her husband? What was his name again? "Alfred?"

Tessa glanced at her, nodded, and folded in on herself like an animal in danger. "Alfred was a hypochondriac. Every sore throat was strep, every headache a tumor, every stomachache an ulcer. I got tired of it. I used to tell him it was all in his head. He could think his way out of it if he tried. 'Get over it,' I would always say."

It took the other ladies a moment to change gears. But Audra saw their faces adjust to the new topic of conversation.

Evelyn spoke first. "I know it can be hard being around people like that. I had an aunt once who —"

Tessa stared straight ahead as if she hadn't heard. "But that last day . . . I was impatient, angry with him. He'd made me miss my class because of one of his spells. And then, just when I was yelling at him . . . he pretended to be sicker. I'd had it. He wasn't going to use his paranoia to get my sympathy. No sir, not this time. I left the house and told him, 'Go ahead. Pretend you're sick. But do it without me. I'm not going to waste my life watching you moan and groan.' "

Audra guessed where this was heading. Her throat was dry, but she managed a swallow. "You left?"

A single nod. "I came back later and found him on the floor." Tessa put the back of her hand to her face and drew one leg off the floor, as if mimicking how she'd found him. "He'd had a heart attack."

"Was he dead?" Mae asked.

"No. Not yet. He regained consciousness long enough to say two words to me."

I love you was three words . . . "What were they?" Audra asked.

"I'm sorry." Tessa's face crumpled like a brown paper bag. "He was sorry for inconveniencing me. While all the time, it was I who should have . . . I can't even say it."

"Asked his forgiveness?" Piper said.

Tessa straightened as if it pained her to move. "That's why I act like such a nasty, bitter person — because that's what I really am, deep down. That's my nature. If a good man like Alfred couldn't change me, nobody can."

Evelyn put a hand on her shoulder. "Oh, Tessa . . ."

"*Are* you sorry?" Gillie asked.

"Of course I'm sorry."

Piper's voice was soft. "Then why stay in the same rut? Why not change?"

"I've tried. Summer was helping . . . I quit thinking about myself — for a little while." The fingers of one hand bit the fingers of her other hand. "But this old fool can't change. It's too late."

"Baloney," Mae said.

"I've tried. But it doesn't work. I didn't even have the nerve to go back to my Bible study today after what happened last week. I was too embarrassed."

"Try harder," Audra suggested.

"But you can't do it alone," Piper said.

"That's right. We'll help," Audra said.

Piper shook her head. "That's not what I mean. We can't force you to change, and obviously you can't do it yourself. So quit trying to."

"Quit trying?" Mae said. "Don't tell her that."

"Let me finish. Quit trying to do it by your own strength."

"Then whose strength — ?" Tessa stopped, and the dawn of revelation shone on her face. "You're talking about God, aren't you?"

Piper looked at Tessa and then at Audra, and Audra knew that whatever was coming out of her mouth was a truth for both of them. It would be her choice to accept it as such or to discard it and stumble on alone.

Piper spanned the space between Tessa's and Audra's chairs with her hands, and they each took hold. Then she knelt to be at their level. "I think King Solomon, the wisest man of all time, said it best: 'Trust in the Lord with all your heart; do not depend on your own understanding. Seek his will in all you do, and he will direct your paths.' "

"Sounds good," Mae said.

"It is good," Piper said.

"That's Proverbs three, isn't it?" Tessa asked.

Piper squeezed her hand. "Yes, it is. See, Tessa? You already know all this — deep down, you know it — you just have to let it come to the surface of your life where it can do some good."

Tessa nodded and Audra took the words to heart too. She wasn't as knowledgeable as Tessa was in Bible things, and she was a true rookie Christian compared to Piper, but she knew that this she could do. She could bring what she knew so far up to the surface and use it. Or at least she could try.

"What happened to my city?" Summer stood in the doorway, one pajama leg riding high, the other low. Her face was that of a homeowner coming home to a ransacked house.

The women looked to Audra. This was her ball game. She picked up the blanket she'd let fall to the floor and held it to her chest. She thought of covering up the tent's destruction by offering some flimsy excuse about redoing it, making it better, but then she realized such a statement might make Summer think she hadn't built it well enough in the first place.

"I got mad. I messed it up. I'm sorry." Audra gathered some clothespins from the floor. "It was a fine tent city, and I ruined it. I was wrong."

Summer helped pick up the clothespins and Audra panicked. "No, honey. You don't have to help —"

Mae picked up one by the buffet. "Of course she does. We all do. And between the seven of us, we'll make the most spectacular tent city in all the world."

And that's exactly what they did.

After repairing the tent, Summer escaped inside, and the rest of the women scattered. Gillie finally had Audra alone. Although she would have loved to present Audra with her TV with everyone looking on, after the giving-fiasco at the bank that afternoon, it was not an option. One-on-one giving was essential. And hard.

Gillie led Audra into the parlor, where Audra slumped onto the couch. Her eyes closed immediately. "Talk about a hard day . . ."

Is that a perfect opening or what? Gillie gathered up the blue box and put it in Audra's lap, forcing her eyes to open.

She sat up, to balance it better. "Oh, Gillie . . . you've got to quit giving me things."

Her words stuck like pins, and Gillie suddenly felt her own bout of weariness. She, too, had had a hard day. "I know I have a lot to learn about giving, Audra, but people can't tell me not to do it. They can't. I *like* to give. I feel good about myself when I give." She flashed a look at Audra. "Is that so bad?"

Audra put a hand on hers. "No, it isn't bad. 'God loves the person who gives cheerfully.' "

Gillie nodded. "Good. Because it makes me happy to give." She slapped her thighs. "And that's that. So open your present, smile, and say thank you."

Audra was good at following directions.

Tessa sat in the rocker on the front porch, both feet squarely on the floor, an arm on either armrest. She braced herself for the pain. Any moment now, her chest would constrict and she would be reminded of her frailty.

Rock, rock, rock . . .

No pain came.

Rock, rock, rock . . .

Tessa turned her total attention inward, exploring every corner of her insides, gauging, weighing, assessing. . . . But there was no pain. None. In fact, she felt amazingly good.

This doesn't make sense. I always get the heart pains when I'm under stress. Always.

"What are you doing, Tessie?"

She found Mae at her side. She hadn't even heard the front door open.

"You appear to be waiting for something. You're in the ready-for-takeoff stance."

Tessa moved her arms into her lap and tried to look more relaxed.

Mae sat on the settee. "I'm really glad you shared about Alfred. I'm glad you trusted us."

"I'm supposed to trust God."

" '. . . with all your heart.' That's a good one. That Piper's a peach. You ladies have got me thinking about God lately. And considering me and Him haven't talked past how-de-do in years . . ." Mae shrugged.

"So you prayed?"

"I wouldn't say that. But I'm thinking about it."

"That's progress."

"A person's gotta start somewhere."

"And end somewhere." Tessa hadn't planned on saying that.

"You talking about Alfred?"

Tessa nodded. "And me." She looked at Mae's face, gauging her sympathy level. There was no mischievous glint in her eye. She looked genuinely interested. "Ever since Alfred's heart gave out, *I've* been the one having chest pains. I don't know how —"

"Sympathy pains, eh?"

Sympathy? "What?"

"I'm sorry. I don't mean to diminish what you're going through, but that was the first thing that popped into my brain, and you know how I am . . . once a thought pops in, it pops out."

Tessa took a deep breath, trying to comprehend the incomprehensible.

Mae was at her side. "You okay? You feeling chest pains now?"

"Actually, I'm not. And that's what I was out here thinking about, waiting for. When I get upset, I've been getting chest pains. But tonight . . . they didn't come."

Mae returned to her seat. "Maybe it's

because you let out the pain — the other kind of pain, the mental pain."

"I confessed."

"There's that word again. Though I prefer the old hippie axiom 'you let it all hang out.' Letting it hang out is good for the soul. Creates good vibes. Taps into good karma."

Since she'd brought it up . . . "Mae, do you really believe in all that karma-vibes gobbledygook? And horoscopes . . . I've seen you reading them in the paper. It's bothered me."

"It's harmless."

"Nothing is harmless that keeps you from God."

"God has nothing to do with karma, vibes, and horoscopes."

"Exactly. He doesn't. It's not what He's about. So if you believe in one, you can't believe in the other."

Mae twirled a strand of hair around her finger. "Can't argue much with that one — even though I'd like to."

"And you just said that Piper and the rest of us had got you thinking about God again. . . ."

"And now you've added more to the mix." She stopped twirling and stood. "I'll think on it, Tessie. But right now, I have a date with our neighbor." She twirled, making her skirt rise and fall. "How do I look?"

Tessa kept her true opinions to herself. She and Mae would never agree on clothing choices. "Isn't he the man who's causing Evelyn so much trouble?"

"*Was* causing. Until I talked to him. And fixed it." She shuffled her shoulders. "Just leave it to Mae."

"But how . . . did you sleep with him?"

"Tessie!"

Tessa put a hand to her mouth. "Sorry. But what with the man in your room and the way you talk."

"That's the clincher, Tessie." She lowered her voice confidentially. "It's just talk. I love men and I love being around them. I may be a flirt, but I'm not the floozy you think I am. God or no God, I've set certain standards." She shrugged. "Face it; they like being around me because I'm good company."

Tessa had to smile. "Yes, you are."

Mae curtsied. "Why, thank you, sister."

"Have a good time." The goodwill in the words shocked her. Tessa was pretty sure she wouldn't have been able to say such a thing a few days ago.

Mae kissed her fingertips and placed

them on Tessa's hand. "Oh, I will. I always do."

As Tessa watched her cross the street, she marveled at all that had been accomplished this day — in her own life and in the lives of the other . . . the other *sisters,* as Mae called them.

It was a start. A good start.

10

Let us go right into the presence of God, with true hearts fully trusting him. For our evil consciences have been sprinkled with Christ's blood to make us clean, and our bodies have been washed with pure water.

HEBREWS 10:22

Tessa opened her eyes. In the moment spanning sleep and wakefulness, she remembered. And smiled.

She was a new woman. A woman without pain — for three whole days now. A woman without the baggage of the past. Well, almost . . . for although she'd experienced the revelation regarding the cause of her chest pains and had confessed to the other tenants her guilt regarding her treatment of Alfred, she had not yet confessed it to the only One who mattered. That had become clear to her in church yesterday. And this morning, she felt she was finally ready.

She pulled back the covers and slipped to the floor beside the bed, the stiffness of her joints reminding her of her age. She ignored their cries. Although she rarely prayed on her knees, this morning it felt necessary. If she was going to humble herself before God, she needed to affect a humble stance.

She clasped her hands on the edge of the bed and dipped her head to meet them. The fresh scent of fabric softener was a pleasant spark to her senses and fit with her goal of starting fresh.

She heard the stirring of the other tenants outside her door and felt a sudden — foreign — need to be with them. But first things first.

"Lord, You know what's been going on these past ten days, and let me tell You, it's been quite a ride. You've made me face my arrogance, stubbornness, and pride head-on. It's not been a pretty sight." She took a deep breath and repositioned her knees on the wooden floor.

I really need a rug right here.

She shook the distracting thought away. She clasped her hands harder, forcing herself to focus on the task at hand. "I've been living under the burden of Alfred's death for a year now." She sucked in a breath as she realized . . . "It's exactly one year today! Too long for a stubborn old woman to ignore the truth that she isn't — wasn't — a nice person."

Tessa felt a tear roll down her cheek. She hadn't been aware she was crying. "That's why I'm here this morning, Lord. To tell You I'm sorry. Mightily sorry. You gave me a good husband and a wonderful daughter and how did I repay You? By treating them like the evil stepmother in *Cinderella*. But I will do better. I *will*. I'll work hard as I can." She flicked the tears away and took a cleansing breath. "Oh, why do You give me such blessings when I don't deserve them?"

Because I love you.

Tessa opened her eyes and repeated the words aloud. "Because You love me."

An outpouring of gratitude and regret fell upon her like a sudden rain, and she fell back on her haunches, grabbing the bedrail for support. "Thank You, Jesus. Thank You!"

Then Tessa let herself cry and be comforted by the One who knew her best. And loved her anyway.

The first image Audra saw upon waking was the face of her daughter. She postponed moving, letting herself study this little girl who loved her — in spite of

Audra's flaws. The big question was why did Audra make it so hard? Here lay a daughter who exhibited the epitome of unconditional love; giving no matter what, with no concern over what she would get in return. And what had Audra given her?

Chores, petty chastisements, and pressure.

Audra had had plenty of time during the past three days to think about her failings. *Lord, help me be a better mother,* she prayed — not for the first time.

She ran a finger along her daughter's cheek, once again marveling at its velvet perfection. Summer twitched, then opened her eyes. Within seconds, she smiled, and Audra realized what a blessing *that* was — to have a child who awoke with a smile.

"Hey, baby."

Summer stretched until her limbs quivered. "Morning, Mommy."

Audra kissed her forehead, then got out of bed. Summer slipped out her side immediately and pulled up the covers in their morning ritual. The fact that she jumped into the routine of their day was a relief but also distressing. Was there too much structure? too many have-to's?

"Mommy, pull your side up."

Audra looked down at the bed. Maybe it

was time for a new routine — or more accurately, a break from routine. "Let's leave it a mess today."

Summer dropped her pillow. "What do you mean?"

"Let's leave the bed unmade."

"But, Mommy, you always say —"

"Never mind that. The world won't come to an end, baby." It was a silly statement that was hard to say. And harder to mean.

Summer stared at the bed as if she couldn't imagine not having it made.

What have I done to her?

Suddenly, Audra had an idea. She picked up her pillow, leaned across the bed, and whapped Summer with it.

Summer's mouth dropped open. "Mommy!"

Audra did it again.

With only a moment's hesitation, as if she'd long been waiting — and craving — for this release from their routine, Summer jumped on the bed and whapped her back. Soon they were engaged in a fierce pillow fight and tickling match.

A tap on the door stopped them. "What are you two doing in there?"

They looked at each other and mouthed a name: *Tessa.*

"We'll be down in a minute, Tessa," Audra said. They heard her feet on the stairs.

They giggled and lay back, exhausted. Then, to the accompaniment of their heavy breathing, Audra felt Summer's hand find hers and squeeze.

She squeezed back. "I know, baby. Me too. Me too."

As soon as Gillie saw Audra come into work she wanted to ask how she liked the new TV. Had she set it up over the weekend? Had she and Summer watched it while cuddling in bed?

But then another thought intruded. *Leave it alone, Gillie. Don't draw more attention to your gift. You've got to learn to let it be.*

She was resolved to follow this prompting until she noticed that Audra was wearing the Hermés scarf. Gillie let her pleasure loose. "My, you look lovely today. You have exquisite taste in clothes."

Audra touched the scarf and laughed. "Actually, I have a fashion consultant who dresses me. She's the talented one." She put her purse under the counter and faced Gillie. "She's also the one who has a generous, giving heart."

Gillie's throat tightened. "Really?"

"Really. And she deserves thanks instead of a scolding for her generosity."

Gillie looked away. "I deserved a scolding."

"Maybe. But you also deserve more thanks than I've given you." Audra reached across the teller stations. Gillie took her hand. "You are a wonderful friend, Gillie. You see a need and you fill it. You shouldn't get flak for that. And I'm sorry for not appreciating you more. Forgive me?"

Gillie felt tears threaten. She was the older of the two by twelve years, and yet she repeatedly felt as if Audra was the mentor, the one who taught Gillie about life and how it should be lived. "There's no need for forgiveness, Audra. We're friends. It's our duty to speak the truth even if it means knocking each other down once in a while."

"Only to help each other back to our feet."

"Exactly. My life is better with you than without you, Audra."

"And I'm better with you than without you."

They exchanged a smile and a nod just as the bank's doors opened for business. It was already a good day.

★ ★ ★

Mae was not busy at Silver-Wear. At other times, that might have bothered her — making her worry about bills and such — but on this particular day, she relished it. The break in business gave her a chance to work on her pet project for the sisters at Peerbaugh Place.

The project that had started as one piece for Tessa had expanded to include four pieces. And she was even considering seven — including Piper, Gillie, and herself in the gang. For even though the other two ladies didn't live among them, they seemed a part of their circle of friends. The bonds of sisterhood extended beyond residence.

Mae arched her spine. Making jewelry demanded tense attention and was tedious work that tired her muscles and eyes. Her first inclination was to take a break. Slack up a bit. There was no timeline for this work. She'd get it done when she got it —

Do it now.

Mae held her breath at the inner command. "Where did that come from?"

Realizing she had just spoken aloud to her empty store, Mae mimicked the musical intro to *The Twilight Zone*: "*Do-do-do-do, do-do-do-do.* You're losing it, Mae."

But as she raised her arms above her head to fully stretch, the thought came back. *Do it now.*

Mae left her hands in the air a moment, suddenly wondering if this inner voice originated beyond herself, beyond . . .

Was it God?

She dropped her arms. "Don't be ridiculous. God wouldn't talk to me. I haven't thought about Him since —"

Since Friday night.

Maybe this wasn't a coincidence. Maybe Piper talking about God, Audra and Tessa talking about God, Mae *thinking* about God, were rungs of the ladder Mae was supposed to climb. The path to good karma. Good vi—

Mae remembered her conversation with Tessa: *"God has nothing to do with karma, vibes, and horoscopes . . . It's not what He's about. So if you believe in one, you can't believe in the other."*

So if the inner prompting to "do it now" was not a part of karma, then it might be, could be . . .

Mae took a cleansing breath, letting the idea seep into her pores. "Okay, God. If it's You telling me to get to it, who am I to say differently? And if it isn't You? What will it hurt to get it done? I'll win either way."

So Mae got back to work, drawing energy from the possibility that maybe, just maybe, God had taken an interest in her life.

And that possibility had the potential to prove more interesting than any karma, vibration, or horoscope.

The first time Mae looked at the clock it was nearly twelve. The girls were expecting her at Ruby's. To think she'd been so engrossed in her work she'd almost missed lunch? It had been a long time since she'd felt such consuming focus. Too long.

In truth, she'd hit a glitch. Although she usually had no trouble designing the patterns to press into her silver, for this project she was stumped. She'd tried a few, but they just didn't seem right. What seemed perfect for Tessa didn't fit Evelyn. And though she could have made each piece unique, she wanted one style for all. One unifying style.

She was just gathering her purse when the phone rang. "Hello?"

"Mae, this is Collier. How are you this fine day?"

"Not as chipper as you. What's up?"

"Hopefully seeing you. You up for another evening in my presence, or did I chase you off the other night with too much talk?"

Mae laughed. Their dinner Friday *had* been consumed with talk, so much so that they'd closed the restaurant. "You can never talk too much for Mae Fitzpatrick — that is, as long as you let me talk just as much."

"And did I?"

"You did."

"So what do you say to my offer?"

"I'd love to see you. But I suggest we pick a different restaurant. The old one may not look kindly on our extensive table-sitting."

"Actually . . . I wasn't planning to go to any restaurant."

"A movie's fine."

"No movie either."

"Carson Creek isn't that big a town, Collie. What did you have in mind?"

She heard him take a breath. "Our church, Riverview Presbyterian, is having our annual May Madness Wednesday night. We get together for potluck and a talent show and —"

"Oh."

"You don't sound enthused."

"Does this involve old ladies getting up to sing 'Rock of Ages' and little Molly Sue playing 'Aura Lee' on the violin?"

"Pretty much."

"Oh, Collie . . ."

He laughed. "It's not that bad. After eating way too much, people perform. I've heard that our ladies singing group — Dallas and the Babes — is planning something big, and *then* Molly Sue plays 'Aura Lee' on the violin."

"That sounds loads better."

"It's fun, Mae. And you're a fun-loving woman. At least I thought you were."

Who was she to judge? One person's fun was another person's torture. "As long as *I* don't have to sing — though I do perform an exhilarating rendition of 'Viva Las Vegas.' "

"I can only imagine. I'll pick you up at seven."

Mae hung up, shaking her head at the thought that she, Mae Fitzpatrick, had not only been open to a prompting from God but to an invitation from a Presbyterian.

Would wonders never cease?

Tessa was on a mission — a mission of reconciliation. First, she needed to buy some wooden buckets. . . .

Tessa was glad to see Evelyn and Summer on the porch when she drove up.

She got out, moving to the trunk. "Who's got strong arms?"

Summer piped up, "I do!"

"Then come help, child."

"Me too?" Evelyn asked.

"I'll take every arm I can get."

Summer ran to the trunk. "Ooh, pretty flowers."

"Can you carry these to the porch for me?"

Summer nodded, but Tessa hesitated just a moment, putting her hand on Summer's forehead. It was warm, but not hot. She looked to Evelyn. "She doing all right today? I don't want to wear her out."

"She's doing fine. Load her up."

Tessa obliged, loading Summer's arms with red salvia, white begonias, and blue lobelia.

Evelyn peered into the trunk. Tessa could tell she was wondering where they would put all these bucket planters at Peerbaugh Place.

"Don't panic, Evelyn. I'm not trying to usurp your gardening plan. These are gifts for my Bible study group."

"What for?"

"Penance. The verse in contention was about drawing up Christ's living water. I got hung up on the details of the bucket of biblical times. I missed the point — until Piper set me straight. Hence . . ." She extended a hand toward the buckets.

"That's very nice, but I'm sure your Bible study doesn't expect —"

"Which is exactly why I'm doing it."

Tessa and Summer pulled in front of Marla's house, and Tessa put the car in park. "Delivery number one, ready to go."

"Do I get to ring the doorbell?" Summer asked. She'd wanted to go along on the deliveries, which had worked out perfectly since Evelyn had some errands she wanted to run.

"I suppose you —" Tessa stopped and reconsidered. Maybe it would be better to set the plants by the door and leave. That way there would be no awkward moment — on the recipient's part or hers. She'd let the note do her talking: *To learn, you must love discipline; it is stupid to hate correction."* *Proverbs 12:1. Please forgive me. Tessa.*

She'd spent a long time picking out just the right verse from the dozens of instances of "knowledge" in the Bible. Calling herself stupid was harsh, but justified. If she was going to move on from this event, she couldn't mince words. She never did with anyone else; why should she do so with herself?

As far as the symbolism of the bucket . . . she'd leave that up to their own discernment. She'd done enough cramming knowledge down their throats.

"You got your running shoes on, little girl?"

Summer lifted her foot so Tessa could see her white-and-pink tennies.

"Let's go, but be very quiet."

Tessa carried the planter to the front door, softening her steps on the porch as much as possible. She whispered to Summer, "Wait until I'm back at the car, then ring the doorbell and run. Can you do that?"

Summer nodded vigorously, her eyes sparkling with excitement. Tessa withdrew from the porch and hurried to the car as fast as her bones could take her. She opened Summer's door, then went around to her own, feeling like a robber preparing the getaway car. Summer had her finger poised near the doorbell, her feet ready to run.

Tessa nodded.

Summer rang the bell and raced to the car. Unfortunately, Tessa hadn't thought of the fact that Summer might have problems closing the huge passenger door. She had to get out and go around to help her. By that time Marla was at the door. She saw the flowers, saw Tessa, and waved.

Tessa waved back. A wave of reconciliation.

God was good.

Evelyn checked to make sure she had her house key in her purse. The Wellingtons would be arriving at any moment to pick her up for her first cooking class. She was excited, but also wary. To go to lessons, knowing no one . . .

A blue sedan pulled up front, and Evelyn's stomach did a flip. A handsome man with a mane of silver hair got out of the car and came up the front walk. Evelyn went outside, shortening his trek. She pulled the door shut and checked the lock. "You must be Wayne?"

He offered a bow. "Here to escort you to the land of haute cuisine." He waited for her at the bottom of the porch steps and shook her hand. He was quite short for a man, five-five or so. Evelyn could look at him eye to eye. "I'm so glad Piper told you about the classes. Wanda and I have enjoyed them immensely." He pointed to the car where Wanda waved from the front seat.

He opened the back door for Evelyn and scurried around to the driver's side, very light on his feet.

Wanda shook hands over the seat. Evelyn could tell she was a petite woman by the size of her childlike hands. Evelyn glanced at Wayne. How did they ever have a girl Piper's size? For Piper was at least five-eight. It didn't match.

Oh well . . .

Evelyn had never known cooking could be so fun. They'd spent the entire class making an enchilada casserole. It was satisfying food that made a person close her eyes and slow her chewing, savoring every bite.

Evelyn checked her notes as they walked to the car. "I wonder if the ladies would eat this."

Wayne opened her car door. "Everyone likes Mexican food."

"My husband didn't. Meat loaf, pot roast, or hamburgers. I made spaghetti once, and he acted like I was feeding him squid."

"So that explains the flush in your cheeks and the grin on your lips. You had a good time exploring new culinary territory. Or is that an understatement?"

"There are no words."

"I can't believe you've never cooked beyond the basics," Wanda said. "You're a natural."

"The aroma . . ." Evelyn took a deep breath, drinking in the memory. "How can a person not be inspired?"

Wayne shook his head. "Like Wanda said, you're a natural, a dormant chef, awakened by the smell of enchilada sauce."

They were right. It was as if the creative cooking had flicked a hidden switch within her, turning on the desire to make something that went beyond sustenance to touch upon delight.

"How did you like Oscar?" Wanda asked, referring to a man who'd grabbed the seat beside Evelyn.

"He's a nice man. A gentleman."

"Which can't be said of all the participants," Wayne said. "I saw Reggie making a play for you."

Wanda laughed. "Before Ingrid claimed him as her property."

"She can have him," Evelyn said. She clapped a hand over her mouth. "Sorry. That was rude."

"But honest. You're much better off with Oscar."

It sounded as if they were pairing her up

for dates. She wasn't ready for that and couldn't imagine being ready for a long, long time. Maybe it would be best if she made her position clear. "I'm not interested in dating."

"Then Oscar's your man."

"Why's that?"

"He's married."

"Why isn't his wife — ?"

"She's sick. Has been for a while. Cancer. She's a great lady. She insists he come to the class because she knows how much he loves it. They used to both come."

"Oh, I'm so sorry . . ." Suddenly, Oscar's gentleman status was upped to the highest rank.

Wanda turned to look at her. "We're sorry about your husband. Piper told us."

"Thanks." Evelyn realized they hadn't really had a chance to talk before now. The trip over had been filled with get-to-know-you's, and then the class had taken over. "Piper's a gem. She's already taught me a lot."

"About what?"

"Faith. She's definitely got her head on straight."

"Yes, she does. We're lucky to call her daughter."

"And she's lucky to call you parents."

"Why, thank you," Wayne said. "We couldn't ask for a nicer compliment. Now . . . how'd you ladies like a fancy iced mocha latte? I'll buy."

"I've never had one," Evelyn said.

"Well, then, Evelyn, it will be our pleasure to introduce you to yet another first in your life."

Bring it on. At the moment, she felt ready for anything.

Audra was glad to see Piper's car at Peerbaugh Place when she got home from work. Last Friday had been so crazy with her outburst — and Tessa's — that Audra hadn't had time to talk to her friend, to explain to her why she'd never previously confided to her the truth about Luke's other children. She'd wanted to call Piper any number of times during the five days since then, but somehow she'd never gotten the chance. Or maybe she just didn't want to talk about something so important over the phone.

Within seconds of Audra's walking in the door, Summer came running, carrying a stuffed bunny with a pink ribbon around its neck. "Looky what Piper gave me 'cause I was sick."

Piper emerged from the kitchen. She

took the bunny away. "But since you're well now . . ."

Summer took it back and hugged it fiercely. "I'm not that much well. I'm still sick just a little."

Piper kissed her head. "I'm just teasing, pip-squeak. It's yours, sick or well." She looked to Audra. "And how was your day?"

"Blessedly normal, but tiring."

Piper took Audra's purse and put it on the front stair. She got behind her and pushed her toward the kitchen. "Come eat. Evelyn's made taco soup and Tessa made bread."

"Homemade bread? Can I have it toasted and slathered in butter?"

"If I had your hips, I'd do exactly that. I told her you needed a loaf just for you, but she said you'd have to share."

They entered the kitchen where Tessa was at the counter, slicing a burnished loaf of fresh bread.

"It smells heavenly," Audra said.

Evelyn ladled the soup from the Crock-Pot into bowls. "I may not be a gourmet cook — yet — but I'm trying. They gave out this recipe at my cooking class today. Sit, ladies." Evelyn set the bowls around while Tessa brought over a plate of sliced bread. It was crowded around the kitchen table with Piper's extra chair, but no one seemed willing to use the dining room, which would have meant dismantling the tent city.

Mae shocked everyone by being the first to take hands for grace. "I'll do the honors this time."

"Way to go, Mae!" Piper said.

"Don't look so shocked, sisters. It's not like I came to the table wearing a purple boa. The truth is I'm going to a potluck dinner after this, yet I simply cannot pass up tasting this aromatic meal. So . . . since I am double-dining tonight and since I've had such a great day in general, I feel the need to be doubly grateful with a little grace." She eyed them all. "May I continue?"

"Absolutely," Audra said.

"Go for it," Evelyn said.

They bowed their heads and Mae began. "Hey, God, I wanted to thank You for these sisters of mine and for the productive day I had doing . . . what I was doing. Add to that a thanks for the fact we're all to- gether for dinner tonight, with delicious food waiting — and me even getting to eat twice. Keep us safe, and wise, and . . . bless us. Amen."

"Amen."

Mae put her napkin in her lap. "So, on a scale of one to ten, ten being that the gates of heaven opened, how did I do?"

"Oh, a ten, definitely a ten," Tessa said.

Evelyn sprinkled her soup with oyster crackers. "Tell us about your 'productive day.' "

"Can't."

"Why ever not?"

"It's a secret."

Summer pointed her spoon. "Mommy says it's not nice to have secrets."

"Well, Mommy is just going to have to deal with this one, because I ain't telling. Now . . . pass that bread."

Audra volunteered to do the dishes, commandeering Piper to help. She shooed the other ladies and Summer onto the sunporch to enjoy a glass of tea.

Piper put her hand under the running water, gauging its temperature. "I'm not sure I agree with this volunteering-for-kitchen-duty business. Shouldn't I have some say in it?"

Audra readied a towel to dry. "Ulterior motives. I wanted to talk to you. Alone."

"Glad to hear it. I've felt apart from you these past couple of weeks. I know you're busy with a new job and all, and I'm not trying to pass myself off as a needy person but —"

"You are a needy person?"

Piper flicked a puff of suds at her face. "Can I help it if I cherish our friendship?"

Audra bumped her, shoulder to shoulder. "Me too."

"But . . ."

"But what?"

"I thought friends were supposed to confide in each other."

So it *had* bothered her. "You're talking about Luke?"

Piper shut off the water and gave Audra her full attention. "Yes, I'm talking about Luke. How come I didn't know his whole baby-in-every-port history?"

Audra folded and refolded the towel. "I was embarrassed. If he was that kind of man — since he *is* that kind of man — the fact I was ever involved with him doesn't say much for my common sense."

"Or your taste in men."

"That too."

"But you know I'm not going to judge you. Never have, never will."

Audra shrugged, feeling sheepish. "I should have told you when I found out. That's one reason I wanted this chance to talk to you. To explain — and apologize."

Piper turned the water back on. "Did Gillie know about Luke?"

"There's no reason for you to be jealous of Gillie. No, she didn't know about Luke either. And yes, she's also my friend, but you're my *best* friend."

Piper shut off the water again. "I am?"

Audra put an arm around her shoulder and squeezed. "Absolutely."

Audra stacked the place mats.

The kitchen door opened and Russell walked in. "Evening."

The place mats slid off-kilter. "Where did you come from?" she asked, her shock at seeing him making her words come out too harsh.

Piper looked up from wiping off the counters. "Nice greeting, Aud."

Audra felt herself redden. "I —"

Russell handed her the last place mat. "Maybe I should go out and come in again?"

"No need," Audra said. "Sorry for the testiness. You just caught me off guard."

"Obviously a dangerous place to be," Piper said.

Russell carried the place mats to the drawer. "I was wondering if you and Summer would like to get some ice cream and go to the park. I read in the paper they've just installed a new swing set. An eight-seater." He looked quickly to Piper. "You're welcome to join us."

She bowed low. "I will defer to the Taylors. Some other time." She picked up the soup tureen. "If you'll excuse me, I have to put this in the dining room."

"I love swings," Audra said in the silence.

"Actually, I'm a teeter-totter man myself. I used to like slides, until I fell off one. Of course, I was climbing *up* the slippery part at the time."

"Always going against the grain?"

"I have my moments."

Evelyn and Summer appeared in the doorway leading from the sunroom.

"Mom."

"Why, Russell. How nice of you to come visit."

Audra saw his blush. She gave him a questioning look, wondering how he wanted to handle it. Was it time to let his mother know about their dating?

Piper chose that moment to return, her voice preceding her. "An ice cream date. How old-fash—" She spotted Evelyn. "Oops."

"What oops?" Evelyn asked. "What's going on?"

Audra grabbed Summer's hand and headed for the kitchen door. "If you'll excuse me, Summer and I will go get our jackets."

"I'll help." Piper left with her.

Russell waited until the door closed. "I —"

Evelyn started to talk but felt a pull in her voice. "Is there something you want to tell me?"

Russell sighed. "Audra and I are dating. Or we've dated once —"

"You only met two weeks ago." She crossed her arms. "I didn't know you were such a fast worker."

He shrugged, looking very much like an eight-year-old in big trouble. He glanced toward the exit. "I can't speak for Audra, but as for me . . . we've really hit it off."

"Obviously."

He studied her face. "Do you approve or disapprove? I can't tell."

"I approve of your choice but disapprove of the fact you kept it a secret from me. Whose idea was that?"

He scuffed a toe on the wood floor. "Mine."

"Oh, Russell . . . why didn't you want to tell me?"

The answer came out in a torrent of

truth. "Because I didn't want you marrying us off after one date."

"Don't be ridiculous."

He raised an eyebrow.

"Okay, okay . . . so I tend to be a bit eager."

"How about *frenzied?*"

She shook her head. "Too strong. I'll accept *fervent.*"

The door opened and Audra and Summer came in. "All ready."

"I want bubble-gum ice cream."

"Ask politely, Summer," Audra said.

Summer lifted her face to Russell. "Can I have bubble-gum ice cream? Please?"

"Would two scoops do?"

"Yay!"

As they left, Russell looked back at his mother, and she could see his need for her approval. She gave him a smile.

It was the least she could do.

"Okay, Evelyn. Spill it," Piper said. "What do you really think about your son dating Audra?"

Evelyn looked out the screen door, listening to the sounds of Russell's car moving away from her. After all her big talk about his settling down, why did she feel like running after him, screaming,

"Come back, come back! You're my little boy!"

"Evelyn?"

She blinked the image away. "I can't think of a nicer girl."

"But she's an unwed mother . . . she's living out a big mistake."

Evelyn swung around to face her. "Don't you ever call Summer a mistake!"

Piper took a step back. "Sorry. I love Summer like my own. It's nothing against the two of them personally. It's just that you, as a mother of a very successful executive, must have had a certain type of girlfriend in mind for Russell."

It took two breaths for Evelyn to calm herself. *Goodness, what brought that on?* But she knew exactly what had caused her outburst: the picture of a tiny baby, hidden in an attic drawer.

And Piper was right. Audra was not the classy, sophisticated beauty that Evelyn had imagined would pair up with Russell. But she was sincere, hardworking, honest, and sweet. What more could a mother ask for?

Piper was still waiting.

"In answer to your question about whether Audra is good enough for Russell . . . I just hope he's good enough for her."

Piper put an arm around her shoulder. "You're a good woman, Evelyn Peerbaugh. It's an honor knowing you."

In a single movement Piper tossed her keys on her kitchen counter and shucked off her shoes. Then she confronted her empty apartment. One more evening, alone.

Although Evelyn had invited her to spend the evening with her and Tessa, Piper had declined. On the way home she'd justified it to herself by pointing out that it wasn't normal for a thirty-three-year-old woman to spend an evening with two much older women. It sounded good as excuses went.

The truth was, Piper hadn't wanted to spend the evening with Evelyn and Tessa because she wanted to feel sorry for herself, and that was hard to do in the presence of good company. Plus, jealousy came into play. Audra had a boyfriend; Mae had a boyfriend; Evelyn was venturing out of her widowhood by taking a cooking class, and Tessa . . . skip Tessa. The lives of the ladies of Peerbaugh Place were turning into a Disneyland compared to her county fair.

Her life wasn't bad, but it was so . . . so

known. One day flowing into another. Work, home, work, home. With an occasional excursion out with a friend. But even that was difficult because most of her friends were married with children. She trudged through life as an odd number. A three in a group of two. A fifth at a table for four.

Why doesn't anything exciting ever happen to me?

There was a knock on the door, and Piper was sincerely glad she hadn't donned her sweats yet. She looked out the peephole. It was Gillie. She opened the door.

Gillie raised a sack. "I come bearing chocolate."

Piper stepped aside. "Then by all means, enter." Piper's mind raced to find a credible reason why Gillie was at her door. They knew each other through Audra, but other than that . . .

Gillie looked around the apartment. "This is nice." She walked toward a piece of furniture Piper had in the eating area. "Is this an Eastlake buffet?"

"I got it at an auction for seventy-five dollars."

Gillie stroked the reddish wood. "My biggest antique bargain has been a set of sterling silver flatware I found at an estate sale for a hundred dollars. It turned out to be circa 1900."

Piper remembered the silver pierced basket she'd found at a flea market and moved to show it off, when she remembered Gillie had never explained why she was there. She pointed to her sack. "You mentioned chocolate?"

"Ah yes . . ." Gillie pulled out a quart of vanilla ice cream.

Piper was disappointed. "Vanilla?"

"I'm not through." Gillie removed a jar of fudge topping and a package of Oreo cookies. "I was in the mood for a little chocoholic fix and thought you might be too." She pulled the carton to her chest. "Was I wrong?"

"No, not at all. I'm just a little curious, that's all. We've never talked much."

Gillie headed to the kitchen. "I know. But after Audra's and Tessa's crises last week . . ." She pried the lid off the ice cream. "You were so wise, Piper. I was impressed."

Piper got out two bowls, two spoons, and an ice cream scoop. "I wasn't speaking out of my own wisdom. It was all God's."

Gillie ran a finger along the inside of the lid and licked it. "Which makes it even better. I liked that trust verse." She shrugged. "It was then I realized I wanted to know you better. And so, *voilà*, here I am." She leaned close. "I guessed on the chocoholic title."

"A good guess."

Gillie filled the bowls to the brim. Then she ripped open the cookie package and crushed three cookies on top of each mound of ice cream.

Piper laughed. "It appears you've done this before."

Gillie brushed her crumby hands over the sink. "Once or twice. How do you think I got through my divorce?"

"Audra told me about that. I'm sorry it didn't work out."

"Me too." She opened the lid of the topping with a pop. "We can get into that after being properly fortified. Heat this up and let's do this right."

It was a grand idea.

There was one cookie left and Piper eyed it, as did Gillie. They giggled at the realization. Then Piper picked it up and broke it in two, handing one half to her new friend.

Gillie popped it in her mouth. "Why does it feel like we've just taken a blood oath by sharing the last cookie?"

It was an apt analogy. "The blood oath

of two sisters, achieved through chocolate. Much less messy and painful than the manly man method."

Gillie licked her fingers loudly. "Amen to that." She leaned back on the couch and patted her stomach. "It's been wonderful to vent with you, Piper. Two single women trying to make their way in a couples world. I feel like I have a compatriot now."

"You do." Piper stacked the bowls. "To tell you the truth, I was feeling a bit sorry for myself before you came. Although I like being alone, sometimes it gets to me."

"As it does to me." Gillie got up and took the dishes to the kitchen. Piper followed, enjoying the fact that Gillie felt enough at home to move about her apartment freely. "You know what's wonderful about tonight?"

Piper put the dishes in the dishwasher. "The fact we found someone else who knows how to binge at our level?"

"Beyond that — and to say that anything is beyond chocolate is quite a feat." She leaned against the counter. "By becoming closer to you, I feel as if I've purchased another insurance policy against loneliness. Not that I'm going to dump myself on your doorstep daily or pepper you with obsessive phone calls." Gillie put a hand to her chest. "And maybe I'm speaking out of turn here, making too much of —"

"No, no," Piper said. "I feel the same way. It's wonderful having another friend to turn to."

"You can't have too many friends."

"Indeed, you can't." Piper felt a satisfaction that went way beyond chocolate.

Mae held Collier's casserole in her lap as he drove. She lifted it, giving her legs a reprieve. "This is hot." She inhaled. "And it smells luscious."

"It's baked ziti with eggplant."

"Gracious garbanzo beans, Collie. How gourmet of you."

"You're surprised I'm a good cook?"

"*Thrilled* is a better word. I love to eat. But at the moment I'm regretting the taco soup I had with the ladies." She patted her stomach. "I want to have plenty of room to eat your cooking."

He risked a glance. "Are you inviting yourself to dinner?"

The church loomed on their right. The parking lot was packed. "Let me get through this Madness thing first."

"Trial by fire."

She eyed the crowd going in. "Why do

I get the feeling I should have worn my asbestos shoes?"

Mae's stomach hurt — and not just from eating too much. Who'd have thought a bunch of Presbyterians could be so fun?

And yes, little Annie Dover had played the violin, but she'd been surprisingly good. Some of the other highlights had been Seth Green on the banjo; a father-son Abbott and Costello team doing "Who's on First?"; a six-person clogging group; and an overabundant woman wearing a shower curtain as a dress while giving a throaty interpretation of an operatic aria. Serious, fun, serious, fun. The pacing was perfect. And it was almost over.

Collier ate the last bite of his strawberry pie and put down his fork. He turned to Mae. "So what do you think of our little church?"

"It's not very godly." She sucked in a breath. "Sorry, that didn't come out right."

"No, it's okay. I think I understand. You think we should be stuffy and serious."

"Pretty much. That's one of the reasons I left God behind a long time ago. He was way too serious for me. And gave me way too many hard times." She felt awkward for saying so much. She barely knew Collier. "You wouldn't understand."

"But I do." His hand swept across the room. "We all do, Mae. The details of our hardships differ, but there's one thing we share."

"Indigestion?"

He smiled. "We share a *yes*."

"For more pie?"

He took her hand, and she could see he was serious. "At some point in our lives, all of us here — all of us who believe in Jesus — have been faced with a question that *He's* asked us."

"What is it?"

"Will you let me do it for you?"

"Do what?"

"Live."

Mae shook her head. "I'm very capable of living on my own, thank you very much."

She was spared his response by a piano fanfare calling people to attention. Collier pointed at the program. "Only two songs left, but you'll love this next one. Dallas and the Babes. They sing for services quite often. But I heard that tonight they have a surprise for us."

"The name of their group doesn't sound very reverent. They actually print that in the Sunday bulletin?"

"Nah. They have another name for that

kind of singing. Quite proper. But we know at heart they'll always be Dallas and the Babes." He pointed to the stage. "Here they —" He stopped chewing and stared. "What the — ?"

A man — whom Mae assumed was Dallas — came on stage wearing a red-and-white-striped jacket and the flapping fingers of a rubber glove on his head. He bowed. "We would like to present to you our rendition of *The 1812 Overture*." He swept a hand toward the stage entrance. "Chickies, if you please?"

Eight women filed onto the stage, wearing matching rubber gloves on their heads, their thumbs locked into their armpits to create wings. An accompanist started playing a rousing rendition of the classical piece while the chickies clucked and squawked to the music. For the cannons in the finale, they used popguns, shooting each other so the song ended with eight dead chickens on the floor and Dallas standing over them, triumphant.

At the last squawk there was enthusiastic applause. Mae found herself saying, "I want to do that!"

She felt Collier's eyes. "It could be arranged. Dallas can always use another Babe."

What was she thinking? She didn't go to church, much less sing in a church group, even if their alias was Dallas and the Babes. She took a drink of tea. "Don't hold me to that. I was overcome by a fit of chicken frenzy."

Collier grinned as if he didn't buy her disclaimer. "I knew Mae would feel at home at *May* Madness. It was inevitable."

"I'm not sure I like you seeing through me so quickly. Transparent Mae."

He patted her hand. "That's a good thing. There's no artifice in you. None."

"Yeah, you got me. What you see is what you get."

His voice mellowed. "And I like what I see."

Mae felt a chuck in her throat. *Okay, how did we get from clucking chickens to romance?* Collier started to say more, but she pointed to the stage. "Shush. The next act is up."

"Now you are acting like a chicken."

She leaned toward him and whispered, "Squawk."

The man at the microphone was Pastor Joe, who'd said the opening prayer. "I want to thank everyone for participating tonight, whether you performed or sat in the audience. I'd like to end with the singing of a song that's very near and dear to thousands." He folded his notes in half, not needing them. "Many of us have heard the story of Horatio Spafford."

There was a communal murmur. It was obvious Mae was in the minority.

"Back in 1871 Spafford was ruined financially in the Chicago Fire. Shortly after, while crossing the Atlantic, Spafford's four daughters were killed in a ship collision. His wife survived and sent a telegram: *Saved alone*. Later, while crossing over the spot in the ocean where his daughters had been lost, Spafford was inspired to write the song we are about to sing. If you'll turn to the back of your program for the words . . ."

There was a shuffling of papers while the pianist started the intro. Then they sang along with Pastor Joe's rich baritone:

When peace like a river attendeth
    my way,
When sorrows like sea billows roll;
Whatever my lot, Thou hast taught
    me to say,
"It is well, it is well with my soul."

During the refrain, Mae's throat tightened, and she had trouble singing the words. How could Spafford write such a thing after his horrible loss? How —

She looked at Collier. His eyes were shut, his forehead tense. He sang from memory, with total conviction.

> Though Satan should buffet,
>   though trials should come,
> Let this blest assurance control,
> That Christ hath regarded
>   my helpless estate,
> And hath shed His own blood
>   for my soul.

Mae looked around the room. There were many like Collier, who sang with their eyes closed. And many who were crying.

Crying over a song? In public? Mae had always thought she felt things deeply. But the depth of feeling that was evident in this room was beyond her experience. Collier opened his eyes and searched her face. He offered a wistful smile as if he understood her turmoil. He took her hand in his and sang on.

> My sin — O the bliss
>   of this glorious thought!
> My sin, not in part but the whole,

408

Is nailed to the cross,
  and I bear it no more,
Praise the Lord, praise the Lord,
  O my soul!

Then suddenly, everything became clear, as if a light had been turned on. All the images of Jesus on the cross Mae had seen throughout her life. All the snippets of fact: *He died for your sins. He forgives you. Trust Jesus.*

Instead of being meaningless, like a jingle she'd unconsciously learned, these truths rose like a billboard in front of her soul. And she knew. She *knew.* It wasn't just a story. It was real. It happened. *Jesus died for my sins. For me.*

She squeezed Collier's hand and felt tears rushing down her face. Crying in public? *Oh yes. How can I not cry? I know what they know. I understand what they've been talking about: Audra, Piper, and Tessie. My blessed sisters. I understand!*

But then her thoughts continued past the cross. Wasn't there more? Wasn't there something about rising from the dead?

Easter, that was it. Wasn't there Easter? Wasn't there eternal life in heaven?

As if on cue, the lyrics answered her.

And Lord, haste the day
   when my faith shall be sight,
The clouds be rolled back as a scroll;
The trump shall resound,
   and the Lord shall descend,
"Even so" — it is well with my soul.

As the last refrain was sung, Mae cupped her face in her hands and sobbed. Collier didn't say a word, but put his arms around her. He held her fast as she gave the most important answer of her life.

Yes. *Oh yes.*

Mae was glad no one was up when she got home. She needed time to digest what she'd just done. What Jesus had just done.

She slipped into her room. She did not turn on the overhead light but walked in the dark to the bedside lamp. She switched it on, feeling comfort in its soft glow. Then she did what she'd been aching to do since the song.

Mae Fitzpatrick got down on her knees to pray.

11

Let Aaron's descendants . . . repeat:
"His faithful love endures forever."
PSALM 118:3

Mae flipped on the lights to Silver-Wear and locked the door behind her. Not that she expected any customers at six on a Saturday morning, but she didn't want to be disturbed.

She put a pot of water on the hot plate for tea and settled behind the workbench. Underneath, from a locked fireproof file, she retrieved a blue felt bag and carefully emptied it onto a padded mat. Seven silver friendship rings.

Except for her own, she was guessing on sizes. But after thirty years in the business she was usually close. Plus, she had an eye for what women liked. And yet, more than the appearance of the jewelry, she hoped the sentiment behind the friendship rings would capture the hearts of the women receiving them.

The idea for the finishing touch had come to her during the night. The perfect symbol of unity among fellow sisters.

She got to work.

Evelyn found Audra, Summer, and Tessa in the kitchen. Although it was a stupid reaction, she felt awkward having them beat her there. As if somehow she'd been a wayward hostess. You'd think by now . . .

Audra and Summer, dressed in grungy clothes, were eating breakfast, and Tessa had the other half of the kitchen table covered with cookbooks. She'd offered to cook the next week.

"Morning, ladies," Evelyn said. "What are your plans for the day?"

"We're building a house," Summer said.

Audra rushed to explain. "We're helping to repair a house. Did you hear about the student from Piper's school whose house burned down, killing his little sister?"

"How awful," Tessa said.

"They didn't have any insurance. We're helping fix it."

"How nice of you," Evelyn said.

There was a moment of silence.

"Russell's coming too. And Gillie."

Summer dipped the corner of her toast in her milk. "Uncle Russell says he hits a mean hammer."

"Wields a mean hammer, baby."

412

It took Evelyn a moment to register the thought of her son doing physical labor.

"You look surprised," Audra said.

"Only because I am. It seems so un-Russell."

Audra laughed. "I thought so too, but when I told him we were going . . ."

Evelyn nodded. *So that's it.*

"Actually, I shamed him into it. I said we were going and if he wanted to spend time with us, he'd have to go too."

"Whatever works," Tessa said.

"And what are your plans, Tessa?"

"I have some errands to do and groceries to buy. I'm taking my turn to cook starting tomorrow evening. It's Mother's Day, so I assume most people will be going out to brunch or lunch. But I'll make a good dinner for us. My daughter called yesterday to say they're taking me to The Crab Shack." She flipped a page and Evelyn caught a glimpse of a luscious slice of cake. "Where is Russell taking you?"

Evelyn had wondered that same thing, but Russell hadn't said a word. In fact, when she'd seen him at the house last night, she'd assumed he was here to invite her out for Mother's Day brunch.

"Did he forget?" Tessa said.

"Of course he didn't forget," Audra said.

"He probably just failed to mention it." It was a good attempt to save the situation, but Evelyn didn't believe it for a moment. She hated herself for having high expectations for a holiday. She was notorious for getting herself worked up to expect flowers or a present or a dinner out, only to be disappointed when Aaron or Russell hadn't read her mind. She'd tried to get into the habit of expecting nothing, but always failed. She expected — she yearned for — the ideal. And no amount of failed attempts would stifle that hope. She could not accept the fact that most of the time she was an afterthought to the men in her life.

"What are you doing today, Evelyn?" Audra asked.

"Piper's coming over and we're going to tackle my room."

"How fun."

"But you sound nervous," Tessa said.

"I'm not good with change."

"That's not true at all," Audra said.

"Sure it is. I like things to remain the same."

"Human nature." Audra drank the last of her orange juice. "But just look at the change you've handled in the past few months. Your husband's death, starting a boardinghouse, dealing with all of us, taking care of Summer." She stood and gave Evelyn a hug from the back. "So don't say you don't take change well. You're doing great."

When she put it that way . . .

Evelyn sat a little straighter in her chair.

Evelyn opened the door to Piper, whose arms were overflowing.

"Ready or not, here I come."

They managed to get the paint, the brushes, the rollers, the wallpaper border, and other equipment into the house, jostling and bumping each other like Laurel and Hardy.

Piper dropped her load to the floor. "We'll have to work on the coordination a bit, or we're in for a long day."

"I didn't know we were painting," Evelyn said. The thought of moving all the furniture did not appeal to her.

"Just the top two feet of the wall — a pretty celery color." Piper retrieved the wallpaper border and unrolled a strip. "Do you like it? We'll paint the top of the wall green, and put this in between the green and the white."

"You can do that?"

Piper put an arm around her shoulder. "Trust me."

Evelyn wasn't sure she had a choice.

Piper had more energy than a dozen Evelyns. She tackled the room like a moving man on a tight schedule. The chintz chair and the bedside tables were carried into the hallway. The high dresser was moved to the middle of the room and the bed pulled away from the wall enough for Piper to squeeze a step stool in between it and the wall. The only piece of furniture in their way was the mirrored oak dresser.

Evelyn eyed it warily, then the doorway. It didn't look as if it could fit through, plus it was heavy. "Are you sure we can move this one?"

"Ah, come on, Evelyn. Are you a man or a mouse?"

"Neither. And right now I'd go for a man *in* the house."

Russell popped his head in the door. "One man, at your service."

"Where did you come from?" Evelyn asked.

"Why are people always asking me that? Actually, the stork brought me."

"Russ—"

"I'm here to pick up Audra and Summer. We're playing the part of good Samaritans." He looked out to the hall.

"Gillie's here too. I've been captured by women, forcing me into doing good deeds."

"It's about time," Evelyn said, though she knew her son's heart was plenty good.

Russell's attention was drawn to the hall, where he had a muted conversation. Though Evelyn couldn't hear the words, she caught the hint of Audra's voice. He turned back to Evelyn. "Sorry." He cleared his throat. "Before I forget, I've been meaning to ask . . . would you like to go to brunch tomorrow for Mother's Day?"

More conversation in the hall. When Russell turned back to Evelyn this time, his face was flushed. "Audra says I should admit that I forgot. I did. I'm sorry. It's just that —"

More muted conversation with Audra. It was odd getting talked to in segments.

One more time. With a sigh this time. "It's just nothing. I forgot. No excuses. Will you forgive me?"

"Of course I forgive you," Evelyn said. "But there's something I'd like even more than lunch."

"You got it."

"Help us move this dresser?"

"No problem." He wiped his hands on his jeans. "Where to?"

"While you've got hold of it, the front porch would be good."

"The porch? Renting out another room, Mom? Alfresco? It does have quite a view."

"I'll call Goodwill and they'll come get it. Unless someone wants it . . ." She checked their faces. There were no takers. "That bad, huh?"

"It's very . . . unique," Audra said.

Piper motioned Russell over. "Unique nothing. The thing's ugly. Evelyn, empty the drawers on the bed. Russell, take an end."

Evelyn spread the last sheet of plastic drop cloth while Piper drew a faint penciled line two feet from the ceiling. She used a level like a pro.

"That was nice," Piper said out of the blue. "Russell. You know . . ."

"It was nice he forgot Mother's Day?"

"It was nice he admitted forgetting. It shows character."

"He had to be prodded by Audra."

"Behind every good man there's a good —"

"It's too soon to say such a thing. They've only gone out a few times — that I know of."

"You're right," Piper said. "And I'm not

trying to marry them off. But it's a good sign that they feel comfortable enough to nudge each other into being better people."

"I never thought of it that way."

"Well, you should. You should." She handed Evelyn the level. "Hand me the tape, will you?"

Tessa had not meant to stop by Mae's shop. But when her errands took her right by the entrance to Silver-Wear, and when Mae looked up from her work at just that moment, Tessa had no choice but to go in.

And yet Mae's reaction was not one of pleasure.

"Tessie!" Her hands scrambled across her workbench like a child trying to hide the candy she'd stolen from the pantry. "What are you doing here?"

Tessa moved farther into the store, wanting to see what Mae was covering up. "You need to work on your welcomes, Mae."

Mae tossed a towel over whatever she was working on and seemed relaxed for the first time. "Sorry about that. You just surprised me."

"Obviously." She nodded to the covered

work. "What are you working on that's so secretive?"

"A commission. I . . . I don't like people to see my work in progress. I only show it after I'm sure it's the best it can be."

"Sounds like an artist."

"I choose to take that as a compliment." She moved in front of the counter, forming an obvious buffer between Tessa and her work. "What are you doing out?"

"You make it sound as if I've been let loose from some asylum."

Mae laughed. "It does get crazy around Peerbaugh Place."

Tessa didn't mention that Piper's and Evelyn's project *had* made the house more chaotic than she liked. "Starting tomorrow night I'm cooking. I'm heading to the grocery store right now."

"What's on the menu?"

"I thought I'd start with ham loaf and broccoli casserole, and —"

"Ugh."

"Excuse me?"

"Oh, I'm sorry, Tessie, no offense to your cooking. I'm sure it will be delicious. But I had my fill of ham loaf Wednesday night with Collier. Could you possibly move that entrée to another week when you cook?"

Tessa put a hand on her purse, protectively shielding her menu inside. "I suppose, but —"

Mae's eyes suddenly lit up. "Actually, I want to share with you something wonderful that happened Wednesday night — above and beyond the ham loaf. I wasn't quite sure how to begin to tell everyone, but you, of all people, will appreciate the change that came over me when Collier —"

"I can't believe you're really dating that man."

"Tessie, we've been through this. He's a nice —"

"You date too much, Mae. With too many different men."

"But this was only the second time I've gone out with Collier. We went to his —"

Tessa raised a hand to stop her words. "Don't share the details of your escapades. I don't want —"

Mae's hands found her hips. "Escapades?"

"Your rendezvous with our neighbor."

"So you're saying it would be better if he lived a block away?"

What am I saying? Tessa realized she had no idea how she had gotten on this subject. She'd stopped into Mae's to be nice and had ended up insulting her.

So much for the new Tessa.

"You know what? You may know a lot about books, Tessie, but you know nothing about life." Mae moved to the door and opened it. "Now, if you don't mind, I have work to do. And make the ham loaf any evening you want. Don't go out of your way for me, Tess-*ah*."

Tessa held her tongue and walked through the open door. If only she'd had such verbal restraint a few minutes sooner.

The door slammed behind her, sounding like a hard slap from God.

Tessa could have used help bringing the groceries in, and thought about going inside and asking Piper or Evelyn. But she didn't. They were busy, and no one else was home. She'd have to do it herself. Slow but sure.

She arranged the handles of two sacks in her hands and headed to the front door.

Suddenly Collier came rushing from across the street. "Can I help you with those?"

"It's *may I*."

He stopped two yards short of her. "*May I help you with those?*"

Why do I have to be so rude? As if the scene at Mae's wasn't enough. "I apologize. I could use some help, thank you."

He started to reach for her bags, but she stopped him. "I've got these. There's more in the trunk."

He nodded but raced up the porch steps in front of her. "Let me get the door for you."

They carried the groceries inside, Collier insisting on retrieving the rest of the bags. "That's the last of them," he said.

"Thank you. I appreciate your help."

He wiped his hand on his trousers. "Collier Ames. Neighbor-at-large."

She shook his hand. "Tessa Klein. Nice to meet you."

"You too."

"So you're the one who kept Mae out so late the other night?"

He blinked twice. "I'm not sure ten o'clock could be considered late."

"Where did you go? Out to some bar?"

Collier's look changed from friendly to incredulous. And Tessa realized — too late — she was doing it again.

"It seems you have the wrong opinion about me, Ms. Klein. And Mae too. If you're angry about my complaints to the city, I've already apologized for that, but I will apologize again — to you. I'm sorry."

A question surfaced in Tessa's head. *No,*

don't you dare. Don't say it. She said it. "I always wondered . . . how did Mae get you to back down?"

He raised an eyebrow. "By being her charming self."

Tessa let out a laugh.

"You don't find Mae charming?"

"It's not for me to judge."

He leveled her with a look. "Not only is Mae charming, she's been charmed — by our church. Though it's none of your business, that's where we were Wednesday night when we were out so *late*."

Tessa's throat was dry. "She's been to church with you?"

"We had our May Madness this week. It was a lot of crazy fun, but also a very serious moment in her life."

"Why's that?"

He studied her a moment. She looked away and started emptying a sack of canned goods.

"I think you need to ask Mae about that. It's her testimony."

She glanced over her shoulder at him. "Testimony?"

"Let's just say that Mae's life will never be the same."

Mae's words at the store came back to her: *"I want to share with you something*

wonderful that happened Wednesday night. . . .
You, of all people, will appreciate the change
that came over me when Collier —"

Tessa finally got it. "You mean she chose Jesus?"

He headed for the front door. "Ask her. Nice to meet you, Ms. Klein. Maybe we can do it again sometime."

She heard the door close. Another door. Another slap.

Tessa's legs gave out. She lurched toward a kitchen chair just as Piper came in the kitchen.

Piper rushed toward her. "Tessa, what's wrong?"

Tessa couldn't answer. She could only shake her head and press her fingers to her temples.

Piper set down the empty glasses she'd been carrying and touched her shoulder. "Was that the neighbor helping you?"

Tessa nodded.

"What did he do to upset you? If he hurt your feelings —"

Tessa removed her hands and let the words flood. "I hurt *him!* I hurt *everyone.* I try and try to be better. I'm willing myself to be a better woman, but I keep messing up. I can't do it. I just can't do it."

425

Piper rubbed her back. "No, of course you can't."

"What?"

"Of course *you* can't. We talked about this the other night, remember? Trusting Jesus? 'I can do everything with the help of Christ who gives me the strength I need.' "

"That's a verse from Philippians."

"Yes, it is."

Tessa's thoughts flew back to a few mornings before, when she'd awakened feeling new. And then she remembered her prayers of confession. All good, except for the part when *she* promised to do better, to work hard at the changes she felt God was trying to make in her. Had she ever asked *Him* to do it for her? Had she ever truly surrendered? Or had she held on to even this, thinking she was strong enough to do it on her own? "I've been trying too hard," she finally said.

"A common mistake."

"I need to let Jesus change me."

"He's much better at it than we are."

"I need to let go."

Piper spread her hands. "That's it."

Tessa felt as if a weight had been lifted. She didn't *need* to be strong. God would be strong for her. *"For when I am weak, then I am strong."* "There's strength in surrender."

"You got it." Piper picked up the glasses she had set down and headed to the refrigerator. For the first time, Tessa noticed she had green paint on her hands and swiped across her cheek. "You want some help putting away the groceries?" Piper asked.

Tessa felt a little dazed. "No, I can do it. I think I need some time alone."

Piper filled the glasses and started to leave.

"Piper?"

"Mmm?"

"Thanks."

"Hey, no problem. I can only teach what I've learned myself."

Teach? Another one of Mae's comments sped front and center: *"You may know a lot about books, Tessie, but you know nothing about life."*

Was that true? Were all the things Tessa tried to teach just *things?* Names, dates, and definitions? Interesting perhaps, but not essential in day-to-day living. In contrast, Piper had just taught her about life — from lessons learned in her *own* life.

Can I teach like that?

"Tessa? You okay?"

Tessa found she was clutching her hands to her chest. But there was no pain; it was just an old habit. "I'm fine. Or I will be fine."

"We're upstairs if you need us."

That was nice to know, but for the moment, the only One Tessa needed was the *Man* upstairs. The two of them had some heavy talking to do. And for once in her life, Tessa vowed she would listen.

Evelyn couldn't believe what a fast worker Piper was. The painting was complete, and Piper said they could put up the border between the green and white portions of the wall later on.

She came in with refills of iced tea. "What do you think?"

"I think I love it. I can't believe the difference a little color makes."

"Just wait until we get the quilt back on the bed." She kissed her fingertips like a Frenchman. *"Magnifique."*

"But what are we going to put on the wall that held the mirrored dresser?" Evelyn asked.

"You have any extra furniture lying about? And some pictures, knickknacks, and lamps? You have a stash somewhere?"

The attic. "Actually, I do." Evelyn went into the hall and had Piper help her move one of the bedside tables out of the way so she could pull down the attic stairs.

Piper rubbed her hands together in anticipation. "Oooh, attic treasures. My favorite."

They ascended the stairs, Evelyn letting Piper take the lead. "I'm not sure about the treasure part, but there's plenty of junk up here."

"One man's junk is another man's —"

"I hope you'll think that after you see it."

Piper reached the top of the stairs and found the light. "Oh my . . . you'll never get me out of here." She made a beeline for the area under the turret where pictures were stacked against a trunk.

Evelyn negotiated the last step. "Don't go too far or I'll lose you. It's quite a mess. I really should go through it." She pulled her blouse away from her chest. "Whew, it's hot."

"I love hot," Piper said. "And as for going through it, why don't you let me do the honors? You could go back down and clean up the drop cloths and such."

It sounded like a great idea. "You sure?"

Piper's face glowed like a kid's at Christmas. "Positive."

Although Piper wasn't looking for clothing, she couldn't resist taking a peek in the trunks. It was like taking a tour through history: floral printed dresses with huge skirts and small waists from the fifties, wool Army uniforms from a world war, crepe dresses from the thirties, filmy lawn dresses from the turn of the last century. She was tempted to try some on but knew once she started, the rest of the day would be consumed.

She reluctantly returned the clothes to their resting place and decided to start her quest by searching for the largest item needed: a piece of furniture to replace the mirrored dresser.

One of the trunks was a possibility, and a bookshelf would always work. But then she saw the perfect piece. It was near the stairs, but she'd walked by it in her first moments of enthusiasm.

A vanity dressing table.

Her eyes caressed the trifold mirrors and the matching bench with a seat cushion that could easily be recovered in a complementary fabric. There were even enough drawers to hold Evelyn's toiletries. In a master bedroom it would have been an extravagance, but in a woman's bedroom, it was precisely right, a concession to a female's domain.

She opened the middle drawer under the

mirror, imagining it lined with a dainty shelf paper —

The drawer wasn't empty.

Piper pulled out a color photo of Evelyn holding a baby in her arms. *It's Russell.*

But, wait. Russell in a pink blanket?

Piper moved closer to the light, needing a better look. There was something odd about Evelyn's face. Instead of being engulfed in a glow of pride, there was a wistful sadness in her smile. As if . . . as if . . .

She looked in the drawer again and found a tiny pink hospital wristband. *Baby Wilson.*

Piper opened the other drawers of the vanity. There were no more pictures. In fact, there was nothing else in the drawers. All had been emptied. Except this one. Except for this evidence of Evelyn and a baby girl.

Where was the girl now? Evelyn had never mentioned her, a fact that wasn't *that* odd because Piper hadn't known her very long. But the photo and bracelet were tucked away, the lone occupants of a vanity in an attic. Purposely hidden? That brought up different explanations. And more questions.

Sounds of Evelyn cleaning the bedroom below filtered up the attic steps. She was oblivious that her secret had been discovered. Should it be a secret that remained a secret? Should Piper slip the picture back in the drawer and pretend she'd never found it? Or should she ask Evelyn about it — ask what happened to the baby girl?

It's none of my business.

Piper pulled the picture to her chest and closed her eyes. *Lord, help me do the right thing, the thing that will help Evelyn, not hurt her.*

She was still a few moments, hoping to feel a sudden urge to race down the stairs and ask Evelyn about the picture. No such feeling came. Just a subtle knowledge that she shouldn't push it, that she should let the situation evolve on its own.

Piper put the picture and wristband back and gently shut the drawer. She went to the top of the attic steps and called down, "Evelyn? Do you want to come up here a moment? I think I've found the perfect piece of furniture."

When Evelyn saw Piper standing next to the dressing table, gesturing to it like a game-show hostess presenting a prize, her heartbeat did a double bounce in her toes.

"What do you think?" Piper asked. "It's a wonderful piece — and very feminine.

Those perfume bottles you had on the other dresser would look great on it. And a doily . . . you've got some doilies around here someplace, don't you?"

Evelyn stood at the top of the steps, staring at the chest that held her secret. To bring it down into the main part of the Peerbaugh house. To move this hiding place to the bedroom where she and Aaron had slept for three decades. A melding of what could have been with what was.

But Aaron's gone. You can bring it down now. You can —

"Evelyn? Are you okay?"

Piper was looking at her funny and was waiting for an answer, but Evelyn couldn't remember the question. She took a step toward the vanity but stopped when Piper put a hand in front of *the* drawer. "It has nice storage, don't you think?"

Storage of my secret.

Piper didn't move her hand, and suddenly that nonmovement had significance. Piper's hand sitting in front of *the* drawer. Her hand, waiting for permission to open it. Evelyn looked at Piper. Piper looked at Evelyn. They shared a moment. Evelyn swallowed. "Did you see it?"

Piper removed her hand and nodded. "I didn't mean to pry."

Evelyn put her hand to her mouth. She felt tears threaten.

"You don't have to tell me, Evelyn."

And Evelyn knew she didn't *have* to. But maybe she *could*. This was Piper, a godly, kind friend. Maybe she *could* tell her.

Evelyn's hand moved toward the drawer. Piper stepped back, giving her room. Evelyn removed the picture and her baby's hospital bracelet. It was so small it slipped around her thumb. "I've never spoken of this to anyone. Ever."

"Why not?"

She knew her shrug was not a good enough answer.

"She's your baby?"

Evelyn nodded and touched a finger to the picture of her baby's face.

"What happened to her?"

Eyes up, then down. "I put her up for adoption."

"Really?"

"I know a lot of girls keep their babies nowadays, but those were different times. Different rules."

"No, no," Piper said. "I didn't say *really* because I didn't approve. I said it because *I'm* adopted."

"You are? Wayne and Wanda aren't — ?"

"Wayne and Wanda *are* my parents.

They raised me. They loved me. The only thing they didn't do was give birth to me."

Evelyn nodded, noting the distinction. "My baby went to good parents too. They provided for her in a way I couldn't."

"So you and Aaron weren't married yet?"

"I hadn't even met Aaron yet. He came later."

"So what happened to the baby's father?"

"His name was Frank Albert Halvorson." Evelyn smiled and felt a blush like the schoolgirl she'd been. "We were in college. He had the most magnificent smile. Frank was a very bright man. Very intense. I was fascinated by the way he could see inside a situation. Everything was so clear to him — even when he was wrong."

"What did he think about your baby?"

Evelyn was pulled to the attic window as if the memories were floating just outside. "He never knew about her. He was sent to Vietnam. I found out I was pregnant a month after he left. And then he was killed." The tears surprised her.

"I'm so sorry."

Evelyn sniffed, got a tissue from the pocket of her jeans, and returned to her place by the vanity. "So there I was, without the love of my life, pregnant."

"Did your parents know?"

"No. And they wouldn't have made it easy for me. I know that sounds so petty, that I gave my baby up because it was the easiest solution, but —"

"You were still in college?"

"I was just starting my last year when I found out I was pregnant."

"At least you didn't abort her."

Evelyn cringed, and Piper looked as if she wished she could take the bluntness back. "I never even considered that. She was alive. A life. I couldn't kill her." She fingered the hem of her sweatshirt.

The moment passed.

She continued her story. "Frank died within weeks of getting to Vietnam. I'd sent a letter telling him the news when he —" She took a deep breath. "The letter was returned. The news of my pregnancy and the news of his death crossed in the mail."

"How horrible."

"With Frank's death, everything changed. What could have worked — awkward though it was — was suddenly impossible. I was so alone."

"Oh, Evelyn . . ." Piper took her hand.

"So what happened after you found out Frank died?"

"I went away, moved across the state, using the excuse that I needed time to get over his death. That was true, but there was so much more because our baby was coming. And though I made the decision to give her up fairly soon into the pregnancy, I wanted that time alone with her *before* her birth since I knew I wouldn't have it after. Does that make any sense?"

Piper nodded.

It was Evelyn's turn to ask questions. "You're adopted. Have you been happy? You turned out great, but . . . were you happy?"

"I've been very happy — and blessed. Mom and Dad are great parents. Just strict enough to rein me in but open enough to make me see the possibilities of life. And they gave me my faith. I don't know what I would do without —" She stopped. "How did you get through all this without God?"

In a moment of revelation, Evelyn answered. "Actually, I didn't. I had God back then. I prayed. And looking back, I think He guided me toward this decision, though I didn't realize it at the time."

"If you believed once, what pulled you

away from Him?"

Evelyn sighed deeply. "I don't want to put the blame — at least not all the blame — on Aaron. But his lack of faith in God things affected my life. He made it easy to forget what I knew. And though I may have depended on God during my pregnancy, it was too easy for me to transfer that dependence over to my husband after we were married."

"What did he think about your baby?"

"He never knew." Evelyn shook her head, her chin set. "I'm not a strong woman, Piper. I wish I were."

She suddenly snapped back to the old Piper. "Oh, pooh. You're plenty strong. Look at what you've accomplished since Aaron died."

Evelyn felt a surge of hope. "That's what Audra told me earlier today."

"See? Two women who care about you, telling you the truth."

Evelyn extended a hand and Piper took it. "I loved my baby before she was even born, Piper. Just as I'm sure your mother loved you." Her voice broke. "I've loved her all these years. No matter where she is."

They let their hands drop and looked toward the hallway, where the sounds of people filtered up the stairs. Audra, Summer, Russell, Gillie, Mae . . . and Tessa were in the kitchen. Everyone was home.

"Mom?" It was Russell's voice. "Olly, olly, oxen free! Where are you?"

"Up here in the attic." She cleared her throat, hoping the next time she spoke her voice would sound stronger.

They heard footsteps on the front stairs.

"What do you want to do?" Piper whispered. "It can be our secret. I promise. Or else . . . do you want to tell Russell?"

The idea shocked her. Evelyn had never considered telling Russell because she had never considered telling Aaron. But now that Aaron was gone . . .

What purpose would it serve? Would Russell think badly of her for having an illegitimate child even though that was another life ago? In the past few weeks Evelyn felt as if she was truly starting fresh. All that was old had passed away.

Including old secrets?

Russell appeared at the bottom of the attic steps. He came up, his man-sized frame filling the narrow space. When was the last time she'd seen him up here? As a child playing forts and castles?

He stood at the top of the steps and

looked around. "I see the old attic hasn't changed much. It was always a great place to capture spiders for science projects." He stopped looking around. "I hope you're not letting Piper discover our family secrets, Mom."

Evelyn exchanged a look with Piper. Piper headed for the steps. "If you'll excuse me, I have some border to put up."

Russell started to follow her, but Evelyn touched his arm. "Rusty?"

He looked at her, immediately concerned. "Rusty? Talk about Memory Lane. I can't remember the last time you called me that."

"Can we sit down?"

"Up here?"

She moved to a trunk and patted it. He took a seat and she stood before him.

"Mom, what's wrong?"

"There's something I have to tell you, and I don't know how. I'm not good at words and I —"

"Mother! Just say it. Simple and sweet."

She moved to the dresser, retrieved the picture and wristband, and handed them to him. He looked at both. "Wilson. Your maiden name."

"Because I was still a maiden."

His eyes returned to the photo. "But this

is you. With a baby girl."

"*My* baby girl."

His eyes returned to the photo as if it could offer more information. "When? Who?"

"It happened before I even met your father. The baby's father and I were engaged. I got pregnant."

His eyes grew wide. "You were an unwed mother?"

"Let me explain . . ."

After she was through with her story, she gave him a moment to digest the words. "I've shocked you," she said.

"How could you?"

She felt as if she'd been slapped. "How could I what, Russell?"

"How could you sleep —"

"I was not promiscuous, Russell. I've only slept with two —" He waved his hands to fend off her words. But she couldn't stop now. This had to be finished. "You're not being fair, Russell. How can you be so hard on me and yet date an unwed mother? Audra made the same mistake I —"

"No, she didn't!"

Evelyn stepped back.

Russell took a deep breath, which seemed to calm him. Somewhat. "Audra kept her child. How could you put yours up for adoption? Your own child."

She looked down, trying to hold in the swell of tears. "Her father was dead, Russell. We weren't married. My family never would have understood. I was all alone. I gave her up because I loved her enough to think about what was best for the child." She lifted her face, letting a tear fall unashamed. "Adoption is the hardest — but often the best — choice for everyone involved. I made every effort to see that my baby would grow up with two wonderful parents who wanted her, ached for her, before they even knew of her. An adopted child is a wanted child."

"Was I wanted?"

There was such insecurity in his tone. She knelt at his feet. "Oh, Russell. Of course you were. You were the child of my marriage. You were very wanted."

He stood and pulled her to her feet. "This is going to take some getting used to, Mom."

"I'm sure it will. But it shouldn't change anything, Russell. This is my past. You are my present."

"So you're not planning on searching for her, or anything like that?"

Evelyn was shocked to find that she'd

never considered it. She'd made a decision thirty-three years ago. There was no reason to change it now. She found she could answer with conviction. "No, I'm not planning to search for her." She cocked her head and looked at him intently. "After the initial shock . . . are *you* going to be okay with this?"

He shrugged, a gesture she'd seen a thousand times.

She cupped her hands around his face. "You are my dearest, dearest child. My boy. My son. Nothing changes that. I love you, Rusty."

He nodded and let her pull him into her arms.

As they went downstairs to join the others, Russell paused. "Are you going to tell the others?"

"Do you want me to?"

He hesitated, then shook his head. "There's no reason to, is there? It's our secret now, right?"

Evelyn considered not telling him that Piper knew but realized that having a secret about a secret might be a double whammy. "Actually, Piper knows too. But she won't tell. She's adopted. She understands."

He seemed to consider this a moment.

"All right. Then just the three of us know. Let's leave it at that."

They found everyone in the kitchen, raiding the refrigerator. Everyone but Piper.

"Where'd Piper go?" Evelyn asked.

Audra was spreading mayo on a slice of bread. "She said she had an errand to run and would see us later."

Piper gave her usual *knock-knock-knock* on her parents' front door, then walked on in. "Hey, it's me."

Her mother popped out of the kitchen. "Hi, honey. Come on back. I'm making popcorn. We're watching that Robert Redford–Barbra Streisand movie."

"*The Way We Were?*"

"That's the one."

The way we were. How appropriate. Her entire reason for stopping by was because of the way they were.

Her mother got another bowl and napkin. "Get yourself something to drink, but hurry. Your father's champing at the bit to push Play."

"He likes this movie? It's a chick flick."

"He's tolerating this movie for me. The true reason he's eager to get it started is that there's a baseball game on soon."

That made more sense. Piper got a diet Coke from the fridge and followed her mother into the family room at the back of the house.

Her father looked up from watching TV. "Hey, Piper girl. To what do we owe this honor?"

Wanda took up three bowls of popcorn and handed them out. Piper took hers, but set it on the coffee table.

"Sit down, honey."

She shook her head and stood in front of them.

Her mother's face clouded. "What's wrong?"

"Can you mute that, Dad?"

He studied her eyes a moment, then aimed the remote around her and turned the set off, giving her his full attention. He was always good at that. Making her feel important. They were such good parents. Which is why she had come.

"I just wanted to tell you thank you."

"For what, dear?" her mother asked.

"For adopting me. For loving me. For being you."

She leaned down and pulled her dad into a hug.

"Goodness, Pipe. We love you too. Having you come into our lives was the

445

best thing that ever happened to us. We've always considered you a gift from God."

Piper moved to hug her mother and then swiped a hand across her wet cheek. "I know I shouldn't get all blubbery like this . . ."

Her mother smelled like White Shoulders perfume. She had always smelled like White Shoulders. She would always smell like White Shoulders.

"You get blubbery anytime you want, honey," Wanda said. "And we always appreciate a hug. But what brought this on? Why today?"

Piper grabbed a tissue from the box by the lamp and blew her nose. "Can't a girl feel a surge of thanks?"

"Of course, but —"

Piper sat next to her mom and took a bowl of popcorn in her lap. "Start the movie, Dad."

"You're going to watch it with us, honey?"

"I need to get back to Evelyn's. I kind of rushed out of there, but I'll watch a little with you. One hanky's worth."

Later that evening, as Piper hung the last picture in the newly decorated bedroom, Evelyn sat on the bed and put one of

Aaron's shirts to her face and inhaled. His scent filled her nostrils, and she marveled at the uniqueness of it. It was a special gift he'd left behind. It was something a person didn't think about, that just *was*.

She folded the shirt and placed it in the last box of his clothes. Her bed was finally cleared of the contents from the mirrored dresser.

Piper glanced over from her work. "You okay?"

It took Evelyn a moment to understand the question. She put a hand on the final box. "It had to be done. There wasn't room for them anymore." She stroked the lid. "Why do I feel guilty about that?"

"About packing things up or about changing the room?"

"About making it mine so soon. It's like I'm glad he's gone. I feel like a greedy teenager pouncing on their older sibling's room before they've backed out of the driveway on the way to college."

"Maybe we should have waited? I hope I didn't push —"

"It was my idea. And I think I went into it knowing it would hurt." She found Piper's eyes. "Isn't it strange? To *choose* hurt?"

Piper straightened the edge of the picture with a finger. "I heard that Mother Teresa said, 'I know God won't give me more than I can handle. I just wish He wouldn't trust me so much.'"

Evelyn laughed. "She must have been a ball of fire."

"A ball of fire for God."

She looked upon Piper with fresh eyes. "Like you."

Piper shook her head. "I try, but I —"

"I've learned so much about God since I met you." She let the words settle. "Since Aaron's death, you've been the one to help me realize God *does* care about me." She stroked the lid of the box once more. "Wanda and Wayne did a good job with you. I hope my own baby fared as well." She sighed. "So many coincidences led me to this point."

Piper shook her head. "I don't believe in coincidence, and neither should you. God is in control. He has a definite plan and is constantly giving us opportunities to be a part of it."

Evelyn shuddered. "Opportunities? That sounds too iffy. Like we can mess it up if we're not careful."

"We can."

"Wouldn't it be better if God just made us do what He wants us to do?"

"Better? No. Easier? Sure. But what would be the point of that? If we were all mindless automatons . . . what a bore."

Evelyn laughed. "I'm sure God would prefer boring once in a while. Sometimes our choices make things *too* interesting."

"But that's the point. It's our choice to follow Him or not. He doesn't want us to say yes to Him because we're afraid of Him or because we think we can get something out of the arrangement. Or even because we think it's the right thing to do. He wants us to say yes to Him because we want to." She put a hand over her heart. "I ache for Him sometimes. As if my heart will burst with my love for Him."

Evelyn touched Piper's arm. "You're too good."

Piper's head shook vigorously. "Not at all! But that's the whole point. I'm not good, but He loves me anyway. God loves *me* — Piper — enough to have let His Son die for me."

Evelyn squirmed. The whole Jesus-on-the-cross bit had always made her feel —

Piper put a hand on Evelyn's knee. "That makes you feel uncomfortable, doesn't it?"

"It does," Evelyn said. "A little. I mean, how could God allow that to happen?

Couldn't He save His own Son?"

"In an instant." Piper snapped her fingers. "But He actually *sent* His Son to die, as a part of His plan."

"Some plan."

Piper sat on the bed beside her, her eyes bright. "But it was. It was a perfect plan. The God who created everything, including you and me, wanted us to have a way to truly know Him, so He sent His Son as a baby. Imagine! Every detail was carefully planned, and an innocent baby was God in human flesh."

"But why did He have to die?"

"So when *we* die we won't have to be separated from God because of our sins. Jesus' death paid the penalty for us. It made us clean — gave us a way to be pure enough to get to heaven to be in God's presence."

"I'm not sure I understand all that."

Piper fingered her lower lip, thinking. Finally she dropped her hand and spoke. "It comes down to this: we are all sinners. We're born with a sinful nature. Because Jesus was born, crucified on the cross, and rose from the dead, anyone can be accepted by God. Jesus is called 'Savior' because He saved us from ourselves."

Evelyn put a hand to her forehead. Piper

made everything clear, but it was almost too much to grasp.

Piper's voice was soft. "Do you believe all that, Evelyn?"

"Yes, I guess I do."

"Then tell Him so."

"What?"

"He's listening. Tell Him you believe in what He did. Just talk to Him like a friend — that's what prayer is."

She took Evelyn's hands, and Evelyn felt her throat tighten. She found a breath and began. "God, thank you for loving me so much. I really do believe what Piper has told me about your Son. Thank you for sending Him to earth. I'm glad I have a Savior and I'm glad You're in my life."

Evelyn lifted her eyes to look at Piper, needing approval for her prayer. Piper said no words, but her look . . . her smile . . .

What a day. What a glorious day!

12

Whatever is good and perfect comes
to us from God above,
who created all heaven's lights.
Unlike them, he never changes or casts
shifting shadows.
JAMES 1:17

Evelyn opened her eyes. A new room looked back at her. A new world.

She sat up in bed, pushing herself against the headboard. The sun peeked into her bedroom curtains, lighting her newly decorated room. She adjusted her pillows so she could sit against them to fully look upon the work. It was definitely not Aaron's room anymore. It was different. Better, maybe, but nonetheless, its newness was a bit disconcerting. So many changes in so short a time.

She'd seen those self-tests where you rated the events in your life in order to figure out a total stress rating. She was positive she'd be off the charts: death of a spouse, financial setback, change of residence — or at least change *within* her residence, meeting new people, continuing her education, getting a new job taking care of Summer. And the pièce de résistance, which even the most thorough test wouldn't dream of mentioning: sharing the truth about a baby she gave up for adoption.

So maybe it wasn't so out of line for her emotions to be undulating like the water of a lake on a breezy day.

A small voice nudged her from within. *But what about Me?*

Evelyn clamped her eyes shut, appalled she'd forgotten the biggest change that dwarfed all the others. "Lord! I'm here! I'm sorry not to mention You. I didn't forget You, not really. It's just so new. Please forgive —"

There was a crash of dishes and a yelp from Summer. Evelyn bolted from the room. Within seconds the other three bedroom doors flew open, their occupants in the hall.

Summer was on the stairs, frantically gathering the fallen dishes. She looked up at her audience, her face stricken. "I tripped."

"I'll get a towel," Tessa said. She slipped into the bathroom.

Audra rushed down to her and righted a glass that had contained orange juice, while Summer frantically plucked up the Cheerios that were strewn over multiple steps. Milk dripped from the second step onto the third. Evelyn tried not to think of the stain on her carpet runner.

"Here." Tessa returned with two towels, one dry and one damp.

"What were you doing, baby?" Audra said. "You know better than to bring food upstairs. You know that's against the rules. You tell Aunt Evelyn you're sorry for making a mess on her pretty carpet. You —"

Evelyn saw tears in Summer's eyes. "I don't need an apology. It's okay, sweetie."

"It is not okay. She had no right bringing that big tray up those stairs." Audra clucked Summer under the chin. "What were you thinking?"

"But, Mommy —"

"Mommy nothing. You have got to be more responsible and follow the —"

"Hey, Audra," Mae said. "Lay off. Can't you see what she was doing?"

Audra pressed a towel onto a puddle of milk. "Making a mess, that's what she was doing."

Suddenly, Summer sat on a step, her cupped hand holding fallen Cheerios. Her shoulders sagged and her chin quivered.

Audra flipped a hand. "Don't stop now,

little girl. We've still got a lot of mess to clean —"

"Happy Mother's Day, Mommy."

They all froze as the truth blared.

Summer raised her face to her mother. "I was bringing you breakfast in bed. I didn't mean —"

With an expulsion of regret, Audra side-stepped the mess to get to her daughter, pulling her into her arms. "Oh, baby. I'm so sorry, so sorry. I didn't understand."

"I didn't mean to fall."

"Of course you didn't."

"What a good girl," Evelyn said.

"You were trying to carry a bowl of cereal and a glass of juice up here, all by yourself?" Tessa asked.

Summer nodded.

Mae rushed to the top of the landing, taking control. "What can be broken can be fixed." She walked down to their step and held out her hand. "Summer, you come with me."

Summer took her hand warily. "Where we going?"

"To make your mom breakfast in bed."

"But Mommy's up."

Mae flashed Audra a look. "She won't be next time you see her, will she?"

Audra stood. She yawned, stretched, and

headed back to her room. "I'm tired. I think I'll go back to bed."

"I thought you looked a little pale." Mae led Summer down the stairs.

Summer remembered the stash of Cheerios in her fist. "What about these?"

"Bring 'em along. Slightly used Cheerios taste the best."

As Mae and Summer disappeared to the kitchen, Evelyn and Tessa fell upon the mess. Audra peeked out from her room. "Need some help?"

Tessa shooed her away. "Get back in there and play your part when she comes back." She pointed with the towel. "You have a gem of a little lady in that girl. I hope you know that."

"I do. I know that."

"Then git."

Audra's door closed.

Tessa laid a dry towel on the wet spot and stepped on it, wicking away the moisture. "Daughters can be such a blessing."

Indeed. Evelyn retrieved the last two Cheerios. "You seeing your daughter today?"

"Sure am. She's taking me to brunch after church. You?"

"Piper invited me to go to church with her and her parents. Audra and Summer go there too. And Audra invited Russell."

"My, my, you are blessed this morning, aren't you?"

Evelyn stood, their work done. She realized that for the first time, she was free to think about *both* her children on Mother's Day. They heard Mae's exaggerated voice coming out of the kitchen. "Now, *shh!* We want to surprise her. . . ."

Tessa and Evelyn hurried into their rooms, but Evelyn peeked through the door to watch the surprise unfold.

A few moments later, Mae tapped on Audra's door. "Audra? You awake? Someone has a surprise for you."

A muted, "Come in."

Mae opened the door so Summer could carry in a tray of cereal and juice. "Happy Mother's Day, Mommy!"

Happy Mother's Day indeed.

Mae had tried to go back to sleep after Summer's mishap but had only managed to lie in bed, very much awake. Everyone else was with their respective families, celebrating Mother's Day.

But it was just another day for her.

She couldn't remember the last time she'd gotten any special attention on Mother's Day. Five years ago? Ten?

And whose fault is that?

Mae flipped to her other side and pulled a pillow to her chest. She'd brought up her children to be independent beings. Was there anything wrong with that?

Independence doesn't have to negate close-ness. The relationships between the women of Peerbaugh Place proved that. They led lives independent of each other, yet were bound by . . . bound by . . .

Love.

Mae subjected her pillow to a strangle-hold. She loved her children. But did they love her?

If they loved me they'd call me on Mother's Day. They'd send me a card, they'd — They can't send me a card if they don't know where I live. What was the last address I shared with them?

Mae tried to remember. Her children didn't know about Peerbaugh Place nor the apartment before that. But she did remember getting a card from Ringo when she lived in that bizarre little apart-ment over the pizzeria. It had taken Mae a good year to tolerate Italian food after that, the smell of marinara permeating her every breath. But it had been even longer ago since she'd talked with Starr. Last she'd heard, Ringo was a roadie with a rock band and Starr was working for some publishing house. Neither was married, though last she'd known, Starr was living with some broker-type. Her children had their lives and she had hers. Wasn't a parent supposed to bring up kids so they could butter their own slice in this world?

But that doesn't mean you shouldn't have contact with each other.

It was a two-way street. They could try to get in touch with her. They could —

They couldn't. Not if they didn't have her address or her phone number. Her self-imposed freedom, instead of offering wide-open vistas, suddenly seemed very closed — with very high walls.

A prison of loneliness.

Mae pulled the covers over her head.

After an hour of brooding, Mae got up. She was just heading downstairs to make herself a cup of tea when the doorbell rang. She froze. Who could it be at nine o'clock on a Sunday morning?

The screen door opened, and the person knocked on the main door. Then a face cupped against the leaded glass, and Mae saw who it was. She raced to open the door, the sudden movement nearly sending

Collier to the floor.

"Morning, Collie. What are you doing?"

Collier took a moment to regain his balance and his composure. "Looking for you. I saw everyone else get picked up for church, but you never came out."

"I was sleeping."

He eyed her muumuu. "This is obviously not subtle Sunday, huh?"

She adjusted her dress on her shoulders. "I am never subtle."

"I wouldn't want you any other way."

She blinked. "You wouldn't?"

"Glow-in-the-dark muumuus are definitely you."

She ran a hand over the hibiscus print. "It does not glow in the dark. It's just —"

"Perfect for you."

She felt herself blush. This man said all the right things. "Care for some tea? I was just on my way —"

"Actually, I'd like you to come to church with me this morning." He checked his watch. "It starts in twenty-five minutes. Can you change fast?"

"You mean I can't wear this?"

"Save it for next year's May Madness. You can do the hula in it."

"You're no fun."

"I beg to differ." He flipped his hands at

her. "Now, shoo. Go get on something Presbyterian."

She was halfway up the stairs. "Will a kilt do?"

"Only if it comes with bagpipes."

"They're in the shop."

"Then maybe next time."

Next time. That sounded good.

Evelyn stood with Russell, Audra, and Summer in the narthex before church.

Summer pulled on Evelyn's hand. "Who are we waiting for?"

"Piper's coming with her parents."

Summer bounced on her toes. "Goody."

Russell looked around, and Evelyn could tell from his fidgeting that he was uncomfortable in this new place. If only she'd brought him to church while he was growing up.

"Shouldn't we go in or something?" he asked.

Audra slipped her hand through his arm. "It's fine. We have plenty of time."

"They're here!" Summer bolted for the door as Piper and her parents came in. She grabbed Piper's hand and pulled her toward Evelyn. Then she took Evelyn's hand, her eyes flitting from one to the other as if she was confused about having them both at her church, and torn between which woman to give her attention to first.

"Now *that's* a welcome," Piper said, flicking the end of Summer's nose.

Summer looked from one to the other. "I like this. You're both here. And Russell is with us." She suddenly pointed to the entry. "And Gillie too!"

Gillie joined them, shrugging away their questions. "Audra's been after me for months. So I figured, why not?"

As Piper introduced her parents to Russell and Gillie, Evelyn found herself looking at the Wellingtons a bit differently. They had adopted Piper just as some other couple had adopted her baby. As the group made small talk, Evelyn watched Piper put her hand around Wanda's shoulders and squeeze, kissing her cheek. An act of true devotion. The fact that Wanda had not given birth to her made no difference in the love they shared.

Was Evelyn's daughter kissing the cheek of her adoptive mother today? Was she laughing with her adoptive parents in the narthex of some church, content in who she was, who she'd been brought up to be?

Evelyn hadn't noticed Russell making his way to her side. He whispered in her ear. "You okay?"

She hadn't realized her thoughts were being so aptly displayed on her face. "I . . ." She didn't know what to say.

He squeezed her shoulders and gave her a kiss on the cheek just as Piper had done to her mother. "It's natural for you to think of the baby, Mom. After all, it *is* Mother's Day."

Evelyn was amazed at Russell's insight. He had never been intuitive in matters of the heart. Or had she underestimated him?

He gave her shoulders another squeeze. "*I'm* here, Mom. Always remember that. I'm here."

Evelyn felt tears threaten. Tears of gratitude.

Gillie wasn't a churchgoer. But after meeting all the wonderful women of Peerbaugh Place, it seemed like a logical next step. Looking around the sanctuary, listening to the sermon and the Scripture verses and the music . . . she saw that these people had something that was missing in her life and she wanted it. Badly.

It was time for the offering. A soprano, who could have been professional, sang a song even Gillie had heard before: "How Great Thou Art." The woman's face revealed the depth of her conviction. She didn't just sing the words; she *felt* them deeply.

As the collection plates started at the front of the sanctuary, Gillie felt a wave of generosity. She pulled her purse into her lap, retrieved her billfold, and pulled out a fifty-dollar bill. She thought that would be sufficient in case anyone was watching.

She saw Summer dig into the tulip-shaped pocket of her Sunday dress and pull out a handful of coins. Probably all she had. It would not be surprising. Summer had a giving spirit.

But then the little girl surprised Gillie as she took an envelope from the pew and dumped her coins inside, licking it shut. *Why did she do that? Why didn't she just put them in the dish with a clink and a clatter, showing everyone that she'd given all she had?*

Gillie readied her fifty-dollar bill, smoothing it on her thigh. *All she had? Is this all you have?*

Suddenly the fifty dollars looked like a penny. Considering her resources, it *was* a pittance. And comparing income to income, it was nothing compared to Summer's sacrifice.

Gillie had the urge to take out her checkbook and write a check for everything she had in her account. But there was something else wrong besides the amount. . . .

Gillie saw Russell glance at the fifty. Their eyes met; then he looked away. Suddenly Gillie felt as if the money was defiled. But why? It was as good as everyone else's money. People should be glad to see —

Gillie sucked in a breath. Was she giving for show again, just like at the bank? Displaying her fifty-dollar bill for all to see? Why, she might just as well get up and shout "See what a great person I am?"

She folded her hand around the bill, crushing it. If she was going to do this, she was going to do it right. She took an envelope from the pew and slipped the fifty inside.

Step one completed.

But there was more — there had to be more. She opened her wallet a second time and removed all the bills, not even checking to see how much was there. She added those to the envelope and quickly licked it shut. She held it in her lap, covered by her hands. Her heart pounded, and she didn't dare look to the right or left to see who might have seen. The whole point was *not* to be seen, right?

The collection plate appeared to her left.

She took it and unobtrusively slipped her envelope onto the top. The plate moved on. And as it did, Gillie felt like a million dollars.

Make that two million.

"Mother, you're not eating. You feeling okay?"

Tessa realized she'd been moving the same forkful of omelet around without picking it up. She set down her fork. She looked at her family: daughter, son-in-law, and grandson. "I don't deserve you," she said. "Any of you."

Her daughter, Naomi, exchanged a look with her family that spoke of worry rather than relief. "Are you sick or something? Are you telling us this because you've just gotten some bad news and — ?"

Tessa had to laugh. She took Naomi's hand. "No, I'm not sick. In fact, I'm feeling healthier than I've felt in months. Maybe years, praise the Lord."

"Then what — ?"

Tessa dabbed her napkin on her mouth even though it had been long minutes since she'd taken her last bite. "Some things have happened since I moved into Peerbaugh Place that have been rather shocking."

Her grandson, Leonard, shoved a piece of bacon in his mouth and began talking. Tessa restrained herself from chastising him. "Shocking stuff? Gee, Grandma, what happened?"

"Have they hurt you?" her son-in-law asked. Calvin had the ability to defend his family with a stern look.

She was heartened by their interest. Had they always been interested in her, but she'd pushed them away?

"It's not a bad shock. It's a good one." She assuaged her dry mouth with a sip of juice. "Though it wasn't easy for me, it was a necessary rite of passage."

"A rite of passage at age seventy-five?" Naomi asked.

"A person never stops learning, you know that."

She shrugged. "So what happened?"

Tessa took a breath that began from her toes and was relieved there was no hesitancy within her. This had to come out. It was time. "I've been a bitter old woman. I've been a know-it-all. And I've been judgmental and nasty to most everyone I've met. That's bad enough behavior done to strangers but inexcusable when subjected upon one's own family. Inexcusable, but hopefully not unforgivable."

"Oh, Mother . . . you're not a bitter —"

"I am. Or at least I was. After your father died, you opened your home to me out of love and concern. And how did I repay you? By making your lives difficult."

Calvin freshened their coffee. "You weren't that —"

"I was. And if you're honest about it, I bet your lives have been a lot calmer and smoother going since I moved out."

Naomi looked at her plate.

"I can play my computer games without muting them."

"Leonard!"

Tessa ruffled his hair. "Exactly. I was a muffler to your home, making you stifle the life you wanted to live."

"I *am* reading that book you recommended," Calvin said.

"Good for you."

Naomi chimed in. "And I reorganized the laundry room. It does work more efficiently the way you suggested."

Leonard licked his fingers. "And Mom and Dad won't let me turn the TV on until seven, just like you told — er . . . suggested."

The listing of these items was well intentioned, but Tessa recognized the true measure of her impact. She'd affected their lives in minimal ways. A few self-help suggestions put into practice. But they had not mentioned missing her presence, or missing any of a thousand ways she could have shown them how much she loved them. They didn't miss these things, because she'd never done them in the first place. She had treated their home like a motel with the three of them as employees meant to serve her. And they had served her — out of duty. But the house had not been a family home populated by people who loved her and who were loved *by* her.

They waited for her to speak, squirming in the silence. "I just wanted to let you know that I'm sorry for how I've acted. I love you all very much, and I plan on showing it from now on."

"But Mother, you don't have —"

Tessa raised a hand, stopping her words. "I do have to. God's made it plain to me. He's been quite patient considering how hard it's been to get through to me, and so have you. But now I see the error of my ways, and I am starting fresh."

Naomi leaned toward her, Tessa met her halfway, and they kissed each other's cheeks. "I love you, Mom."

Mom. Not Mother. "I love you too. Now eat your food before it gets cold."

★ ★ ★

Sitting in the church service with Collier, Mae got the idea to top off everyone's Mother's Day by presenting the women of Peerbaugh Place with their gifts. She realized this must be the reason she'd felt such a nudge to get them done. A God nudge?

Though Mae wasn't in tune with such things, she was pretty sure it was true. And if it was, it was much more satisfying to give God the credit rather than chalking it up to karma.

She'd declined Collier's offer of brunch at a restaurant, needing to get home so she could prepare her presentation. She needed to be there when the rest of them returned from their Mother's Day celebrations to rein them in, just in case they had other plans and were suddenly spread to the wind for the afternoon.

But first, she asked Collier to swing by the shop, where she picked up the jewelry. Then she promised to make him the best omelet he'd ever eaten if he would help her prepare her project. "I need your mind and your Bible," she said. How could he refuse?

So while she cracked the eggs and chopped the green peppers and onions, he slipped home and got his Bible. They ate in the kitchen. Then Mae cleared the table except for their tea.

She brought over a paper and pen. "Okay, here we go. Body fueled?"

"Check."

"Bible open?"

He opened it. "Check."

"Writing utensils ready?"

He pointed to her paper and pen. "Check, check." He took a sip of tea. "I must say you have my curiosity piqued. What do you have in mind for these unsuspecting ladies?"

"Sisters. That's what we are, and that's the key. I need a Bible verse that fits each sister in this house — plus Piper and Gillie. As I'm new to this Christianity thing, I've chosen you to be my able assistant."

He made a bow from his chair. "I am honored."

"Rightly so." She pointed at the Bible. "Now let's get started. They could be home any minute."

"So how do we do this?"

"I tell you about the woman, and you magically come up with a Bible verse that fits her personality, who she is."

Collier shook his head.

"What? A mutiny so soon?"

"Oh, I'll do it. Gladly. But I reject your use of the word *magically*. There's no magic involved in faith. When we get the right verse, it's going to be because God's given it to us."

"Sounds magical to me."

"It's called faith." He took her hand and closed his eyes. "Lord, Mae wants to do a very nice thing for her new sisters, her sisters in Christ. Help us find the verse that You want to give each woman. Amen."

Mae shivered. "Sisters in Christ. I like that. Amen on my end too. You're sure that prayer will work?"

"Absolutely." He ran a hand over the opened page. "One thing we know for sure is that God wants us digging into His Word. He blesses such times. One hundred percent."

"Can't beat that."

"No, you can't. So," Collier said, coming to attention, "who first?"

"Let's begin with Evelyn, since she started all this." Mae looked to the ceiling, finding the words. "Evelyn is a sweet lady who feels things deeply and feels what other people are feeling deeply. Actually, sometimes those very same feelings get in the way of her taking a stand, and she has

472

to be nudged one way or the other and —"

"And you're quite willing to do the nudging?"

"We'll get to me later."

"I can hardly wait."

Mae had asked Collier to stay for the ceremony, but he declined — though he *did* request a play-by-play later. Mae was stunned by the verses he'd found, both at their perfection in fitting her friends' personalities and at his ease in finding them. The Bible was a huge book, and yet Collier seemed to know right where to look. Of course, that concordance thingy in the back helped too.

Mae held her basket of goodies on her arm and paced the parlor. Maybe this wouldn't work. She had no guarantee everyone would come back anytime soon or at the same time. Maybe they'd decide to go to a movie or shopping or run a marathon or some other time-consuming diversion.

After she'd stopped at the front window for the tenth time, she couldn't stand the iffiness of the situation any longer. She raised her hands to the sky and yelled, "God, help this come together!"

Before her words faded into silence, Mae

wondered if she'd been a little pushy with the Almighty. Maybe He didn't like women who yelled at Him in such a demanding way. She lowered her voice and added, "Pretty please?"

She heard a car in the driveway. Hurrying to the window, Mae saw that it was Russell's carload. And then came Gillie and Piper. She gave God a high five. "Thanks!" And then, before the car doors had shut, Tessa pulled up. Mae had to laugh. This praying business was cool. Very, very cool.

Mae positioned herself at the front door, trying to calm her excited stomach with a deep breath.

Summer was the first in the door. She looked up at Mae, then at her basket. "What are you doing, Aunt Mae?"

Mae put a finger to her lips. "*Shh*. It's a surprise."

As the rest entered in a gaggle, Mae greeted them. "Welcome home, sisters — and brother — I invite you to come into the parlor and take a seat."

Audra eyed the basket, and Mae was glad she'd covered the contents with a napkin. "Mae, what's going — ?"

"No peeking. Sit like a good boy and girls."

There was a general murmuring and a friendly discussion about what Mae could be up to now. She waited until they were settled: Tessa in the rocker; Evelyn, Piper, and Gillie on the couch; and Audra in a chair, with Russell and Summer at her feet.

Mae took a place in the center of the room. "In honor of our meeting here at Peerbaugh Place, in honor of the friendships that have been born or enhanced here, I have a presentation to make."

"Is it candy?" Summer asked.

"No, it's not candy. But I hope you'll consider it sweet." She cleared her throat, hoping she could get out the words she'd planned to say. "Although we've only known each other this short time, we've grown close in a way that only women can." She winked at Russell, hoping he'd forgive his exclusion. "Remember one of the first discussions we had in this house? About how quickly women bond and share the important details of their lives?"

"That was the first night, wasn't it?" Evelyn asked.

"Exactly. We were like strays, all needing something. There is a unique quality about women. We have a knack for getting to the heart of things — to the heart of each other. Just think of how diverse the seven of us are; yet I've come to believe we were sisters before we even met. Once we met, that sisterhood took root and blossomed as our need for one another was fed. We nourish one another. And sometimes we even do a bit of weeding."

"You got that right," Tessa said.

"But it's weeding done out of love." She put the basket on the other arm, hoping this next part came out right. "This morning Collier helped me see that there is another bond to our sisterhood that I hadn't thought about. He said we were sisters in Christ." She looked to the carpet and shrugged a toe back and forth. "And though I'm new at this faith stuff, I've got to agree with him. From what I've overheard, all of us have had some God moments during this time together." She scanned the room. "Right?"

Nods all around.

"Exactly right." She took a deep breath. "I find that terribly exciting." It was time. "And so . . . I've been working on a project that will cement this bond of sisterhood." She pulled the napkin back and picked up a ring. Through the ring was a long strip of paper containing the verse, stapled at the end. "I would like to present to each of you a friendship ring, a sister ring. The ring is in the shape of a circle that has no beginning and no end — just like our sisterhood."

Evelyn put a hand to her chest. "You made us *rings?*"

"Yes, ma'am. And I've even attached a Bible verse to each one — thanks to Collier — a verse we think illustrates the special people you are." She looked at the name on the ring in her hand. "Evelyn. How appropriate for you to be first." She handed Evelyn her ring. "Read the verse so everyone can hear."

Evelyn pulled the paper apart and read it. "Psalm 31:24: 'Be strong and take courage, all you who put your hope in the Lord!'"

"You've been through so much lately, Evie. And yet, we've all seen you grow stronger."

"Through Him," Piper added.

"Amen to that," Audra said.

"Try it on."

"Let me look at it first." Evelyn held it close. "It's beautiful. A vine wraps around, interspersed with little crosses."

"I thought of the crosses last week after having a revelation moment at Collier's church. The vine symbolizes our growing friendship, branching out, spreading."

" 'I am the vine; you are the branches. Those who remain in me, and I in them, will produce much fruit. For apart from me you can do nothing.' " Tessa looked up as if surprised she had spoken aloud. "John 15:5."

"Wow," Piper said. "There is more symbolism present than you knew."

Mae felt a shiver. This was going better than she ever could have imagined.

Evelyn tried her ring on. "It fits!"

Whew. One down. Mae dug through the basket. "Since Tessie knew that wonderful verse, we'll get hers next." She found it, but paused before handing it over. "Actually, all this started because of Tessie."

"Me?"

"You. You and me. You and me arguing. I felt bad and decided to make you something as an I'm-sorry gift."

"You didn't have to —"

"I know. But I wanted to. And then the whole idea took off . . ." She shrugged and handed Tessa her ring.

Tessa hesitated. "I certainly hope this isn't Proverbs 26:12 — though I would deserve it."

"What's Proverbs 26:12?" Audra asked.

Tessa closed her eyes and sighed. " 'There

is more hope for fools than for people who think they are wise.' "

Evelyn leaned over and squeezed her hand. "Oh, Tessa. You're too hard on yourself."

"Actually, I'm not, but thanks for saying so."

"Read it, Tessie. I promise you'll like it."

Tessa read the verse. "It's Psalm 143:10: 'Teach me to do your will, for you are my God. May your gracious Spirit lead me forward on a firm footing.' " She lowered the verse. "Firm footing. And *Him* lead *me*. I like that." She looked at the ring and put it on. "Thank you, Mae. For the jewelry and the verse."

"You're welcome." She pulled out the next. "Gillie."

Gillie's eyebrows raised. "You made one for me?"

"Of course. Sisterhood isn't restricted to how long a friendship, but how close. Yours is Luke 12:48." She handed Gillie the ring and verse.

Gillie read it aloud. " 'Much is required from those to whom much is given, and much more is required from those to whom much more is given.' " She lowered the paper. "If that isn't a challenge, I don't know what is."

"Next is Piper," Mae said.

"I don't live here."

"Neither does Gillie. But both of you are like one of the family."

Piper read her verse. "From Philippians 1:9–10: 'I pray that your love for each other will overflow more and more, and that you will keep on growing in your knowledge and understanding. For I want you to understand what really matters, so that you may live pure and blameless lives until Christ returns.' " She folded the verse in half. "Wow. Thank you. I'll try to live up to its words."

Evelyn patted her hand. "I'm sure you will."

Piper put on her ring. It also fit.

"Three for three," Mae said.

"How did you know the sizes?" Audra asked.

"I didn't. I'm usually good at guessing sizes, but not this good." She chose the next ring. It was the smallest. "Summer, this is for you."

Summer scrambled to her feet. "I get a ring too?"

"Of course. You're one of the girls, aren't you?"

Summer carried her ring back to her

mother as if it were the Holy Grail. "Read it, Mommy."

Audra unfolded the paper, holding it so Summer could see the words. "It's from Romans 12, verse 11: 'Never be lazy in your work, but serve the Lord enthusiastically.'"

"What's en-thooz-as-tik-ly?" Summer asked.

"With energy," Audra said.

"Eagerness."

"Excitement."

Summer nodded, understanding. "I like that."

"Put it on."

"I have a big-girl ring too!" She ran to Mae, wrapping her arms around her waist. "Thank you."

"You're welcome, doll face." One more. She picked up Audra's ring. "And for Audra . . . our organizer. Our confident perfectionist."

Audra laughed nervously. "I'm not sure those are all good traits." She opened the paper. "My, it's a long one. Jeremiah 17:7–8: 'Blessed are those who trust in the Lord and have made the Lord their hope and confidence. They are like trees planted along a riverbank, with roots that reach deep into the water. Such trees are not bothered by the heat or worried by long

481

months of drought. Their leaves stay green, and they go right on producing delicious fruit.' "

"You *have* been through a lot," Piper said. "And gained confidence from it because of —"

"Because of your help."

"I was going to say because you put confidence in Him."

Audra blushed. "You're right. He is my confidence."

"But what about Russell?" Summer said. "Doesn't he get a sister ring?"

Russell shook his head. "No, Summer, this isn't for —"

Mae stepped forward. "Although I don't have a sister ring for brother Russell, I do have a verse for him."

"You do?"

"Absolutely." She handed him the next to the last slip of paper. "I couldn't believe how much this one fit you, Russell. It's from Proverbs 4:3–5."

Russell read it out loud. " 'For I, too, was once my father's son, tenderly loved by my mother as an only child. My father told me, "Take my words to heart. Follow my instructions and you will live. Learn to be wise, and develop good judgment. Don't forget or turn away from my words." ' "

Audra put a hand on the back of his neck, a touch of endearment noticed by all.

He carefully folded the verse and put it in his pocket. "Thanks, Mae, for including me."

She curtsied. "My pleasure."

"But what about you, Mae?" Evelyn said. "Did you make a ring for yourself?"

Mae plucked the last item from the bottom of the basket. "Actually, yes. And at Collier's insistence, I even have a verse." She cleared her throat to read. "It's from 1 Thessalonians 5:11. 'So encourage each other and build each other up, just as you are already doing.' " She closed the paper. "Collier said it fit. I'll leave you to decide if he's right."

Audra pumped a hand in the air. "Mae the motivator!"

Mae felt herself blush. She could think of no better compliment. "Well, that's it," she said. "Like it or not, we're bound for life now. Sisters forever."

Audra pulled Summer onto her lap. "You know what's interesting? None of us are the same. We don't have the same gifts, the same way of looking at things, or the same temperament."

Evelyn nodded. "But if you put us all to-gether, we —"

"Become whole." Tessa nodded twice. "Very nice."

Piper stood. "Can I lead us in a prayer?" She held out her hands. The group formed a circle and Mae couldn't help but notice they formed a circle like their sister rings.

"Dear Father, we thank you for this circle of faith, this sister circle. We know you are the one who has brought us together to be a part of each other's lives — for whether sisters by birth or adoption, we are all adopted in Christ. How special that we have been brought together to encourage, motivate, serve, lead, teach, discern, and give, each as we are able. Bless us as we live our lives and help us to serve each other — and You — with all our hearts. Amen."

"A sister circle," Mae said. "That's perfect."

She got no arguments, not a one.

After a spectacular dinner à la Tessa — which was *not* ham loaf — Evelyn sat on the front porch alone. Tessa was washing dishes; Piper, Gillie, and Russell had gone to their respective homes; and Audra was getting Summer ready for bed.

It had been a momentous day. The best Mother's Day she'd ever —

The front door opened and Mae emerged. "Can I join you?"

"Of course." Evelyn moved over on the settee and patted the cushion beside her.

Mae fell into it with a sigh. "Quite a day, wasn't it?"

"Thanks to you."

"Ah, shucks, it weren't nothin', ma'am."

Evelyn touched her ring. "It was everything, Mae. It was a Mother's Day we'll never forget." She suddenly remembered that Mae had children. While the rest of them had gone to church and brunch with their kids, had Mae . . . ? She hadn't mentioned hearing from them. Evelyn wondered if she should ask or remain silent. *But as sisters . . . maybe I can help.* "Speaking of kids, did you hear from yours?"

Mae picked at the orange nail polish on her left thumb. "Nope. And I didn't expect to. Though it's not entirely their fault. I haven't been too good about keeping them apprised of my whereabouts."

"They don't know where you live?"

"Not unless they're psychic. Strike that. Not unless God has sent them an e-mail from heaven."

"Then *you* need to call *them.*"

"What?"

Although Evelyn's instruction had burst forth without thought, it was a good idea. "All your talk of closeness and sisterhood today . . . what about motherhood?"

"We haven't been close in a long —"

"Then do something about it. Don't get stuck on who calls whom. Just do it." Evelyn thought about all that had happened since she'd opened Peerbaugh Place. "If we've learned anything from living together, it's that we shouldn't go through life with regrets. We need to pursue our dreams, own up to our mistakes, and say what needs to be said to the people who need to hear it. We've discovered new sisters. Now it's time for you to go rediscover your children."

"But what if — ?"

Evelyn stood and pulled Mae up beside her. "You've been harping on me to take a stand. Well, I'm standing. And so are you." She pointed toward the house. "Go do it, Mae. Do it now."

Mae looked at her a moment, and Evelyn could tell by the gleam in her eyes she'd gotten through. Then Mae engulfed her in a hug. "Thanks, sister." She went into the house.

Evelyn sat down again, so full she could burst. She felt totally content for the first time in . . . for the first time ever? She started thinking of her own regrets, but pushed the thoughts away. The past was past. She couldn't change it. She could only make her apologies to God and move forward.

But what about the future?

A breeze drew up behind her, brushed past, and made the Peerbaugh Place sign sway.

Or nod. Yes, that's what it was doing. Nodding to her, just as it had done that first morning when she found it in the attic, assuring her that she'd made the right decision in opening her home to these women, these sisters.

What would come next? She hadn't a clue. But whatever was around the corner, she knew she'd be able to handle it, through the help of the sister circle and the God who had brought them together.

**Bless the one who comes
in the name of the Lord.
We bless you from the house
of the Lord.**
PSALM 118:26

A Note from Vonette Bright

My dear husband, Bill, has always believed that I could do the impossible. And after his suggestion, I usually bend over backward to prove that I can so as not to disappoint him. He had such success with his first novel and later his allegory that when Helmut Teichert introduced me to Nancy Moser, I believed this book possible. Nancy has been so creative, so patient with me, has taught me much about fiction writing, and has been quick to take my suggestions or come up with even better ones. She has become a real "sister" and a delightful co-laborer.

Brenda Josee has been a pleasure to both Nancy and me — dreaming, strategizing, and envisioning an outcome in which this book will touch many lives and result in dramatic life changes.

My original Sister Circle came together to support and encourage me when I moved to Orlando ten years ago. I called them "the committee." They helped to provide everything I needed in meeting new people and becoming acclimated into a new community. They even came to help unpack nearly a hundred boxes, washing silver, china, and crystal and putting them into drawers and cupboards. They unwrapped bric-a-brac and collectibles and placed them in strategic places. Through the years they have continued to be like sisters. Now we will call them a Sister Circle, as they not only support me but also support each other. Some of them meet weekly for prayer and are always ready for a potluck brunch or lunch when there is something special to be shared.

The people of Tyndale, especially Ron Beers, Becky Nesbitt, Anne Goldsmith, and Kathy Olson, have become friends and ministry partners, so enthusiastic in helping us to reach our goals and to maximize our opportunities. We have the highest respect for the Tyndale family and thank them for taking us on.

Nancy joins with a big hug and kiss on the cheek for all these people who have given us the courage to believe we really do have a ministry in the Sister Circle series. We will be interested in your response too.

God bless you as you read.

A Note from Nancy Moser

Only God could arrange for Vonette Bright and me to join forces. There was little chance our paths would ever cross. And yet they did. Meeting Vonette and Dr. Bright, spending time with them (and making and eating Vonette's fabulous taco soup) has been a highlight of my life. Such godly people tuned in to His will . . . they continue to be an inspiration. Thank you for the chance to be a part of your lives.

Through the Brights I met three other fabulous people: Helmut Teichert (an amazing idea man who made that first phone call that opened the door of opportunity for me), John Nill (who is the epitome of a gentle godly man), and especially Brenda Josee. Have you ever met someone and known within minutes that somehow you've been waiting to know her all your life? Or felt as if somehow you *have* known her in every way except the detail of meeting? That's Brenda and I. Sisters on contact.

At the Christian Booksellers Convention in Atlanta during the summer of 2001,

Brenda and I had a chance to brainstorm the nugget of Vonette's and my idea for these novels. The goal was to find a way to nurture the special bond that is unique to women. As we started to talk, we connected in a way that was divine (if not Divine). We got to talking faster and faster, and got more and more animated, and *voilà!* The term "Sister Circle" was born. We were eager to share with Vonette, and as we did, more ideas flowed. How ironic that in brainstorming the idea of Sister Circles we created our own Sister Circle! And when Tyndale got involved, we added more sisters to the group: Becky, Anne, Kathy, Danielle . . . and some brothers too: Ron, Travis . . .

A note about the group Dallas and the Babes mentioned in Chapter 10. They exist. I sing with them. We're actually called The Seeds of Faith, but when we're at our zaniest, we like to refer to ourselves as Dallas and the Babes. And one time (before I joined their forces), they actually did squawk through a classical song dressed like chickens. So to all my fellow Seeds: It's down on paper now. No chance of ever forgetting it. Not that we could.

In closing, I want you, the reader, to come to know deep down that women are special. We possess a unique, God-given talent (that men often cannot fathom!) to bond, to fellowship, to share. I pray that *The Sister Circle* and the rest of the books in this series will lift you up and bring you closer to being the best woman you can be. Through Him. Through Jesus Christ.

About the Authors

Vonette Bright is the coauthor of *The Joy of Hospitality* (with Barbara Ball) and *Building a Home in a Pull-Apart World* (with Bill Bright); editor of *The Greatest Lesson I've Ever Learned*; and author of four devotional books in a series entitled *My Heart in His Hands*. Since cofounding Campus Crusade for Christ with her husband, Bill Bright, in 1951, Vonette has maintained a rigorous schedule as hostess, evangelist, discipler, and author. Founder of Women Today International, she is widely recognized as a spokesperson for Christian women.

Nancy Moser is the author of three books of inspirational humor and five novels, including *The Seat Beside Me* and The Mustard Seed Series. She teaches writing at a regional college and is a motivational speaker. She and her husband have three nearly grown children and three corresponding nearly grown cats.

Scripture Verses in *The Sister Circle*

Chapter	Topic	Verse
Chapter 1	Trust	Psalm 62:8
	Worry	Matthew 6:25–33
Chapter 2	Hospitality	1Peter 4:9–10
	Quarrels	Proverbs 25:24
	Providing	1 Timothy 5:8
Chapter 3	Tolerance	Ephesians 4:2
Chapter 4	Love	1 John 4:11
	Love	Luke 10:27
	Judging	John 8:7
	Gossip	Exodus 20:16
Chapter 5	Joy	Jeremiah 31:13
Chapter 6	Blessing	Psalm 115:12–13
	Peace	John 14:27
Chapter 7	Humility	Ephesians 4:2
	Woman at the Well	John 4:5–30
	Wisdom	James 1:5–6
	Grace	Ephesians 2:8–9
	Pride	Proverbs 16:18
	Love	Matthew 19:19
	Pride	Proverbs 16:18
	Creation	Psalm 139:13–14

The employees of Thorndike Press hope you have enjoyed this Large Print book. All our Thorndike and Wheeler Large Print titles are designed for easy reading, and all our books are made to last. Other Thorndike Press Large Print books are available at your library, through selected bookstores, or directly from us.

For information about titles, please call:

(800) 223-1244

or visit our Web site at:

www.gale.com/thorndike
www.gale.com/wheeler

To share your comments, please write:

Publisher
Thorndike Press
295 Kennedy Memorial Drive
Waterville, ME   04901